Ex-National Hunt Champion Jockey John Francome is now a broadcaster on racing for Channel 4 and is fast establishing himself as one of the front runners in the racing thriller stakes. John Francome lives in Lambourn, Berkshire.

His previous bestsellers have been highly praised:

'Thrills, twists and turns on and off the racecourse. Convincing and beguiling'   *Irish Independent*
'A thoroughly convincing and entertaining tale'
Daily Mail
'The racing feel is authentic and it's a pacy, entertaining read'   *Evening Standard*
'Irresistibly reminiscent of the master . . . a most read-able yarn'   *Mail on Sunday*
'Francome knows how to write a good racing thriller'
Daily Express
'Pacy racing and racy pacing'   *Horse and Hound*
'Francome can spin a darn good yarn'   *Racing Post*
'Mr Francome adeptly teases to the very end'
Country Life
'Move over Dick Francis, here's competition'
Me magazine

High Flyer

John Francome

HEADLINE

First published in 1997
by HEADLINE BOOK PUBLISHING

First published in paperback in 1998
by HEADLINE BOOK PUBLISHING

10 9 8 7 6 5 4

ISBN 0 7472 5606 3

Typeset by
Letterpart Limited, Reigate, Surrey

Printed and bound in Great Britain by
Mackays of Chatham plc, Chatham, Kent

HEADLINE BOOK PUBLISHING
A division of Hodder Headline PLC
338 Euston Road
London NW1 3BH

High Flyer

Chapter One

Barry Mannion looked at his watch. It was eight-thirty on a warm Monday morning in late May, six days before the French Derby. He should have been getting back to his office but, shaking his head to dislodge a lingering hangover, he picked up the local paper and started to flip his way to the racing pages.

Halfway through, a headline caught his eye. He glanced at his employer, Joey Leatham, sitting on the other side of a green cast-iron table in Joey's garden.

'Freddie Fielding's Circus, didn't you used to work there?' Barry said in his soft, Tipperary accent.

Until Barry innocently asked the question, Joey had been sitting happily, dealing with his post and the day's business. Almost ten years had passed since the young jockey had last heard the name mentioned; a period which had helped slowly to numb his conscience without deadening it completely. As he looked up from the letter he was reading, his face showed none of the guilt that flooded into him. 'Yes. Whatever made you ask that?'

'They're mentioned in this rag.' Barry nodded at the paper.

'What does it say?' Joey didn't want to hear, whatever it was.

1

Barry chuckled. 'One of their giraffes escaped and fell into someone's swimming pool. They're only over in Cambridge. Did you know?'

News of the giraffe came as a relief. After all this time, Joey was certain no one would come looking for him, but the mere mention of the circus was enough to set his pulse racing.

He managed to smile. 'They never could keep their animals under control!' He was aware that his Scouse accent was stronger than usual in his effort to sound unruffled.

Barry didn't notice. He looked at his watch again. 'Ah, well, you'll have your work cut out keeping Isle de Rey under control.' He dropped the paper on the table and stood up. 'I'd better get back to the office to ring Zamowski and tell him you'll take the ride.'

Joey nodded absently. 'Okay.'

A look of concern came over Barry's broad, red face. 'Are you sure now? He is a bit of a monkey?'

Joey nodded again. 'Yeah. Sure.'

As his agent padded away across the velvet turf to his office beside the house, Joey's throat felt suddenly dry. He closed his eyes to wipe away a vision from his past. The action only made the scene worse – brought it back to haunt him, as vivid now as it had been ten years ago.

He snapped his eyes open and sought reassurance from the timeless view of flat meadowland beyond the brook which burbled along the eastern edge of his garden.

He had woken early to find a bright sun already shafting through the light mist over the water meadows. The weather was unusually hot and when Barry had arrived, they'd decided to have breakfast outside.

Joey's black and white springer spaniel, Roger, was flopped at his feet in semi-slumber with a lazy eye on the cereal bowl which would soon come his way – half full if he was lucky.

They were sheltered from the sun by a canopy of dangling yellow laburnum blossom and a row of young poplars. The rustle of tiny silver leaves provided a background to the spring song of thrushes and warblers hidden in the bushes around the finely mown lawn.

Joey pushed back a lock of his curly black hair from his forehead and turned to look at Roger. The animal wagged his shaggy tail and sprang to his feet.

Joey passed his untouched cereal bowl down to the dog, who buried his nose in it with noisy gratitude. He leaned back and wished that the memories of Freddie Fielding's Circus hadn't come back to spoil such a perfect morning.

A jay cried loudly in a stand of massive beeches in the corner of the garden. Joey stood up and walked out from under the laburnum. He drew in a lungful of meadow-scented morning air, his nostrils twitching appreciatively. He stretched and absently, almost unconsciously, threw back his arms in a routine exercise.

His well-tanned, hard-muscled figure showed beneath a light cotton shirt, giving the impression of a compact Roman sculpture, with almost implausibly fine features – features which, with his exceptional shortness, looked pretty rather than handsome, and had made him the butt of countless jokes for much of his young life in Liverpool.

Even now, at twenty-eight, his dark, tousled hair and sea-blue eyes set above high cheekbones gave him a look of guileless innocence which was not entirely false – an attribute which a lot of rivals envied.

Joey finished stretching and stood quite still while his eyes followed a heron flapping up the brook. When the bird had disappeared behind a clump of willows, he gazed around his garden, determined to dispel the sense of foreboding that had descended on him.

After all, he told himself, if he discounted his lack of height, life couldn't have been better at the moment. He was supremely fit, healthy and good-looking, and for the last two seasons had been one of the most sought-after jockeys in Europe. He had worked hard to get to the top, and he'd been lucky, too. Almost everything he'd touched – or, in his case, sat on – had turned to gold. As a result, he now lived in a beautiful old Suffolk farmhouse, drove a Ferrari Testarossa and owned a new Cessna 800 five-seater plane. He was, by almost any standards, a very wealthy man.

Taking a retainer with Dick Seabourn at Crowle House had been a major decision given the success Joey was already having as a freelance. But the first few months had worked out better than even Barry, the congenital optimist, could have predicted.

Dick's three-year-olds were on fire and Joey was reaping the benefits. Added to that, his appointment as senior jockey had attracted half a dozen more top-class horses to the yard. He'd already ridden thirty-eight winners that season; they'd had a runner in each of the Guineas and both had been placed. The colt Scaramanga had finished so strongly to take second that he was now favourite to win the Derby in a fortnight's time. And this morning Barry had announced that Joey was booked to ride Isle de Rey in the French classic, the Prix du Jockey

Club at Chantilly, the following weekend. Joey had never seen the colt race but if Barry had booked it then it was certain to be in with a chance. His agent and mentor from the days when they had been apprentices together was a wizard with the form book.

As he looked down at Roger pushing the empty bowl around the lawn, memories of Fielding's big top danced across his mind again and led, as they so often did, to bitter-sweet memories of Nina.

Joey wished, not for the first time, that somewhere among the thousands of beautiful women who had paraded past him at racecourses around the world, he could find just one to match her. Nina Korsakov had been very special to him.

For a moment he allowed himself to reminisce, then he shook his head and returned to the comfort of the present. He had no intention of letting a past that held so many unhappy memories spoil anything for him now. Barry returned a few minutes later, by which time Joey had his thoughts back on track.

'I don't suppose you'd want another, slightly tricky ride before the French Derby?' Barry said almost triumphantly. He swayed from side to side in an attempt to disguise his eagerness, then pulled up a chair.

Joey laughed. 'Why are you so keen?'

'Listen, Joey, it's up to you. But this is a horse called Sudden Spin – a six-year-old. He's been away at stud for the last two seasons.'

Joey nodded. He remembered the horse from the couple of times he'd been sent over to run in England. He'd been a top-class stayer and had won the Gold Cup at Royal Ascot. 'How come he's back in training?'

'I've just been talking to Michel Lacroix's assistant

and according to him, they'd nothing but problems with the horse. To begin with, he wasn't interested in any of the mares; then he turned the other way and didn't behave quite like a gentleman. He got so vicious they just couldn't handle him. Anyway, they decided not to cut him, and to put him back in training for a season or two to see if he calms down a bit.'

'How's he done so far?'

'He hasn't run yet, but if he starts in one piece, he'll walk all over the rest of them at Chantilly.' Barry paused and nodded. 'And if anyone can get him to the start, it's you.'

'I'll check him out and let you know,' Joey said. 'I'm not too keen on blind dates with loonies. You never know what they'll lead to.'

The racing was typically moderate for a Monday, and Joey had taken the day off – the first since early March. He felt that a morning doing nothing would freshen him up. Recharge his batteries. He pottered around the garden while Barry returned to his office to do his job of finding and booking rides for Joey and the four other jockeys he now handled. Joey was pulling some weeds from a bed of roses when he heard the familiar sound of his Range Rover scrunching across the gravel driveway.

Danny Leatham was returning from doing morning stables at Dick Seabourn's yard. He was looking forward to lunch. He'd been up since five-thirty, mucking out and riding work. Mondays were always harder than any other day of the week because with only half the staff working on Sundays, the stables were never mucked out properly.

He turned the vehicle into a courtyard with the buildings to three sides and parked it next to his brother's red Ferrari. To either side of him, thatched barns stood at right angles to the corners of the big timber-framed farmhouse. The barn on his left, Joey had converted into a cottage for Danny. The other served as a garage, beneath Barry's office.

Danny stepped out of the Range Rover and breathed in the quiet air. Until Joey had come along and his riding had taken off, Danny had resigned himself to living in Seabourn's hostel. Then, he'd shared a room with three other lads and struggled to run a clapped-out Mini. Now, he had a two-bedroomed cottage to himself and the use of either of Joey's cars. Life for the brothers these days was unrecognisable from their childhood.

He debated for a moment whether to go to his cottage or look for Joey. Making up his mind, he walked towards the sturdy oak front door of the house. He'd find his brother and give him the good news.

Roger spotted Danny's arrival first and bounded off across the lawn, barking hysterically with a frantic quivering of his body.

Danny fended him off with a laugh. 'Get down, you soppy bugger.'

The two brothers, handsome in their individual ways, bore little resemblance to one other. As well as being nine inches taller, Danny had a much heavier frame. His hair was fair, where Joey's was black as coal, and through years of careful eating, Joey's face had an altogether sharper look. The one feature that might have caused a stranger to connect them was a tiny upturned nose. Their looks were the only thing that their parents had ever given them.

Joey watched his brother walking towards him and wondered why he had come back from Crowle House in the middle of the day. Usually, if he wasn't at the races with a horse, Danny spent his lunch hour at the pub with the rest of Dick's lads.

Joey felt a twinge of concern. He'd learned from long experience that his brother was fine so long as he stuck to the routine of his job.

On the occasions – mercifully few – when he succumbed to a bout of gambling or drinking, everything got out of synch for a few days, and Joey would find himself having to make excuses for Danny.

Of course, people were inclined to accept Joey's apologies, though it made neither brother happy.

But that morning – Joey thought – Danny looked well enough. 'All right?' he called over Roger's noisy greeting. 'How's Scaramanga this morning?'

'If you don't win the Derby this year, I'll shag Dick Seabourn's donkey,' Danny said confidently, grinning at his own peculiar sense of humour.

Danny looked after Scaramanga and his excitement was because, for the first time that season, the colt had genuinely relaxed while cantering. 'Normally he's tugging on the bit and doing more than is necessary but if he settles like he did this morning, he'll win by a mile! I wish I was riding him.'

Danny often ribbed his younger brother that if he'd been his size, he would have been a top jockey too. He only ever said it in jest, but if he took it too far, Joey was quick to remind him that it had taken only one ride over hurdles to discover that, when it came to a race, Danny just didn't have the nerve. Despite this, he was an excellent work rider and knew what he was talking about when it came to judging a horse.

Joey was intrigued to know why Scaramanga had suddenly decided to settle. The colt had been keen since he'd first set a hoof on the Newmarket turf. Danny had done a good job with him, but up until now Scaramanga had never learned to relax completely and wasted valuable energy because of it. 'So, what do you put that down to?'

Danny held up his hands as if they were pieces of priceless porcelain. 'You couldn't buy a pair of these in the shops, Shorty.'

Joey winced. Even now, at the pinnacle of a career where his size was a vital asset, he was still hung up about his height. But he didn't like his feelings to show, not even to his brother, so he smiled broadly.

Danny spotted the cover-up. He shrugged and said more quietly, 'I think he must be growing up, that's all.' With that he turned and walked towards his cottage, taking Roger with him.

Michel Lacroix had been shocked when Sudden Spin had returned from stud at the end of the previous summer.

The horse had always been quite difficult to handle, but as Sudden Spin leaped from the horse-box that delivered him back to Lacroix's yard in Lamorlaye, the whites of his eyes flashed with an anger that the trainer had not seen in a horse before.

The stallion tugged menacingly on the bridle through an old leather muzzle strapped tightly to his head. He pounded the ground with his hooves, using every ounce of strength he could summon from his huge chestnut frame, and dwarfing the two grooms who struggled to

hold him. '*Ce cheval est taré!*' the older groom yelled in
fear and anger. He yanked the sharp steel bit harshly
across the bars of the horse's mouth and managed to
bring him back to his feet and under control.

Michel watched apprehensively as Sudden Spin
snorted defiantly through the thick muzzle. The trainer
had lived sixty-one years and spent the last fifty-five
working with horses. He'd handled probably over two
thousand in his time – everything from show-jumpers to
trotters – but they could still surprise him. That, he
admitted, was sometimes the pleasure and often the
frustration of dealing with them.

As the two lads wrestled Sudden Spin across the yard
towards his old stable, Michel guessed that getting this
horse back on to a racecourse would test his skill to the
limit.

He knew from the owner that the horse's problems
had developed while he had been away at stud. It wasn't
unusual for stallions to become aggressive when they
covered mares, often kicking and biting them. For that
reason, a mare was always protected with thick leather
padding. But Sudden Spin had managed to rip off the
pad and savage a mare viciously.

Thierry Grazac, the lad in charge of him, had panicked and lost his temper. He had picked up a mash pole
and given the stallion such a violent thrashing that one
of the other lads had had to drag him out of the
covering shed.

As a result, Sudden Spin had become impossible to
handle, and Thierry had been sacked. Soon after that,
Michel had received a call telling him to expect the horse
back at his yard.

Watching him now, nine months later, quietly picking

grass on the lawn beside the house, Lacroix wondered at
the transformation.

It had taken over a month before anyone could go into
his box without first hooking on a muzzle. But Marlon,
the young Turkish lad now standing at the horse's head,
had shown limitless patience with him. He had spent
every spare hour talking to him, stroking him until he
had begun to gain his confidence. No one but a fool
would have trusted the animal completely, but at least he
could now be handled more easily.

He was also working better. The year off had allowed
him to mature, and he was much stronger.

Lacroix had just heard from Barry Mannion in
Newmarket, confirming that Joey Leatham would ride
the horse. With the little Englishman on board, he
thought, the race at Chantilly would be simple.

Two days after Barry had booked Joey's rides at Chantilly
for the following Sunday, he arrived at the house with a
videotape of Isle de Rey's previous races.

He and Joey sat on the sofa in the study and played
the tape until Joey felt as though he'd ridden the horse
himself. He experienced a moment of sympathy for the
young jockey who had ridden him in all his races but
who was now sidelined with a broken ankle. The horse
had an electric turn of speed and if he was close enough
at the furlong pole, Joey doubted anything would be
quick enough to go with him. It was also clear from each
race that Isle de Rey had a mind of his own.

It was a fact that when people whom Joey had never
ridden for contacted him out of the blue, it normally
meant they had a talented horse but with a quirk. He
knew how to ride a tactical race as well as any other

jockey on the circuit; but it was his reputation for handling the tricky animals that made him a cut above the rest.

However, in the five years that Barry had been his agent, Joey had urged him always to weigh the odds between talent and danger and so far Barry hadn't let him down.

On the morning of the French Derby, Barry had arranged for Joey's pilot to pick him up in the Cessna 800 on Newmarket racecourse at nine-thirty. The flight to Chantilly would take a little under two hours, which would give Joey plenty of time to walk the course, and to relax before his two rides.

A friend of his who lived in the next village was booked to ride the pacemaker for an English runner. He had rung earlier in the week and asked if Joey could give him a lift to Chantilly. Johnnie Redmond was a good jockey, but wasn't a winner and would never be top-class. He was good company, though, and Joey had told him he'd be glad to have him on the trip.

Johnnie hadn't put the phone down at once.

Joey guessed what was coming. Since he'd owned the plane, he'd grown used to people asking outrageous favours.

'Is Barry coming too?' Johnnie had asked.

'No. Why?'

'Well, I wondered if there'd be room for one more?'

'Depends who it is.'

'You don't know her.'

'Oh, no,' Joey said, well aware of Johnnie's form. 'Not another of your conquests?'

'She's not,' he said quickly. 'I've never even . . . well, I hardly know her myself. She's a French girl who wants to get back to Paris. And I just said . . .'

'All right,' Joey agreed with a laugh. 'We'll squeeze her in.'

He had put the phone down wondering what Johnnie had got himself into this time.

Chapter Two

Joey's nose was buried in the sports section of *The Sunday Times* as Barry pulled up the Ferrari beside the small plane.

'Jesus! Would you take a look at that!'

Joey knew without raising his eyes that there had to be a girl nearby. He'd heard the lusty Irish voice produce similar invocations a hundred times before. Anything female in a skirt could set Barry off.

But this time Joey found himself gazing at a girl who could have stepped right off the cover of French *Vogue*. She was standing talking to Johnnie, but looked over and smiled as they arrived. She wore a fitted cream linen dress that stopped six inches above her knees. With a grin, Joey noticed Barry craning his neck to get a better view of her legs.

There was something about the way French girls dressed that always made them stand out. But this one had more. Joey couldn't decide whether it was her violet-blue eyes, her flawless, slender limbs, or her soft, full mouth that made the greatest impact.

She couldn't have been more than twenty, about five foot ten, with dark hair cut neatly to her shoulders. In her hand she held a wide-brimmed hat and a matching linen jacket, folded carefully to avoid creasing.

Embarrassed, Joey became abruptly aware that his eyes must have been popping out of their sockets. He blinked, blushed and turned away to stroke Roger who was squashed on to the back shelf, while Barry eased himself out of the driver's seat and ambled over to say hello.

Joey stayed where he was, looking around the inside of the car, self-conscious and nervous about meeting a woman who was just too beautiful for words. It was at times like this that he most wished he was taller. And it didn't do any good reminding himself that if he were, he'd probably still be living in the back streets of Liverpool.

Taking a deep breath, he swung open the car door, climbed out and walked the few yards to where the girl stood with Johnnie and Barry. Joey was determined not to let the difference in their height matter, though his eyes were at the same level as the simple pearl necklace that hung round her neck. It helped that Johnnie wasn't much taller, and didn't seem to be having any trouble communicating with her.

Joey gave her a grin. '*Bonjour. Ça va?*' Before she had a chance to reply, he added quickly, 'I'm Joey Leatham and I'm afraid that's all the French I know.'

She held out one slim, brown hand. 'That's not much,' she said with an upturn of her wide mouth. 'How are you going to tell the horse what to do?'

'With these.' Joey lifted his hands, much as Danny had to him at the beginning of the week.

'For me, you can speak in English . . . Stephanie Ducas.' She spoke in a soft French accent that made Joey's skin tingle. 'It is very kind of you to give me a lift.'

'No trouble. Do you have any bags?'

'Just that.' She nodded at the small briefcase by her feet.

The pilot had climbed out of the Cessna to join them. He picked up Stephanie's bag to stow it with the jockeys' kit-bags in the small hold and they all walked towards the plane.

Watching them, Barry wished he was going to Chantilly now, instead of returning to his office to book rides for the coming week. He waited to see the French girl negotiate the step up on to the wing of the plane, the two jockeys having gallantly let her go first. He was rewarded with a tantalising glimpse of stocking top. Johnnie caught his eye and grinned like a naughty schoolboy.

Barry let out a long sigh. 'Well, best of luck, boys. I'll be here this evening to pick you up at eight-fifteen, so don't be late.'

Joey gave him a wave, and clambered in behind Johnnie. Barry watched the plane taxi away across the turf and take off. He climbed back into the Ferrari, turned to Roger and sighed. 'Some guys have all the luck,' he chuckled and swung the car in a big arc across the grass and drove back to Three Elms Farm.

Joey found the journey to France passed quickly. Sitting opposite Stephanie, he realised she was just as beautiful as on first impressions.

She seemed relaxed and, to their surprise, was well informed about French racing. It turned out that her father had over a dozen horses in training with various yards around the French capital and one of them was racing that day – a four-year-old, Duveen, who was declared to run in the staying race against Sudden Spin.

He was already the top hurdler in France and if Joey's mount was still rusty after his lay-off, looked the most likely to win instead.

From the moment he had set eyes on Stephanie, Joey had accepted that, however friendly she might be, she was out of his league.

Girls like her had a queue of men to choose from, all at least as rich as he, more sophisticated, and almost certainly taller.

While Johnnie prattled on, Joey sat back in his seat and thought of Nina.

He remembered how the first time he'd seen her his heart had pumped so hard, he thought it would show. He was only fifteen when he'd first seen Freddie Fielding's Circus in Liverpool. He'd sneaked in without paying and found a spare seat right next to the tunnel. Nina had appeared riding a grey stallion which Joey had thought absolutely magnificent. As she'd waited her turn to enter the ring, she'd been so close he could almost have touched her.

Within a month, he'd joined the circus and she'd become his best friend. It was she and her mother who had taught him to ride – not just to sit on a horse, but to do anything he wanted with one. For two years, Nina had been the centre of his existence and although he'd never told her, she was the first and only person he had ever truly loved.

She wasn't as beautiful as Stephanie, but looking at the girl opposite him now, he decided that Nina was no less striking – unless time and memory were playing unfair tricks on him. After all, he hadn't set eyes on Nina in over ten years.

Since he'd left the circus, he'd often thought of going

to look for her, but every time he'd found an excuse not to. In his heart, he knew that the real reason was fear of rejection.

Another reason was guilt.

But maybe it was time he confronted it. Maybe this time he really would go to look for her. Perhaps when he got back from France . . .

Stephanie's laughter brought Joey back to the present. He looked at her and managed a smile.

'Tell me, Stephanie, what have you been doing in Newmarket?'

'I was only there for one night, staying with Lord Leamington.'

'Moving in the right circles, then.' The Leamingtons were owners and breeders who entertained on a grand scale.

Stephanie shrugged. 'He wants to sell some pictures to my father.'

'Her dad's got a big gallery in Paris,' Johnnie said. 'Specialises in sporting pictures. Leamington wants to sell him a pair of Herrings.'

'He'll be wanting a few bob for them,' Joey said, impressed. He'd looked at a lot of racing pictures himself over the last few years, since he'd had money to invest, and he'd taught himself a lot about the art market. 'Are you buying them?'

Stephanie smiled and tapped the side of her nose with her index finger.

'You work for your dad, then?' he asked.

'He says he works for me. Are you interested in paintings?'

'Yeah. I buy a few, but only when I know they're

selling for less than they should be.'

'Then you will not buy anything from us, but I'm going back into Paris straight after racing. Why don't you both come with me and have a look at the gallery, if you want?'

Johnnie looked eagerly at Joey, like a dog who was about to be thrown a bone.

Joey shook his head. 'Sorry, I'd like to, but I've got to get back tonight.' He didn't have to be anywhere that night, but he was certain he wasn't ready for Stephanie Ducas yet; he doubted that he ever would be.

Bitterness had been festering in Thierry Grazac since he'd been unfairly sacked by the stud where he'd looked after Sudden Spin.

But today he was going to exact his revenge. He'd found another job easily enough, but only as a stable lad. He'd always been a loner and at the stud he'd had a cottage to himself; now he was living in a hostel, sharing a room. His wages were a third of what they'd been. But he wasn't brooding about the money; in his time working with the stallions he'd saved most of what he'd earned and had the advantage of being single, with no one to support but himself.

What had incensed him was the injustice done to him; that he'd been dismissed for doing a job he was good at, which he loved and in which he took great pride.

Maybe he had gone a bit over the top with Sudden Spin, but he'd been around horses long enough to know just how much you could safely let them get away with.

He'd seen savage stallions before. He had previously worked at a stud with a stallion so unpredictable that no one ever went into his box. Once, when they were trying to shoe him, they decided to hold him secure between two heavy timber boards, but as the blacksmith stepped into the box, the horse had gone berserk; he'd bent the boards as if they were flimsy ply. Next, they'd attempted to lasso him and half suspend him from a beam over his stable. The lad with the rope had been tugged right off the stable floor, and the horse attacked him so viciously with hooves and teeth that he'd spent six months in hospital.

Thierry was in no doubt that the beating he'd given Sudden Spin was for everyone's protection. The horse was evil and if he'd let him get away with savaging one mare that way, he'd only have become worse and maybe ended up killing another.

He was angry, too, because after the incident he had told the stud manager that he thought the horse's behaviour had been triggered by the disinfectant they were using. He'd thought for some time it was making the stallion worse and had made no secret of his theory. Two months later, he was told by another lad that Sudden Spin had started to turn savage while he'd been at a spelling yard, before he'd come to the stud, and that his first real beatings had happened there. When Thierry also discovered that they'd used the same disinfectant, he was sure the horse associated its smell with serious pain.

Even after he had been fired, ignominiously and without notice or wages in lieu, he'd written to the stud owner, who also owned Sudden Spin, to tell him what he thought had happened. But, despite Thierry's five years' service at the stud, the owner hadn't even had the courtesy to reply.

Now Sudden Spin was due to run again, and Thierry

was looking forward to finding out if his theory about the disinfectant was right.

If it was, the owner could kiss goodbye any chances of winning. If the horse behaved badly enough he might even be warned off, which would make him worthless, and the arrogant pig who owned him would get what he deserved.

If Thierry was wrong and nothing happened, there'd be nothing lost; he'd soon find another way to repay his old boss.

His plan was simple, and depended on the network of lads who worked in the dozens of training yards around Chantilly.

Thierry had once worked with Georges Kerlidou, a wiry little Breton who was now travelling head lad for Eric Clauzel, and Clauzel's yard had a runner in Sudden Spin's race. Thierry found him in the racecourse stables.

'Georges, how's it going?'

'Fine, except for this bloody heat. How about you?'

'I'm still doing my two, and flogging fly repellent for some extra cash. Have you got anything you want to try some on? It's the best I've come across.' The enthusiasm in his voice sounded genuine.

'They'll all need some today, particularly Duveen. He's like a magnet to every insect in Picardy.'

'It's a disinfectant, actually, and I'm supposed to be flogging it on commission for the makers.'

'Sure, let's give it a try,' he agreed.

'If you think it's any good, get your guv'nor to buy some and we'll both make a few bob.'

'If it helps Duveen to calm down, I don't give a damn about any commission.'

22

★ ★ ★

Michel Lacroix had Joey's saddle and weight-cloth tucked neatly under his arm. He was looking around the pre-parade ring for Sudden Spin when the dapper figure of Freddie Long, his English travelling head lad, appeared, walking briskly towards him.

'The horse has started getting on edge and showing himself,' he told his boss anxiously.

Michel shook his head slowly, knowing that the news shouldn't have come as a surprise. 'Where is he?'

Freddie pointed to one of the enclosed saddling boxes. 'I put him in there, hoping he'd quieten down a bit.'

The two men walked across the neatly mown grass and into a dimly lit stable. Sudden Spin was on his toes, rattling the concrete floor and gazing wildly about him as his young Turkish lad struggled to calm him.

The trainer took one look at the stallion's extended penis and sent Freddie for a large bucket of cold water.

When his head lad returned, Michel made sure he closed the door and took the bucket from him.

'Right. Hold him tight.'

In a single, decisive movement, he threw every drop of water over the colt's genitals. Sudden Spin tried to rush forward but found nowhere to go. His head crashed into the thick wooden door. The deluge of cold water and hitting his nose seemed to shock him into temporary submissiveness. His penis retracted and he stood in the middle of the stable shaking.

'I just hope that keeps his mind on the job for a while,' Michel muttered as he stepped back. But he knew that all the valuable hours spent settling the truculent stallion had been undone in a few minutes. He watched the water forming a puddle around Sudden Spin's feet. 'What set him off?' he asked without looking up.

Marlon shook his head dejectedly.

'I don't know. As soon as we walked out of the stable yard, he was twitchy, and then he started to go mad, just like he used to when he first came back.'

For the next few minutes Sudden Spin stood still and allowed Michel and Freddie to saddle him and rinse his mouth and nostrils with water. But when Michel pulled the door open and let the bright sunshine flood in, the stallion immediately tried to bolt outside.

Michel snatched the bridle and yanked him back. Sudden Spin turned his head to bite him, but feinted at the last moment.

'Freddie,' Lacroix muttered through gritted teeth, 'get round the other side of him and keep a good hold of that chifney. If he steps out of line, let him have one. Marlon, take this side.' He handed the rein to the anxious Turkish lad.

'Do you want us to take him into the parade ring yet?' Freddie asked.

Michel thought for a moment, weighing up the options, watching Sudden Spin tugging on the bit.

'No. Lead him around here, away from the others. He'll be better off if we bring him into the paddock late.' He looked down through his race card. He didn't need to tell Freddie not to walk the stallion behind the one filly in the race, but he was looking for something he knew was quiet. 'Tuck him behind the hurdler, Duveen. Number four.'

Michel left the two lads hanging on to Sudden spin and started to walk towards the parade ring. He was thinking about the trouble they'd had when the horse had arrived back from stud. He stopped and for a moment considered going for a muzzle. But he decided against it. Once Joey Leatham was on board Lacroix was confident the horse would behave.

As Joey stepped into the tree-shaded paddock he glanced around for his trainer. There were twenty runners, the parade ring was crowded, and it was a few moments before he spotted Michel's silver hair.

Lacroix was with a group of people less than twenty yards away. As Joey walked towards him, he scanned the myriad colours in the ring, looking for an elegant splash of cream linen. But Stephanie was nowhere to be seen.

He was shaking hands with Sudden Spin's owner when he caught a glimpse of her walking into the paddock. Michel and his owner followed Joey's gaze. The trainer looked down at Joey with a grin on his face. 'So you've met Harry Ducas' daughter?'

'I gave her a lift from Newmarket this morning.'

As she walked in his direction with her head slightly bowed, Joey sensed that she was embarrassed by the number of people staring at her. This was something he'd experienced too, only in his case because he was so short.

Stephanie saw him, smiled and mouthed 'Hello' as she carried on to join some people nearby. She started chatting to a tall, greying man in a well-cut, light-weight English suit. As he listened, absorbed in every word she said, Joey guessed from the pride on his face that he was her father. Of the others in the group, Joey recognised only Duveen's trainer, Eric Clauzel.

'I would train Ducas' horses for nothing, with a daughter like that,' said Michel with a mischievous grin. Seeing that his owner wasn't amused, he quickly added that Duveen was a very versatile horse, and the one Sudden Spin had to beat.

Joey angled himself so that he could watch Stephanie while still listening to Michel. In the heat of the afternoon sun she was using her race card as a fan-cum-fly-deterrent. A welcome breeze briefly rippled the leaves of the trees but vanished almost as quickly as it had come. Eric Clauzel turned and uttered a few words to a skinny lad standing a couple of yards away with his hands behind his back.

Georges Kerlidou nodded and went off to draw Duveen into the middle of the ring. He removed the gelding's thin paddock sheet as he'd been told. He had previously dampened it with Thierry's disinfectant to keep the flies at bay, but now the heat was promising to be more of an irritant than the insects.

When the girl who looked after Duveen had led him away again, Georges carried the sheet and roller back to Clauzel who was still talking to Harry Ducas and Stephanie.

Another gust of wind brought some reprieve from the sticky heat. Most of the horses and jockeys had come in. Trainers were issuing final instructions and thinking about getting their jockeys mounted.

Suddenly, the quiet murmuring of pre-race speculation was rent by a thunderous roar. Every head turned to see a large chestnut horse charging into the paddock, completely out of control. Two lads were struggling to hang on to his bridle. The animal's neck was held high and his small ears lay flat against his skull.

The crowd scattered all over the parade ring in the rush to get out of his way. Two owners tripped and crashed into each other. One elderly lady slipped and fell to the ground in front of her trainer, who stooped to help her up. But the horse was already on top of them and trampled across them as if they weren't there. A scream of pain escaped the woman's lips as a large rear hoof crushed her ankle. The animal charged on as if locked on to some kind of homing device.

Georges Kerlidou stood for a moment wondering if there was anything he could do. But the animal was rushing away from him and there were other lads closer, already running to help. Abruptly, he realised where the horse was heading. He screamed to Duveen's girl to look out.

An instant before the stallion hit the gelding head-on, two more lads and a tall, silver-haired man grabbed it and dragged it to a standstill.

The animal stood snorting noisily. His eyes rolled angrily at the restraint finally imposed by five men holding him. Georges arrived, panting, and yelled at the girl to get Duveen well out of the way. With the maverick horse apparently under control, other trainers quickly got their own horses mounted and clear of the paddock while a pair of paramedics ran in with a stretcher for the old lady, who was still lying on the ground, crying in pain.

Joey had watched the whole scene with disbelief. If he hadn't thought he knew better, he'd have said that Michel Lacroix had known what was going to happen as soon as Sudden Spin entered the paddock. The trainer had moved almost before the stallion's roar had finished. By the time Joey and the owner had realised that it was their horse which was causing the fracas, Lacroix had got the animal under control, and it was all over.

They hurried across to where the trainer stood holding the quivering stallion.

'Get on him now.' Michel's voice invited no debate. 'He'll be fine once you're on him.'

Joey hesitated, feigning difficulty with the buckle of his helmet. He'd forged his career riding moody horses, but this one looked positively evil. There was something almost sinister about the animal – the way he strained at the reins while a lathery sweat drenched his massive frame. Every vein and muscle seemed to bulge in defiance and his manic eyes beamed pure hatred.

Joey had seen a horse behaving like this only once before, when he'd first arrived in Newmarket. The animal had developed an abscess which had been causing it pain for weeks. Joey was in charge when the vet came to treat him. With no warning, he had sunk his teeth deep into the man's side and lifted him right off the ground as if he were a doll.

Joey vividly remembered the vicious wound he had caused, the torn, ragged edges where the skin had been severed. He had wondered how any doctor was ever going to stitch it back together.

He looked at Michel, and shook his head. 'Forget it. I'm not riding him.'

Michel glared back at him in amazement. 'What do you mean?'

In a job where subservience to trainers, owners and stewards was second nature to every jockey, it took courage for Joey to say what he had. A lot of people who didn't know him would call him a fool.

But he knew that getting up on Sudden Spin was too great a risk to take. Damn what anyone else thought! he told himself, it was his neck!

'I mean what I say, and anyway, he's not going to run any sort of race now. Just look at him.'

The trainer continued to stare down at Joey. He realised that he had no choice. There was still a crowd of people in the paddock, waiting to see what Sudden Spin would do next.

'I'll see you never get another ride in France,' Lacroix hissed with such venom that Joey almost reconsidered. But the chance was lost. 'Take him back to the stables,' the trainer snapped at the horse's nervous young lad.

'Let me take my saddle first.' Joey slipped smartly round the seething trainer. He slid his tack off the stallion's still-heaving back and wrapped the girth and circingle neatly round the saddle. As he stepped away, he caught sight of Stephanie walking back from the course.

Joey felt his stomach turn at the idea of her seeing what had gone on and thinking him a coward. She had no idea how many horses he'd ridden that other jockeys had turned down – all those tearaways with nothing on their minds beyond getting the rider off their back and on to the ground; the horses on which he'd made his name.

He was rehearsing what he would say to her when Sudden Spin's anger seemed to be triggered again by another gust of wind.

He lunged forward half a stride, slackening the reins. Before the two boys holding him could adjust their grip, he snatched his head away to the right, knocking one of them over. Unrestrained on that side, he whipped his back-end round and lashed out his near-hind to land a hefty kick on the boy's thigh. The sharp crack of break-ing bone filled the air, and was followed by the boy's terrified scream.

The other lad tried to yank the horse away but Sudden Spin sprang at him, using his head like a battering ram and lifting him off the ground. The lad's arms flailed through the air. He dropped the reins as he struggled to regain his balance, but failed.

The horse sensed at once that he was free and tossed his big head. The lead rein swung loose in a broad arc. Michel made a grab for it, but as his right hand got to within an inch of the leather, Sudden Spin thrust away and was gone.

Stephanie stood mesmerised, not knowing what to do. She'd watched Duveen go out on to the course, and had come back to see what had happened to Joey and Sudden Spin. After his kindness in giving her a lift that morning, she was concerned for his safety.

Coming back into the parade ring, she'd spotted Duveen's paddock sheet where Georges had dropped it earlier. She'd picked it up and taken a few paces towards the group beside Sudden Spin when the trouble had begun again. When she'd seen the lad being kicked she'd run forward, wanting to help, but common sense drew her up short. She wasn't used to dealing with horses, and their size frightened her.

She waited to see what would happen. Suddenly, without warning, she realised that the horse was loose and charging straight towards her.

Joey dropped his saddle and began sprinting the moment he realised Sudden Spin was free. His first few strides took him towards the paddock entrance to head off the horse and prevent him from getting in amongst the crowd.

But the horse had dropped his nose to the ground and

it was clear that he wasn't trying to get out. Roaring and snorting, he snaked across the ring towards his quarry.

Someone screamed at Stephanie to run, but her legs wouldn't work. Her brain told her to move, but she was paralysed with fear.

She could feel her grip tighten on the paddock sheet as she lifted it up in front of her to protect herself. But still she couldn't move until Sudden Spin was only a few feet away; then an inner will to survive took over and she spun round.

The stallion timed his attack to perfection, knocking her over as his toes stabbed into the turf, bringing his huge frame to a sudden halt. Stephanie crashed to the ground and winded herself. Sudden Spin's bulk cast a shadow over her where she lay, but she couldn't move. The horse raised his head in triumph and dropped to his knees.

Stephanie opened her mouth and screamed as the horse's weight pinned her legs to the ground. She struggled with every ounce of strength, utterly terrified now, as she felt his coarse sweaty hair press against her soft skin.

Her heart almost stopped as she wriggled her upper body round and came face to face with his gaping mouth and huge jagged teeth, inches from her face. She was still clutching Duveen's paddock sheet tightly in her hands; she pulled back, yanking it over her head, just as Sudden Spin took his first bite. The force of his assault drove her face into the grass with a thud. His weight as he thrust his mouth towards the back of her head kept her pinned there. He tugged the sheet violently, trying to tear it away.

Joey was in full flight as Sudden Spin opened his

huge jaws. He forced his legs to move faster as a vision of the vet's ravaged side flashed through his mind. Stephanie was screaming, twisting her body with only the sheet between herself and Sudden Spin's massive jaws. Joey was almost there when the animal snatched its head viciously towards him with the thin cotton material still between his teeth. The sheet had been pulled away enough to expose Stephanie's tangled dark hair. Joey dived forward and forced his strong fingers behind the rings of the bit. His right shoulder hit Sudden Spin just behind the ear, but the strength and momentum of the animal's downward lunge were too much for him.

Stephanie twisted her neck just as Sudden Spin thrust his mouth forward again. She yelled as she felt the sharp edges of his teeth scrape her ear. She sensed him turning his head to take a proper bite; then a hand slapped against her as more weight piled into her back.

Joey caught hold of the chifney with his left hand and pulled it as hard as he could, using the bottom half as a lever. The pressure inside Sudden Spin's mouth forced him to keep it open. The next moment Michel Lacroix had joined Joey, and they were both grappling to get the horse under control. But even their combined strength was no match.

Michel relinquished his hold on the reins for a second, drew his fist back and hammered the animal in the eye with an almighty punch. The horse hesitated for a moment, before springing up with the two men still clinging on to him.

Michel administered three ferocious jabs to Sudden Spin's mouth, bringing him to submission, and as suddenly as the drama had started it was over.

With the weight gone from her legs, Stephanie crawled painfully to her feet.

Joey was immediately by her side. 'Are you all right?' he asked, looking at her anxiously. Her face was pale with a wide graze down one side and there was blood on the other side of her head. She was obviously in shock; he wanted to hold her but felt too awkward. She sniffed deeply, trying to regain her composure.

'I'm fine,' she said, smoothing her grass-stained dress and combing her dishevelled hair with her fingers. She opened her mouth to speak again but instead burst into tears.

Joey stepped forward and wrapped his arms around her hunched shoulders. As her whole body heaved uncontrollably, he held her closer, oblivious of the watching public, the pressmen and the cameras until her father arrived and took his place.

Grateful for the smile that shone through her tears, as they walked away, Joey looked around and found that Sudden Spin had already been led out of the paddock. He collected his saddle from where he had dropped it and walked quietly back to the weighing room.

The story of Sudden Spin's attack spread rapidly, and for the remainder of the afternoon Joey found himself besieged by press and TV. Ironically, his subsequent win on Isle de Rey later on in the French Derby seemed of minor importance.

That evening, after he'd checked on Stephanie and was heading home, the story of an Englishman who refused to ride for a French trainer before courageously saving a beautiful girl was headline news. It was a story that would lead from bravery to blackmail.

Chapter Three

Joey looked out at the heat still shimmering above the runway at Bernes-sur-Oise. There was no one in the Cessna besides him and the pilot. Johnnie had disappeared after the races, leaving a message that he would be making his own way home. Joey sighed. He didn't even have a newspaper to read.

As they took off, he settled back, dozing, half dreaming of Stephanie. She had come looking for him in the weighing room to congratulate him on his win on Isle de Rey, and he'd thought he had detected a tear in her eye as she'd thanked him again for saving her life. She had repeated her invitation to come back to Paris with her, to look at some pictures and dine with her father, but he'd stuck to his original plan.

Now he was wondering why.

He pulled out his wallet and looked at the gallery business card on which she had written her home phone number. He gazed at it for a moment, before putting it back thoughtfully.

Among the bits of paper and receipts nestling in his wallet was a newspaper cutting. He plucked it out now and carefully unfolded it. It was the report about the runaway giraffe at Freddie Fielding's Circus which Barry had found. Joey read it, and his thoughts turned inevitably to Nina.

He hadn't seen her since he was eighteen. And in the few years he'd known her then, he hadn't so much as kissed her. Although on the flight over that morning he'd seriously thought about going to look for her in Cambridge, it seemed inconceivable that she wouldn't be married and even, perhaps, a mother by now. He wondered if she knew what he was doing, if she ever followed racing or had read about his success; if she was even aware that he was the same Joey Leatham who had turned up as an undersized fifteen-year-old at Freddie Fielding's Circus.

It was Nina who had first put him up on a horse – on one of the Lusitano stallions which her mother, Tatyana Korsakov, used in her troupe of Cossack Riders. Within two years of arriving at the circus, he could ride at a full gallop round the arena, hanging on to the underside of a horse's belly, then pull himself round until he was on its back. He could perform handstands on a horse's quarters, ride backwards, sideways, blindfold, and with his wrists and ankles bound and the reins between his teeth.

They didn't tell him at the time, but the Korsakovs had recognised as soon as they'd seen him on a horse that he was an intuitive rider. He loved the animals, and seemed to understand them instinctively. He had an extraordinary natural balance and a pair of hands that any horse could trust.

Looking down over the Channel at the English coastline appearing in the evening sun, Joey wondered if Nina knew that those same hands had gone on to steer more than six hundred winners past the post.

36

A few minutes before they landed, Joey picked out the red dot of the Ferrari, parked on the Newmarket turf beside the Rowley mile.

Barry was standing by the car, watching the small plane land and taxi to a standstill. He walked over as Joey climbed out and jumped to the ground. There was a huge smile on Barry's face. Above the smile, his eyes were dancing.

'Congratulations! How was La Belle France?'

'As belle as ever, but I'm glad to be back.'

Barry opened the boot in the front of the Ferrari and Joey dropped his bag into it. 'Do you want to drive?'

'No.' Joey shook his head and opened the passenger door. Roger, crammed into the tiny rear, stuck his head between the front seats and wriggled in ecstatic greeting.

Barry climbed in beside Joey. 'Are you okay?'

He nodded, but said nothing.

'So,' Barry went on. 'What on earth happened to Sudden Spin? I didn't see it on the telly, but I've heard he started misbehaving in the paddock.'

Joey grunted. 'What an understatement! He damn' near killed three people – including Stephanie.'

Barry started to drive the car slowly across the undulating turf. 'So what happened exactly?'

Joey told him, as objectively as he could.

'Well, I don't blame you for not riding him.'

Joey glanced at his agent. 'Thanks. I'm afraid Monsieur Lacroix wasn't so understanding, though I'm pretty sure he was expecting something like that to happen.'

'I won't book you for any of his horses again, I promise.'

'I don't think we'll be asked.'

Barry shrugged it off. 'Ah, well. So, how's Stephanie? Is she grateful to you?'

'I suppose so. She wanted me to have dinner with her and her father.'

'And you didn't go!'

Joey shook his head with a rueful grin. 'No, she gave me her number, though.'

'You lucky bastard. Mind, I reckon she fancied me more.'

Joey laughed, wondering if Barry was being serious. 'I'm not giving you her number then. By the way,' he wanted to change the topic, 'is that circus still in Cambridge?'

'What circus?'

'Freddie Fielding's. You told me about their giraffe falling into a swimming pool, remember?'

'Oh, yes. Your old outfit. I haven't got a clue. Why? Do you want to look up your old mates?'

'I just wondered, that's all.' Joey sat in silence as Barry drove out on to the road and headed for home.

'What have I got on for tomorrow?' Joey asked after a few moments.

'You should win the sprint. There's not much left in and Zapata Bianca's well drawn.'

Joey perked up. Barry seldom exaggerated their chances. 'You said she worked well last week?'

'Yeah, she did. The only thing is, Dick thinks she's better than she is. He's entered her in all the top races. Really he should keep her to Leicester and the smaller tracks. But then,' he shrugged, 'I'm just a humble jockeys' agent.'

'You're not humble.'

'No,' Barry agreed. 'It's the jockeys I'm referring to.'

38

'I suppose you told Seabourn what you thought?'

'I mentioned it.'

Joey grinned. Not many people told Dick Seabourn what to do.

Seabourn was an old-fashioned, gentleman trainer, in his late-fifties, who occupied one of the most venerable yards in Newmarket. Crowle House had been left to his wife by her late father, who had himself been one of the great racing names of the forties and fifties. It was Barry who had advised Joey to take up his retainership with the yard, while keeping it open-ended.

Seabourn had been spectacularly successful in his first dozen years, but more recently his yard had been plagued with a virus. Showing real grit, Seabourn never gave up, and after four wretched seasons, his fortunes had started to change.

He was hauling himself back into the limelight and the previous season had had an impressive crop of two-year-olds. But Graham Street, his stable jockey of six years' standing, had been beaten on some of them when it mattered. Barry had spotted a chance for Joey to move in. It hadn't taken him long to persuade the trainer to engage Joey as Graham's replacement. The move had benefited Seabourn in more ways than one. Joey's appointment as stable jockey had immediately attracted a handful of top-quality new horses to the yard.

'Doesn't he bite off your head when you try to tell him his job?'

Barry nodded with a grin. 'He does, but then I remind him that taking you on was my idea and he becomes more co-operative. After all, it's worked for him, and it's worked for you. I was totting it up while I was waiting for you this evening: it's nearly thirty winners you've ridden for Dick so far this year.'

The downside to the glory was the guilt Joey felt about replacing Graham as Seabourn's jockey. He knew that if it hadn't been him, it would have been someone else, but he hadn't realised until it was too late just how devious Barry had been in bringing it off.

Graham Street was a few years older than Joey, an apprentice already winning races when Joey had first turned up in Newmarket. A handsome, rough-hewn young man, full of natural verve and charm, he'd made Joey welcome, shared a room in his digs, and encouraged him in his pursuit of success on the racecourse. Their friendship had started to sour as Joey had begun to attain the success that Graham originally encouraged him to achieve.

Graham hadn't taken his dismissal at all well. He had blamed Seabourn's lack of winners on anything other than his own performance.

But whatever the cause, Joey had proved it didn't apply now, and, as a result, he was bearing the full brunt of Graham's resentment.

Graham was almost the first person Joey saw when he and Barry drove into Leicester racecourse the next afternoon.

As Joey climbed out of the passenger seat of Barry's car, Graham was in a huddle with Mike Wade, another jockey, not ten yards away. There was some kind of row going on, but whatever it was about, both men clammed up as soon as they saw Joey. Whatever their disagreement, there was no mistaking their joint feelings for him. Joey shied away from their scornful stares.

'Ignore the eejits,' Barry said, seeing them.

Although Mike Wade was a perfectly competent flat jockey – not one of the best, but not one of the also-rans – he was also thoroughly disreputable. For years, he had been known as the man to contact if a jockey wanted to earn a wedge for hooking up a horse. He had relationships with several heavy-weight punters and a few bookies. Now it looked as if Graham Street was going down the same road.

The Jockey Club had never been able to pin a single act of malpractice on Mike when he'd stopped horses himself; and even when other jockeys, acting on his instructions, had been caught and punished, they had never pointed the finger at him. Not because they liked Mike, but because they were afraid of the people he knew.

He had once, in carefully ambiguous terms, asked Joey to fail to win on a favourite in a handicap. Joey had always kicked any suggestion clean out of court. But having told Wade to get out of his life, Joey had failed to win on his horse and Wade compounded the loss by putting it around that he'd paid Joey. He made a show of handing him an envelope in clear sight of three or four other jockeys. But Joey had torn the envelope open, in front of everyone, and flung the thousand pounds it contained back into Wade's face.

Since then, Wade had been one of his most committed enemies. Joey always did his best to ignore him.

Ten minutes after he had seen Mike in the car park, he heard his voice, right beside him in the changing room.

'Fucking chicken.'

The words were hissed over Joey's shoulder, loud enough for most of the other jockeys in the changing room to hear.

Joey didn't let his head turn a single degree.

'You're giving us a bad name, bottling out of a ride like that. Lacroix says he'll never book an English jockey again.'

Joey thought of simply shaking his head, but Wade would consider even that a triumph. He carried on buttoning up his silk.

'Yeah, Joey.' He recognised Graham's hectoring tones. 'Call yourself a pro?'

A few other jockeys, smelling a good scrap in the air, tittered and waited for the follow-up.

But still Joey said nothing. There wasn't a sound as Mike and Graham waited for his response.

It was Johnnie Redmond who broke the silence.

'If either of you had been there, you'd have run a fucking mile. It was Joey who pulled the horse off the girl when it went berserk.'

'Only because he was getting jealous,' Mike guffawed, until he noticed he wasn't carrying the rest of the changing room with him.

Joey turned and stared at him. 'Piss off, Wade,' he said with disdain.

Barry watched Zapata Bianca canter to the start and marvelled at Joey's hands. He had set off with the normally flighty filly on a long rein and now she was on her way to the start like an old hack.

Barry had recognised Joey's special gift from the very first time he'd seen him ride at Sammy Samson's yard. When Danny had introduced them, announcing that Joey had spent the past three years in a circus, flying a trapeze and trick riding with Korsakov's Cossack Riders, the other lads had looked at him and laughed. Within a week, the laughing had stopped.

But Joey had never forgotten it.

He remembered it almost every day, and he saw each race as a way of proving that he was no joke, even now, after six hundred winners.

This was his first race on Zapata Bianca. He'd ridden work on her for Seabourn on Newmarket Heath, but her earlier runs had been under Seabourn's claiming jockey.

He pulled up as they approached the starting stalls and walked her the last fifty yards with his feet out of the irons and his legs hanging loose at her sides. Joey did everything he could to let her know she was in safe hands, talking to her all the time and patting her muscled neck until she was inside her stall.

When the gates sprang open, she half missed the break and Joey had her settled at once.

Barry Mannion stood alone, packed tightly among a crowd of spectators in the stand. He watched quietly without any display of raucous triumph as Joey and Zapata Bianca sneaked up and stole the race. He, like Joey, was a winner, but he'd had the sense to accept early in his career that he hadn't been born with the natural skills of a successful jockey. Besides, he liked his food and drink too much.

However, he possessed one characteristic that was essential in the racing world. He had the capacity to retain a clear mental picture of almost every race he'd ever seen. As soon as Joey's riding career had started to progress, Barry had appointed himself the young jockey's unofficial adviser, which had turned out to be a critical factor in a career where luck, timing and judgement were as important as talent.

As Joey brought Zapata Bianca to a trot, and winning punters whooped and congratulated themselves, Barry calmly calculated his winnings.

Joey had always liked Di Lambert and was glad to see her walking out on to the course with Zapata's lad to lead in the winning filly. She was Dick Seabourn's secretary, a strong fit, lively girl in her mid-twenties. Her long legs and spectacular shape made up for her mousy hair and a nose which was a little too long. In racing circles, she was known for her forthrightness. Among the devious and duplicitous, who made up a large part of Newmarket's racing community, Joey found her a breath of fresh air.

Dick and Veronica Seabourn often brought her with them to the races, where she enjoyed helping out. Like the daughters of thousands of English gentlemen farmers, she couldn't remember a time when she hadn't had a horse of her own to look after. Even now, she still kept a hack in a small stable on the edge of town and, on the long summer evenings when all the expensive bloodstock had been put to bed, she liked to ride out on the heath.

Today, at Leicester races, she looked up with a broad grin on her face as the lad clipped a leading rein on to the winner's bit.

'Brilliant riding, Joey,' she said. 'I thought you'd never get her through that gap.'

He smiled back.

'Thanks. It was probably wider than it looked from the stands. I was lucky.'

He always felt more secure, high on the back of a horse where his size didn't show – especially on a horse that had just won.

Di had never made him feel inadequate; in fact, he had had an almost adolescent crush on her earlier in the year, but somehow they'd never quite found themselves in a position where anything developed. Now, as Di walked with her long stride beside the filly and her hand on Joey's thigh, he felt a sudden rush of heat to his groin.

'You've recovered from France, then?' she asked, perfectly aware of the effect she was having on him.

Joey grinned. 'Just about.'

'It all looked very dramatic in the papers . . . and rather romantic,' she added wistfully.

Dick Seabourn had watched the race from a box lent to him by one of his owners. Today he had invited several others to join him – mostly well-heeled, old Etonian types like himself, who lived and hunted nearby. When he had arrived back from unsaddling Zapata Bianca, they were patting his back and booming congratulations which he accepted with typical modesty.

'It's the jockey you should be congratulating, not me. He's wonderful with a young horse.'

'That last chap of yours, Street, was a crooked little bugger, I'm certain,' a white-haired Lincolnshire land-owner chortled tactlessly. 'I reckon he was stopping half the good horses he rode.'

'Not mine,' Seabourn said. 'I'm afraid last year they were more than capable of losing without any help from my jockey. The virus did a pretty good job all on its own.'

'I should think some of those big owners will come back, now the horses are winning for you again,' another man in the party suggested.

Seabourn's wife Veronica – grey-haired and neatly dressed in an emerald green linen suit – pursed her lips. 'I think not. Dick's rather burned his boats with most of them. Nearly all our new horses are owned by people we've gone out and found.'

Seabourn looked embarrassed. 'I did tell them what I thought of them, I must admit,' he said with a quick laugh.

Veronica raised her eyebrows almost imperceptibly and inwardly sighed. She looked out on to the course where the runners were being led out for the next race and spotted Graham Street leaning on the rails, watching them.

Chapter Four

Joey walked into the Seabourns' drawing-room at Crowle House in Newmarket, three hours after leaving Leicester races.

A hundred or so assorted friends, relations, owners, trainers and hangers-on were assembled with the Seabourns and their teenage daughter, Laura, to celebrate their twentieth wedding anniversary.

Dick Seabourn pressed a glass of champagne into his hand. 'Very well done, Joey,' he said.

'On Zapata?' he asked with a grin.

'Of course. She hardly knew she'd had a race. But I suppose we ought to drink to your French win, too. Next time, though, can you please make sure it's on one of ours?'

'Of course. By the way, Captain Zamowski sends his regards. He's a good trainer to ride for.'

'But not Michel Lacroix, what?' Seabourn laughed.

'No. I can safely say he's not my favourite!'

Barry Mannion joined them and they talked for a while about French horses and forthcoming racing events. As the party settled down, groups forming and dissolving, Joey found himself alone for a moment.

Laura Seabourn, seventeen and precociously confident, made her way through the crowd to him. She was wearing a little black dress so short that half her height seemed to consist of slender brown legs. She leaned down and kissed him on the lips, with a possessive air. Joey had the impression that she thought, because her father retained him, he was a piece of family property, available for her amusement.

'Bloody brill bit of riding in France, Joey,' she said in a public-school accent slurred by champagne. 'Did you get laid afterwards?'

'Of course not.' Joey smiled. He was not in the least bit interested in the likes of Laura Seabourn, but he knew it would be rude not to flirt back. 'There wasn't time, and I'm saving myself for you, aren't I?'

'Well, don't save yourself for too long, will you, or you might find someone else has got there first.'

'Don't worry. I'm good when it comes to a tight finish, you should know that.'

She gazed down at him with undisguised eagerness. 'Why don't you take me out to dinner tonight?'

'I expect your father will want you to eat here this evening.'

'For God's sake, Joey, I'm not a ten-year-old kid, you know,' she expostulated with a pout.

'I'm sorry, Laura,' he said, 'but tonight I feel like an old man. I'm exhausted and am going straight to bed as soon as I leave here.'

'God! You're so boring,' she said, trying to laugh off his rejection.

As she flounced off with an attempt at a steamy look over her shoulder, Dick Seabourn spoke from behind Joey.

'Don't encourage her, there's a good chap.'

'I wouldn't dream of it, sir,' he replied, and to himself

he thought, she doesn't need any encouragement.

The trainer shook his head in mock despair and turned away to talk to his vet.

Half an hour later, Dick stood on one of his wife's Chippendale dining chairs, brought the room to silence and delivered a short eulogy in praise of Veronica. He followed this up with a handful of compliments about Joey's riding skills and proposed a toast to his health.

Joey listened with the uncomfortable feeling that the trainer's heart wasn't quite in it; perhaps he was just peeved at Joey's winning a classic, albeit in another country, for another trainer.

By nine-thirty, Joey had spoken to almost everyone in the room; he'd done his duty and was ready to go. When he found a natural break in a conversation, he extricated himself and started to walk towards the door. He had nearly reached it unhindered when Veronica saw him and touched his arm, turning away from the group to whom she was talking.

'Are you off then, Joey?'

He nodded. 'Yes, I am. Thanks for a good evening.' He found that he always wanted to tell Veronica the truth; her manner was so unthreatening, one never felt the need to disguise anything. 'I don't want to make a fuss, and with my size, I can usually slip off without anyone seeing me.' He grinned.

'I don't blame you.' Veronica had changed from the green suit she'd been wearing at the races into a plain beige silk blouse and a skirt with a fine gold chain around her neck. She was at least ten years younger than her husband and still a good-looking woman in a traditional English way. 'Thanks for that win today; in fact, thanks for all the wins this season. It's been a huge boost to Dick's business.' Her voice dropped to a whisper. 'I'd been telling him from the word go that Graham wasn't up to the job.'

'He really used to work hard at it,' Joey said, being fair. 'I think he was getting frustrated. You know, weight problems and all that.'

'Frankly, Joey, you're being too kind, and you know it. Though why,' she went on with a hint of sadness, 'I should discourage a bit of kindness in this jungle, God knows. Anyway, you escape now, and thanks for coming.' Unexpectedly, she leaned down and gave him a gentle kiss on his cheek.

Joey stared at her for a moment, slightly embarrassed, before she turned away. Two minutes later, with a sense of relief, he steered his Range Rover out of the Seabourns' gates. He was grateful to them for inviting him to the party, but even after ten years in racing – the last two as a major figure – he still didn't feel comfortable with most of the people at that sort of function. Except Veronica, of course; he would always have time for her, though he suspected he'd read more into her kiss than he should have done.

He sighed to himself. It was time he got his love-life sorted.

There had been several girls – he was no saint; some he'd taken out three or four times. But in the end he always compared them to Nina, and often lost interest once that had happened. Sometimes, he dreaded the thought that maybe his memory was flawed and the Russian horsewoman would turn out to be nothing like the person he had so firmly fixed in his mind. He might find out if he could just pluck up the courage to look for the circus in the first place.

★ ★ ★

It was just before sunset when Joey parked his car in the courtyard at Three Elms Farm. He stood listening to the noises of roosting birds, took a deep breath and walked towards his front door. As he reached it a dark shape separated itself from the deep shadows in the far corner of the yard.

'Hello, Joey.'

'Danny? What are you doing lurking there?'

'I've just been for a stroll in the garden. Good party, was it?'

'Not really. Well, not the sort of party you'd have enjoyed.'

'I wouldn't know – lads never get asked to things like that.'

'Well, you weren't missing much. Do you want to come in and have a cup of coffee?' asked Joey, getting his keys out.

'Okay. But I'd rather have a drink.'

Joey didn't think Danny needed another drink but that wasn't his problem. As he unlocked the front door, he heard Roger snuffling and scratching in the kitchen. Joey let him out and the dog bounded towards them, leaping up at the two brothers.

'Fancy a game of snooker?' Joey asked, ruffling Roger's floppy ears.

'A pound a point and you're on,' Danny grinned.

They walked through into what had once been the farmhouse dairy, before Joey's predecessor had converted it into a grown-ups' games room. At one end of the long room was a fake rustic 'bar', which Joey hadn't got round to replacing. Joey poured them each a good measure of Jack Daniel's while Danny set out the snooker balls.

'So,' he said, swallowing a mouthful of whisky, 'they say you were a bit of a hero in France?'

Joey shrugged. 'Did you see the race?'

'Nope. I was busy trying to get a few quid from somewhere. Lenny Williams has taken a bundle off me in the last few weeks.'

'Come on, Dan. That's what bookies are for. Anyway, more likely you gave it to him.'

Danny laughed. 'Yer right. It's a joke, isn't it? The punters on the outside think we lads know it all.' He hammered the cue ball at the triangle of reds, scattering them all over the green baize, leaving his brother with a choice of half a dozen shots.

'The trouble with you,' Joey said, lining up an easy pot, 'is that you can judge a horse as well as the next man, but you don't spend enough time studying the races and the form. That's what Barry does, all the time, and he wins. But you'll never make money punting until you learn to work at it.'

'Yeah,' Danny sighed. 'I guess you're right.'

They played and gently ribbed each other until Joey had won and Danny was forty pounds down. Joey looked at him.

Danny shuffled his big feet and looked away from his brother's enquiring eyes. 'Double or quits?' he suggested.

Joey shook his head. 'Keep your money. Don't worry about it; it's only a game.'

Danny nodded gratefully. 'Say, Joey, I don't like to ask, but could you lend us twenty quid till Friday?'

Joey slipped a hand into his rear pocket and pulled out a bundle of notes. He peeled off a twenty and handed it to his brother. 'There you go. Don't spend it all at once!' There was neither accusation nor recrimination in his voice.

Danny sometimes wished there were.

'Thanks, Joe. Friday – I promise.'

Joey sighed as he shut the front door behind his brother, wondering for the umpteenth time how best to treat him.

Danny seemed to have no idea how to run his life and Joey seriously doubted he would ever survive on his own. He didn't want to put him down, but being a permanent soft touch wasn't going to help him, either.

The French Derby was followed by a normal enough week in the lead up to the English Derby. Scaramanga, the big prospect at Crowle House, had been visibly improving week by week since the Guineas.

Joey's arrival at the start of the season had given a real boost to morale in the yard and, for almost the first time in his life, he didn't feel that everyone around him was laughing at him or looking down on him.

Danny seemed extra buoyant when Joey turned up to ride work on Scaramanga two days later.

'How's he doing?' Joey asked as his brother legged him up on to the big, brown colt.

'He's brilliant. Doesn't he look great?'

Joey nodded. 'Let's hope he doesn't peak too soon.'

'Let's hope,' Danny agreed.

The larks were up, quivering their wings and trilling above Newmarket Heath. The morning sun, already strong, cast twenty-foot shadows behind the horses and riders as they hacked up from the stables in the town.

Dick Seabourn was on the Heath by the time his first

string arrived. He stood beside his spotless old Mercedes with a pair of battered binoculars in his hands, their case dangling at his hip. Tall – six foot three – and handsome in an unmistakably English way, he wore a flat cap over his tanned forehead and thick, dark grey curls, a tweed jacket, cavalry twill trousers and brown brogues. He squinted his clear blue eyes into the sun to watch his horses walk on to the Heath.

Scaramanga was an uncomplicated individual, a beautiful conformed animal who simply loved to gallop. After six furlongs at three-quarter speed, Joey pulled him up, as Seabourn had instructed, and trotted across to the trainer where a lad had turned up to ride the horse back.

Joey jumped down, feeling conscious of his size, as always, and losing confidence as soon as his feet touched the ground. Seabourn towered over him but, unlike many men, he seemed to understand Joey's complex about his height. He managed somehow to talk to Joey as if they were eye to eye.

'He's looking good. If we can win at Epsom . . .'

He seemed suddenly reluctant to tell Joey what the benefits would be – apart from the obvious ones – if Crowle House managed to send out the winner of the Derby. Joey didn't press him. If they pulled it off, he thought, that would do for him: two Derbys in one year.

'I think we might,' he said, without too much emphasis.

Seabourn nodded again. 'How does he feel?'

'Plenty in hand at the end, and I wasn't doing anything to help him.'

'Good. Well, let's keep our fingers crossed.'

Joey's last ride at York was at four-thirty-five. Forty minutes after he'd picked up his prize – his only trophy that day – he was strapping himself into a seat in the Cessna. The plane took off and followed the A1 south towards Newmarket.

By six-thirty, Joey was driving his Ferrari into the converted thatched barn beside his house, underneath Barry Mannion's office.

Barry's Porsche was still parked outside, along with the Range Rover and a BMW Joey recognised as Barry's old car.

He ran up an external wooden staircase and let himself into the office which was a large open room with exposed beams and rafters. There was an oak desk, where Barry sat, and a smaller pine one for his secretary, though currently occupied by Di Lambert. There were several indoor plants positioned between the desks and a long sofa in green and white checked linen, on which Danny was flopped with Roger curled up asleep beside him. A coffee table in the middle of the room was covered in magazines and newspapers.

A television opposite the sofa was tuned loudly to the Racing Channel. Barry was shouting happily down the telephone and Di Lambert was on another line, giggling to someone.

'Hello, team,' Joey called over all the noise. Hearing Joey's voice, Roger awoke, eased himself off the sofa and padded over to sniff approvingly at his master.

Barry glanced across and nodded with the phone wedged between his cheek and shoulder while he thumbed through a pile of papers. Di smiled at him and carried on her conversation.

'All right, Joey?' Danny said, without taking his eyes

off the TV screen. 'God! This guy's going to get a suspension! He's hit that horse ten times already.'

Joey pottered about while he waited for Barry to finish his call. For a couple of minutes he glanced at the next day's declarations before picking up a bundle of post lying on the coffee table. He pulled off the rubber band which was wrapped around it to see if there was anything interesting for him. At the bottom of the stack was a Jiffy bag bearing a French stamp, which made him think of Stephanie.

He peeled off the sticky tape and pulled apart the staples that secured the envelope.

As he'd assumed, there was a videotape inside.

Di finished her conversation and put the phone down. 'Hi, Joey! What've you got there?'

'It must be the French Derby. Zamowski said he'd send a tape.'

'Great. Can I have it after you?'

'We can watch it now, if you want?'

Di looked at her watch. 'I wish I could but I've got to run, I'm meeting my mother in Cambridge.'

Barry, at his desk, had also put down his phone. 'Well done, Joey boy. I didn't think you'd get the trip,' he said, referring to Joey's York winner.

'That horse'll go a mile and a half; I told you.'

'Well, I can't always be right.'

Joey laughed. 'I never thought I'd hear you admit it, though.' He waved the tape in his hand. 'Do you want to have a look at this?'

'Sure. I've been meaning to all day.'

'Danny?'

Danny was absorbed in the next race replay. 'What?' he grunted.

'Do you want to see my win at Chantilly?'

'There're a few more races I want to watch here first.'

'I'll take it back to the house and watch it there, then,' Joey said, resigned, and turned to Barry. 'Come over when you've finished, if you want?'

He nodded. 'Will do.'

'By the way, what's your old BMW doing outside? I thought you'd sold it?' Joey asked as he headed for the door with Roger bounding behind him.

'Graham wants to buy it,' Di said with a lift of her brows.

'Yeah,' Barry said. 'The cheeky bastard said he wanted to test drive it, so I brought it in specially, he took it for a spin and then dropped it back here saying he'd have to think about it first.'

Joey glanced at the old BMW as he walked across to his house. It must be worth about ten grand, he thought. Where the hell was Graham going to get that kind of money from?

Joey couldn't help feeling some sympathy for him, but Graham had ridden for the bookies too often recently. Good jockeys could get away with not trying occasionally, especially if they were also producing plenty of winners. Graham seemed to be doing it every afternoon. It was only a matter of time before his licence was rescinded.

Joey unlocked his front door and went in. He was always glad to get back home. The house was furnished in a simple, country style with old pine, oak and elm. The wife of one of the smaller trainers had set herself up as a decorator to supplement her husband's recession income. She had understood exactly what Joey wanted, and he was more than happy with what she'd done for him.

He made a cup of tea, took it through into his study and pushed the videotape into the VCR. He settled down on one of the sofas to watch himself winning the Prix du Jockey Club on Isle de Rey.

Eighty seconds later, he was staring at a blank, fizzing screen, limp and helpless with shock.

He had been expecting Chantilly and his first success in a French classic, but what he had just watched were two scenes from a world he'd hoped never to see again.

The first short clip provoked only a mild mood of nostalgia, even a smile, as he saw himself riding out into the arena beneath Freddie Fielding's big top in his first public performance as one of Korsakov's Cossack Riders. It wasn't a bad performance, either, he thought to himself, for a sixteen-year-old Liverpool kid who had never so much as touched a horse six months before. The sight of Nina Korsakov cantering round with perfect poise and a cool smile on her face evoked some unsettling memories, though.

But it was the second clip which left him shaking with horror. Starting with a sequence of shaky shots of him rehearsing a spectacular act with the Korsakovs' trapeze troupe, it turned into a replay of the worst, most terrifying event of his life.

Slowly, as his senses returned, so too did vivid memories which he'd been trying to wipe from his consciousness for years; memories of a time when he had been bullied and frightened, and desperate loneliness had clouded his judgement.

What he had seen was a minute from his past, recorded ten years before, caught and perfectly preserved like a specimen in formaldehyde – a minute that was the very nadir of the two lonely years he had spent with

Freddie Fielding's travelling circus.

In the final few seconds of the short sequence, the unsteady but sharply focused camera zoomed in on the floor of the big top, where a broken safety net lay, draped around the two inert figures of Mikhail Korsakov and his father Ivan.

Ivan Korsakov. Even now, the thought of the man made Joey shudder with fear.

Ivan was the first person he had seen when he'd crept into Freddie Fielding's Circus compound, plucking up the courage to ask if they had any work.

Joey had been to the circus a few days earlier in Sefton Park, near Liverpool, where he lived. A picture of the blonde goddess on the grey stallion, both with manes flowing, had never left his head since and that day he'd followed them to their next pitch on the edge of Stockport, just south of Manchester.

He had put on his best clothes – a white cricket sweater, a pair of almost new cord trousers, and his old shoes polished as bright as he could get them. He was feeling hot and awkward, dreading instant rejection, but had made up his mind that the circus was going to be his way out of Liverpool.

Danny had already gone, and had written to Joey from Newmarket – working with horses was a breeze and freedom was fantastic, he'd said.

It was mid-morning and several hours before the first performance when Joey wandered uncertainly from the road, in among the cluster of tents, pick-ups and trailers behind the big top. He saw no one until he rounded the corner of a large, grubby marquee emitting aromas of unfamiliar animal dung.

A tall man, stripped to the waist and wearing only black tights which showed every sinew of his well-muscled legs, was standing with his back to Joey outside a long, four-wheeled caravan. He was shaving in front of a mirror dangling from a hook on the side of his trailer.

Knees trembling, Joey walked up to him. He stood there unseen until he cleared his throat. The big man spun round. Joey couldn't help cowering at the sight of the hard, muscular torso and the cruel, flashing dark brown eyes. The man's sheer physical presence almost knocked him off his feet. Even his moustache was viciously pointed so that it seemed more of a weapon than an adornment.

'Who are you?' He towered over Joey's slender four feet ten inches. 'What do you want?'

'I want to work . . . with the horses, please?'

'What do you know about horses?' the big man challenged in a rumbling, foreign voice.

'Not much,' Joey admitted. 'I just know I like them.'

'Do you?' the man said with heavy cynicism. 'Many, many people want to work in the circus, you know.' He gazed down at Joey between the wings of his huge moustache. 'You are just a mouse of a boy, but you have something. Maybe I can use you on the trapeze. If I want you, the boss will have you. If not . . .' He heaved his shoulders dismissively. 'That's his trailer – over there. Tell him Ivan Korsakov sent you.' He nodded at a caravan elaborately finished in chrome and gold-flake paint. 'If I want you, you will be something. If I don't, you are nothing. And I won't ever let you forget it.'

And – Joey reflected bitterly now, stricken with horror in front of his television – he never had.

Even ten years after Ivan Korsakov's vicious bullying

had stopped for good, Joey felt a faint nausea at the memory. Automatically, he stumbled across his study to the television. He rewound the tape in the VCR, started it again and fell back on to the feather cushions of his chesterfield to gaze at the screen again in incredulous horror. Hard though he had tried to erase it from his memory, he found he hadn't forgotten a single second of the sequence it showed.

The terror Joey felt now was as vivid and debilitating as on the day it had happened. When the film clip had finished for the second time, he leaned back his head and closed his eyes, drained, utterly appalled that the one discreditable moment in his personal history had been recorded and reproduced on videotape, capable of duplication for anyone to see.

He groaned and swore as the questions began to pound inside his head.

Who the hell had sent it?

Ginger Calaval?

No, Ginger had always been his friend.

But if not Ginger, who?

Who else could have done it?

Why had they sent it? Why now?

Who else had seen it?

He screwed up his face and gritted his teeth as the true horror of it hit him.

There was a loud bang on the front door.

Joey started. It would be Barry coming to watch the race. He gasped with relief that he'd managed to watch the tape before Barry had arrived.

He leaped to his feet and crossed to the television. He ejected the tape and stuffed it into a waste-paper basket. Going into the hall, he forced a smile on to his face before opening the front door.

Graham Street was standing on the door step, fastidiously picking fluff from the lapel of his smart blue blazer.

'Oh, hello, Joey,' he said, as if surprised to see him in his own home. He pushed a fringe of fine blond hair off his forehead. 'Can I come in? I want to ask you a favour.'

Joey wasn't feeling up to seeing anyone, least of all Graham, but he forced himself to open the door wider and let the other jockey in.

'Do you want a drink?' he asked, hoping he was making it clear he didn't want the offer accepted.

'Yeah. Brandy . . . please.'

Joey led him into his study where he'd just been watching the horror show on tape. He glanced guiltily at the waste-paper basket.

He poured his guest a much larger drink than he would normally have done, and a small one for himself.

He waved Graham into one of the easy chairs, and sat himself on a sofa. 'Well, what can I do for you?'

Graham took a noisy swig of his brandy and gazed at the blank television screen. He tried to look directly at Joey but turned his eyes away at the last moment. 'I was going to ride Sheila's Shebeen in the ten-furlong race at Epsom tomorrow.'

'I'm riding her now. But I didn't know you'd been jocked off. I'm sorry.' Joey shrugged his shoulders. 'What can I say? I didn't chase the ride.'

'No, I'm not saying you did. That fat bastard, Leeming who owns her wanted you.'

Joey made a regretful gesture with his hands. 'Not my fault, Graham.'

'Could you tell him you've changed your mind? Say

you can't ride her for some reason?'

'Why? I suppose you could do with a few winners.' Though Joey had already guessed that winning wasn't what Graham had in mind.

Graham looked at him for a few seconds, and Joey saw the shame in the other man's eyes.

'It's just that,' he forced the words out, 'I really need to ride her.'

'So you can stop her?'

Graham bit his lip nervously. 'I need the money, Joey.'

He hardened himself to the catch in Graham's voice and the desperation in his eyes.

'I can't do it. I'm sorry you're in trouble, but I'm not going to help you get yourself deeper into it by dealing with people like Lenny Williams. If you get really stuck, let me know.'

Graham flicked back his hair and glared at Joey. 'I don't want your fucking charity!' He drained the rest of the brandy from his glass and stood up a little unsteadily before walking out of the room.

Joey followed and said nothing as he watched him heave open the front door to let himself out.

Graham left the door ajar and strode across the yard to a clapped-out Subaru. He jumped in, revved up and drove out, narrowly missing Barry, who had just stepped down the stairs from his office.

Joey waited as he walked towards the house.

'What's up, Joey boy? You look as though you're about to throw up.' He nodded in the direction Graham had driven off. 'How he thinks he can afford to buy my BMW I'll never know,' he snorted. 'If that toe-rag's been giving you a hard time about Sheila's Shebeen, don't take any notice. He was on at me about it too – accusing me of nicking the ride for you.'

'That's not the problem. Maybe I ate something.'

'You want to take some medicine then. I'll leave you to it. I just came to say I haven't time to see that tape now. I'll have a proper look tomorrow, okay?'

He gave his customary nod and a wink, and walked over to his car.

Joey watched him go, glad of the extra time to think of a good reason why Barry couldn't see the video the next day either. He went back to his study and took it from the basket. He plucked at the tape with his fingers, pulling it from the spool until he'd extracted it all and scrunched it into an untidy bundle. He carried it through his kitchen to the back door, picking up a box of matches on the way, and took it out to the incinerator in the garden.

He dropped the tape in, lit it and watched it flare up. He knew that wasn't the end of it. There would be other copies of it somewhere, but the act relieved him for the moment, deluded him that any danger it threatened was past, for the time being at least.

He went back inside to change for a reception the auctioneers were holding at Tattersall's and tried to block out of his mind the agonising question of who had sent the tape.

Before he went out, he picked up the Jiffy bag in which the tape had been sent. It was post-marked Paris, 3 June 1996.

Chapter Five

For a brief moment, inside two furlongs from the Epsom finishing post, Joey thought he was going to land his Derby double. He was lying second and gaining ground when, despite Joey's intense efforts, the leader fought back and deprived Scaramanga by a short head.

For the next week and a half, Joey heard nothing from whoever had sent the tape. He felt like a man wandering through a minefield, waiting every second for the explosion that would inevitably finish him off.

He carried on his work automatically, giving scarcely any hint of the turmoil inside him. Dick Seabourn asked him once if something was the matter, but Joey fobbed him off with a story about a dose of food-poisoning.

On the tenth morning, he came home from riding work. There was a stack of post scattered on the seagrass flooring in the hall.

He picked it up, carried it through to his kitchen and dropped it on the old pine table in the middle of the room. He ground some dark Costa Rican coffee beans and made himself a large espresso. He glanced at his watch: eight-thirty. Barry would be round in twenty minutes to go through the declarations with him.

It was Tuesday, the first day of the Royal meeting – the biggest week in the flat-racing calendar – and the bookies had made Joey Leatham favourite to win the jockeys' title.

Scaramanga's finish in the Derby, a few inches behind the winner, and comparable form among several of Dick's horses, made Joey optimistic about his fifteen chances over the next four days.

He turned the television on to the Racing Channel to see a preview of the day's events while he drank his coffee. At the same time, he started to open his post.

When he opened the fourth letter, it took him a fraction of a second to register that it was neither typed nor hand written, but scrappily composed with Letraset.

There was an accurate estimate of his earnings for the year, and a demand for £100,000, which was approximately twenty-five percent of that sum – followed by an uncompromising threat to despatch copies of the video-tape to interested parties if he did not comply precisely with the instructions he would receive.

Joey read the scruffy message several times before he picked up the envelope. It was addressed by hand in block capitals, dated the previous day and stamped with a Nottingham post-mark.

Joey stared at it, absurdly trying to put a face to the sender. At the same time, he shook with a deep, physical fear of exposure, blame and public opprobrium for an eighteen-year-old's innocent prank that had ended in tragedy. For two weeks he'd been hoping and praying he wasn't going to hear anything more about the tape. Now, as he'd always known it would, it had come back to blight his life until somehow he could find who was responsible.

As Barry drove him to Ascot, he tried unsuccessfully to make a link between the two post-marks: Paris and Nottingham.

The first race of the Ascot meeting promised to have an extra edge to it. Graham Street was riding the favourite while Joey was on an unfancied outsider called Pistachio, from another yard.

In the absence of a Seabourn runner, Barry had persuaded the doubtful owner that he should run the colt, with Joey up.

As he cantered down to the start of the seven-furlong course, Joey acknowledged to himself, as he often had, how Barry's skill in spotting underrated horses had done so much for his own career. It was the first time the horse had run short of a mile.

He also knew that Barry had backed Pistachio to win a lot of money.

Joey pulled up behind the starting stalls beside Graham Street, who was already circling on an athletic chestnut colt. The animal had a lot of class and had already won two big races that season. Joey knew that Graham's winning percentage was more than he could have earned for stopping it.

As far as Joey knew it was Graham's only ride for the whole meeting. All the press had tipped the horse that morning; for once, he would be desperate to win. But Joey was determined to beat him – not out of any malice towards Graham, but simply because that's what gave him a buzz.

And a buzz was what he got, with Graham Street's mount half a length back in second.

Joey and Pistachio were led in by Samantha Peacock, whose Australian husband owned the exhausted, sweating colt. There was a ragged cheer for the jockey and his unexpected winner. After the first race of Royal Ascot, for a few untroubled moments Joey felt the same elation he had in his earliest wins for Sammy Samson. Then he saw Graham glowering at him from beneath his bushy eyebrows, and his thoughts sharply back-tracked to the letter that had arrived in the post that morning.

He'd had several hours to think about it, only half listening to Barry's analysis of every runner in every race that day as they'd driven down from Newmarket, and his head was full of possible suspects – dozens of people who he thought might be resentful enough, desperate enough, malicious enough, to want to damage him and benefit themselves.

Rationally, though, he concluded that it must have come from someone at the circus. But why had they waited so long? He had been earning good money for three or four years. However hard he tried to deny the possibility, Ginger was still the most likely culprit.

Ginger Calaval had been the elder of the two clowns at Freddie Fielding's. The pair performed their own crazy juggling act and filled in time between the others. When Joey had arrived at the circus, Ginger was living on his own in a small caravan. However, he had a spare bunk in a tiny compartment at the end of his trailer and when Ivan Korsakov had agreed to take Joey on, he had offered it to Joey.

Ginger was a Czech, a few inches taller than Joey and about fifty years old, though he could easily have been ten years more or less.

He greeted Joey with voluble irritation.

'Why on earth,' he asked in his thick accent, 'have you come to this bunch of wandering misfits?'

'I dunno. Maybe I'm a bit of a misfit meself,' Joey said. 'My mum came over from Ireland and dumped me and my brother. I don't even know what my real name is.'

'So you're an Irish boy?'

'I suppose so, I haven't a clue who my dad was. The council gave us our names. We were sent to an orphanage then fostered by some people called Mr and Mrs Roberts.'

'And now you've run away from them?'

Joey nodded. 'They're not like real parents; they were paid for keeping us and never let us do anything. We couldn't watch telly or go to the films. They're Methodists, ever so strict. I even had to sneak off to come to the circus.'

'But you should still be at school, shouldn't you?'

'Not for much longer. I'm sixteen next month. Our kid's gone off to work in Newmarket and I don't think the Robertses wanted me for much longer. Anyway, I hated school. I was smaller than everyone in my class and I kept getting thumped for it. It was all right for Danny . . .'

'Who's Danny?'

'My brother. He's a year older than me and twice the size. Anyway, I did a bit of a paper round so I had some money to come to the circus.' Joey shook his head. 'I'm glad I did. I was knocked out by it, you know. I mean – I couldn't believe the trapeze artists and the tigers! But it was the horses, the Cossack Riders, I liked the best.'

Ginger made a sour face. 'And the clowns?'

'Oh, yes, of course. D'you know, when I saw you and all those midgets, it made me feel better. You see, I'm never going to get any taller, for sure, but you're even smaller and it doesn't seem to matter to you.'

Joey had regretted the words as soon as he'd spoken them.

The hurt on the clown's face was almost tangible. 'Not now it doesn't. As you get older you learn there's no point denying the inescapable. It doesn't really make it any better, though.'

Ginger had been right about that, Joey thought. But what could have made the clown turn against him now?

The tape had been sent from France, which was why, when he'd first seen the package, he'd assumed it was the French Derby recording. Joey recalled that there'd been a rumour when Ginger had left the circus that he'd gone to join some old colleagues in France, though no one knew for sure.

He didn't want to believe that his old friend had harboured any kind of animosity towards him. After all, the whole plan to make Ivan Korsakov look a fool had been Ginger's. Finding him now was Joey's top priority.

'Are you all right, Joey?' Samantha Peacock asked, leading him into the paddock.

He forced a smile and glanced down. The owner's wife was regarding him with unexpected concern. 'Yeah, sure. Suffering from shock.' He grinned. 'Didn't think we'd that much of a chance.'

'Barry did.'

'Well, I hope you followed his advice.'

'We did.' She laughed happily. 'And you deserve a big thank you.'

Joey didn't answer. The trainer had joined them at the gate to the paddock and was patting the horse's neck, congratulating the jockey. They pulled up in the winner's slot; Joey jumped down and unbuckled his girth. He heaved the saddle over the horse's back, stopped for a moment for a photograph then hurried off to weigh in.

Afterwards, with no ride in the next race, he got a cup of tea from the small canteen in the changing room and tried to decide what his next move should be.

When Joey was still an apprentice, Jimmy McMahon had been the first owner to insist that Sammy Samson put Joey on his horses. He had recognised the young jockey's skill and grit right from the start and had moved six horses to Crowle House when Joey had taken his retainer there.

Over the years, they had become good friends with a strong mutual regard. It was now a tradition for Joey to spend Ascot week in the McMahons' house, a convenient few miles from the course.

Jimmy McMahon was the boss of a major construction company and a big character in every way: a first-generation Irish immigrant who disguised his shrewdness beneath eighteen stone of overindulged flesh and booming Celtic bonhomie.

If Joey had had a weakness for alcohol, he'd have been hard tempted during his four nights with Jimmy and his wife Molly, a tiny Kerry woman. Every evening was a party, whether they'd won money or lost; Jimmy McMahon never divulged which.

Getting back that evening, Joey managed to slip away

for the first hour with the excuse that he was going to take a nap in his room, which was furnished like a five-star hotel with phone, fax and modem.

He picked up the phone and asked directory enquiries to give him the number of Cambridge police.

As he had hoped, they were able to tell him at once where Freddie Fielding's Circus had gone. After Cambridge, they had a two-week run in Nottingham.

Joey dialled the number of the only man he knew in Nottingham – the retired cavalry officer who was clerk of the racecourse there. If he was surprised by Joey's question, he didn't show it.

'A circus performing near here, did you say?'

'Yeah, sounds a funny question, I know,' Joey said, 'but is there?'

'Yes, there certainly is.' The major gave a curt, faintly disapproving laugh. 'Right here on the racecourse, for the next ten days.'

'And what's it called?' Joey asked unnecessarily.

'Freddie Fielding's Cir—' The ex-soldier's faintly supercilious voice faded into an embarrassed grunt. 'Er . . . didn't I read that you were once with them?'

Joey laughed. 'Yes, you did. That's where I learned trick riding: with Korsakov's Cossack Riders.'

'They're still on the bill,' the clerk said. 'Lovely girl running the show.'

'Really?' Joey replied, finding it hard not to show his excitement. 'Not a girl called Nina?'

'That's the one.'

'Well, I may be up to see them soon,' Joey said. 'Thanks for your help.'

He put down the phone, wanting to jump into his car and leave at once.

Nina and the Cossack Riders, Ginger, Giulio and the midgets, Mr Wimsatt the ring-master . . . He hadn't seen any of them since he'd left the circus. Nina had been the only reason he might have gone back, but a nagging doubt that she would ever return his feelings had always stopped him. That and his own awful feeling of guilt. As soon as Royal Ascot was over, he was going to put that aside and go in search of her.

Joey decided he wasn't ready to put on a front for the party-goers downstairs. Instead, he lay on his bed and thought about Freddie Fielding's Circus.

He wondered if Ivor Wimsatt was still owner and ring-master. Wondered too what he would have made of Wimsatt if he had met him at this age, not as the completely unsophisticated fifteen-year-old he had been then. He recalled the first time he had met the strange little man . . .

After his encounter with Ivan Korsakov, Joey had knocked on the door of the trailer which the big Russian had pointed out.

It was opened by a woman with hair dyed the colour of straw. She was wearing leopard skin leggings and a short purple halter top. Joey thought he'd never seen so much make-up around a woman's eyes.

'Hello. I . . . I'm . . .'

'What is it, pretty boy?' the woman asked, not unkindly.

'I want to see Mr Wimsatt,' he said in a rush.

'He's not here.'

With a lurch of disappointment, Joey turned and saw the big Russian, fifty yards away, glance up from his shaving and stare at him.

Joey swallowed. If everyone in the circus was like that man, he was damn' sure he didn't want to stay.

He turned back to the woman. 'Oh, well, never mind. I think I'll leave it.' He started to climb down the steps.

'Hang on, love. They're not all like him, you know. If you want to see Mr Wimsatt, you come back up and stop here a few minutes.'

Joey looked at her for a moment before making up his mind. He clambered back into the caravan, amazed by the flashy luxury of the interior and its spaciousness.

The woman waved him to the sofa and gave him a can of Coke to drink. 'You'll be all right here,' she said with a wink, and clattered off down the steps in her high-heeled mules.

Joey gazed at the ornately framed photographs of circus acts that covered the walls, and wondered what Mr Wimsatt would be like, and what he should say to him. He remembered seeing the archetypal ring-master when he'd come to watch the circus perform; a man like Ivan but much smoother.

The reality was a disappointment. The only thing Mr Wimsatt had in common with the Russian was his moustache – and this was an insignificant little growth compared to Ivan's.

'Who are you? Sharon said you've come for a job.'

'I never said that,' Joey started, peeved that he had been pre-empted.

'Well, she didn't think you'd come to sell me life insurance.' Mr Wimsatt was a small, busy man, wearing tartan trousers and a red cardigan. He sat down at a table and shuffled through some papers as he talked, giving the impression that he was allowing the boy about a quarter of his attention. 'How old are you?'

'Fifteen, nearly sixteen.'

'You look about twelve. What's your act?'

'I . . . I haven't got an act,' he said. 'But I'll learn. I want to work with the horses and I'll do anything while I'm learning – for no pay,' he added recklessly.

'I've got plenty of people here already working for nothing,' Wimsatt said bluntly.

'Ivan said he could use me on the trapeze,' Joey offered reluctantly.

Wimsatt looked up from his papers and thoughtfully rattled a wooden pencil between his teeth. 'Did he? You look keen and fit. Maybe, if someone will give you some space in a van, we can find something for you – if Ivan wants you. If anyone'll teach you to ride, that'd be a bonus.'

Joey lay back in the luxury of the McMahons' Virginia Water mansion and found himself wondering, not for the first time, what his life would have been like if Ivan Korsakov had not wanted him.

After half an hour, his conscience got the better of him and, reluctantly, he started to dress. Putting on a classic Prince of Wales check suit, he tried to put a good face on his inner turmoil and went down to join the festivities below.

Joey had decided to ride at Warwick on the Saturday, rather than Ascot Heath. After racing on Friday, he hitched a lift back to Newmarket with Johnnie Redmond. He picked up Roger from Danny's cottage and, with a sigh of relief to be away from the permanent party atmosphere of Ascot, let himself in at his front door while the sun was still well above the horizon.

He walked through to his kitchen, dumped his bags on

the table and switched his television on to the Racing Channel to watch a replay of the day's races while he opened a tin for Roger.

It had been one of the best weeks ever in his career, and he'd crowned it with a double that day. He'd won the week's championship. Everyone wanted him to stay and celebrate. There was nothing he wanted less, not, at least, until he'd found out who had sent that tape, and with a demand for £100,000.

The phone trilled. A racing journalist wanted to interview him about his week.

Joey managed to answer his questions for five minutes and get rid of him without saying anything too personal. As soon as he'd put down the phone, it rang again.

'Hello?'

'Hello, Joey. Not out celebrating then?' He didn't catch the words at once, the sound was indistinct. 'No, maybe not. Got a pen and paper?'

Joey's blood chilled as he realised the significance of the whispering voice which had been deliberately distorted to avoid identification. He leaned over and picked up a Biro and the *Sporting Life* from the dresser. 'What is it?' he croaked.

As he listened, Joey tried to discern some recognisable characteristics or accent in the voice, but it was impossible through whatever device the man – if it was a man – was using.

He was told to deposit £100,000 into an account at any branch of the Southern Counties Building Society, by the following Tuesday. If the money didn't arrive, or he went to the police, the voice told him, he would find that every national newspaper's sports desk would receive a copy of the videotape.

Joey felt all the strength drain from his limbs. The phone line clicked and reverted to a dialling tone. He banged down the receiver and took a deep breath.

He tried to imagine the man, maybe ringing from Nottingham, somewhere near the circus.

He looked at his watch. It was after nine; too late to start out now. He would go after racing tomorrow.

The telephone by his elbow rang again.

He picked it up warily.

'Hello.'

'Hi, Joey. It's Di.'

A picture of Di Lambert instantly came to mind: bright-eyed, reliable, good-natured – and, above all, in possession of a fine body in full working order. Suddenly Joey realised how much he needed some female company to distract him from the looming crisis.

'Hi, Di.' Joey smiled to himself. 'Where are you?'

'At home . . . at a loose end. No one's back from Ascot.'

'You sound lonely. Come round and have a drink.'

'Can we have dinner first?'

' "First"? I like the sound of that. Sure I'll treat you to dinner. Book us a table at Le Picasso and I'll pick you up in twenty minutes.'

Joey studied Di in the candle-lit, Art Deco surroundings of Le Picasso. She wasn't as beautiful as Stephanie, or as striking as Nina, but tonight she was looking her very best. Carefully applied make-up made her eyes look bigger than normal, her nose more pert, and her chin smaller. A soft, smooth, well-tanned cleavage was clearly visible over the sheath of black silk-satin she wore. A sweet, musky scent wafted from her warm skin.

But Joey's natural diffidence wouldn't let him plunge straight into the kind of blatant innuendo other men might have been tempted to try on her.

Although they'd been to dozens of the same parties and had spent hours in the same bars and boxes at the races, this was the first time they'd had dinner alone together; the first time they'd really been one to one; and, as far as Joey could judge, she was as pleased to be there as he was.

But she sensed his reticence. 'Well, didn't you fancy staying in Ascot for a celebration with Mr McMahon?'

'No, I did not.' Joey grinned. 'Until you rang, I'd made up my mind to stay in and celebrate with Roger. I'm riding work first thing, I've got three rides at Warwick and then I'm driving to Nottingham.'

'Nottingham? But there's no racing there tomorrow night.'

'I'm not racing – I'm going to the circus.'

He got a perverse amusement from the effect this had on Di. His old life in the circus was fairly common knowledge; most people in Newmarket knew about it, but seemed to find the idea rather embarrassing and were reluctant to mention it or ask him about it.

'The circus?' Di said with surprise. 'What for?'

'Come on, don't tell me you didn't know I once worked in a circus?'

'Well, I suppose I had heard . . .'

'For God's sake,' Joey laughed, 'it's not as if it was a leper colony.'

'No, of course not.'

'I'm not ashamed of my time there.' This wasn't entirely true, but he had a point to make. 'It's where I learned to ride.'

'What – trick riding?'

'That's right.'

'Who taught you to race ride, then?'

Joey didn't answer at once. He gazed around the restaurant – a popular place but only half full that evening. A lot of Newmarket people weren't back from Ascot. A cross between folksy and minimalist in harebell blue and lemon yellow, the restaurant served expensive food in such small portions that even the most weight-conscious jockey could eat safely. But Joey was the only jockey there. As he thought about the answer to Di's question, his mind flashed back to his first few months in Newmarket.

'There's a touch of irony there, actually,' he said. 'It's funny how relationships – friendships – change over a few years. You wouldn't believe how terrified I was of this place when I first came here . . .'

'What? Of Le Picasso?'

'No. Of this town. It seemed to me like an entirely separate world, with its own rules and codes – its own language, almost – which you had to learn before anyone would take any notice of you. It makes outsiders feel very alien and unwanted. You wouldn't know that – you've been around here all your life. But people like Sammy Samson, Mick Mahoney – Sammy's first jockey then – Graham Street, were like people from another planet to me. Even Danny my brother, for God's sake.'

Joey didn't need to point out to Di the obvious reversal in their respective fortunes.

'And I couldn't believe the amount of money around – what the jockeys were paid, and driving around in Ferraris, and fellas paying millions for yearlings . . .

'The funny thing was, though, in a tacky sort of way

the circus was quite glamorous, too. You know – spotlights, sequins, cheering crowds and all. The main difference from racing was the performers earned a pittance. They'd have got more on the dole, half of them, but that didn't matter – not inside the circus. There was a kind of religious commitment to the way of life.

'But here, where there's all this money, bullshit and jargon – all this hierarchy and snobbery, as if they're dealing with matters of vital world importance – all it's really about is making your horse run faster than anyone else's. Not very important in the scheme of things, is it? But you get sucked up into it until it's the be-all and end-all.'

Joey looked at Di with a wry grin. 'You were asking who taught me to race ride. I don't suppose you knew Sammy Samson – my first trainer? He taught me a lot, but I learned most from Graham.'

'Who? Graham Street?' Di said, amazed. 'He never told me.'

'Didn't he?' Joey sounded surprised. 'Well, he was a bloody good teacher, and he really wanted me to succeed.'

'Not quite to the extent you have, though, I suspect.'

'No. I'm afraid he probably wishes he hadn't taught me a thing, especially after Pistachio's race on Tuesday. He didn't look too chuffed after.'

'He had all his punters on it, apparently.'

'You don't say.' Joey thought of Graham, dead broke, with a nag of a wife, two snotty-nosed kids, a mortgage you couldn't count the noughts on, and no regular income.

It wasn't the first time since the blackmail demand had come in that he'd thought of Graham – resentful, and certainly desperate, enough to look anywhere for a large lump of easy money. If Joey hadn't opened the French Jiffy bag himself, Graham would have been prime suspect. Logically, though, Joey was still convinced that if it wasn't Ginger, it must have been someone else from the circus. And he hadn't yet ruled out his old circus friend.

He shook his head.

'What?' Di asked.

'Sorry – thinking of something else. Did you get to know Graham well while he was at Dick's?'

Di seemed reluctant to admit it. Finally she said: 'Yes, I suppose so. He's had a tough time, really, and his wife's a bitch.'

'What did he marry her for, then?'

'God knows, but he did and they've got those kids, so he won't leave her now. And anyway, lots of men marry bitches. Don't ask me why.'

'You're right,' Joey mused. 'I've often wondered about that, too.'

'So,' Di said abruptly, reverting to their original conversation, 'how did you end up at Samson's?'

'Through my brother Danny. Then when Sammy gave up I persuaded Dick to take him on at Crowle House.'

'He's not at all like you, is he?'

'He is in some ways,' Joey said, automatically defensive. 'We were very close when we were kids.'

'Were you? But you're complete opposites now. He's big, thick and charmless.'

'Oh, come on, that's not fair. But I suppose the comparison's flattering for me – except for the size.'

'You're paranoid about being short, aren't you? I can't think why you're so worried about it; you wouldn't be

where you are if it weren't for your height. Besides –'
there was a mischievous gleam in her eye '– I hear you're
not so small in certain other departments.'

'For God's sake,' Joey said. 'Who the hell told you
that?'

'I've forgotten,' she laughed. 'Anyway, I thought I
might find out for myself one of these days.' She opened
her big, candid eyes and drank Joey in.

He succumbed, pouring himself a large glass of wine.
'Well, maybe you will.'

'Tell me something . . .' Joey was lying naked on his
stomach, diagonally across his bed. He looked at the
black dress and lacy underwear abandoned on the carpet
and leaned over the edge of the bed to pick up a bottle
of champagne from the floor. He topped up two glasses
standing beside it and lifted them, turning over as he did.
'How did you learn to make love like that?'

'I don't know,' Di murmured with matter-of-fact confidence. 'It sort of came naturally.'

'Like you just did?'

'Mmmm. I can see why you get on so well with the
fillies.'

Joey laughed out loud. 'I only talk to them, for God's
sake.'

'Well, you're hung like a horse, so it wouldn't be a
problem.'

He laughed again. 'Talking of horses, do you realise
that in precisely two hours from now, I'm supposed to be
galloping one across the Heath?'

'And you need some sleep. Okay, I'll go. But first, I'll
just give you a little goodbye kiss.'

She turned and placed her left knee beside his right

ear, leaning forward until Joey felt her lips brush his stomach.

She crouched lower so her mound was a few inches above his face. He felt her hands on his hardening penis and the soft suction of her lips around it.

He reached up and wrapped his arms around her soft buttocks, drawing her down so his tongue could stretch up and probe, and she began to tremble again while her own busy mouth brought him to another shuddering climax.

Di's words the previous night came back to Joey as he walked his horse from the end of the gallop towards Dick Seabourn's waiting Mercedes. It had been a great evening but with all the hallmarks of a one night stand. Besides racing, he and Di had little in common.

She was a good-natured, well-constructed Sloane Ranger, who would probably revert to type and marry an Old Etonian banker, while he was a four-foot-ten-inch orphan from the wrong end of Liverpool.

Of course, since he'd arrived in the traditionally aristocratic world of flat-racing, he'd taught himself to fit in – or at least, not to stand out – in the Newmarket crowd. He didn't find it difficult to dress like something out of the Hackett's catalogue, not to hold his knife like a pen, and to tone down his native Scouse.

After ten years in the business, he realised he was actually more intelligent than many of the senior racing figures he met. Occasionally he would regret he'd left school before he'd had so much as a sniff of a GCSE paper, missing out on what minimal qualifications were on offer at his Liverpool comprehensive. But he wasn't so naive as to believe that paper qualifications were the only kind. On a racecourse, he knew, he could achieve things undreamt of by even experienced jockeys.

As he pulled up the young horse, relaxed and balanced now, he saw the appreciative look in Dick Seabourn's eyes.

'I think she could be a bit special. Did she feel as good as she looked?'

'Yeah. Brilliant. She stopped fussing after a furlong and settled beautifully.'

'Well done,' the trainer said as Joey took his feet out of the stirrups and swung his leg over the horse's quarters.

When his feet touched the ground, he handed the reins to a waiting lad, legged him up and watched him walk the horse over to the rest of the circling string. He unclipped his bobble-topped helmet and took it off with relief.

'You look a bit rough, Joey. I thought you missed all the celebrations in Ascot and went home early last night?'

'I did, but Di came round. We went to Le Picasso and . . . you know, one thing led to another.'

'Did they indeed?' Dick nodded his head. 'I wondered when you'd get round to it.'

Joey grinned, a little relieved. He'd thought his boss might be touchy about him sleeping with his secretary.

'At least it wasn't *my* daughter,' Seabourn went on. 'Mind you, Graham Street won't be too pleased.'

Joey stared at him. 'Graham? You're kidding! He's already married. I should have thought he had enough problems, and you wouldn't think he was her type, would you?'

It was only later, when Joey was alone in the house and the effects of his night with Di had worn off, that the menace of the blackmail threat crept back into the forefront of his mind. But now he'd worked out the beginnings of a campaign to deal with it. As he changed, he was almost looking forward to his visit to the circus.

Chapter Six

The familiar red and blue stripes of Freddie Fielding's
Circus tent loomed inside the last long bend of the turf
track as Joey drove his Range Rover into Nottingham
racecourse.

The evening sun blazed obliquely across the faded
canvas, exaggerating folds and ripples so the tent looked
like a great colourful, wrinkled elephant, with its sides
heaving perceptibly in a strong evening breeze.

Joey felt a surge of contrasting emotions: fear and
nostalgia; affection and apprehension. He parked his car
unobtrusively, some distance away.

He walked around the back of the stands and on to
the course. He leaned on the running rail and gazed at
the familiar bustle around the big top. It was ten years
since he had last seen it, but suddenly it all came vividly
back to him.

Joey could remember clearly how, once he had stowed
his meagre possessions inside Ginger's caravan, he had
gone off with a thumping heart to find the Korsakovs.

He couldn't guess what sort of reception he'd find. He
knew only that Ivan had agreed with Wimsatt that he
would see if Joey showed ability on the trapeze – which

his size suggested – and, as they were short-handed, he could also help out with the horses.

Joey wandered among the lorries and trailers, looking at the bizarre collection of people who scurried about their business. Some cast him curious glances and faint nods of greeting. Most ignored him and he carried on until he reached the long khaki tent where Mr Wimsatt had told him he would find the Korsakovs with their horses.

He stopped at the entrance and drew a deep breath, sucking in through his nostrils for the first time the particular smell of horse dung and sweat which would pervade the rest of his days here.

Hoping that Ivan wouldn't be there, he walked into the gloom of the canvas stables and looked around. Eight white horses were tethered in temporary stalls made from timber panels and iron rails.

At first he couldn't see anyone until, in the darkness of the far end, he spotted the round denim-clad bottom of someone bending over, pulling apart a bale of hay.

Joey's pulse quickened. He couldn't deny that for him the biggest attraction of the Cossack Riders' show had been the fiery blonde girl who seemed to be the leader of the troupe. When he had seen the circus in Liverpool, he'd been struck by her skill and mesmerised by her coolness as she careered round the arena with her long golden hair flying behind her.

He knew at once that the firm shapely hips belonged to her. He stopped a few feet inside the tent and a moment later the girl straightened herself, holding a thick wedge of hay and an empty hay-net which she started to fill. She turned and walked towards one of the stalls near the entrance where Joey stood. She saw him at once, but acknowledged him with only a brief nod. She squeezed her way to the horse's head and tied the net on to an iron ring. When she edged out of the stall and walked up to Joey, he was still gazing at her with an awed expression which she ignored.

'Are you the boy my father took a liking to?' The girl spoke with a throaty accent which was a cross between Russian and rural English.

'Yes,' Joey said, coughing nervously. Close to, she looked more stunning than he'd dared imagine. Her dark eyes were set above soft, porcelain pale cheeks with just the hint of a flush from her exertions over the hay, and silver-gold hair fell in soft waves to her shoulders. An embroidered cotton top and denim jeans did nothing to hide the curves of a body in which not a single contour was overstated or out of place.

'What's your name?' she asked.

'Joey Leatham.'

'I am Nina Ivanovna Korsakov. My father . . .' Joey detected a hint of dislike in the two words '. . . says you will help with the horses until he has time to train you on the trapeze.'

'I'll do anything to help,' Joey blurted out eagerly, unable to believe his luck.

'Don't say that to people here or they'll all have you doing their jobs.' She turned and walked back to the stack of bales at the end of the tent. 'You can start by filling the rest of these hay-nets. I'll show you how to do it.'

As she demonstrated and Joey followed all her actions, she carried on talking – matter-of-factly, never losing a slight aloofness.

'Where are you going to live?' She asked the question as if she didn't much care.

'With one of the clowns.'

Nina stopped what she was doing to turn and look at him, and made a face. 'With Ginger?'

'Yes.'

'How old are you?'

'Nearly sixteen.'

'But you're so small,' she said with no attempt at tact. 'I thought you were about twelve.'

'That's just the way I'm made,' he said with rare defiance. 'How old are you then?'

'I'm nineteen, if you want to know. Anyway, don't worry about being small – it might help you,' she said. 'What do you know about horses?'

'Which is the head and which is the tail; not much else.'

'Have you ever ridden?'

'In Toxteth? No way.'

'You'll learn.'

Joey smiled, looking forward to it.

'You won't smile like that when my mother's teaching you,' Nina said, with her first sign of sympathy.

With these memories fresh in his mind, Joey walked across the Nottingham course where he'd ridden and won dozens of times and joined the short queue outside the circus box-office van.

When he came face to face with the well-remembered, elongated and slightly bulbous features of one of the midget clowns, it was as if he'd seen him just a few days before.

'Hello, Joey. Been on holiday then?' the little man said with a sardonic grin.

Joey smiled back. 'How're you doing, Charlie? You haven't changed.'

'You have. You look like a man with a few shillings in his pocket.'

Through the strange, faintly archaic accent and idiom which the circus seemed to foster in its performers, Joey thought he heard an edge of resentment which set his mind racing and reminded him why he was here.

'Here's your ticket,' Charlie said. 'No, you don't have to pay. I'll tell the others you've come.'

'Don't do that. I don't want to disturb anyone. I just want to watch, like an ordinary punter.'

'Mexican flyers we've got now. Brilliant – much better than those Russkis you were mixed up with.'

'That's good.' Joey hesitated a moment. 'What about the horses – the Cossacks?'

Charlie immediately picked up the nuance in Joey's voice. 'Oh dear, still in love, are we? Don't you worry. The lovely Nina's still with us. Her mum died, though.'

'Tatyana?'

'That's the one – tough old boot. But Nina's done a good job.'

'Is she . . . er . . .'

'Is she married?' the clown pre-empted him. 'Is that what you were going to ask? No. She was, mind, but it didn't last long. We didn't think it would. A great oaf, he was. Weight-lifter, waste of time. Magnificent physique and all that, handsome too, but, oh, was he dim!'

There was a perceptible grumbling from the queue piling up behind Joey.

'Right,' said Charlie. 'I'll see you later. I've got to deal with these eager punters.'

Joey took his ticket and gave a quick smile of apology to a mother and three children behind him.

'Hey! It's the jockey, Joey Leatham,' said a man

behind her. 'Come to ride them Cossack horses, I should think!' He cackled and beamed at his own joke.

Joey gave him a half a smile. Not enough to encourage him, but enough to stop him saying to his friends: "That Joey Leatham is a right miserable sod when you meet him. No sense of humour."

He was used to total strangers treating him with familiarity, assuming he'd know them simply because they'd recognised him.

Charlie, he'd noticed, had made no direct reference to his recent career. Joey still didn't know if the circus people knew what he'd been doing since he'd left.

He followed the steady trickle of people entering the musty gloom of the big top. The smell of elephant droppings, sawdust and damp canvas took him back ten years in an instant.

He climbed a few steps up one of the gangways in the bank of seating and sat down beside a group of children. He gazed around the tent, recognising almost everything as memories flooded in. Nothing seemed to have changed.

Even the diminutive Ivor Wimsatt, elongated by his top hat and red tails, looked the same as he'd always done while he announced the first act in his booming voice: Nina Korsakov and her Cossack Riders.

Joey held his breath as the six Lusitano horses cantered into the arena, ridden by five men followed by Nina.

She, like the others, wore Russian breeches and an embroidered jerkin, but where the men wore small fur *feskas* on their heads, her long blonde hair flowed free behind her.

Joey found that time stood still as he watched them

gallop through the routines he knew so well. A few manoeuvres and tricks had been added but generally the show was much the same as it had always been, until Nina got up to stand on her horse's back, without reins or any other support, and cantered her beautifully balanced animal around the ring. Her golden hair and high cheekbones showed clearly in the spotlights, and a broad confident smile revealed her gleaming teeth.

It came to Joey with a sharp jolt that this extravagantly beautiful and talented woman was pathetically wasted in a tacky, tawdry circus, performing every night to a few hundred punters who wouldn't have any idea of the quality they were watching.

Whatever else he was going to find out tonight, he'd at least had the satisfaction of seeing that Nina looked even better than he remembered.

When the Cossacks had cantered off to a burst of applause, Joey settled into a kind of reverie as he watched the other acts – including a few new ones – until at last Mr Wimsatt announced the men on the flying trapeze.

In the ten-minute interval before, while they were setting up the safety precautions, Joey watched with grim fascination as the guys and stays which supported the net were put in place.

The Flying Ferraras, a family of five Mexican brothers, had appeared earlier in the show, clowning around on a trampoline with comic skill. But on the trapeze, Joey had to agree with Charlie, they were at least as good as the Korsakovs, and a brilliant act.

For the twenty minutes the Mexicans' show lasted, Joey completely forgot his purpose in coming to the circus.

But by the time they had taken their last flamboyant bow and the ring-master was singing their praises before the final parade, Joey was waiting restlessly to get on with his investigation.

He left the big top with the public, but peeled off outside and made his way round the side to the encampment of tents and trailers at the back.

He guessed Nina would still be with her horses, checking that they had everything they needed for the night. He identified the long, low khaki tent – a relic of the days of cavalry warfare by the look of it – which would be the mobile stable block.

She was still there, and Joey was relieved to find her alone. She was strapping on the horses' rugs and settling them down for the night.

Joey watched her for a moment before he spoke.

'Hello, Nina.'

She glanced towards the entrance where he stood obscured by darkness.

'Who's that?'

Joey took a few paces in. Light from a dim, naked bulb dangling from the apex of the tent caught his face.

'Joey! My God! Little Joey Leatham!' She walked up to him with a beaming smile, flung her arms around him and hugged him. 'Where have you been?'

He breathed in the smell of her fresh cotton blouse and the light scent she wore. He hardly dared believe her apparent pleasure in seeing him again, but couldn't stop his pulse from racing.

'Don't you know?' he asked.

'No. Why should I? You never came back and told us anything. Someone said you went to ride racehorses, but I never knew for sure.'

'I did.'

'And now you're back?'

Joey shook his head, smiling, touched by her innocence of the outside world. He'd almost forgotten how insular circus life could be. 'No. I've only come to visit. Can I give you a hand?'

'I've just finished.' Nina hesitated for a moment. 'I was going to have something to eat. Do you want to join me?'

'Sure.'

'Come to my caravan then. There's goulash and Georgian wine.'

Joey had forgotten the strong Russian accent she'd inherited from her parents, and her husky voice, surely lower than it used to be. He followed her to what he recognised as Ivan's old trailer, transformed inside with Indian cottons, kilim rugs and a display of fine Russian pottery. Joey guessed from the look of the place that Charlie was right about her living alone.

'Here,' she said, handing him a bottle. 'Open that while I heat up the goulash.'

He filled two glasses of wine and sat on a tapestry-covered bench. Nina perched on a chair opposite. Joey had his first real chance to look at her. She must be about thirty now, and her looks had lost nothing since he'd last seen her. There was an elusive softness – perhaps an increased tolerance of others' failings – about her which he didn't remember.

She smiled at him. 'It's good to see you again, Joey. Why's it been so long?'

'There hasn't been a reason to come back – not really. I never belonged here, did I? And after your father and Mischa died, it didn't feel the same. I knew what happened was partly my fault . . .'

'Joey, no one ever blamed you. Accidents happen on the trapeze. Of course, I loved Mikhail – I still miss him.'

'And your father?'

'No,' she said without a moment's hesitation. 'In his case, it was an accident I'd been praying for.'

Everyone in the circus had known that Ivan beat his wife. Joey had suspected that Nina and Mikhail and their brothers had also been victims of this brutality. Although Joey had loathed Ivan, he hadn't realised that the big Russian had been so disliked by his own family. This no doubt explained why he himself hadn't suffered more recriminations at the time.

'What about your mother?'

'She despised him. Nobody missed him. Wasn't it obvious?'

'Maybe it was, but not to me. I was young; I don't think I really knew what was going on half the time and I could never relax after it had happened. When Ginger left, I just didn't feel like staying on. He was the person I knew best – I thought. Though maybe I didn't know him at all really.'

'I always thought he'd picked you up somewhere and brought you back to the circus.'

'How do you mean?' Joey asked, shocked and uncomfortable at the implication.

'I mean, I thought you were gay. Well, you were so pretty and . . . not very big.'

'You mean, a little squirt?'

Nina looked at Joey in a way that made his heart race. 'I never thought of you like that. But people believed you and Ginger were an item. It was only when he left that we found out he'd been carrying on with that partner of his, Giulio. Poor old Giulio was in tears for months afterwards. But Ginger had got upset because Giulio had a scene with someone else for a while.'

'Someone in the circus?'

'Yes,' Nina said with a grimace. 'My father,' she added with disgust. 'Now you can see why my mother wasn't unhappy when he died.'

'Are you saying your father was *gay*?'

'It's not unheard of, you know,' she said without any apparent embarrassment.

'But what happened to Giulio after that? I didn't see him tonight.'

'No. He went, only about a year ago. He was never the same after Ginger left.'

'I'd like to see him again.'

Nina looked surprised. 'Would you? Why?'

'Well,' Joey said carefully, 'he might know where I can find Ginger – for old times' sake. Unless you know?'

'No. No one knows where Ginger went. He had friends in France, though, and most people thought he'd gone there. But no one ever heard from him again as far as I know. Hang on.' She glanced at the gas range behind her, where a pot of stew was bubbling with spicy aromas. She got up and turned it off. She spooned some on to two big willow pattern plates. 'So, why have you come back now? What have you been doing since you went?'

'Don't you ever read the papers?'

'No, why should I?'

'Or watch the telly?'

'Only the soaps and old films. But what's that got to do with you?'

'Well, I haven't done too badly in racing. I won the

French Derby this year, and I rode the most winners at Royal Ascot this week.'

Nina stopped what she was doing, holding a spoon in mid-air. 'I don't believe it!' She dropped the spoon into the ghoulash and spun round to look at him. 'That's it! I heard them mention Joey Leatham. I never thought it was *you*, though. Fancy that – little Joey, a champion jockey!'

'I've never won the championship. But,' he added quietly, 'I am in with a chance this year.'

As they spoke, Nina put two plates and some fine silver knives and forks on the table, and he refilled their wine glasses.

'Then you're rich and famous now.' Nina looked at him with pride, and a little envy. 'And I taught you to ride! You didn't know which end the bit went when you came here.'

Joey laughed. 'I haven't forgotten that, but if you're after a percentage, you're too late. I've already got an agent.'

It was obvious to him that Nina was relaxed and happy in his presence and the easy rapport between them was stronger than ever.

She was looking at him now with wide eyes.

'It's funny,' she said. 'You haven't grown, but somehow you're bigger, more manly. Are you married to some beautiful model or something like that?'

'No.' He blushed. 'Of course not.'

'Oh, well, never mind.' Nina grinned. 'It's fantastic everything else has worked out so well for you, Joey. D'you know, I sometimes think I'm wasting my life here, but . . .' she heaved her shoulders philosophically '. . . my family's been in the circus for four generations and it's hard to break with tradition. Anyway, what else would I do?'

'You could do anything,' he said, 'with what you know about horses, and your grit and looks. You're not tied down by anyone, are you?'

Nina shook her head slowly. 'No. There was a guy, six years ago – Diego. I married him.'

'The weight-lifter?'

Nina nodded.

'Charlie told me,' Joey said. 'But he went?'

'Yes, he went.' She gave a short laugh. 'He was very good-looking, like Arnie Schwarzenegger, and very stupid, like a big baby. I was dumb, too, to marry him.'

Joey had the crazy idea of asking her, then and there, to leave the circus and marry him. He could almost have convinced himself she would do it, too.

But before he brought anyone else into his life – even if they wanted to come – he knew he had to get rid of the blackmail which was threatening to take it over and destroy all the fruits of his success – everything he'd achieved since he'd last seen Nina.

Instead, he asked her about the assorted bunch of eccentrics who went to make up the circus community, and sat only half hearing her answers. He could have stayed there all night, watching her, listening to her soft, throaty voice, but at one o'clock, after a couple of hours in the warmth of the caravan and Nina's personality, he eased himself off the plush bench and stood up. 'I'm going to have to go, but before I do, can you tell me where Giulio is now?'

Nina looked at him curiously. 'I don't know.'

'Is there anyone in the circus who does?'

'I'll ask, if it's important. Tell me where I can call you and I'll let you know.'

'That would be great! I was hoping you'd do that for me. I've got to find him – and not because he's an old boyfriend, either,' he added with a grin.

'I'm glad to hear it. I wish I'd never thought you were gay. But I suppose when people tell me things, I just believe them.'

'Now who's being naive?' Joey leaned over to give her a kiss on the cheek. 'It's been great to see you again, and give me a ring if you find out about Giulio. In fact,' he added with a faint blush, 'give me a ring anyway.'

'I promise.'

Joey successfully disguised his pleasure at her answer. He sensed she didn't want him to leave. 'Here's my phone number,' he said, scribbling on a card. 'Thanks for a fantastic dinner and a great evening. Talk to you soon, okay?'

Nina smiled at him and nodded slowly. 'Okay.'

Joey opened the door of the caravan, gave her a wave and jumped to the ground.

He strolled back through the tents, caravans and trailers, remembering all the sights and smells, and thought of how things had changed, and how they'd stayed the same.

He thought of Ivan Korsakov, and his wife Tatyana.

Joey had learned soon after meeting her that Nina's mother never smiled. She showed no obvious reaction when Nina had taken Joey to meet her in their caravan – merely looked him up and down and pronounced that he might be worth teaching.

She told Nina to tack up one of the white horses with

a lunging rein and take it to the scrubby patch of grass beside the camp. She and Joey followed more slowly while, in her strange guttural English, Tatyana began to lecture him on horsemanship.

They arrived at the little field at the same time as Nina, who gave Joey a leg up. Tatyana's manner once he was on the unfamiliar animal suggested that she considered him to be no different from a new horse that needed training.

She stood in the middle of a circle made by the horse trotting on the end of the long rein, giving an occasional flick of her long whip. Joey sat astride the horse, with no stirrups or saddle, clutching a neck rein while his mount trotted, walked, trotted again, was gingered into a canter by the hissing cord of the whip – and all the time the poker-faced Russian woman barked instructions at him to sit up, straighten his legs, push down his heels, keep his chin up and point his toes in.

She carried on mercilessly until unused muscles in his legs screamed for relief. Circus people passing saw him and smiled sympathetically, despite his unfamiliar face.

But together with all the discomfort and embarrassment, Joey was experiencing something entirely new, and unbelievably thrilling. Like millions of young people before him, he was relishing the sensation of being on an animal that moved and carried him, within the restrictions of the lunging rein, where and when he wanted in response to instructions from reins and legs.

When at last Tatyana told him to dismount, he felt a pang of disappointment, for despite his wobbling legs and the humiliation of having this crabby woman shouting at him, he'd loved every moment of his first ride.

Tatyana restricted her assessment of his efforts to a

few words. 'Maybe I can teach you something, if you will work hard.'

He couldn't wait for his next lesson.

Joey was still immersed in memories as he drove home from Nottingham. When his thoughts returned to the present, they careered between the sublime and the deeply depressing.

One thing was sure: until he found the blackmailer, his life was blighted by the fact that the damning videotape could end up in the wrong hands – like with the police or the national press – at any moment. And, although after the accident the police had let him go soon enough, on the tape, whose existence had been unknown at the time, it was patently obvious that Joey's actions had been deliberate. It would be only a step from there to the conclusion that he'd also been responsible for the collapsing net which had caused the death of the two men.

A good prosecuting counsel would have had no problem creating a plausible motive – from what Nina had just told him, a seamy one of homosexual liaisons and jealousies which would attract millions of tabloid words.

It made Joey tremble and sweat just imagining the results of an onslaught like that.

In contrast to this horrible prospect, though, was the amazing discovery that Nina had been pleased to see him again.

This made the need to deal with the blackmail threat even more urgent, for though she hadn't shown much regret over her father's death, she'd loved her brother Mikhail. Joey guessed that if she were to see the tape, she'd find it hard to forgive him for his part in her brother's death, however often he told her his intention had been merely to humiliate Ivan, never to kill him.

The next day was Sunday, and there was no racing. Joey thanked God. He was physically and mentally exhausted from the pressure of trying to win the jockeys' championship at the same time as coping with blackmail.

He slept late and spent an hour in a hot bath, purging himself of feelings of guilt he didn't deserve but couldn't get rid of.

He had planned to spend the day alone, but was just out of the bath when the phone rang.

Joey picked it up, still towelling himself.

'Joey? It's Dick Seabourn here. Veronica wondered if you'd like to come and have lunch with us? We'll be out in the garden, by the pool.'

Off the cuff, he couldn't think of a plausible reason not to go. Besides, he liked Veronica. 'Thanks. That'd be great. What time shall I come?'

'Any time after midday.'

'See you then.'

'By the way,' Seabourn added quickly before he hung up, 'there's a big article about you in the *Sunday Mirror*.'

Joey felt as if the blood had been drained from him. His mouth was suddenly dry.

'What does it say?' he asked nervously.

'Quite a good profile: the likely champion, all that sort of stuff.'

Joey let out a long breath. He had known it was ridiculous to expect any fall-out from the tape already, but this had brought sharply home to him just what role the press could play if the time ever came.

Joey put the phone down with a groan. Maybe lunch

at the Seabourns' would be better than brooding on his own all day.

But he felt stifled. He wanted air. He pulled on some clothes and called Roger, and they walked out into the garden and across a small bridge over the brook into the meadows beyond.

The walk and the peace of the morning helped to calm his fears until he was coming back through the courtyard, when the Ferrari powered through the gates and came to a slithering halt in front of the house, next to the Range Rover.

When he had come home at half-past two that morning, Joey had noticed that the car wasn't there, and recalled that Danny had asked if he could borrow it.

Despite his misgivings, and a tentative suggestion that it might be wiser to get a taxi home, he had let his brother take the Ferrari, on the understanding that he wouldn't get back into it if he was even slightly drunk.

At least it looked as though Danny had heeded the warning – something he wouldn't have done a year ago.

Danny opened the door of the car and heaved himself awkwardly from the low-slung seat. He banged the door shut and leaned against the roof of the car, apparently to keep his balance, then straightened himself with difficulty.

''Morning, Danny.'

He swung round, more rapidly than he should have done, and shook his head with pained regret. 'Hello, Joey.'

'Bloody hell, Dan, you're still plastered!'

'No, I'm not. I've just got a hell of a hangover. I wouldn't have driven if I was still pissed.'

Joey shook his head. 'At least you made it back in one piece. Come on in and have some coffee.'

Danny smiled his gratitude. 'I'm sorry, Joe, I won't do it again.'

'That's what you said last time.'

In the kitchen, Roger flopped into his basket and Danny sank into a venerable old elm carver at the head of the table while Joey shoved a kettle on the Aga and heaped a few spoonfuls of dark Costa Rican coffee into a cafetière.

'Where d'you go last night, then?' he asked.

'I promised a couple of lads I'd give them a lift to Cambridge. Billy's brother's got a tattoo place. They wanted to have it done, so I took 'em in.'

Joey poured a mug of coffee and slid it across the table to his brother. 'What the hell did they want to get tattooed for?'

'Why not? Why shouldn't they?'

'Because it'll cost a bomb and a load of grief to get it off once they're old enough to wish they'd never done it.'

'I had one done too.' Danny glowered into his coffee.

'Oh my God!' Joey laughed. 'What does it say?'

His brother sat back and rolled up his right sleeve to reveal a crudely drawn heart with the word 'Mum' in thin, curly letters.

Joey stared at it a moment and shook his head with a sigh. 'You're pathetic sometimes, Danny. You don't even know our mum.'

'So? Doesn't mean we haven't got one.'

'Oh, well, no more short-sleeved shirts for you,' Joey said with a laugh.

'It's my bloody arm!'

'You're right. It's none of my business.'

'No. And, anyway, where were you last night?' Danny asked.

Joey hesitated before he answered. He had never kept any secrets from his brother, except one.

'I went up to see Freddie Fielding's Circus.'

'Bloody hell! What for? Some nostalgia trip?'

'Something like that.'

'I'd have come with you, if you'd said. I never saw them, but I can remember you writing to me, soon after you'd run away there. I've still got the letter somewhere.'

Joey nodded. 'Yeah, I can remember writing it. I felt so lonely. It was strange really, in some ways I was in seventh heaven, being away from the Robertses, but I think I already knew I'd never really be one of the circus people.'

'Did you see that bloke you used to stay with? You said you liked him.'

'Ginger? No, he left before I did.' Joey laughed ruefully. 'Someone told me last night that he was gay – and I never knew.'

'What?' Danny expostulated. 'You lived in his caravan all that time, and he never tried anything?'

'No. Never even a hint. That caravan was a happy home to me. Ginger was tricky, mind; full of it one minute, gloomy as hell the next. If I ever did him favours – you know, did a bit of shopping for him without him asking – he used to look at me in a strange way, like I was the son he never had. I asked him once why he never married, but he just looked at his funny little body and shook his head. I thought he had a girlfriend in the circus because sometimes he didn't come back at nights. Now it turns out he was having it off with the other clown! I was so bloody innocent, in two years I never realised.'

'Where did he come from?' Danny asked.

'He was a Czech. Used to tell me fantastic stories about when he was a kid in Prague. I didn't believe half of them but they were great yarns, and bloody funny. Better than telly any day.'

'What do you think happened to him?'

'I don't know. They say he went to France.'

As he spoke, Joey was reminded of the post-mark on the package which had brought the videotape.

Joey drove the few miles to Crowle House wishing that he could have told Danny more. He longed to share his secret – and his guilt – with someone else, but he knew that he couldn't be sure who to trust.

He arrived at the Seabourns' to find Di Lambert already there.

'Hi, Joey,' she greeted him off-handedly, as if they hadn't been in bed together only two nights before.

In a way he was relieved, after seeing Nina and realising what he still felt for her, but like most people he didn't enjoy losing an admirer either. And he'd found Seabourn's suggestion that Di was having a scene with Graham Street – if it was right – oddly disturbing.

Di was pouring champagne at a table beneath a pergola of well-weathered wrought iron. Joey joked with her while he tried to avoid Laura Seabourn's advances, but her manner towards him didn't thaw for the rest of the afternoon.

He was relieved when Veronica appeared and kissed him, taking him by the arm to lead him out across a velvet lawn to a seat beneath the sprawling boughs of a large blue cedar.

The day passed comfortably enough between the tennis court and swimming pool. It was only as Joey drove home alone that his anxiety began to resurface.

His answerphone was flashing at him when he walked into his kitchen. He played back a few messages about his work, until his attention was grabbed by Nina's throaty Russian accent.

'Joey, this is Nina. I can tell you where Giulio is – it's not far. He's at Summertown Holiday Village at Great Yarmouth. He's a sort of compère there, poor man!' she added with feeling. 'Come and see me again soon. 'Bye.'

'I will.' Joey spoke aloud into the empty kitchen. 'For sure.'

He opened his diary. As if providence had arranged it specially, he was riding at Yarmouth the following Thursday.

But he couldn't wait that long.

He changed into a pair of worn jeans, a T-shirt and dark glasses, climbed into his Ferrari and headed for the Norfolk coast.

He knew it was a mistake to be so hasty and prepared himself to be disappointed. After all, on Sunday night there was a good chance Giulio would be in town, doing whatever off-duty clowns did in their leisure time.

He tried to think back, to remember what he could about the man.

During the season, from spring to autumn, the circus would move sites about once a week. When they were on the move, Ginger and Joey used to travel with Giulio, a lugubrious Italian who was the other half of Ginger's act. Joey couldn't imagine one ever performing without the other. Despite the ominous purpose of his trip, he was almost looking forward to seeing how Giulio coped on his own.

Summertown Holiday Village had the weary, unloved

look of a refugee camp, with a high chain-link fence, designed, pointlessly it seemed to Joey, to keep gate-crashing punters away from all the free rides and jollity within.

He parked his conspicuous car a long way from the holiday camp and walked up to the main gates.

If anyone recognised him, they gave no sign. He bought himself a day ticket and wandered over to the Pavilion where the evening's entertainment was due to start soon. He checked on the posters in the foyer to find that 'Giulio, Internationally Acclaimed Circus Clown' would kick off the proceedings in half an hour.

Joey went into a large auditorium where a virtue had been made of the heavy structural RSJs by painting them with thick coats of red gloss paint to match the steel-framed windows, which were themselves framed in orange folk-weave curtains thirty years out of date. He sat at a table, ordered fish and chips and buried his head in a paper, hoping he wouldn't be recognised.

When Giulio appeared, he looked much as he had when Joey had last seen him. His movements, always slow, were a little more ponderous and his lined face thinner and even more lugubrious, but his routine with a bicycle, which kept collapsing every time he mounted it, was the same, stroke for stroke. It was, Joey thought, still a brilliant piece of comic mime, and worthy of a far more appreciative audience than the Summertown holiday campers.

Since the first blackmail letter had arrived, Joey had considered the possibility that Giulio might have sent it. He, of all the people in the circus at the time, had perhaps been best placed to record Ivan's fall.

Alternatively, as he and Ginger had been in and out of

each other's pockets so much, he might simply have found a tape Ginger had made, and stolen it. Adding to this what Nina had told him about their long-standing relationship and the row over Ivan, Giulio became an even more likely prospect.

Joey slipped out of the garish room as soon as the clown's act was over and left the camp to find his car. He decided that it would be much more productive to wait and confront Giulio on Thursday, after the first blackmail payment had been made.

On the Monday morning, Joey deposited a bank draft for £100,000 in the building society account he'd been instructed to. Doing it, he was determined that he would see all or most of the money back. But in the meantime, he was taking a punt on having more chance of identifying the blackmailer by paying up now without a fuss.

He spent the day performing with a mechanical competence that evoked no particular curiosity in the people around him. He convinced himself that it was only a matter of time and determination before he identified his blackmailer. The field was so narrow. And in two days' time, he would be able to see for himself if Giulio had been a beneficiary of the £100,000. He couldn't reconcile the clown's heavy Italian accent and use of idiom with the distorted voice in the phone call, but it seemed possible, even likely, that the old clown would have an accomplice to make the calls for him.

Joey shook his head. It was hard to be certain of anything at this stage. He'd have to wait until Thursday, when he'd meet Giulio and confront him.

★ ★ ★

Joey rode a winner at Brighton the next day and afterwards joined Jimmy McMahon, the winning owner, at a
French restaurant in Kemp Town. It was an expensive
place, though not particularly exclusive; the first person
Joey saw when he walked in was Mike Wade. And
opposite him, beside a girl who looked as if she'd just
walked off the Baywatch set, was Graham Street.

Joey tried to reach his table without being spotted, but
Graham leered at him and beckoned him over.

''Ere,' he said to the girl, 'meet the man of the
moment, Joey Leatham. This is Sammy.'

Joey saw that Graham was drunk, which wasn't unusual. He guessed that Wade was picking up the tab from
the restaurant and Graham was making the most of it.
Joey nodded at them both, and carried on to join Jimmy
McMahon at his table.

'Who's the tart, then?' Jimmy asked.

Joey shook his head. 'Trouble, I'd say.'

'For me? A happily married man? No – my interest is
academic. She's a rare species, in danger of extinction. I
didn't know they still made women like that.'

'Whatever she is, she looks expensive to run,' Joey said
thoughtfully. 'I wonder who's paying?'

The gateman at Summertown Holiday Village looked at
the short, handsome Irishman with tousled hair and
over-sized dark glasses. He didn't doubt that the little
man was what he said he was – some kind of trick rider
looking for a job. He was also pretty sure the so-called
director of entertainments wouldn't want to see him. But
that wasn't his problem. He nodded the man through
and told him where to go.

Joey walked unnoticed among the crowds of holiday-makers, with just the glasses and an Irish accent for a disguise. He didn't go to the entertainment director's office, but asked a camp official where he could find the other performers. He found an old comedian he'd seen in the Sunday night show drinking in a staff bar which had clearly missed out on the last few camp refurbishments. The man was half-cut already, slouching at a table, nursing a bottle of Newcastle Brown. Joey guessed that he would be happy to talk as long as there was a steady supply of free drinks.

On the subject of Giulio, he was voluble in his disdain. 'Miserable sod! I don't know why they keep him on.'

'I saw him on Sunday night. He looked pretty professional to me,' Joey said.

'Maybe he is, but when you've seen his act four hundred times, you begin to wish he was a tad more versatile.'

'Do you see him around much?'

'Why? What do you want to know for?'

Joey shrugged. 'I was just interested in what happens to these old performers.'

'I see him most days, before the show. Had a drink with him today – I bought as usual and he was as gloomy as ever.'

'Where does he go after the show?'

'Look, what is this? Why the fascination for an old Italian poof? Or are you one of them too?'

'No, I'm not. It's like I said, I was just wondering how a fella like that copes.'

'Well, he usually goes straight back to his cabin.'

When Joey guessed he had teased as much useful information as he was going to get from the cantankerous old comedian, he didn't ask him which Giulio's cabin was. Anyone would be able to tell him that.

As he extricated himself from the comic, Joey was already feeling disappointed about his mission. It didn't sound to him as if Giulio was behaving like a man who had just come into substantial funds. Reluctantly, Joey was preparing to scratch him from the list of potential runners, as easily as he had made him favourite on Sunday night.

When he walked into the clown's stuffy room five minutes later and saw his face, Joey knew he had to discount him.

Giulio's cabin had the damp, musty smell of a badly built pre-fab occupied by a man less than diligent about washing. The squalid little room contained a rickety wardrobe, a chest of drawers and a narrow bed beneath a grimy Indian bedspread. The stained walls were well covered with framed photographs, which seemed to span half a century of Giulio's life in various circuses. A dusty bronze statuette of a classic clown – some kind of award – stood on the chest of drawers alongside a greasy comb and a half empty bottle of Grappa.

Joey had taken off the dark glasses just outside the cabin door. Giulio, sitting hunched on his bed, looked up to see him standing in the doorway.

'*Dio!*' he gasped, eyes momentarily animated as Joey closed the flimsy door behind him. 'Joey? What are you doing here in this Godforsaken corner of Hell?'

'Is it that bad, Giulio?'

'Oh, yes, and I don't care any more. That makes it even worse.' His face grew longer and his dark eyes misted over. 'But why have you come here? Not to work, I hope?'

'No. To see you.'

'Why do you want to see an old clown like me?'

'To tell you the truth, Giulio, I want to find Ginger.'

Giulio's face puckered, as if at some painful memory. He stood up and walked a pace to the chest. He opened one of the drawers and took out two small, beautifully cut crystal liqueur glasses. 'Have a little Grappa with me?' he pleaded.

'Sure,' Joey nodded. 'Do you know,' he said, when he'd taken a sip of the bitter, herby fluid, 'when I was at the circus, I never knew you and Ginger were lovers. I never even realised either of you was gay.'

Giulio looked back at him. 'I know. Ginger never wanted you to know or feel threatened. You were so innocent.'

Joey nodded. 'I don't think I even knew what gay meant.'

'Ginger liked you very much, you know, but he didn't want to frighten you away by telling you. He knew you weren't like us, nor ever would be.'

The idea that Ginger had been harbouring this affection for him all the time they had shared the trailer hit Joey hard and uncomfortably. And yet, if Giulio was telling the truth, Ginger had disguised his feelings very convincingly.

Joey tried not to think about Ginger's intentions. 'Where is he now?' he asked.

'Why do you want to know?'

'It's . . . something I gave him before he went. I need it back.'

Joey knew it sounded lame, but Giulio didn't press.

'I don't know for sure,' he said. 'But he went off to Le Grand Cirque Fantastique du Midi. There were people there he'd worked with in Czechoslovakia, but that was

ten years ago. Now . . .' Giulio heaved his shoulders
sadly. 'I don't know. I haven't seen him or spoken to him
since he left. He never even wrote. It was someone else
who told me where he'd gone.'

As Giulio talked, Joey thought.

The demands had been made over the phone, and
could have come from anywhere; the letter was from
Nottingham, where the circus was. But the tape had
come from France, postmarked Paris, which still left a
wide field of possibility.

But Le Grand Cirque Fantastique du Midi was surely
not going to be too hard to find in France in mid-
summer.

Without hurting the feelings of the old Italian, Joey
managed to bring their conversation to an end. He even
evoked a pathetic smile of gratitude from Giulio by
producing two fifty-pound notes.

'Here, I've had a bit of luck recently. Get yourself a
nice present.'

'*Grazie*, Joey. You are a fine boy.'

'I'll come and see you again.'

'I may not be here, though.'

'Why not?'

'Can't you see? I'm not well. Look how thin I am.' He
extended a dry, sinewy hand on a bony wrist. 'I've got
AIDS,' he whispered. 'Don't tell anyone here, please.
They don't know yet. They'll throw me out when they
do.'

'Giulio, I'm sorry.' Joey knew how inadequate it
sounded but the old clown had caught him unawares.
'How long have you had it?'

'From Ginger. That's another reason he would never
touch you. But he was a flirt, he went with other boys.

115

That's why I went with Ivan.'

Joey held his breath. He hadn't dared ask directly about that relationship.

'With Ivan?' he prompted.

'Don't act like you didn't know. Ginger told you for sure. That's why he asked you to play that trick on Ivan: because he knew Sol Werner would come to watch that new routine, and then Ivan would be made to look a fool.'

Joey's heart stopped. He said nothing. He looked straight into Giulio's black eyes and tried to quell his trepidation.

'What did he tell you?' Giulio went on.

'He just said Ivan was such a bullying bastard, he deserved to fall and look a fool. I thought he'd tumble into the net – with nothing hurt but his pride.'

Giulio nodded, and sighed. 'I saw Ginger unclip the guy ropes,' he said quietly.

Joey could hardly believe what he was hearing. 'Are you telling me Ginger planned Ivan's death?'

'Oh, yes. He admitted it all to me afterwards, when I told him I'd seen him with the ropes.'

Joey couldn't contain the surge of shameful relief that suffused him. 'Giulio, thank God you told me this. For years I've blamed myself for Ivan's death.'

'This is why you want to see Ginger, I suppose?'

Joey nodded.

The clown put his hand on Joey's arm.

'If you still want to, and you do find him, tell him you saw me looking well and happy – not like I really am. And don't say where.'

Joey nodded sympathetically.

'You know something else?' Giulio went on. 'Ginger

never told anyone, but he boasted to me afterwards that he filmed the whole thing.'

Joey's face turned ashen. 'But what did he do with it?'

'I don't know. I never saw it. Is that what you want to find?'

'But you said Ginger liked me? He wouldn't use it against me, surely?'

Giulio shrugged. 'Who knows? Sometimes the distance between love and hate is very small.'

Joey drove home with these words pounding in his brain as he tried to fathom an aspect of human behaviour he hadn't encountered before. At the same time he realised that Giulio had been honest with him, and if it ever came to defending himself against a charge of murder, the old clown was the one vital witness who could tell a court the truth about what had happened.

Joey was already five miles from Yarmouth when a sudden thought occurred to him. He turned the car around and went back to find the old man and persuade him to write down everything he had said.

But when Joey got back to the holiday camp, Giulio wasn't in his room and no one knew where he'd gone. After half an hour of fruitless search, Joey slipped a note under his door with his phone number on it, asking him to get in touch.

It was after one, dark and moonless, when Joey reached home, but there were still several lights on in his house. As he put his car away in the garage, he guessed that Danny must be there.

He unlocked the front door and stood in the hall for a

moment to work out where he was, but only the ponderous 'tock' of a long case clock broke the silence.

The door to his drawing-room stood ajar, showing a crack of light.

Joey seldom used this room; it was more suitable for large gatherings. He wondered what Danny had been up to.

He walked across the oak floor of the hall as quietly as he could, pushed open the door and looked inside.

In the middle of the room, sprawled across a large kilim rug, was the body of a mini-skirted woman. She wasn't moving, and from where Joey stood, she wasn't breathing either. For a few seconds, he feared the worst.

With his heart pounding, he hurried across the room and crouched beside the slender female form.

With a flood of relief, he saw the girl's chest rise and fall, lightly but regularly, and a strong smell of alcohol suggested the cause of her condition.

The relief was short-lived when he saw that it was Laura Seabourn.

He stood up and looked around for her companion.

Danny was lying full-length on a deep chesterfield. His mouth was open, emitting stertorous breaths. Lodged beside his head was an empty bottle which had contained double strength Russian vodka, presented to Joey by some misguided owner.

Before he tried to wake his brother, Joey checked around to see if there were any obvious signs of damage or disaster. Nothing appeared to have been disturbed.

Joey sighed. He thought of leaving them both where they were and dealing with them in the morning, but didn't relish having to tell her father what had happened. The first priority was to get Laura home.

He knelt down beside her and shook her gently, until her eyes flickered open. The confusion that first showed turned quickly to pleasure.

'Joey, where've you been?' she murmured. 'I've been waiting for you for hours.'

'You chose a great place to go to sleep,' he said.

Laura looked around her. 'Oh my God! It must have been all that vodka Danny gave me. It was really strong.'

'You should be tucked up in bed by now.'

She nodded in mock remorse. 'Well, we can go up to your bed, if you like?'

'Oh no we can't,' he said as firmly as he could. 'I'll run you home, before your dad finds out you're missing.'

'For God's sake, Joey, I'm not a schoolgirl. He knows I stay out.'

'Maybe, but not with me. Come on.'

'Don't you want to sleep with me, then?'

'Not tonight, and not when you're drunk.' He helped her from the ground with his hands under her shoulders.

'I'm probably better when I'm drunk,' she said, half turning so her face was just under his.

Joey's more basic male instincts needed little encouragement, but he stopped himself.

One kiss, he knew, and he'd be in all sorts of trouble. At the back of his mind, he was glad he'd had no more than a single glass of Grappa all evening.

'Well, I'm not going to find out tonight,' he said wryly. 'Come on, let's go.'

He half led, half dragged her from the room and across the hall. Once the cool of the night air hit her, she woke up a little and seemed to accept the inevitable.

She sank into the passenger seat of the Ferrari without arguing. Coolly, she hunted in the glove box for a

CD she liked, slotted it in and leaned back as he drove the few miles to Crowle House.

'Is Danny *really* your brother?' she asked.

'Yes. At least, we had the same mother.'

'He's completely different from you. I mean, he's such a nerd. When I turned up at your place, he thought I'd come to see him. He insisted on staying with me while I waited for you. Still,' she added, overlooking his short-comings for a moment, 'he had some bloody good drink.'

Joey swung the car into the Seabourns' drive and pulled up in front of the house. He turned and looked at Laura.

'Danny's got strengths you'll never have, but he's vulnerable too, so just leave him alone, okay? If you promise me you won't come round again, I won't tell your father I found you pissed on my drawing-room floor.'

Laura didn't say a word as she climbed out of the car and flounced up the steps to let herself in through her parents' front door. It closed behind her and Joey drove away, hoping he hadn't woken the Seabourns.

When he walked back into his drawing-room, Danny was stirring. Joey looked down at him, shook his head with a weary smile and tip-toed from the room.

Chapter Seven

''Allo, Joey?' said a French voice.

His nerves were so on edge he jerked the cup he was holding and splashed coffee on to his jodhpurs. His first thought was that it was his blackmailer.

'Yes,' he croaked, and cleared his throat.

'I 'ope you are not ill, Joey. I want you to ride Isle de Rey for me again.'

Joey was so wrong-footed for a moment, he didn't know who was speaking to him, or even who Isle de Rey was.

''Allo, Joey? Are you there?'

'Yes, yes. Sorry, Captain. I was miles away. Where do you want me to ride him?'

'In the Grand Prix de St Cloud, next Sunday.'

Joey didn't need to look in his diary. 'You're on. How is he?'

'Missing you,' the French trainer said with a laugh.

Joey checked the travel arrangements with the French trainer and loosely discussed the possibility of a few other rides for him during the long Deauville meeting in August, before ringing off.

Joey picked up the phone again and dialled Barry's home number.

The Irishman answered after one ring and didn't sound as happy as usual.

'Hi, Barry,' Joey said as brightly as he could. 'I'm just phoning to let you know I've told Captain Zamowski I'll ride Isle de Rey in Paris on Sunday, and I've decided to stay on in France for a couple of days afterwards.'

'What!' he exploded. 'You can't do that! How am I going to make you champion jockey if you're not here?'

'Barry, I'm going.'

'But . . . where exactly are you going?'

'It doesn't matter where. I've got a couple of things I have to do, that's all.'

'My God, it's that Stephanie!' Barry laughed.

'Don't be ridiculous, of course it isn't. Look, just fix it for me, please. Say I'm taking a short break.'

'Joey . . .'

'Barry, you're supposed to work for me, remember?'

Joey could almost hear the resentment crackling down the line. But Barry backed down.

Joey got up from the table. He had half an hour to spare. Normally he would have used the time to take Roger for a quick run through the beech woods opposite his front drive. He decided he was damned if he'd give in to the pressure he was under, and whistled to his springer spaniel.

Roger leaped to his feet and bounced around his master's legs all the way up the drive. They had reached the gate and were about to cross the road when Danny arrived in the Range Rover.

He stopped the car when he saw Joey and wound down his window, emitting a barrage of house music.

Joey winced. Danny switched off his ignition.

'What are you doing back here now?' Joey asked.

'I'm ill. I've got a thumping headache. I told Mickey I was coming home.'

Mickey was Seabourn's head lad.

'He won't let you off for a hangover more than a couple of times,' Joey warned.

'I haven't got a hangover,' Danny said.

'Well, you deserve one.'

His brother ignored him. 'What did you do with Laura last night?'

'I found her asleep on the floor, so I picked her up and took her home.'

Danny pulled a face. 'Thanks. Did her dad catch her?'

'I don't know.'

'He'll go ape-shit if he hears about it. He'll sack me – even though I'm your brother.'

'I'd keep out of her way in future, if I were you. She's trouble and always will be.'

'How do you know?'

'She's just the type of girl who thrives on other people's failings.'

'Thanks,' Danny muttered sarcastically. 'I know what you mean, but I still wish I hadn't passed out.'

'Don't worry, she was beyond any action by the time I found her.'

Danny laughed like a man who has failed to get his bet on a horse that has just lost and drove on down to the house.

Joey looked after him for a moment before he turned and crossed the road into the woods with Roger.

Half an hour later, he walked back through the front of his house. As he pushed it open, it brushed over a small envelope. He picked it up. It was addressed in thick marker pen with the single word "JOEY".

With a sinking stomach, he tore it open and pulled out the inevitable Letraset note.

'We've had one hundred grand but you earned seven and a half last week. We'll have three. Same place – by next Tuesday.'

Joey was still staring at the note, feeling as helpless as a man drowning in quicksand, when he heard a car drive up to the house and a knock on his front door.

He pulled himself together and, putting on a smile, went to answer the door. It was Di, looking vaguely sheepish.

'Hi,' she said, head drooping in obvious embarrassment. 'Are you in?'

'What's it look like?'

'I mean, are you alone? Do you mind if I come in?'

'No, why should I?' He opened the door wider and beckoned her in.

'I wasn't too friendly at lunch last weekend, was I?'

'Weren't you?'

'You know perfectly well I wasn't, but Dick had given me a hell of a bollocking.'

'He suggested to me that you're having a scene with his former jockey.' Joey shrugged.

Di had followed him into the kitchen by now.

'Joey, I can't think why he said that. Of course I'm not having any kind of scene with Graham. I did fancy him once, but nothing ever happened.'

'It's none of my business anyway. Do you want a drink?'

'A quick glass of wine?'

Joey nodded and took a bottle of Chablis from the fridge. 'Anyway, did you want anything in particular?'

'I was just passing so I thought I'd pop in and apologise.'

'Apology accepted.'

'Oh, come on, Joey, don't be so uptight. That was a great night we had and you know it.'

He smiled at the memory, despite himself. 'Yeah, it was.'

'I suppose you'll be seeing the lovely Stephanie when you're in France for the Prix de St Cloud?'

'Not necessarily.'

'You mean, you haven't arranged anything?'

Joey grinned. 'If I had, do you think I'd tell you?'

'Sorr-ee.' Di drained her glass. 'Don't worry, I'm going. Thanks for the drink.'

Through his study window, he watched her get into her car and drive off faster than she had to, and wondered why she had really come to see him.

At the last minute, Barry decided to come to Longchamps with Joey, who couldn't reasonably refuse him a seat on his plane.

Nevertheless, despite a rational deduction that Barry couldn't have any part in blackmailing him, Joey was feeling strangely uncomfortable about the Irishman's presence.

But Barry was in his usual ebullient form once they reached Paris on the Saturday evening before the race.

'Far be it for me to lead you astray, Joey boy,' he said as their taxi pulled up outside the Bristol, 'but I think I might treat myself to dinner at the Taillevent tonight. You can watch and I'll tell you what it tastes like. How does that grab you?'

'You greedy bastard,' Joey laughed, knowing he could eat what he liked and still draw the lightest weights. 'Serve you right if I have to put up overweight tomorrow.'

In the morning, he rode work for Captain Zamowski. Later, Barry and he went shopping before heading off to the race course.

'I wonder if the lovely Stephanie will be here? I see her old man's got two runners today,' Barry said as they pulled into the jockeys' car park. He glanced sharply at Joey for his reaction.

Joey shrugged. 'As long as that bastard horse Sudden Spin isn't.'

The principal race was the third on the card. Barry had managed to fix up three more rides for Joey, but it wasn't until the Prix de St Cloud that, with conflicting emotions, Joey saw Stephanie.

She looked every bit as stunning as she had at the Prix du Jockey Club. She caught Joey's eye and smiled. Without thinking, he found himself smiling back.

He had not thought about her a lot since their first meeting. There was no doubting his physical attraction to her, but he suspected it would be short-lived once he made the inevitable comparison to Nina.

The Russian girl was much more his type; so much so that he couldn't think of anything about her that he didn't like. He still wasn't sure, though, that she felt the same about him.

When he came face to face with Stephanie, he found a surprising paradox: the more politely and charmingly he kept her at bay, the more eager she seemed.

Isle de Rey won his race on the bit and was ready to go round again. Joey earned a five-thousand-pound bonus (including five hundred for Barry) and went to join Zamowski and the grateful owner in his box.

He wasn't surprised to find that Monsieur Ducas and his daughter were already there. Zamowski had told him

Ducas was an old friend. There were several other girls in the box who all seemed keen to try out their English on Joey. He obliged, but had to call in Barry to help him out.

As they talked and joked, he tried to imagine how Nina would have coped in these surroundings. He was determined to find out very soon. That evening, though, he was saved from any temptation to stray by Barry's announcement that he wanted to get back to England. Joey left with him to return to the Hôtel Bristol and then saw him off in a taxi to Charles de Gaulle airport for a scheduled flight.

Back inside the hotel where Isle de Rey's owner had put him up, he pushed thoughts of Stephanie to the back of his mind and settled down to ring round and find out where the Cirque du Midi was currently performing.

On a Sunday night, there was no official body operating to tell him. With growing frustration, he dialled Nina's mobile number in England.

She sounded pleased to hear from him.

'Did you find Giulio?' she asked.

'Yes. Thanks for the message. I meant to ring you before. He's not too well so it wasn't much of an evening, but he told me to look for Ginger in Le Grand Cirque Fantastique du Midi. I'm in Paris now, trying to find out where it's pitched, but I can't find anyone to tell me. Do you know anyone who'd know?'

'Sure. There's an agent called Sol Werner who always knows where everyone is. I've got his number in London.'

Sol Werner. Joey hadn't thought of Werner for years until his name had cropped up in the conversation with Giulio the other evening.

Sol Werner, who had come to watch the Korsakov trapeze troupe's new routine the night Ivan and Mikhail had died.

Joey rang him.

'It's Joey Leatham here, Mr Werner. Nina Korsakov gave me your number.'

'Joey Leatham? The boy who was in the accident with her father? What can I do for a jockey who's making millions? I'm just a humble circus agent.'

'I'm in France, and I want to visit the Le Grand Cirque Fantastique du Midi.'

'Why do you want to do that?'

'I'm looking for someone.'

'Are you? Who is that?'

'A clown from Freddie Fielding's called Ginger.'

'Ginger. Heinrich Calaval. He's not there any more.'

Joey's heart fell. 'Do you know where he's working now?'

'No. In fact, I doubt he works. He's very sick – AIDS.' Sol Werner hissed the word with distaste. 'People can't risk a man like that in the circus.'

'Have you any idea about where he went?'

'No. It's of no interest to me when people have left the circus.'

'Who would know, then?'

'Maybe someone at the Cirque du Midi.'

'Okay. So where's it pitched now?'

'Somewhere near Paris, I think. Hold on.' Werner was evidently consulting a calendar. 'Yes. Near Versailles – between St Germain-en-Laye and Versailles. It shouldn't be hard to find.'

'Thanks, Mr Werner.'

'Sol – call me Sol. And maybe you can do something

for me. I've got other boys from the circus who would love to do what you have done. Maybe you could come and see me sometime.'

'Maybe,' Joey said, without conviction.

'Good. I'll be in touch.'

Joey wished he'd spent enough time at school to have learned a few words of French, at least enough to have understood the various and apparently contradictory directions he was given from the centre of Versailles to the circus. It took him an hour to find it, pitched in a woodland glade on the edge of the town.

He parked his unobtrusive rented Peugeot among a sea of cars and walked across to join the noisy throng heading for the big top.

This French circus was a much bigger, more diverse affair than the smaller outfits that still toured Britain. There were fewer restrictions or public bodies in France imposing bans on wild animal acts, and the French still took the circus seriously.

Joey had arrived just before the afternoon show. He thought he might as well go in and watch it: maybe he would see someone he knew.

Once again, sitting inside the big top, he found vivid memories of his circus life flooding back – most potently when the trapeze artists finally took over.

Joey had never become a fully fledged flyer himself, though he was close to it by the time his career in the circus came to its ignominious end, but watching the lithe figures of the young men gliding so gracefully through the air, he was soon reliving his own experiences.

Joey had started on the trapeze at the same time as

Tatyana Korsakov had been putting him through his
paces with the horses. Ivan had taken on the much
lengthier and more dangerous process of teaching him
how to fly.

It was unusual for one family to be involved in two
such different acts, but Ivan Fedorovich came from a long
line of trapeze artists and Tatyana's family had performed on horses for several generations. It would have
been a waste not to use both skills. So the Korsakovs had
strengthened their hand considerably by being able to
offer circus bosses two pivotal acts.

On the trapeze, Joey's size was in his favour. Ivan
ordered him to get up and swing until any residual fear
of heights had evaporated and he could swoop across the
big top like a swallow, almost to the highest point of the
canvas.

He had learned a few beginner's steps in flying – like
letting go of his trapeze to grab a static bar – but it
would be several years before he could perform twists
and somersaults well enough to fly effectively in public.
But once he had experienced the intense thrill of flying
and was beginning to get it right, Nina's brothers offered
him the encouragement normally reserved for family
members.

They also started to tease him about his crush on
Nina. Their father, as he put Joey through his paces on
the trapeze, took every opportunity to tell him what he
thought of his romantic ambitions.

'Do you think I would let my daughter have anything
to do with a midget like you? A menial with no circus
blood in his veins? Forget it, you little shrimp!'

As a result, the resentment Joey had developed for
Ivan deepened every day. There was no let up in the

abuse. The big Russian was well established as the circus bully, by far the strongest man there and probably the worst tempered. It was tacitly accepted that no one ever pushed him too far.

Once, when Joey had been alone with Giulio during a stop-over between pitches, the Italian had muttered reluctantly that the jugglers in the trailer next to the Korsakovs had heard Ivan beating his wife, his sons, even his daughter. When Joey pressed him for details, the clown clammed up; if stories like that found their way back to Ivan, it would only mean trouble and pain for the informant.

There was another, better known story of his beating a man to death in a Hungarian circus, so that he and his family had been forced to run, even managing to dodge the wary border guards on their way to the West.

Tatyana never spoke of it and her children claimed they were too young to remember what had happened. Besides, Nina and Mikhail had been born later, in France.

But the stories about Ivan the Terrible had persisted.

When the tormenting became too much for Joey, he would tell his friend Ginger. Ginger's attitude was ambivalent. There was no doubt, he agreed, that Ivan was a bully, but the little clown seemed to take the view that he was such a magnificent man that he was entitled to be one.

As the performance of Le Grand Cirque du Midi came to an end, Joey emerged from his recollections, sweating at the thought of the man who had made life such hell for him. Now it seemed, even from the grave, he was going to do it again.

Joey shivered and looked at the audience around him.

They were cheering and clapping happily, reluctantly preparing to leave. Joey had other plans.

Although he had recognised no names or faces among the performers, he still felt he had something in common with them all. He had no trouble blagging his way into the camp with pidgin English and a lot of smiling and nodding.

Once he was among the caravans and trailers, he spotted one of the clowns, still in make-up and costume.

'Hello,' said Joey.

''Allo. Do you want something?' the clown asked with a thick French accent.

'Yes.' Joey grinned. 'I'm looking for another clown, one called Ginger. Do you know him?'

The man stopped and looked at him. 'Ginger?' he said. 'He was 'ere, but 'e 'as gone since. Maybe one year.'

'I have to find him, it's very important,' Joey said urgently.

The performer shrugged the pointed shoulders of his emerald satin costume. 'Maybe I can find out where he is. Come.'

The man, with a milk-white face and huge black semi-circles over his eyes, led Joey to a small trailer on the edge of the camp. He beckoned him up the steps. Inside, he took a bottle down from a shelf. 'Calva?'

Joey had never drunk Calvados, despite his annual visits to Deauville, but thought he'd risk a glass of the Normandy cider brandy, out of politeness.

The clown poured an inch of the clear, viscous fluid into a tumbler which he plonked on a table in front of Joey. He turned back to his shelves and took down one of the three books there and handed it over.

'I don't read good. Maybe you find his name. He write it for me when he went.'

Joey racked his brains, trying to remember the real name and surname that Sol Werner had used for Ginger.

'What was his real name?' he asked.

'Heinrich.'

'That's it,' Joey said with satisfaction. 'Heinrich Calaval.'

He thumbed to the 'C' section of the address book, which was full of names, addresses and telephone numbers – all in different hands and mostly with what looked like a job description; each, as far as Joey could tell, in a different language.

He found Calaval, scrawled in a script he recognised at once, with an address in an outer suburb of Paris.

Joey read it out.

The clown nodded. 'Yes 'e tell me. Is a cheap *pension* 'e used to stay.'

Joey copied the address into his diary then knocked back the Calvados at a gulp, and regretted it as soon as he had.

He thanked the clown warmly, resisted the offer of another drink, and walked from the circus compound as fast as he could.

He was standing in the crowded car park, trying to remember where he had put his car, when an old Citroën van, grey and corrugated and coming from the opposite direction, trundled past him and stopped.

Joey didn't give it a thought, until two pairs of hands grabbed him, spun him round and hurled him through the open back doors of the low-slung vehicle.

His face scraped along the dirty floor and he breathed

in familiar smells of hay and animal feed. The doors were banged shut behind him. Before he could turn, the weight of two men crashed down on his back and shoulders and an old hessian sack was pulled over his head.

Joey lay trembling in the dark, wondering what was going to happen. He tried to lift his head, despite knowing he couldn't see anything through the sack.

He lay there for a few moments, waiting for someone to say something, but no one spoke. The van was still jolting slowly across the lumpy field where the circus audience had parked their cars.

Abruptly and without warning the assault came. Joey was kicked viciously in the lower abdomen, below the diaphragm, until he was left gasping and helpless while his pockets were rifled. Then one of his attackers finally addressed him.

'You wanna be careful.' It was an Englishman – a voice Joey didn't know and a gravelly Essex accent. 'People don't want you to go looking for trouble in case you get hurt. But if you do, next time you won't go home alive.'

The doors were opened and a moment later he felt himself being picked up and heaved from the back of the moving van.

There was a split second before his head crashed on to the rutted track, then nothing.

He came round a few seconds later and dragged the musty sack off his head. His preliminary check for injuries identified nothing more serious than a sore shoulder and a headache. He looked around. There didn't seem to be anyone about to witness what had happened. He stood and searched through his pockets.

Everything had gone. Wallet, car keys, passport.

Joey looked up and gazed across the fast emptying car park. There was no sign of the van, and he hadn't seen any of the people who had attacked him. He hadn't heard them either; they had been very careful, very professional. He wondered who the hell they were.

If Ginger was the main man, it wasn't surprising he wanted to stop Joey pursuing any investigations in France.

But the only people who knew he was actively looking for Ginger and could have warned him were Giulio, Sol Werner and Nina. And at least one of the heavies had been English.

He bundled up the old sack and ran up to some higher ground to get a view over the remaining parked cars and orientate himself. He still couldn't see the Citroën van, or his rented Peugeot.

He thought for a moment before walking briskly towards the gate where the cars were still streaming out. He started thumbing a lift, and almost at once a Mercedes with two or three people in it stopped for him.

The driver, with his window down and a cigarette hanging from his lip, looked at Joey, making an instant appraisal. He nodded and muttered something over his shoulder. A back door was opened and a sultry, dark-haired girl beckoned Joey inside.

He leaped in gratefully and pulled the door shut just as the car reached the gate and turned on to the road.

'*Merci*,' he said, exhausting most of his vocabulary in one hit.

'English?' the girl asked at once.

Joey nodded.

'Are you with the circus?' she asked in an American

accent, indicating with her big black eyes that his size suggested it.

Joey shook his head. 'Not any more. I went to look up an old friend. Then I was mugged – just now. They took everything: money, passport, car, the lot. I need to get back to my hotel in Paris to make some phone calls.'

The driver turned and glanced at him in the mirror. 'Where are you staying?' Although obviously native French, he also spoke with a slight American accent.

'The Bristol,' Joey answered.

'We can take you there. But if you want to make some calls, use this.' He passed a cell phone over his shoulder.

'Thanks,' Joey said, and passed it to the girl. 'My French is lousy. Can you get the number of a place called the Ducas Gallery for me? It's in the Faubourg St Honoré.'

'Sure,' the girl said, and tapped into enquiries.

A minute later, Joey was talking to Stephanie, who sounded pleased he had rung, though surprised to hear he was still in France.

'Yeah,' he said, 'there were a couple of things I wanted to do, but I've got a bit of a problem. I hoped maybe you could help me out?'

'Of course I will – you saved my life. And you gave me a lift from Newmarket,' she laughed.

'I've been robbed, out near Versailles,' he said, feeling slightly foolish. 'They took everything. Of course, I could just go back to my hotel and get the plane to pick me up at Bernes but I've got a couple more things I need to check out first.'

'No problem. Where are you now?'

Joey turned to the girl beside him. 'Where are we?'

'On the A13 into Paris.'

'Whose car are you in?' Stephanie asked.

'Some good people who say they'll take me into Paris.'

'Put me on to the driver, I'll ask him if he can drop you at my father's place in St Germain-en-Laye and tell him how to get there. It's not too far. I'll meet you there in an hour. You could stay for dinner,' she added.

'Thanks.' Joey handed the phone to the driver.

Twenty minutes later, the Mercedes turned off a quiet tree-lined road into an elliptical drive that swept up to a classic French mansion in stone and slate. They stopped before a broad flight of stone steps leading up to the front door.

Joey was impressed. He'd been to dozens of big flashy houses – like the McMahons' – endowed with all the trappings of wealth: ostentatious pools, snooker rooms, cocktail bars, gyms and Jacuzzis. These were the things people had often already acquired before they started owning expensive racehorses. But this house, a kind of mini-château set in a story-book garden, showed impeccable taste.

Joey thanked the people who had driven him and got out of the car, just as the front door was opened by a tiny Indo-Chinese woman who appeared to be expecting him.

He waved goodbye to his rescuers and walked up the steps to the fine stone portico. When he reached the top, he found himself, for once, towering over the maid by an inch or so.

'Mam'selle Stephanie say you come.' She opened the door wider and led him across a wide hall into a pleasantly cool, dark salon where the smell of piquant pot pourri lingered.

The maid left him, to reappear five minutes later with a tray of tea and cakes.

Joey thanked her and drank the tea, wondering about Stephanie and her father. Monsieur Ducas was evidently a very wealthy man. The room in which Joey sat was full of exquisite furniture and pictures.

These were things that he had learned to appreciate in recent years, for themselves, not the mere possession of them. But these surroundings, the quiet air of old money, he knew he could never aspire to, and Stephanie was undeniably part of this world.

Nina, despite her exotic Slav origins, would always be closer to him in temperament and experience – though that didn't mean the French girl was without her attractions.

But for now he had more pressing problems to deal with.

He guessed that the attack in the circus car park was meant to be a low-key beating, just a warning to let him know that his blackmailer was keeping close tabs on him. While he hadn't personally told many people he was going to stay in France for a few days, his presence at Longchamps on Sunday would have been announced in the racing pages of hundreds of newspapers across Europe.

To have had someone follow him after racing the day before would have been easy to arrange, especially when he was off his guard.

But what was puzzling him was that the people who'd temporarily hijacked him must have assumed he hadn't found out anything. Or that they hadn't been concerned about any information he might have gathered at the circus.

He knew for certain that no one had followed him from the circus to St Germain-en-Laye. He'd had plenty of opportunities to check from the back seat of the Mercedes.

His next task was to trace the address he had been given for Ginger. He was hoping Stephanie would give some help with that.

He crossed the room to the sweeping floor-length windows which overlooked the drive. As he surveyed the formal beauty of the Ducas' garden, spread out below, a gleaming Aston Martin convertible appeared through the gates. Stephanie was driving, her hair loose and tangled from the wind.

Joey watched her park and run up the steps. He heard her footsteps click across the hall and a moment later she appeared in the doorway. A smile spread across her face. 'Oh, good. You're here.'

She walked over to Joey by the window and stood close to him, accentuating the difference in their heights.

'Hello,' he said. 'Thanks for letting me come. When I was in trouble, your name was the first that came into my head.'

'What happened to you?'

'I went out to Versailles to track down an old friend – and I got mugged when I was leaving.'

'They even took your car?' she asked.

'Yes.' Joey gestured helplessly. 'They dumped me out of a van. I hit my head and blacked out.'

'My God, some mugging! But they were crazy. They won't be able to use the car for ages after you've reported it.'

He shrugged. 'I don't know about that. They could change the number, respray it – whatever. Anyway, that's the first thing I have to do, report everything I lost: my passport, my credit cards, and ten thousand francs I'll never see again.'

'Use my father's office, if you like?' Stephanie showed him to a room across the hall. 'And you can stay the night here if you don't want to go back into Paris,' she added.

'Thanks, that'd be great, but I need to borrow a car as well. I got an address for this guy I'm looking for – a little hotel in Clichy – and I want to follow it up before . . .' Joey hesitated.

'Before what?'

'Just as soon as I can.'

'That's fine. Make your calls, have a shower and freshen up, then I'll drive you, Okay?'

Joey stripped off his clothes and stepped gratefully into the shower. He realised he was far better off staying away from the Bristol tonight. He must have been followed from the hotel this morning and it seemed more than likely that someone would still be watching for him there.

Back in the bedroom to which Stephanie had shown him, he checked himself for injuries. There was nothing worse than a few bruises. He'd hit his shoulder badly as well as his head when he'd been chucked out of the van, but it hadn't stiffened up. He lay down on his bed feeling that even if he hadn't won the first round, he hadn't lost it either.

His final show-down with Ginger, though, might turn out to be another matter altogether.

As dusk fell, Stephanie drove him up to Clichy on the western outskirts of Paris. Joey hadn't told her why he wanted to see his friend, but had warned her that there could be some trouble, and still she had insisted.

With Joey map-reading, she turned her car into a dull street of villas built in the early nineteenth century. The place had evidently taken a few steps down the social scale since then. The Aston Martin looked much too opulent among the old cars that lined the road. Joey checked the address he'd been given for the *pension*'s number. It was a house slightly larger than the others, with a freshly painted front door and respectably clean if fussy lace curtains in the front windows. Joey couldn't reconcile this fastidious gentility with his memory of the outspoken, rebellious Ginger.

Wondering if their arrival had already been observed, he asked Stephanie to carry on to the end of the street and park a short distance away. He let himself out of the big sports car and walked back but stopped a hundred metres short of the *pension*. The only other pedestrians were a pair of old women creeping home nervously with a bag of shopping. A few more people came and went but it was a quarter of an hour before anyone emerged from Ginger's lodging house. Then a middle-aged woman walked briskly towards Joey. She passed him with hardly a glance. He called after her.

'*Madame*?'

She turned warily, ready to run, until she took in his unthreatening size and appearance. '*Oui*?'

'Heinrich Calaval? You *connais*?'

'English?'

Joey nodded.

'You ask, do I know Heinrich Calaval?'

'Yes.'

'I did. He lodged in our house for a short time, about

141

one year ago. But he is ill. My mother send him to some other place, where they look after him.'

'Do you know where?'

'No. My mother has died now, but if you want I can find out. If it is important?'

'It is.'

The woman hesitated a moment then declared, 'Okay.'

Joey had to make up his mind, on the strength of this very brief acquaintance, if she could be trusted or was simply tricking him into coming into the house.

He decided to follow her back to the *pension*. Inside, she asked him to wait on an upright chair in an old-fashioned, brightly tiled hall. A minute or two later she reappeared with a small piece of paper on which she'd scrawled an address in a town on the Seine, fifty miles west of Paris.

'Thanks,' he said, and from his pocket pulled out one of the five-hundred-franc notes Stephanie had given him, which he handed to the astonished woman.

She was still staring at it as he turned and walked out of the front door, back to where Stephanie was waiting.

'Well?' she asked, excited by the prospect of a chase.

'He's gone – to some kind of hospice, fifty miles west of here.'

'Let's go, then,' she said eagerly.

Joey shook his head. 'No, not tonight. It's a convent. I'll go in the morning.'

'Okay. I'll take you.'

Joey wasn't so sure. 'You want to go and see some old guy dying of AIDS?'

'No, but I'll drive you there. Now if we go home, my father will be back and we can have dinner. He will be pleased to see you and talk about horses.'

Joey smiled to himself. He'd almost forgotten that he made his living riding horses.

He enjoyed dinner more than he had expected. They talked widely, all three of them, about pictures and racing. Monsieur Ducas was uncondescending about art and showed a genuine respect for Joey's own talents. No mention was made of a Madame Ducas – whether she was alive or dead – and Joey didn't ask, but he sensed that Stephanie and her father were very close.

After a large glass of the softest old Cognac Joey had ever tasted, he and Stephanie went upstairs. When they reached his bedroom door, Stephanie lingered only a moment and, unprompted, kissed him on the lips before slipping away.

In his room, Joey felt relieved. For though his physical excitement was undeniable, he couldn't ignore an absurd but deep sense of loyalty towards Nina. He lay in bed, thinking of her and longing to rid himself of the black cloud which hung over his future.

In the morning, Joey persuaded Stephanie that she wouldn't enjoy the next stage of the search for Ginger. Privately, he thought it more than possible that this was when things would get nasty.

She agreed reluctantly, but insisted that he keep in touch with her via her mobile. She gave him the keys to a small spare BMW, and he promised her he would be back again for dinner that evening.

Joey drove away from Paris against a fierce incoming tide of impatient commuters, but once he had broken free from the clinging suburbs, quickly reached the small town where the convent hospice stood, on the outskirts and set still further apart, as if the local people were anxious not to rub shoulders with a place dedicated to housing the incurably ill and dying.

Joey watched the building from a few hundred yards away before he made up his mind what to do.

It had occurred to him that someone might have become alerted to his presence after his visit to the *pension*. Although he had performed a few simple manoeuvres on the way and was sure that no one was behind him, they might still have pre-empted his journey here.

There were few people coming and going from the hospital besides the nuns who ran it. It was the sight of them, serene and at peace with themselves despite their daily contact with the terminally ill, which finally gave Joey the confidence to go in. It seemed to him very unlikely that he would be attacked in a place like this.

He had noticed a pair of nuns, surprisingly young, he'd thought, carrying a fork and hoe down to a vegetable garden.

Skirting round the perimeter of the convent's grounds, he found the two women with their habits tucked into rubber boots, hoeing between rows of healthy-looking onions.

'Hello, sisters,' he ventured. 'Does either of you speak English?'

'*Anglais*? *Non*.' Both of them shook their heads.

Joey's face must have shown his frustration.

'*Attendez*,' one of them said, and walked back up the path to the convent buildings.

Joey smiled with conscious restraint at the one who had stayed behind, and was relieved when a few moments later the other reappeared with a third nun, clearly older and presumably wiser.

'Hello? What can we do for you?' she asked him in fluent, lightly accented English.

'Well, sister,' he said, 'I had heard there's a man I want to see living here, but I hadn't arranged a meeting and didn't want to just arrive unannounced.'

'Who is it you want to see?'

'Heinrich Calaval.'

The nun shook her head slowly. 'I'm afraid he is no longer here.'

Joey panicked. Ginger must have heard that he was on his way.

'When . . . when did he go?'

'The first week of June.'

Before the first blackmail letter! No wonder the heavies at the circus hadn't bothered to stop him coming here. He guessed this must be where the trail stopped.

Unless this nun knew, and was prepared to tell him where Ginger had gone?

'Do you know where he went?'

She looked upward and pointed a finger at the thick grey clouds above them. 'To heaven, God willing. He had done everything to purge himself and make his peace with the Lord before he went.'

'You mean,' Joey said fatuously, 'he's dead?'

'Yes.' The nun nodded. 'He has gone to join his Lord; he is happy now.'

Joey's mind went blank.

For a few desperate, irrational seconds, he thought that maybe this beatific-looking woman was in on the blackmail plot. After all, he thought, it must cost a mint of money to keep a Gothic pile like this going.

He looked at her again, and rejected the thought.

But to learn Ginger had died five weeks ago!

'When was it exactly, sister?'

'I can tell you, because I know who you are now. Heinrich saw you on television, saving the young woman from the mad horse. He was so pleased and proud of you. You are Joey, are you not?'

He nodded.

'He didn't know until then that you had become a famous jockey. But he found out where you lived and asked me to post a parcel to you. Something very precious, he said. Something he wanted you to know that he was sorry for.'

'Yes,' Joey said. 'I got the parcel. But when did he die?'

'The very next day.'

The words hit him like a punch to the diaphragm.

Not only had Ginger never received the £100,000, but even if he had been responsible for the original black-mail letter, he was dead long before it was posted from Nottingham.

And from the way this nun was talking, he had hardly been in the frame of mind for blackmail. It seemed to Joey from her expression that she had been fond of Ginger, even approving, certainly prepared to forgive a man the kind of life that led to a death such as his.

The nun seemed to sense his surprise. 'He may have done some terrible things in his life, Joey, but in the end he found God, who forgave him. You must believe me, he died happy.'

He tried to understand what the nun was saying but couldn't make sense of it.

He had no doubt now that Ginger had sent the tape. But, if the nun was right, it was someone else who was extorting money from him. Somewhere, though, there had to be a connection with Ginger.

As Joey stared up at the grey stone walls of the convent, he felt the first drops of a summer shower fall from the heavy clouds overhead.

'Sister,' he said, 'Ginger was a good friend to me once. Will you tell me where he's buried?'

'Of course.' She glanced at the sky. 'Come inside.'

Ten minutes later, the rain had set in and Joey was in his car, following directions to the fourth and final address he'd been given for Ginger.

The cemetery was on the other side of the Seine. He drove through the damp little town, over an ancient bridge and up the bank on the far side to the walled graveyard perched near the top.

He parked outside a pair of high, rusty wrought-iron gates and got out of his car. The wind whipped up the river valley, howled up the bank and spat rain into his face. He pulled his jacket closer around him and let himself into the gloomy burial ground.

He found Ginger's grave where the nun had told him he would – a humble mound of earth still, with a small cross at one end. The remains of one modest bouquet of flowers drooped from a plastic vase – placed there, Joey guessed, by the saintly sisters.

No one else had been at the burial, the nun had told him. The tragic man must have led a life full of setbacks and disappointments. And yet, Joey realised now, Ginger had been nothing but kind and considerate with him, and had asked very few favours in return.

Help in getting his revenge on Ivan Korsakov had been one of those few.

Two years after Joey had joined the circus, it was pitched

on Putney Common. This was a popular site among the circus people. They played there for ten days and liked the chance to get into the middle of London. It was early autumn; the evenings were still mild but shortening fast – usually a good time for the circus.

Three days after they had arrived there and the big top was up, Ginger came back to the caravan late one night while Joey was watching television, exhausted from a strenuous day's rehearsal. The trapeze troupe had been working for over a year on a new, potentially spectacular routine in which two smaller 'flyers' – Joey and Mikhail – caught the big catcher – Ivan.

Although to aficionados of the circus the idea of the catcher himself flying and being caught was crazy enough to be exciting, the movement still lacked finesse and drama and Ivan was getting impatient, as much with his own performance as with the boys'. Nevertheless, the day before he had announced that he had persuaded Sol Werner, one of the leading London circus agents, to come for a private preview of the sensational new act.

Joey switched off the television when he saw Ginger's face. The clown looked as if he had seen his mother's ghost – simultaneously terrified and mystified.

'The shits . . .' he hissed. 'The lying, cheating, sons of whores!'

'Who? What?' Joey asked. He'd never seen Ginger so openly upset or heard him complain so bitterly.

'That big stupid bastard Ivan Fedorovich thinks he can take whoever he wants . . .'

'What's he done?' Joey asked, glad to hear anything disparaging about the man in the circus whom he most thoroughly disliked.

Ginger pulled himself up, as if abruptly aware of

having committed an indiscretion.

'I can't say, but I tell you, that man deserves to be completely humiliated.' Ginger fell silent and gazed speculatively at Joey. 'I have an idea,' he said slowly. 'Maybe you can help me.'

And Joey had helped.

Joey looked at the pathetic oblong of grey-brown earth and contemplated the irony of what Ginger had since, unwittingly, unleashed. He thought of that evening with him, and all the other long evenings when he had first arrived at the circus, and Ginger had told him story after story: of acrobats, elephant trainers, lion tamers and trapeze artists; of how he and his family had survived then fled the stifling communism of post-war Prague.

Joey found himself close to tears. Decisively, he turned and walked out of the cemetery to the BMW, drove back down to the town and found a florist's shop.

He managed to convey to a confused assistant that he wanted a dozen arum lilies and a tasteful disposable vase. Once he had them, he took them back to the cemetery and placed the vase in the middle of the hummock of earth that covered his dead friend.

He wondered why he was doing it. He didn't believe in life after death, but maybe Ginger did, and Joey was doing this for him.

Feeling better for leaving his tribute, he walked back through the drizzle to the car and set off for St Germain-en-Laye. He would see Stephanie to thank her, excuse himself from dinner, and arrange to go home on the next scheduled flight.

Now that he had traced Ginger, Joey was almost relieved he could scratch him from his list of suspects.

But he was still no closer to finding his blackmailer. With an effort, he resigned himself to starting the search all over again, back at square one, when all he had to go on was a Nottingham post-mark, an unidentifiable voice – and a list of people who might, just possibly, have played Ginger's video before he had.

Joey tried to reach Stephanie on her mobile phone and at the gallery, without success. To fill in time, he stopped at a riverside café for lunch. When he came out, the rain had blown off and the clouds had broken to unveil a strong sun. He tried Stephanie's number again. This time he got through.

'Hi,' he said. 'I've done all I can here.'

'Did you find your friend?'

'In a manner of speaking – in a cemetery.'

'Oh. What are you going to do now?'

'I have to get back to England and do some work.'

'I see.' Stephanie's disappointment was obvious. 'But I'll see you when you bring back the car?'

'Will you be there?'

'I will.'

She appeared at the front door as soon as he turned into the drive.

He left the car at the bottom of the steps and walked up to greet her. 'Thanks for all your help, you've been brilliant. You must tell me what I owe you?'

'A dinner, just the two of us, soon.' She walked before him into the cool of the dark hall.

Joey smiled. 'I think I could manage that. Sorry about this evening, but my agent's going mad that I'm not riding.'

'When are you leaving?'

'I couldn't get a scheduled flight tonight, so my plane's coming over to an airfield outside Versailles in about three hours. The Bristol is sending my bags over now.'

'Great! So you don't have to go right away?'

'Not for a couple of hours.'

'It's a beautiful afternoon. Would you like a swim?'

'Now that's a good idea.'

Joey glanced up at her. Just a slight wrinkling of her perfectly shaped nose gave the hint that, maybe, there was more than a swim being proposed.

'Got any spare swimming trunks?' he asked.

'Who needs them?' Stephanie half turned her head and raised her eyebrows a fraction. 'There's no one around. Come on.'

She glided down the hall to a grand old conservatory. They passed through the palms and spice bushes, out on to a broad, stone-flagged terrace. Beyond this, a large swimming pool had been situated unobtrusively, encompassed on all four sides by a high yew hedge. A margin of soft, beautifully tended grass surrounded the paving stones at the edge of the pool.

In one corner of the enclosure stood a mock Chinese pavilion which served as a changing room.

Stephanie evidently didn't need to use it. She reached one arm behind her back and unzipped her short chiffon dress. It floated down round her ankles on to the grass; she stepped out of it, kicked off her sling-back shoes, unclipped her bra and dropped it on the dress.

Joey had followed her through the gap in the perimeter hedge. Without realising it, he had stopped in his tracks and was gawping at her like a teenager. She wriggled seductively out of her pants and turned round to face him. He couldn't tear his eyes from the sight of her long, tanned body; the proud-nippled breasts, soft but self-supporting.

He had seen beautiful naked women before, but Stephanie's body had been presented to him so unexpectedly that, for a moment, he didn't know how to react.

She knew it, and grinned. She said nothing, though, just turned to take three quick strides and dive elegantly into the water. Joey still hadn't moved when her head broke the surface at the other end of the pool.

'Aren't you coming in?' she called.

Joey, embarrassed by his awkward reaction to her nakedness, was still rooted to the spot.

The girl had turned and was drifting in a leisurely back stroke. Joey felt excitement course through him at the sight of her legs lazily opening and closing; her nipples and pubis breaking the lapping surface of the water.

He turned away, acknowledging that, right then, the man in him wanted nothing more than to make love to her, as she evidently assumed he would.

But he resented that assumption; and the idea of his abandoning control before such unsubtle tactics. He turned and looked up at the magnificent house.

'Come on, Joey. It's lovely. It will cool you down,' Stephanie's voice floated to him across the water.

He looked back at her and shrugged. 'Okay. Why not?'

He took off his clothes until he was standing in a pair of sky blue briefs on the edge of the pool, presenting a well-tanned, hard-muscled figure.

'Joey,' Stephanie admonished, 'you can't swim in those.'

Ignoring her remark, he lifted himself on to his toes,

flexed his knees and sprang up to perform a neat jack-knife into the cool blue depths. Hugging the bottom of the pool, he looked up through the glittering water to where two long brown legs trod water. He swam well past the girl and broke the surface at the other end.

When he turned, there was no sign of her. The sun was striking the water and it was impossible to see through the glare.

Suddenly, the touch of her hands on his thighs had him caught between conflicting thoughts and desires. He used his hands to grab his pants as she tried to slip them down.

She tickled him under his arm. He laughed and let go. She had the pants down over his calves before he knew it and she faced him with a mischievous smile. Now, unlike on land, their eyes were level.

Stephanie put a hand on one of his buttocks and squeezed. 'What's the matter, Joey?'

He plunged sideways to escape her, reached the side of the pool and heaved himself up the ladder.

He snatched up his shirt and wrapped it round his waist to conceal the effect she had had on him. Part of him was thankful for his lucky escape from committing a major indiscretion; another longed to plunge straight back into the cool water.

She followed him up the steps, dangling his pants from her index finger.

Joey hesitated. To run would have been absurd, but he knew if she touched him again, his resistance would ebb.

He put up a hand like a policeman on point duty. 'Stephanie, I'm not ready for this, not now anyway. I've got too many other things on my mind.'

She stopped short as if she had walked into a wall.

Then, regaining her poise, she gave a small regretful pout and shrugged her shoulders. 'Okay. But I thought you wanted to.'

'Have you any towels?'

'In the pavilion.'

Feeling ridiculously guilty, Joey tried to walk with some semblance of dignity to the decorative building. He opened the door and found several towels on a rack. He wrapped one around himself, picked one up for Stephanie and went out to mend bridges, wondering what he had done to get himself into this position.

She was smiling, still naked, still holding his pants. He passed her the towel. When she started to rub herself down, he had to look away.

'Well,' she said, 'I guess the swim cooled you off more than I meant it to.' She started to walk back towards the house. 'We'd better get you packed and over to the airfield, or you might have to stay another night.'

Joey was relieved to find his pilot already waiting in the Cessna when he and Stephanie arrived at the small airfield.

He gave her an awkward kiss and mumbled that he would see her soon.

She gave him a wry smile and lifted one eyebrow a fraction. 'I hope so, Joey. Good luck.'

Ten minutes into his journey, he was hit by a thought that made him feel sick with anxiety. He had been so sure of finding Ginger, and that his old friend was the culprit, that he had done nothing about paying the additional three thousand pounds into the building society, as the blackmailer had instructed. And he'd been told to get it there by Tuesday at the latest. It was already

Tuesday, but he couldn't do anything over the phone; he didn't have the number of the building society account. And by the time they got back to Newmarket, the banks would be closed.

He realised with a sinking stomach that now he would find out just how serious these people were.

Chapter Eight

Joey arrived in Newmarket as the sun sank towards the dark ridge of the Devil's Dyke. A taxi was waiting at the racecourse to take him home.

He was thankful that neither Barry nor Danny was at the farm. He needed more time alone to sort out his thoughts.

There was a string of messages on his answerphone and half a dozen faxes waiting for him, but nothing from the blackmailer.

He looked up the account number of the building society and immediately faxed instructions to his bank for the transfer of three thousand pounds from his own account first thing next morning.

When he'd done that, he relaxed a little and rang back all the people who had left messages. The last call he made was to Dick Seabourn. Di Lambert answered.

'You're working late, Di.' Joey laughed to disguise the pressure he was under.

'Yes, there was a whole lot of entries to finish off. How was France?'

'Great,' he lied.

'I hope it was worth it. You missed two winners here.'

'I know, but you've got to leave a little for the rest.'

'Don't get too cocky.'

'Is Dick there?' asked Joey. 'I wanted a word about tomorrow.'

'No, but I'll ask him to call you as soon as he's back. He'll want you out in the morning, I expect.'

Joey put the phone down, wondering how the hell he was going to cope with riding while the threat was still hanging over him. He didn't want to sit on another horse or do anything else until he'd dealt with the extortionists. At that moment, more than anything, he wanted to confide in someone about the mess he was in.

He thought of Nina. He could have skirted round the facts and used her as a sounding-board, but he needed specific advice; as much as he longed for her comfort, he knew she wasn't the one to give it. In terms of wisdom and experience, Dick would have been the ideal person, but Joey could hardly go to his boss and tell him he was being blackmailed – for killing a former boss!

There was Giulio, of course. Although he hadn't contacted Joey since their conversation in Yarmouth, he had seemed sympathetic enough and knew exactly what had gone on at the circus. Joey still wanted to get his testimony down on paper and, besides, the clown might have an idea who else could have found out about the existence of the videotape.

The sad old clown wasn't an ideal candidate for a supportive role, but Joey ruefully had to accept that he was all there was. After racing at Yarmouth next day, Joey decided to go round to Summertown – assuming the tape hadn't been revealed to the world by then.

He switched on the TV but it failed to take his mind off the horrendous prospect of the tape's being released. He stood up and wandered about, trying to think what was missing, until he realised Roger wasn't there.

When Danny was looking after the dog, he usually took him into work with him, to exercise him during the day. If he went out in the evenings, he left him in his cottage, although sometimes he'd been known to forget about Roger and the poor dog had been found sitting by Joey's front door, waiting for his master's return.

Joey picked up a bunch of keys and walked out of the house and the few yards to the cottage. He let himself in, waiting for the usual noisy, hyperactive greeting. But there was no sign of Roger. He looked in the kitchen and saw that the dog bowl was empty. Danny would have filled it up earlier that evening before going out, so at least the dog had eaten; maybe Danny had taken Roger with him.

With a sigh of disappointment, Joey went out. Although the sun had set, it was still light, and instead of going back into his own house, Joey decided to walk round the outside to the garden and see how his roses were doing.

He found Roger on the stone-flagged path outside the back door, lying on his side, quite still.

Joey didn't have to look closer to know that he was never going to move again. With tears welling in his eyes, he ran the last few steps and knelt down beside him. A pair of opaque staring eyes seemed to reproach him as he stroked his hand across the shaggy coat and felt the body, still warm underneath.

Joey looked up and scanned the garden. It was empty, save for a few birds singing their evening finale.

'Bastards!' he hissed in fear and anger.

This was the next, inevitable development of the

endless nightmare he'd found himself in; he wondered where it would end.

Brimming over with guilt, he leaned down and slid his hands under the stiffening corpse. He lifted Roger and carried him slowly, almost ceremonially, to the large beech tree on the far side of the lawn.

He laid the dog gently on the ground beneath the spreading branches and walked back to fetch a spade from the garden shed.

When Joey had buried his old friend, he walked from the garden into the kitchen and heard his phone ringing.

'Found your dog yet?' Joey heard the distorted voice with a shudder of dread. 'I thought after Monday you'd have got the message. But you've been a naughty boy, haven't you? I said by Tuesday, remember? You must understand that I'm serious.' The strange distortion of the voice gave the words added menace. 'I don't know what you think you were up to in France yesterday, but you found you were wasting your time, didn't you? When you should have been doing as you were told. Now, I'm just putting a copy of the tape into a Jiffy bag but I can't decide whether to send it to the *News of the World*, the Jockey Club or the DPP. What do you think?'

'I transferred the money this evening,' Joey blurted, ashamed of his fear but with a picture of Roger in his head. 'It'll be in the account first thing tomorrow.'

'That's good.' Joey thought he detected relief in the hollow, grating voice. 'Don't keep me waiting, or next time it won't be just a lethal injection in a dog.'

When he'd put the phone down, Joey took a deep breath to calm his jangling nerves. He went back out to his garden and the warm dusk. He wanted to yell, to vent his frustration, grief, anger and shame in a mighty scream; instead, in silence, he walked across to Roger's freshly dug grave and stood for several minutes below the great beech.

It seemed impossible that a life could be turned upside down so suddenly and so completely by something that had happened more than ten long years before, but from where he stood now, Joey couldn't see any way out. He breathed deeply, hoping the evening air would calm thoughts that were running out of control. He wondered if now was the time to call the police. If he told them to go and see Giulio, the old Italian could tell them exactly what had happened in the big top the day Ivan Korsakov died.

Decisively, Joey walked back into the house. He picked up the phone while he pulled a directory from a shelf. He found the number of the police station in Newmarket; his finger hovered over the buttons. He thought of the police watching the tape, then remembered he didn't have a copy of it. There was no point going to them and saying someone was blackmailing him, without being able to show them why.

Of course, he could alert them that it was coming and get his defence in first. But, eventually, they would see the tape and Joey couldn't believe they'd be prepared to accept that his intention that day had been nothing more serious than to make the Russian trapeze artist look foolish.

He put the phone down without dialling.

Tomorrow he would go and see Giulio again, and tell him what had been happening.

In the meantime, he sat down and made a list of everyone he could think of who might be tempted to blackmail him, given the opportunity.

Ten minutes later, Joey gazed at the dozen or so names on the pad in front of him. It seemed to him that any of them could have been willing to extort money from him, and several were poor enough to need it badly. Although none of them had any connection with the circus, there was one, and only one, who knew that Ginger existed and that Joey had lodged in his trailer for nearly two years.

Danny, his brother.

Reluctantly, Joey turned over the possibility in his mind. In common with several other names on the list, Danny was also in a position to judge fairly accurately what Joey's earnings were; but then, anyone with a reasonable knowledge of racing and the daily papers could have done the same.

He sighed. Danny may have had his difficult moments, but Joey was sure that his heart was in the right place. He admitted that, as a lad who couldn't ride work, Danny was paid a wage which was less than he would have received in unemployment benefit. True, he was housed for free, but as far as Joey could see, most of what he earned went on drink, cigarettes and gambling.

Maybe, Joey found himself thinking, Danny had decided it was time to strike out for himself; but he stopped pursuing this line abruptly. Even if Danny was harbouring an unreasonable and well-disguised resentment, there was no way he could have got hold of a copy of the tape. It was impossible that he had been to France to see Ginger – he'd have been missed from the yard. And what would his relationship be with the man who had spoken to Joey on the phone?

With relief, he concluded that his brother simply was not a suspect.

He thought back to the moment he had first seen the tape. He had found it in a padded envelope which had not been open – or had it been and then carefully resealed? After the four weeks that had passed since he had destroyed it, he simply couldn't remember if it had shown any signs of tampering.

He wasn't in any doubt that it was Ginger who'd sent it; the nun at the French hospice had confirmed that.

He tried to remember who had been in Barry's office on the day the tape had lain about on the coffee table.

Barry, Di, Dick and Graham – maybe a few others, as well as Danny.

Graham Street was on Joey's list, and it wasn't the first time his name had featured in the parade of suspects. Graham was up to his neck in debt, and patently disliked Joey for taking his job.

But if Graham had opened the package and seen the tape on the day it arrived, he wouldn't have had the patience to wait three weeks before asking for money.

In the end, Joey came to the conclusion that there was no certainty that his blackmailers had anything to do with racing, although there was obviously a local contact.

At the same time, if it was someone from the circus, why had they only now decided to use their knowledge?

He was still sitting at the table in his kitchen, staring at the names he had scrawled, when Dick Seabourn rang.

'Hello, Joey. Feeling better?'

'What?'

'I thought you had the 'flu? Barry said that was why you didn't come back from Paris on Sunday night.'

'Oh, yes. I'm fine now, thanks. Di said you may need me tomorrow morning?'

'Yes, please. Scaramanga – first lot.'

'Fine. I'll see you then.'

'Are you all right, Joey? You sound rather agitated.'

'No. I'm fine, guv'nor, I promise.'

'Good. I'll see you tomorrow then.'

Joey put down the phone with a shaking hand and, breaking one of his own rules, took four sleeping pills and went to bed.

He went to see Giulio straight after racing the next day. He had taken the Range Rover and parked it in the town, not far from the holiday camp. He made his way to the old clown's cabin, unchallenged until he reached it.

There he found a policeman standing outside the flimsy door with its flaking paint.

'What's going on?' Joey asked.

'I'm sorry, sir, you can't go in there. There's been an accident.'

'But I've come to see Giulio. He's an old friend. What's happened?'

'I'm afraid Mr Santini was found dead in here this morning, sir. A murder enquiry is currently in progress. The DI looking after the case will want to talk to you if you were a friend of the deceased.'

Joey was still rocking on his heels from the shock.

'Are you all right, sir?' The policeman stepped forward solicitously.

'No,' he said. 'Of course I'm bloody not! What else do you expect? I've come to see an old friend for a chat, and you tell me he was murdered last night.'

'I'm sorry, sir. Though we're not confirming it was a case of murder yet,' the policeman backtracked. 'The medical officer said he died from cardiac failure, but someone was round earlier and gave him a thorough hiding which triggered the heart attack.'

'Oh my God!' Joey groaned. He already had a horrible suspicion that this was connected with his own recent visit. 'Where is he now?'

'They took him away, once they'd done the photos and that.'

'If I can help . . .'

'Hang on. I'll tell DI Jacobs about you. He's in one of the offices here.' The policeman unclipped his radio and got through to the detective. When he was finished, he told Joey how to get to the temporary incident room, where the DI was waiting for him.

As Joey followed the directions, he felt like a drowning man. In the last few days, he had built Giulio up as his principal witness for the defence, the lynch pin of the case for his innocence, not just in a court of law but in his own eyes, too, and ultimately Nina's. He cursed himself for not having come back sooner.

Joey was trying to face up to the fact that the only two people besides himself who'd known what had really happened to Ivan and Mikhail were now dead.

He pushed open the door to some kind of accounts office, furnished with a pair of steel desks and shelves full of files and cash books.

The policeman in charge of the investigation was sitting at one of the desks, with a junior plain clothes man at the other. DI Jacobs was a Londoner – an East Ender, Joey guessed, from his sharp, nasal accent. He had the fast talk and quick gestures of the inner city.

They seemed out of place in the sleepy semi-rustic air of the Norfolk coast.

As he waved Joey impatiently towards a battered metal chair, he seemed to be raking in every visible detail and nuance of his appearance.

'You're a jockey, aren't you? What's your name?'

'Joey Leatham.' He nodded at them both.

The detective constable gave an embarrassed smile.

'And what brings a top jockey to a seedy dump like this – to visit an elderly homosexual entertainer?'

'He was an old friend. I used to work with him years ago.'

'Where was that?'

'At Freddie Fielding's Circus.'

'You used to be in the circus?' Jacobs said with disbelief.

'He was, guv,' the DC butted in importantly. 'I read it once, in one of the papers.'

The DI raised his eyebrows. 'Really?' He turned back to Joey. 'Did you often come and see him?'

'No. When I visited him last week it was the first time in about ten years. I was trying to track down another fella I knew – he'd been a friend of Giulio's, too.'

'Okay,' Jacobs said. 'Now, I've dealt with a lot of enquiries like this in my time and I can tell you that when a man dies in these circumstances, and I hear someone who hasn't seen him for years has come visiting the week before, everything tells me there's a connection.' He looked straight into Joey's eyes without blinking.

Joey stared back. 'And is there always?'

The DI gave a hint of a smile. 'No, not always, but nearly always.'

'Well, this must be one of those rare exceptions.

Because my coming to see him, and his being attacked, are a total coincidence. There's nothing to connect the two.'

'And you've come back, which isn't par for the course,' the detective added. 'You knew Giulio, you say, though you hadn't seen anything of him in the last ten years? So, tell me, why do *you* think somebody might want to harm or frighten him?'

Joey shrugged his shoulders and shook his head. 'I haven't got a clue. He was gay, as you know. I suppose that might have something to do with it. Or maybe someone was trying to rob him.'

'There wasn't a lot to steal, was there?'

'I gave him a hundred quid last week. People have killed for less than that, haven't they?'

'Yes, Mr Leatham, they have,' Jacobs said impatiently. 'Now, let's get down to business. Where were you last night?'

Joey shivered and felt himself turn pale. He had seen and spoken to no one between talking to Seabourn on the phone at about eight-thirty and meeting him on Newmarket Heath just after seven the next morning.

'I was at home, alone. The last phone call I got was at eight-thirty and I didn't see anyone until about seven this morning.'

'So, you had plenty of time to drive up here, do the deed, and scarper off back home?'

'Yes.'

'Is that what you did?'

'No.'

DI Jacobs laughed. 'All right. Let's have your dabs. Constable?'

The junior officer opened an ink pad and placed a

pair of fingerprint cards on the desk in front of Joey.

'D'you mind, sir?'

He shook his head slowly and allowed his finger and thumb tips to be pressed on to the soft black pad and gently rolled from side to side on the small squares provided.

'And now, would you expectorate into this beaker, please?'

'Would I what?'

'Spit – into this plastic cup.'

'What for?'

'I don't have to tell you, Joey, but I will. It looks as though old Giulio had a drink with someone. There were a couple of glasses with the remains of some filthy Italian drink in them.'

'Grappa. I had a glass with him when I came to see him.'

'That was nearly a week ago, you said, wasn't it? I doubt we'll get much of a reading from them, then. Let's hope not anyway. Now, let's just get your version of events down on paper, to make sure I haven't made any mistakes.'

Twenty minutes later, inwardly in turmoil but calm on the surface, Joey left the stuffy office and walked to his car as quickly as he could.

He was back home in an hour – speeding seemed a negligible offence compared to the horror he was facing. As soon as he was in the house, he picked up the phone and dialled Nina's number.

'Nina? It's Joey.'

'Hello.'

He stiffened at the coldness of her voice. 'Are you okay, Nina?'

'I'm okay, but I just heard about Giulio.'

Joey didn't reply at once. He could tell that he would have to put his case very carefully if he didn't want a major misunderstanding to develop.

'That's what I was ringing about. I've just come back from Yarmouth.'

'What were you doing over there?'

'I went over to see Giulio again. When I got there, the police told me he'd been attacked and had died.'

'Look, Joey, you're going to have to tell me what's going on. Why you've been running around looking for him and Ginger when you hadn't been near the circus for years?'

'That's why I rang,' he said again. 'To tell you. I've found myself mixed up in something that goes back a long way – to when I was in the circus. I thought I could deal with it on my own, but now it's turned nasty.'

Nina didn't answer at once. 'Okay,' she finally relented. 'But I wish I hadn't heard about Giulio from someone else first.'

'Can I come up and see you tonight?'

'Do you know where I am?'

Joey had rung her mobile; it hadn't occurred to him that the circus might have moved on from Nottingham.

'No, I don't.'

'You'd better get your skates on, then. We've just arrived at a pitch in Lichfield, north of Birmingham. Do you know it?'

'I think so. I can look it up.'

'Are you still coming, then?'

He glanced at his watch. 'Yeah. I'll see you in an hour or so.'

'Don't kill yourself, Joey.'

The gently uttered words lingered in his mind as he powered his Ferrari up the Midlands motorways to the small Staffordshire city.

He found the circus in a municipal park near the town centre. It had only arrived that day and the big top was half up. He drove across the thin grass and stopped his car beside the collection of lorries and trailers that made a temporary village for the circus people.

He found Nina in her trailer.

She looked to him as spectacularly attractive as she had last time, but greeted him so icily that his heart sank.

'Come on, I'm taking you out,' he said as brightly as he could.

'But I've got to deal with the horses.'

He got the impression she was nervous of going outside the circus – surroundings which had always cocooned her from the real world. It had never occurred to him before that Nina could be nervous about anything.

'Get someone else to do it,' he suggested. 'I really need to talk to you away from here.'

She looked at him for a moment, undecided.

'I'll have a walk round for ten minutes while you change,' he urged.

Nina opened her mouth to object, then with a sigh changed her mind. 'Okay.'

Joey left her trailer knowing that she was going to want a plausible explanation for what he'd been doing – a convincing reason for his search for Ginger and Giulio.

He looked around, recognising many of the caravans and trailers from the old days. As on his last visit, a wave of intense nostalgia washed over him, but this time mingled with a dread of ever having to go back to make his living here, if the other, thriving career he had made for himself was brought abruptly to an end. And overall there was the nagging fear that somewhere within this strange nomadic community, someone was watching him; laughing as Joey waited, sick with frustration, for the next demand. Someone who had had no scruples about killing Roger, and Giulio.

He suddenly felt a fool for coming.

He couldn't tell Nina enough to answer her doubts about him – not without admitting his own part in the accident – and, if he was being watched by someone in the circus, it wouldn't help her if they thought she knew what was going on. He was going to have to pick his way very carefully through the truth.

'Still carrying a torch for Nina, then?' a familiar deep voice said just behind him. Joey spun round to find Ivor Wimsatt watching him.

He hadn't seen the ring-master closely or to speak to on his last visit. Wimsatt hadn't changed much; he had a few more wrinkles and the grey at his temples had spread to cover most of his head.

'Hello, Mr Wimsatt. I just thought I'd come and see how everyone was.' Joey tried to speak lightly.

'Didn't take too long to get up from Newmarket in that nice little red car, I shouldn't think. If you're waiting for Nina, come into my trailer.'

Joey didn't want to talk to Wimsatt, but couldn't think of an excuse fast enough so followed the boss into his lavish caravan.

'Drink?' Wimsatt's hand hovered in front of a cluster of bottles on a shelf.

'No, thanks. I haven't got time.'

Wimsatt shrugged off the refusal. 'I heard you were

back the other week,' he said, faintly accusatory, 'but you never came to see me.'

'That was a quick visit, too.'

As Joey's eyes ranged around the caravan, recalling the first time he'd seen it the day he'd arrived at the circus, they landed, almost without registering it, on a padded envelope with a French stamp and a Paris post-mark.

His heart lurched.

'Maybe I will have a drink,' he said huskily. 'A vodka.'

Wimsatt turned back to the shelf which contained bottles of every conceivable shape and colour.

Joey waited until Wimsatt handed him a glass of Stolichnaya.

He cleared his throat. 'What's this you've had from France?' he asked as lightly as he could, reaching over to pick up the package.

Wimsatt threw him a puzzled, faintly resentful look and took the package from him. He put in his hand, pulled out an unlabelled videotape and shrugged his shoulders.

'It's nothing; just a tape of an act I said I'd look at. Sol Werner said I should see it.'

Joey stiffened.

'Sol Werner?' he asked, almost unconsciously.

'You must remember Sol?' Wimsatt said testily. The tape is of a riding act – no use to me, of course, as long as I've got Nina. Anyway,' he went on brusquely, 'I heard last time you came you were looking for Ginger.'

'Yeah,' Joey answered blandly.

'And Giulio.'

He nodded.

'I could have told you Ginger was dead.'

'How come you knew when no one else here did?'

'He used to send me a card now and again. The nuns at the hospice wrote to me.'

'You mean, he kept in contact with you after he left?'

'We went back a long way, me and Ginger. But never mind that. What I want to know is what the hell happened to Giulio? I heard you were looking for him, too, then last night somebody beat him so badly he died, just after you'd been to see him for the first time in years. Why was that?' Wimsatt was glaring at Joey by the time he finished the question.

'That's what the police asked me, and I told them – God knows.'

'Oh, no.' Wimsatt shook his head. 'There's got to be a connection.'

Joey saw a sudden coldness in the ring-master's eyes and tried to hide his own uneasiness. 'All I did was ask him where I could find Ginger. I followed it up until I found the hospice outside Paris, but Ginger had died there about a month ago.'

'And why were you so keen to see him?'

'Because he wrote to me – it must have been just before he died. He'd seen me on French television, the nuns said. It was the first I'd heard of him in years. When I knew I had a few days to spare in France, it seemed like a good idea to look him up.'

'I didn't know jockeys could just take days off when they wanted?' Wimsatt said sceptically.

Joey dredged up another lie. 'I had the 'flu, not badly but enough to keep me off peak form.' He wondered why he owed Wimsatt an explanation. 'But I was sorry to miss Ginger; he was a good friend to me when I first came to this circus.'

'Maybe he wasn't such a good friend as you think.'

Joey looked sharply at Wimsatt who seemed to be having second thoughts about what he'd just said.

'What do you mean?' asked Joey.

'It doesn't matter. But I have to tell you, there are a lot of people here wondering who killed Giulio.' Wimsatt paused, eyes narrowed and knuckles protruding whitely. 'And if you don't want to make any more enemies than you've got already, take my advice and keep away from Nina Korsakov.'

Joey recognised that the chips were down.

'Thanks, Mr Wimsatt, but I don't think I'll listen to your advice.'

He turned and opened the door to let himself out. He didn't look back, stamping down the wooden steps, seething with angry suspicion.

Nina was overdressed, but Joey didn't care; with a woman as stunning as she, few men would have minded if she'd worn a ball gown to McDonald's.

She looked at the Ferrari distrustfully before lowering herself into the bucket seat. 'I hope this thing isn't as fast as it looks?'

'Only when I want it to be.'

They crawled out of the circus compound and on to the road outside the park. Joey headed for the centre of the small city. He'd looked up a guide and found a small Italian restaurant listed.

The waiters beamed when he walked in with Nina; beautiful women were always welcome, especially on a quiet Wednesday.

Joey wished their first dinner together could have been at a less fraught moment in his life, though he was well

aware of the irony that it was precisely because of the
blackmail threat that he had finally returned to the
circus – and to Nina.

They sat either side of a small round table with a
candlestick in a wax-dribbled bottle as the main source
of light. When they'd dealt with the business of ordering
dinner, Joey leaned back and looked at Nina.

She seemed surprisingly vulnerable – sad and uncertain.

'What's the matter?' he asked.

She forced a smile and straightened up. 'I'm okay,
really. It's Ivor . . . the trouble is, ever since Diego went,
he's been trying to get me to move in with him.'

'What happened to Sharon?'

'Oh, she walked out on him five or six years ago.'

Joey saw now why Wimsatt had been so hostile, and
his hunch that the ring-master might have been behind
the blackmail plot suddenly seemed less likely.

'Have you . . . you know, been out with him much?'

'You mean, have I been to bed with him?'

Joey nodded and held his breath.

She shook her head. 'No way. But he's been coming on
very strong recently. He bought me this ring.' She wag-
gled her right hand at him to show off a large diamond
with a cluster of small rubies round it. Joey didn't know
much about jewellery but he guessed he was looking at
something worth several, if not tens of thousands of
pounds.

'When did he give you that?'

'Last week. And he's booked a house in Barbados for
a month in the winter, and wants me to come.'

'He's splashing out a bit! The old circus must be
making a few bob at last.'

'I don't know about that. I think the audiences have been down, and they don't seem to be getting any better.'

Joey looked at her. He spoke as lightly as he could. 'Has he been buying much else for himself recently?'

Nina laughed. 'Yes, a bloody great car – a Bentley – and he was showing me pictures of a farm back in Essex he says he's going to bid for.'

'How the hell's he paying for all this?'

Nina shrugged. 'He'd never tell me anything like that. But there always was a rumour that he had money somewhere.'

'Would you choose this life-style, if you had money?'

Nina looked back at him, hurt. 'Do you think it's such a terrible life I lead?'

'I'd like to show you another one,' he said.

She didn't answer. A waiter had arrived with their first courses and placed them on the table with a lot of prattle. Joey acknowledged him, but didn't speak.

Nina's eyes had dropped to her hands for a moment. Joey saw her fists tighten before she lifted her eyes to meet his. 'Don't mess around with me,' she said quietly when the waiter had gone. 'I've found out more about you since you last visited. I could hardly believe it but they say you're a rich man now, and famous.'

He dismissed this with a shrug. 'Only to people who follow racing.'

'That's quite a lot of people. Anyway, you must be living a life-style that's miles from the circus. That's why I want to know why you suddenly turned up, and why Giulio's dead?'

'What makes you so sure I had anything to do with that?'

Nina looked guilty. 'Ivor – he said you had good

reasons for stopping Giulio talking about old times.'

'But, Nina, if I wanted to stop him talking, I'd have done it years ago, wouldn't I? Did you tell Wimsatt I was coming this evening?'

'No, but he knew you'd been before, to Nottingham.'

'Look, I've seen the police; they took my fingerprints and everything. They don't think I had anything to do with Giulio's death or they'd have charged me. If Wimsatt says I did, maybe it's because *he's* got something to hide.'

'Like what?' Nina asked.

'Well, there was a rumour that someone had deliberately loosened the guys to the safety net when your father and Mikhail were killed.' Joey felt guilty that he was suggesting Wimsatt was involved, when he already knew it had been Ginger.

Nina looked at him sharply, then shrugged her shoulders. 'There would be, wouldn't there? Anyway, if someone had loosened them on purpose, how the hell did they know he was going to fall that day? He hadn't fallen doing that act for a year or so, had he, since you'd first started practising it?'

'No . . .' Joey tried to think fast, ashamed that he still didn't have the courage to tell her the truth.

Nina shook her head. 'I think this is all a fairy story.'

'Then why did someone kill Giulio? I went to see him because Ginger got in touch with me just before he died, but he didn't tell me where I could find him. Remember, that's why I came back to the circus in the first place? So, Giulio tells me where I can find Ginger and I follow it up. But he also tells me his theory about those rumours and when I come back to tell him what I've found, he's dead. In other words, someone doesn't want him repeating what he'd told me.'

'Who do you think it is, then?'

'I don't know. I wish I did,' he added with feeling.

'Those poor old clowns,' Nina said. 'They were always such sad characters, weren't they? But to die like that, in a grotty little holiday camp, with no one around to care . . .'

'I care, and I'm going to find out who killed him,' Joey promised. 'If you hear anything about it, you'll tell me, won't you?'

'If it means I'll find out the truth about what happened to Mischa, then of course I will.'

Joey winced at that thought. Only when he was sure he could convince her of what he had agreed with Ginger at the time would he tell her the whole story, in the hope that he hadn't overestimated her capacity for forgiveness.

'Have you got a gap between shows coming up?'

Nina nodded. 'Yes, we've got three days off after we finish here. We've got to park up out in the country near Chester before we pitch there.'

'Come on down and see me then. Just ring me, and I'll pick you up from the station – unless you've learned to drive?'

'No, I bloody haven't.' She laughed at herself. 'The boys do it all for me.'

'The boys?'

'The Spanish boys who ride for me.'

'Are all the Cossack Riders Spanish, then?'

'Yes,' she laughed again.

After that, Joey tried to keep the conversation off the threat which had been looming over his life for the last month. To his surprise, it was easy to forget, for a while, that he wasn't just enjoying himself, catching up with an old friend with whom he'd shared a lot of youthful experiences.

They were the last customers lingering over a glass of Sambucca when Nina said they should go.

'Haven't you got to be up exercising some racehorse first thing in the morning?'

'Probably.' He grinned. 'You should come and do it too, some time.'

Nina nodded. 'Yes, I think I'd like that. I've started watching the racing on TV,' she admitted. 'Your riding's improved.'

'Thanks! Come on, I'll drop you back at your trailer.'

Joey stopped the Ferrari outside the park and turned off the engine. 'I hope I'll see you next week?'

Nina looked at him by the dim light of a street lamp twenty yards away. She leaned across and gave him a quick kiss on the cheek. 'You will.'

She turned and let herself out of the car and disappeared into the darkness with a little flick of her wrist in parting.

Barry Mannion let himself into Joey's house, wondering where his friend and client had gone. Joey had disappeared after his last ride at Yarmouth races without a word about where he was going.

Barry was nervous; Joey's behaviour had been strange recently. He seemed permanently distracted and kept forgetting what he had been told. He was producing results by instinct rather than design.

And then there was the bizarre business of Roger. The spaniel, Joey had said, choked on a bone and died. No vet had been involved. Danny said the animal was as right as rain when he'd gone out at eight-thirty on

Tuesday night, an hour before Joey himself had got back from France. And no one had left any bones out.

Barry rummaged around Joey's desk, trying to find the Ferrari's insurance policy which was running out, and which he had promised to renew for half the price.

On top of the desk, a parking ticket caught his eye.

It had been given in Yarmouth – three hours after Joey had left the racecourse that day, and on the other side of town.

Barry wondered what on earth he had been doing there, and out of habit tried to guess the reason.

He still hadn't thought of anything plausible by the time he was climbing into his old Porsche to head back to Newmarket for some rest and recreation. He let the problem drop.

In the big hotel in the town, where he regularly met a few like-minded friends for the first part of the evening, the subject of Yarmouth cropped up again.

'Evening, Barry.' Di Lambert was just leaving with a wad of papers under her arm. 'Have you seen Joey?'

'I have not. He left after the fourth and I never saw him again. Why?'

'One of his old colleagues has been in the news.'

'Who's that?'

'Some old clown – Giulio something or other – found beaten to death at a holiday camp in Yarmouth.'

Barry's eyes nearly popped out. 'Yarmouth? Good God!'

'What about it?'

'Well, we were racing there today, for God's sake.'

'So?'

'So, Joey disappeared early, and I know for a fact he was still in Yarmouth three hours later, and over the side of town where that place is.'

'Maybe he'd heard.'

'Then why didn't he tell me? I wonder what in hell he's up to?'

'Barry, what are you talking about? Why should he be up to anything?'

'Listen, let me get you a drink. I want a word. Do you have time?'

'Okay,' Di gave in. 'A large vodka and I'm all yours.'

A few moments later they were installed with drinks at a corner table.

'What did you want?' Di asked.

'The fact is, I'm worried about Joey. He's been acting really strangely for the last few weeks. Then he took those days off in France, and his dog died, and he shot off to that place where that fella was killed. And he keeps disappearing – being careful not to tell me where.'

'Come on, Barry – you're his agent, not his nanny. Why should he tell you everything he does?'

'It's just that he always used to.'

Di grinned at his forlorn expression. 'Look, Joey's riding as well as ever – better, if anything. I shouldn't worry about it. I'll keep an eye on him for you.'

Chapter Nine

'Joey, they want you up in the commentary box for an interview,' Barry said, poking his head round the door of the jockeys' changing room at Sandown. Joey got up from the bench and walked over to him.

'I told you, Barry, I don't want to do any interviews.'

He had had another phone call at six-thirty that morning. The blackmailer knew he'd been to Summertown; he felt as if he were living in a glass box, like a stripper he'd once seen in a club one of his owners had taken him to. It was as if the whole world was spying on him, watching everything he did, while under the spotlight behind the glass he couldn't look out and see the watchers.

'Come on, for Christ's sake!' Barry was saying, close to losing his temper – something he seldom did. 'You've just won a big race and you're twenty-four winners ahead in the championship. The punters have a right to hear what you've got to say.'

'Well, I'm not saying it today. Sorry, Barry. I told you this morning – no interviews for the time being.'

'But why the hell not?'

'Because I've got a few things on my mind that need sorting out.'

'Joey, you don't have that option. You're in the entertainment business now, and entertainers have to please their public.'

'That's crap, Barry. The punters are interested in what horses win, and marginally interested in who's ridden them. They couldn't give a damn about my views on the meaning of life. Now, I've got a big race to ride in a moment, so if you don't mind, I'll get changed.'

'. . . and this must be one of the most spectacular rides ever seen in British racing!' The television commentator took a deep breath and resumed his excited coverage of the race from the commentary box at Sandown. 'Joey Leatham was *spun round* Scaramanga by a slipping saddle! He ended up *under* his horse's belly! In the most dazzling piece of horsemanship I personally have ever witnessed, which must surely hark back to Joey's days as a circus rider, he pulled himself back on to Scaramanga's back and still managed to ride the finish of a lifetime, to force the colt home by a whisker!'

Nina gazed, incredulous, at the television in her caravan. She knew many circus riders but few who could have pulled off the stunt Joey just had – and on a galloping three-year-old thoroughbred, not a highly schooled, ten-year-old Lusitano.

She was more impressed by what she'd just witnessed than anything she'd heard about Joey's career.

She was almost scared by what she was feeling for him. It wasn't something that had happened to her before. Even with Diego, with whom she'd been briefly infatuated, she had always been in control, known that she called the shots and could choose to have him as and when she wanted.

But Joey, younger than she, and smaller, was so talented, positive and energetic, his compact physique at least as beautiful as Diego's. More than that, it was a new and exciting experience for her to talk to a man with an active mind, who listened to her and was ready to open up and be honest with her without making it seem like weakness.

Circus people tended to think that admitting a problem of any sort was admitting their own failure, and the whole ethos of the big top was centred on complete abnegation of the idea of failure.

Joey, Nina had noticed, wasn't scared to admit his problems, but didn't appear any less of a man because of that.

She was still thinking of him when she went to the stable tent later that evening. One of the Spaniards was already there, giving the horses a final check.

'It's all right, Miguel. I'll finish them off.'

'Okay, Señorita Nina. Two of them not too good; others fine.'

'I'll have a look.'

When he had gone, Nina took her time inspecting both ailing horses. She guessed they were suffering from a cold, which was easy to treat.

She enjoyed the smells and quiet sounds of the stable tent, and the distant sounds of the circus people enjoying their leisure for a few days while the circus wasn't performing.

She went to the back of the tent and opened up a trunk of animal medicines beside a stack of hay bales.

She ignored the sound of flapping canvas at the entrance to the old military marquee. The soft footfalls across the grassy floor were lost among the stamping and snorting of the ten horses.

It was only when she stood up with a bottle in her hand and turned around that she found herself looking straight into the staring, intoxicated eyes of Ivor Wimsatt.

'Hello, my beauty,' he hiccuped.

She winced at the waft of sour brandy on his breath. She took a step back and to one side, automatically lifting the bottle to protect herself. 'Mr Wimsatt! What do you want?'

'Don't call me *Mr* Wimsatt. I'm Ivor, remember?'

'Sorry, Ivor, but I'm busy. Two of my horses are sick.' She tried to step round him. He moved with her, blocking her way, advancing slightly so that she was pressed back against the hay bales. 'What are you trying to do?'

He chortled. 'You don't want to stop me. You know you want me.'

Nina squirmed between the stocky little man and the teetering pile of hay. 'For God's sake!'

'Come on.' Wimsatt's cajoling tone turned nasty. 'You can't stop me anyway.'

He grasped her blouse in both hands and tore it open. Nina dropped the bottle and tried to strike him. But Wimsatt was too strong; he thrust his hands clumsily behind her back, breaking the flimsy clip of her bra, dragging it off together with the blouse.

He almost drooled as he looked at her naked breasts jutting proudly. Before she had time to get her breath, he grabbed the waistband of her jeans and, with startling strength, ripped the zip apart.

She pummelled him with her fists but made no impression. He was leaning heavily against her now, and she felt the whole stack of bales begin to shift until suddenly they collapsed and he was horizontally over her, then leaning back briefly to snatch at her jeans and pants and pull them off her legs, taking her shoes with them.

She felt the hay scratching her legs and naked back under the impact of his body, crushing hers again as he fumbled with his flies in a lustful frenzy.

At the same time, he muttered a breathless litany of savage endearments, oblivious to her wildly hammering fists.

Grunting angrily, he was trying to thrust himself into her. She wanted to scream but gagged instead, almost choking in disgust, as he failed and semen spurted over the inside of her thighs.

Once spent, he collapsed, panting and wheezing, temporarily weakened. Nina grabbed the chance to heave him off and shove him to one side.

Her first instinct was to scream and beg for help from anyone who would come, until she stood up and looked down on her naked, degraded body, and shuddered with shame.

She turned and looked at the man who had all but raped her. The sight of his leering sweaty face was too much for her. She picked up the discarded medicine bottle, lunged forward and brought it smashing down on his head.

Wimsatt's eyes closed and he fell back, comatose.

In the brief respite that followed, she turned her attention to herself. She felt filthy, in urgent need of a wash. She grabbed the nearest water bucket and tipped the cold contents over her thighs, scouring herself afterwards with a rough cloth.

She dragged her clothes back on, praying that none of

the Spaniards would come in and see what had happened.

When she was dressed in her ruined jeans and ragged blouse, she looked down at Wimsatt who was beginning to stir. She picked up a metal feed scoop, crashed it down on his head and left him bleeding on the straw.

Later, on her own in her trailer, she let herself go. She sobbed until she was calm enough to pick up the phone and dial Joey's number in Newmarket.

To her bitter disappointment, she was connected to a recorded message with Joey's voice inviting her to ring a mobile number if she wanted to.

Joey was just starting up the M11 the next morning, on his way back from Jimmy McMahon's. He'd spent the night there after winning the Eclipse at Sandown.

'Hello?'

'Hello, Joey?'

'Nina?' He tried to keep a tremor of excitement out of his voice.

'Yes. Joey . . . something horrible's happened here.'

He heard the frightened note in her voice. 'What is it?' he said, brought down to earth at once.

'I was attacked last night.'

He immediately thought of Roger, and Giulio.

'Attacked? How? Why?'

Nina found she was struggling to explain. 'Sexually,' she said finally.

'Oh my God!' he gasped. 'I'll come up. Where are you?'

'Near Chester, on the Wrexham road. But don't come to the pitch. There's no point. I haven't told anyone here, and I don't want to.'

'But . . .' he started to protest.

'No,' she said. 'I beg you.'

Joey fought back his frustration. He burned to deal viciously with the man who could do this to Nina. 'Where can I meet you?'

'Outside Chester. There's a Little Chef on the ring road. How long will it take you?'

'I'll see you there at about one. Is that okay?'

'Yes, thanks – that's fine. And, Joey, I saw your ride yesterday afternoon. It was fantastic.'

He laughed, relieved that Nina could think of anything other than her own appalling experience. 'It's amazing what fear of fast-moving ground and galloping hooves will do!'

Joey drove home first, where he changed and checked his messages. He was on his way out of the house again when Danny left his cottage.

'Morning, Joey. Great ride yesterday! We all cleaned up in the yard.'

'I knew it was worth hanging on.' Joey grinned as he walked towards his car.

'Where are you off to now?' his brother asked.

'Just to see a friend. Why?'

'Di Lambert was round earlier, looking for you.'

'What did she want?'

'She didn't say, just asked me to let her know when you got back. I suppose the guv'nor wants to get hold of you.'

'I'll ring him from the car.' Joey opened the door of the Ferrari and got in. 'See you.'

Among the crowd of drab Sunday travellers, Nina stood

out like a beacon – looking even brighter when she saw Joey.

He sat down opposite her and ordered a cup of coffee, glad not to have been recognised.

Behind her smile, Joey could see she was really scared. 'What happened?' he asked quietly.

'Last night, when I was dealing with the horses, Wimsatt turned up . . .'

'I *knew* it! The bastard!' Joey was almost choking with anger. 'Ever since you told me, I thought it must be him. I could see he was obsessive about you when he tried to warn me off at Lichfield. What the hell are you going to do? Have you told the police?'

'No . . . no. I couldn't do that, not to all my friends. If he was arrested, the circus would close and they'd all be out of a job – at least for the rest of the season.'

'But you can't let him get away with it!'

'I may have to. But you never know, maybe sometime I'll get even.'

'But you can't stay on at the circus.'

'No, I know. I never want to see him again, after what he did . . .' She shook her head and Joey saw that she was shaking at the memory. 'I couldn't believe how strong he was, even though he was so drunk. It was disgusting . . . horrible.' She shuddered.

'Do you know why it happened now? After all these years of knowing you.'

'But he's been much keener on me recently, and with you turning up, I think he's become jealous.'

'There's no reason why he should be jealous of me, is there?'

Nina held his gaze for a moment. 'Don't be dumb, Joey.'

'I thought at first he was warning me not to talk to

you about what happened to your father and Mischa.'

'But, Joey, why should he? What *did* happen?'

He shook his head slowly. 'I can't tell you anything else, but some people are trying to implicate me.'

She stared at him. 'But why, Joey? Why now? After so long?' She stopped abruptly, gazing at him. 'I know – it's because you're famous now . . . and you've got a lot of money.'

'Nina – I can't tell you, I'm sorry.'

She tried to look behind the sparkling blue eyes, to see if she could detect any fear or guilt. Joey smiled sadly back at her, his face unreadable.

'You know you asked me if I wanted to come and see you in Newmarket?' she said.

He nodded.

'Is the offer still open?'

'Of course it is.'

'I'll come back with you tonight, then.'

Nina took a taxi to the circus pitch. She sneaked in and found the Spaniards to make arrangements for the horses. Half an hour later, she met Joey in the car park of the Little Chef with a single tote bag for luggage and a smile on her face.

On the drive to Suffolk, she seemed determined not to be crushed by the ordeal of the night before. Almost as if it hadn't happened, she asked Joey about everything he'd done since he'd left the circus. She listened, enthralled, to the story of his climb to the upper ranks of one of the world's most competitive sports.

They stopped at a pub outside Cambridge for dinner. It was a quiet Sunday evening with little to distract them from each other.

As Joey carried on talking about his love of racing and natural affinity with the horses he rode, Nina was ready to concede, for the first time in her life, that the world outside the circus might have something to offer.

Joey was glad to be side-tracked into telling her the story of his racing career. Resolutely, he pushed to the back of his mind the fact that his whole future was being threatened by one ill-judged action in his distant past. He was expecting another demand any time now, and dreading it. Besides everything else, it was getting difficult to get his hands on the ready money.

But with an effort, he ignored his own problems and played the easy-going, story-telling jockey he liked to be.

As they drove the few miles further to Newmarket, he could feel that the attraction between them had reached a point where something was about to happen, and the first move would be up to him.

Joey drove his car into the yard in front of his house. The buildings were bathed in a glow of orange flood-lighting and Nina fell silent for a moment, dazzled by such opulence.

'My God, Joey, this is like something out of the films.'

He grinned. 'It's pretty modest by Newmarket standards, I can tell you.'

He opened the front door for her, ushering her through to the small sitting-room.

'What do you want to drink?'

'Anything,' she answered with a grin, 'I don't care.'

Joey put a CD on his player and went through to the kitchen for glasses. As usual, his answerphone was flashing at him. He hesitated a moment and reluctantly gave in.

There was only one message that mattered: a short

promise from the blackmailer that he would be in touch again that night.

Joey tried to pretend that he hadn't heard it, tried to push away his certain knowledge that the call would come. He didn't let Nina know, though, and kept her talking. He was longing for the moment when they might go to bed together, but sensed that she needed time to get over the ordeal she had suffered.

And then there was the next phone call. How could he focus on Nina, give her the love and attention she needed, when he was waiting for the next demand from his blackmailer?

The call came at last, after midnight; before Joey had been able to consider making love to her with a clear conscience.

He started when the phone rang. Nina noticed his unease as he went to the kitchen to answer it, carefully shutting doors behind him as he went.

'Go to your front door.'

The line went dead. The caller was taking no chances on being traced, or on Joey's phone being tapped.

Guiltily, he crossed his hall on tip-toes so Nina wouldn't gather what was happening.

He wasn't surprised to see a plain white envelope lying on the coconut mat in the hall. If Roger had still been alive, he would have barked the house down at anyone walking up the drive, but then, these people knew the dog was dead.

Joey picked up the envelope and took it back into the kitchen where he tore it open.

This time it had been produced by word-processor.

'If Colombian Prince wins tomorrow, the police get the tape and you'll be banged up within a week.'

Joey's knuckles whitened as he stared at the letter, seething with dread at the demand he'd prayed would never come.

He had been asked – subtly, occasionally overtly – to stop horses in return for various rewards, sometimes huge. But he had chosen never to take that route. It could only be a one-way street once you'd started down it.

There was to be no reward this time. He was being offered the stick instead of the carrot: Do as we say or the tape gets shown around. Joey felt sick.

He walked slowly back into the sitting-room where Nina was waiting for him. He couldn't pretend any more that nothing was up.

'I'm sorry,' he said. 'I've got a couple of things to deal with. Do you want to go to bed?'

Nina looked at him, confused. She didn't know if he meant his bed or not.

'I'll show you where to go,' he said regretfully, and led her up to an immaculately decorated spare bedroom which had seldom been used. He said goodnight and left her there without so much as a kiss.

Downstairs he put his head in his hands, wanting to weep.

Later, alone in his room, he barely slept. He had arranged to ride work for Seabourn at half-past six the following morning. He got up early and went into Nina's room. She was still asleep, her clothes draped neatly over a button-back chair. Joey saw a pair of small, pink pants on top and guessed she must be naked between the white linen sheets of his spare bed. He longed to get in beside her.

'Nina?' he said quietly.

She stirred and gave him a long, curious look. 'Hello.'

'I'm sorry,' he said simply. 'I've got to go out for an hour or so. We'll have breakfast when I come back, okay?'

She didn't answer.

When Joey came back from the Heath ninety minutes later, Nina wasn't in the house.

He looked all over for her, feeling foolish at first, then starting to panic. He had a sudden wild idea that the blackmailers had decided to strengthen their hand by kidnapping her.

Cursing his crazy fantasies, he nevertheless hunted for her all round the garden, even drove up and down the lane a few times to see if he could find her, until, angry with himself for mishandling things, he went back to Barry's office above the garage.

'Morning,' the Irishman boomed. 'Who was that lovely creature I saw leaving just now?'

'Did you see her go?' Joey asked, sharply enough for Barry to know something was wrong.

'Did you blow it, or what? That's not like you, Joey boy. Especially with a girl who looks like that.'

'Well, I did blow it. How did she leave?'

'She went off in a taxi from town.'

'Oh.' Joey felt utterly deflated, but at the back of his mind was sure she'd be back sooner or later. Once he'd dealt with his own problems, he'd go looking for her again.

He checked his calendar with Barry and found he wasn't committed to anything before the three-ten at Kempton that afternoon. He made two phone calls, climbed into the Ferrari and drove to London, now prepared to try anything, however remote a chance, to discover who was hounding him.

Joey had never visited his solicitor's in London's West End. He had often wondered how they could justify charging a hundred pounds for twenty minutes' work; when he saw their offices and the bevy of female assistants, he understood why their bills were so large.

But he had often met Bruce Trevor in Newmarket and was inclined to trust him. He hadn't told him much over the phone – just that he needed some discreet enquiries made and a first-rate investigator to do it.

'Good morning, Joey.' Bruce Trevor greeted him with a firm handshake and waved him to a chic little sofa in a corner of his Georgian panelled room, while he went back behind his gleaming mahogany desk. Discreetly, he glanced at his watch and scribbled a note of the time on the pad in front of him.

'So, how much do you want to tell me?'

Joey looked into the lawyer's shrewd eyes. 'No more than I have to.' He had thought this over on the way down from Newmarket; all his instincts told him to trust nobody more than he had to. 'Basically, I'm being blackmailed – for something I didn't do. Trouble is, they've got a videotape that makes it look as though I was to blame, and the only two people who could say what really happened are both dead.'

The lawyer's eyes opened a fraction wider. 'Recently?'

Joey nodded. 'One died of AIDS at the beginning of June. The other was beaten up and died of a heart attack – last Tuesday.'

'Mmmm,' Trevor murmured with studied impartiality. 'He was . . . murdered?'

'There's an inquest to come, but the police are treating it as murder in the meantime.'

'Do you think it's connected with this blackmail?'

Joey shrugged and shook his head. 'I don't know. Probably.'

'Presumably the police don't know anything about that?'

'No, they don't. The fella who had the heart attack was an old clown I used to know at the circus. He was working in a holiday camp in Yarmouth. I was racing there and went to see him, the day after he was killed. The police interviewed me then.'

The lawyer leaned back in his big Chippendale carver chair. 'If, as you say, you were entirely free from blame over whatever happened, why don't you either call your blackmailer's bluff or take your chances with the police?'

'I told you – the evidence on the tape would be hard to disprove and the scandal would finish me. I'm not going to go into details, but I've worked my butt off to get where I am. You know the score in my game; it's not just a matter of being a little bloke with a good sense of balance. People need to be able to trust me: owners, trainers, punters. I'm not going to let anything come along and rock the boat, or put my licence at risk.'

'No. I quite understand.' The solicitor didn't press for any more details. 'As you asked, I've arranged for a very discreet private investigator to see you. He will have arrived by now. Would you like to talk to him in here?'

'Yes, that's fine.'

Trevor buzzed his secretary in the adjoining room. 'Ask Mr Allen to come in, please.'

Nick Allen wasn't anything like Joey's idea of a private detective. He had long black hair and was wearing jeans and an Italian leather blouson. When Bruce Trevor introduced them, he took off dark glasses and shook Joey's hand. 'Pleased to meet you,' he said with a faint South London accent. 'I've won a few bob on you over the years.'

'Well, if you can do what I want you to do, you might be able to save me a few.'

'I'll do my best. What's the story?'

Joey sat down on the sofa and Nick dropped into an armchair opposite, while Trevor stayed at his desk.

'I'm being blackmailed. You don't need to know the details. I have to pay the money into an account at the Southern Counties Building Society. Their head offices are down in Croydon. I want you to see if you can find someone there who can tell you the identity of the account holder.'

Nick nodded. 'I know the place. I'm sure I'll find someone who *can* tell me; whether they *will* or not is another matter. I've had dealings with the building societies before, and I wouldn't hold out a lot of hope. The only people they'll open up to are the Inland Revenue, Customs and Excise, and the police. But I'll see what I can do. Then what?'

'Let's get the name first.'

'Frankly, Joey,' Nick said with easy familiarity, 'it's a perfect scam he's organised. He can pull out five hundred quid a time, as many times a day as he wants from holes in the wall at any of two hundred branches all over southern England. He'd be almost impossible to catch, even if the police were involved. And suppose I do manage to extract a name – it's bound to be an alias, isn't it? Probably with a false address. But let me have the number and I'll get on with it.'

Nick stood up.

Joey took out a pen, wrote the account number on a slip of paper and handed it to his investigator. 'What do I do about paying you?'

'I bill Mr Trevor, and report to him. You pay him. Saves a lot of hassle. Right, good to meet you.' He stuck out his hand again and was gone as quickly as he'd arrived.

Joey drove on to Kempton feeling satisfied that if anyone could get the information he wanted, Nick Allen could. He always rated people who kept the talk to a minimum and acted fast.

Joey's mount in the three-ten, Colombian Prince, started odds on in a field of eight, and finished second. There were a lot of surprised faces in the paddock as Joey steered the horse towards the second slot.

On the walk back to the weighing room, Barry Mannion could barely contain himself.

'What the hell happened?' he hissed.

Joey tried to look him in the eye, but had to resort to fiddling with his silks. 'He just didn't have anything left.'

'But he was still well on the bit when he hit the furlong post, and you never moved!'

'He just wasn't going,' Joey hissed back, hating himself. 'Sorry if you've dropped a packet, but you're a big boy now.'

Later, he was walking across the car park to his Ferrari.

'Joey. Joey Leatham.'

He spun round and found himself facing Mike Wade. He was about to spin right back and carry on, when Wade said, 'That was an interesting ride you gave Colombian

Prince this afternoon. I didn't know he wasn't supposed to win. You really should tell your colleagues, you know. Still, I'd heard you'd got problems.'

'And you standing here in front of me is one of them.' Joey was startled by Wade's last statement but didn't let it show.

'But maybe I can help,' he went on, oozing insincerity. 'And maybe you can do my associates a little favour in the King George and Queen Elizabeth.'

'Listen, and try to remember so we don't have this conversation again: I don't have any problems. Colombian Prince got beaten fair and square. There's nothing you can do to help me and I'm not doing you any favours – ever, in the King George or any other race.'

This time, Joey turned on his heel and headed for his car. He wouldn't even look in Wade's direction as he drove out of the racecourse.

Driving back, he reviewed the day's events.

For one thing, he had decided he was never, ever going to stop a horse again, no matter how much pressure was put on him. It had been bad enough with Barry, and he'd hardly been able to look the stewards in the face after Colombian Prince's race. He would rather lose all his money than an ounce more of his integrity.

Which brought him back to the unremitting problem of the blackmailer. He had decided to tackle things from the inside through the building society when he'd realised that almost everyone he could think of was a potential suspect, including Mike Wade. He was no nearer knowing who it was – apart from eliminating Ginger and Giulio – than he had been since the first demand had arrived through the post.

At the same time, he knew he was dealing with people

ready to go to almost any length to maintain their threat. They had known exactly what effect they would achieve when they'd killed Roger, and Joey didn't doubt that Giulio had been attacked to stop the old clown from coming to his defence.

He wished he had seen Nina before she'd gone that morning; wished he'd had the guts to tell her the truth. He was concerned that by keeping this from her he'd threatened the rapport that was steadily growing between them.

But he couldn't help that – not yet.

For the next two days, every time the phone rang, Joey sweated.

But the three calls he was dreading or wanting didn't come.

The blackmailer's – to make more demands, and give him the name of the next horse to stop.

Bruce Trevor's – with any news from Nick Allen.

Or Nina's.

But on the third day, when he arrived home feeling fleetingly pleased with himself after scoring an unexpected double on a pair of two-year-olds, there was a message from Nina on his answerphone.

He had resisted the urge to call her over the last couple of days. Now he picked up the phone and rang her back before he played the rest of the tape.

'Hello, it's Joey.'

There was a moment's silence before she spoke. 'Sorry I left without saying goodbye.'

'I don't blame you. I'm sorry, too. I've been having the kind of hassles that make you forget about other people sometimes. What have you done?'

'I've left the circus. I haven't seen Wimsatt.'

'But you can't just let him get away with it.'

'I've told you, Joey, I'm not dragging the police into it. I won't see all my friends out of work. They know I'm leaving because of Wimsatt, maybe they can guess why. They know what a complete bastard he is – that'll do for me.'

'But, Nina, what are you going to do with your horses?'

He was astonished to hear her laugh. 'I've sold them to the Spanish boys. They reckon they can run the act themselves.'

'Then what the hell are you going to do?'

'First, I'm coming to see you. It sounds to me as if you could do with a bit of help. I've got some things to sort out first, but I'll be in Newmarket tomorrow. You needn't worry about putting me in your spare room, I've sent one of the boys on with my trailer. He'll find somewhere to pitch it.'

Joey thought of the immaculate verges at the sides of the roads for miles around Newmarket, and thought of Nina trying to find somewhere to park a wagon which no one would be able to distinguish from an out and out gypsy's.

'I've got a couple of paddocks. You can put it in one of them.'

'No thanks, Joey. I like my independence too much.'

'Don't stay too fond of it if you don't find anywhere to park! They're not too keen on people turning up and parking caravans all over the place round here.'

'I'll let you know.'

'But why are you coming?'

'Don't you want me to?'

'Of course I do. But what are you going to do?'

'Try and sort out my life, for a start. Also,' she paused, uncertain of his reaction, 'I thought I might have a go at this racing game.'

'What?'

'I was looking at the state of some of those horses out on the Heath; I could produce fitter animals than that, and have them better ridden. Some of those lads I wouldn't let sit on a garden wall. And I thought I might have a go at riding racehorses, instead of my Lusitanos.'

Joey was taken aback, but supposed it wasn't such a crazy idea. She certainly knew how to get the most out of her horses and she'd been doing it a long time.

'Why not? I'll give you a few lessons.'

'I taught *you* to ride, remember?'

He laughed again. 'I remember.' He wondered what Newmarket would make of a jockey who'd learned her trade riding bare-back, wearing a sequinned leotard with an ostrich feather headdress. 'I think you could have a lot of fun.'

For a while, after he'd put the phone down, Joey felt as carefree as a teenager, and all the hassles of the last month seemed suddenly less important.

Chapter Ten

When Nina turned up on Saturday evening, Joey felt as if he'd been holding his breath for the last forty-eight hours. He hadn't really believed she would come – it had seemed too improbable that she would go as far as chucking in her old career. It was more than understandable that she wanted to get away from Wimsatt, but she could easily have taken her team of horses to any other circus in Europe.

It was clear, though, from the moment she arrived at Three Elms Farm that whatever else she may have lost, she didn't intend to give up her freedom.

She arrived in the passenger seat of a horse-box. Joey guessed she must have hitched a ride; he was watching her from the window of Barry's office where they'd been reviewing a successful day's racing over a bottle of wine. She jumped down from the cab, waved a sunny goodbye to the driver and vaulted over the post-and-rail fence.

'Jesus, Joey. That's an athletic bird you've got yourself,' Barry observed over his shoulder. 'Are you up to the job, man?'

'I doubt it,' he laughed. 'But I'll give it a damn good try.'

He went downstairs to greet Nina and brought her

back up to the office to be introduced to Barry. He gave
her both barrels of his Celtic charm, and even had the
good manners not to laugh when she told him she
wanted to take up training and race riding.

'She's serious, by the way,' Joey said. 'Would you get
her fixed up with an amateur rider's licence?'

'No problem. I might even be able to fix a ride or two,'
he added. 'If it's not a cheeky question, what's your
riding weight?'

'I haven't decided yet,' she declared grandly.

Barry roared with laughter and looked her up and
down. 'Nine stone, two pounds, with a breast plate, I
reckon.' And she'd need a hefty one of those, he thought
appreciatively.

A look from Joey told him to keep the thought to
himself.

In the house, Joey made coffee and they sat at his
kitchen table.

'So,' he asked, 'where's your trailer? I thought you
were bringing it with you.'

'Not far from here. In a field on one of those big
flashy studs you pass coming into town. I found a young
toff who goggled like a rabbit and said I could park there
for a few days. I told him I wouldn't make a mess.'

Joey couldn't help being impressed with her brazen-
ness, a trait which always went down well in Newmarket,
especially in long-legged blondes. 'But how did you get it
there?'

'One of the Spaniards towed it for me.'

'Oh. Where is he, then?'

'Sanchez? He's gone.'

'And you haven't got a car?'

'No. I haven't even got a driver's licence.'

Joey laughed. 'You're crazy. You'll be really stuck, out on some stud with no car. I know you want to be independent and all that, but at least park your caravan on my land, then there'll always be someone to take you around.'

Nina looked at him consideringly. 'I need privacy, and water, too.'

'There's a great spot at the bottom of one of the paddocks, well tucked away about three hundred yards from the house, and right by the brook.'

'If you show me tomorrow, I'll make up my mind then.'

He accepted that was as far as he was going to get for the time being. 'How do you feel now?' he said, changing the subject.

Nina pushed her black coffee across the table. 'Put a bit of brandy in it, please.'

Joey found some Cognac and sloshed a generous measure into her mug.

She took a long swig, and spoke in her low, husky voice. 'I tell you, now it's happened I'm so happy. For years I've wanted something to force me out of the circus. It was beginning to seem like a prison. But, you know, I was scared to leave. I've lived in a circus all my life – I was born in a bloody circus trailer! And to the circus people it's sacrilege to want to get out. But when Wimsatt attacked me the other night – that was enough.'

Joey nodded. 'It must have been horrible, but I still don't understand why you don't want him to pay for it? I can hardly believe he'd do such a crazy thing.'

'Believe me, he *is* crazy. He kept saying he loved me, yet what does he do? Try and rape me! He risked the police, and me leaving his circus – even when he knows how many people come to see me ride.'

'There may have been more to it than that,' Joey said, not wanting to scratch Wimsatt from his list of suspects too soon.

'What are you saying?'

'I'm not sure yet. Nothing, probably.'

He struggled with his conscience, wishing he had the guts to tell her about all the guilt and confusion that weighed him down.

Since his visit to Lichfield and Wimsatt's attack on Nina, Joey's suspicions had turned in a new direction. For a while, after he had seen the tape which had been sent from France in Wimsatt's trailer, he had been utterly convinced that the ring-master was his blackmailer.

But now, in trying to rape Nina, the circus boss had committed what was obviously the act of an insanely obsessive man, not a calculating extortionist. Reflecting on Wimsatt's reaction when he had asked about that tape, Joey had to admit to himself that he hadn't shown the slightest sign of guilt.

He felt gloomily that his reluctance to confide in Nina was weakening the bond between them. But as she was leaving shortly afterwards, he was encouraged when she told him the name of the stud where her caravan was, and asked if he would come and get it the following day. She would take his word on the quality of his site.

Joey came and watched her walk out of the gate, impressed that she insisted on making her own way back.

The phone started to ring as he went into the kitchen.

'Hello?'

'Is that Joey Leatham?'

'Yes.'

'It's Nick Allen here. We met at Mr Trevor's.'

'Yes, of course.'

'Can I come up and see you?'

'What? Now?'

'Yeah, if it's convenient.'

It was a rare free Saturday evening, which Joey had hoped to spend with Nina. 'Sure,' he said gloomily.

'Great. I was hoping you'd say that. I'm only forty minutes away.'

The private investigator turned up just after nine. He declined Joey's offer of a drink, opted for strong black coffee and sat down at the kitchen table.

'Right,' he said, opening a folder. 'I made contact with an employee of Southern Counties Building Society. A young clerk, male, about twenty-five.'

'Great! What did you get?'

'Nothing. I explained who I was and what I was doing, though of course I couldn't reveal your name. I offered him a monkey if he could come up with a name and address from the account number you gave me.' Nick paused. 'I had a second meet with him this afternoon, and I'm afraid he was scared shitless of getting caught. Like I said, unless the police ask, there's no way the building society will identify the account holder.'

'So?' Joey asked impatiently. 'What do you suggest?'

'Tell the police.'

'I've told you, I can't.'

'In which case, these guys can carry on milking you and getting their hands on the cash without coming up for air as long as they like, until you run out of money.'

He stopped, and glanced up sharply. 'Is it only money they're looking for?'

Sitting at the table opposite him, Joey looked down at his hands. 'Not entirely.'

Nick gave a dry laugh. 'I guessed as much. Look, if these people are asking you to stop horses, isn't it likely they're in the business?'

'Not necessarily. It's pretty obvious that's one way of exploiting what they've got over me.'

'As long as they think you'll do it.'

'How do I convince them I won't?'

'Just don't – next time they ask – and see what happens.' Nick started shoving pieces of paper back into his folder and stood up.

'Listen, they've already killed my dog and gave another friend of mine such a hiding he died afterwards. He was the only person who knew the full story. But these guys got him, and then they followed me over to France and gave me a serious hammering. I don't think I want to see what happens next.'

'They'd be crazy to do you any serious damage because then you'd stop riding and lose your income. People don't kill the goose laying golden eggs or maim it either. That's bad for the laying process.' Nick picked up his folder. 'Anyway, sorry I couldn't do a lot for you – as far as the building society's concerned. If you think you'd like some more intensive work done in tracing these people, let me know and I'll be happy to oblige.'

'What else could you do?'

'I'll tell you that when you've agreed to take me on. Do you want to talk about it now?'

'No, but I'll let you know. Have you got a card?'

'You can get hold of me through Mr Trevor. He'll send you a bill for the couple of days I've done.'

The three-week spell of fine weather had come to an abrupt end. Thunder storms on Saturday night and a steady downpour which followed into the middle of Sunday morning were either too much for anyone who had planned a barbecue lunch, or too little for any trainer with horses that needed a cut in the ground.

Joey was giving Dick and his wife a drink on their way to lunch with one of their bigger owners who lived nearby. Di Lambert was with them.

'I hope you don't mind?' she said. 'I'm not going on to lunch afterwards. What are you doing?'

Joey noticed a slight and uncharacteristic raising of Veronica Seabourn's eyebrows. This was the first time he had noticed anything critical in Veronica's attitude to Di. He wondered what was causing it; whether, perhaps, Dick had told her about Joey and Di sleeping together.

He opened a couple of bottles of Krug, and caught himself wondering what his strait-laced, teetotal, penny-pinching foster-parents would have thought if they could have seen him filling his guests' glasses with such an expert hand.

He was just passing the glasses round when a short rap on the front door was followed by Barry's entrance.

'I'm sorry to interrupt your party, Joey, but I need a word with Mr Seabourn and Di.'

'Sure,' Joey said, surprised. 'Use my study.'

'If you don't mind, Dick,' Barry addressed the trainer, 'could we go over to my office? We've got into a real mix-up over next week's rides and we need to sort it out now.'

Seabourn agreed. 'Di, have you got your organiser with you?'

'Yes, it's in the car.'

They went out, leaving Joey and Veronica alone together. 'I can't think how Dick managed in the old days without Di and her little organiser.'

Joey picked up a hint of bitterness in her tone, which surprised him. 'I suppose when you had to keep everything in your head, you just did.'

'I always used to. It was one of the things that kept us close.'

Joey didn't like the direction the conversation was taking but guessed if Veronica needed to talk, he should be flattered to be her confidant. 'Aren't you still involved in the running of things?'

'Hardly at all now. My sole contribution seems to be providing meals for owners when they come.'

It was strange, Joey reflected. On the face of it, most women would have found Veronica's life-style thoroughly enviable. She lived in a large, comfortable and beautiful house with plenty of help. Her husband was handsome, charming and successful in his field. She had a busy social life, and a bright, good-looking daughter.

She had had the will and the money to age very gently, and was still an attractive woman. Yet now it seemed to Joey she was deeply unhappy.

'Maybe Dick felt you deserved a break from all the stress of running the yard?' he suggested.

'I'm afraid to say that would be unusually considerate for him.' She lifted her chin defiantly. 'Anyway, let's not talk about it. Why don't you sneak us another glass of champagne before they get back?'

A few minutes later, Seabourn and Di returned with

all the booking problems sorted out. Veronica showed no further signs of the anxiety she had expressed privately to Joey, and they carried on talking much as usual about racing and the horses in the Crowle House yard.

As they talked, Joey found himself wondering what Nina was doing and wishing she were here with them. He wanted to show her off to the Seabourns, and everyone else in Newmarket.

Later, they were getting up to leave when there was a flurry of gravel in Joey's drive. He went across to the drawing-room window and looked out to see a bright aquamarine Bentley skidding to a halt.

Ivor Wimsatt burst from the driver's door and strode purposefully towards the front of the house.

Joey went and opened the door to him and was slammed back against the wall almost before he turned the deadlock.

'Right, you little sod, where is she?' Wimsatt bellowed. He wasn't a tall man but he towered over Joey and his eyes bored into him with undisguised hatred.

'D'you mean Nina?'

'Of course I fucking do!'

'She's not here.'

'Yes, she is. The Spanish boy who brought her told me.'

'He didn't bring her here.'

'Where did he take her trailer then?'

'I don't know, and if she'd wanted you to know, she'd have given you a forwarding address.'

Wimsatt puffed out his chest. His sharp black eyes narrowed. 'Listen, you jumped up little tit, I know where you came from, remember. So just get out of my way!'

'She's not here!' Joey shouted back, close to losing his

own temper. 'Do you seriously think she wants to see you after what you did to her? You must be mad even to think of coming to look for her here!'

'What's she been saying, then? Look, I gave the ungrateful bitch a ring worth ten grand, for Christ's sake! *That's* what I've done to her. And I know she's here!' Wimsatt lunged forward so suddenly he caught Joey by surprise. He barged past him and looked around the hall before charging into the empty kitchen.

Joey stood and watched while he checked the other rooms until he reached the drawing-room, where Di and the Seabourns sat with drinks in their hands, trying to suppress their astonishment.

'You can look upstairs, too,' Joey invited, feeling in control in the face of Wimsatt's obvious derangement, 'as long as you don't make a mess.'

Wimsatt glared at him, then at the others.

Abruptly, he let fly a left hook which caught Joey on the tip of the chin and sent him staggering back into a drinks table. Bottles and glasses crashed and tinkled across the room. Joey stumbled to his feet, rubbing his jaw.

'She's far too good for you, you little wimp,' Wimsatt roared at him in his ring-master's voice. 'God help you if I ever find her here.' He turned on his heel and strode from the room.

Nobody spoke until they heard the car pulling away with a noisy scattering of gravel.

'Who on earth was that?' Dick asked.

'Believe it or not, he used to be my boss. He owns the circus I was in.'

Dick's eyebrows raised. 'Your old boss? But why's he suddenly turning up here? And who was he looking for?'

'Nina Korsakov. She had a riding act in his circus.'

'But what did he do to her?' Di asked excitedly.

The Bentley had gone, but a movement outside caught Joey's eye. 'I'll tell you another time. She's just arrived.'

The front door-bell rang. He went to answer it. A few seconds later he showed Nina into the drawing-room.

'This is Nina. Nina, this is my boss, Dick Seabourn, his wife Veronica, and this is Di Lambert who runs the office for Dick.'

Dick looked at Nina with open approval; Veronica with curiosity. Di, at first sizing her up like a jealous rival, quickly assumed a friendly smile and came over to take her hand in greeting. 'We've just been hearing all about you.'

Nina glanced at Joey. 'What have you been saying?'

'Only that you've come to set the racing world alight,' he said quickly.

He gave her a glass of champagne and soon the others were questioning her, fascinated by her bizarre career and plans to move into racing.

While the Seabourns were there, no mention was made of Nina's eccentric living arrangements and the proposal to move her into Joey's paddock, but once they'd gone, she asked, 'Do you still want to bring my trailer here?'

'What's that?' Di asked with a grin. 'Have you brought your horses with you? They'll stand out from the crowd on the Heath.'

'No, I've sold them, but I've brought my living trailer – my home.'

'And you're going to park it *here*? What a laugh, Joey! The locals will go crazy. They'll think you're starting a caravan site.'

'Well, I'm not,' he said sharply and turned to Nina.

'We could go and get it now, if you like?'

She nodded. 'That would be great.'

'Provided Danny hasn't gone off in the Range Rover.'

'D'you need a hand?' Di asked.

Joey could see she'd be hard to dissuade. 'It's stopped raining and it looks as though the sun's here to stay for a bit, so if I light the barbecue you could get everything ready to cook when we get back. We'll only be gone half an hour or so.'

'Fine,' Di said brightly. 'Let's get on with it.'

While they were fetching the trailer, Joey was able to tell Nina about Wimsatt's whirlwind visit. When he mentioned the punch he'd taken on the chin, she looked at him with deep concern.

'Joey, I'm so sorry you've got caught up in this.' She put a hand on his arm.

'It's okay,' he said, 'but we've *got* to teach the bastard a lesson – make sure he doesn't come round pestering you again.'

'Just so long as other people in the circus don't suffer.'

Nina loved her new pitch. It was a quarter of a mile from Joey's house, screened by a belt of birch and oak. Even in high summer the brook gushed and tinkled crystal clear over a small weir a few feet away. It was on the far side of a flat pasture, a hundred yards from a road gate, tucked in among the trees.

'This is so beautiful,' she said. 'Thank you very much, Joey. But I must pay you rent.'

'If it was a grazing horse, I'd charge twenty quid a week, so we'll call it that, okay?'

She pulled a note from her purse and made him take

it. 'And don't think that just because I'm pitched on your land, you can come round any time you like. Only when I invite you.'

'Fine. When can I come, then?'

'I'll see,' she laughed.

Although Joey had been irritated by Di's inviting herself to hang around, when he got back to the house, he decided she'd earned her lunch. Everything was prepared and the barbecue was glowing like a furnace.

Joey was also impressed by the canniness with which she treated Nina. Nina was more beautiful, almost certainly more talented and with an obviously more impressive physique, but somehow Di managed to present herself as more worldly and sexually aware.

A lot of this was lost on Nina – at least, if she saw it, she wasn't prepared to be affected by it. Nevertheless, the feeling prevalent was that they were two women of equal attractiveness and knowledge of the world, and on the whole Joey was relieved by this. It was better than out and out competition.

The sun was beginning to gleam through the clouds and they decided to eat outside. It was an enjoyable al fresco lunch, helped by two bottles of Burgundy.

After a couple of hours of eating and talking lazily, Di rose decisively to her feet.

'Okay, Joey, I expect you've got lots of dreary phone calls to make – at least for an hour or so – so I'm going to whisk the lovely Nina away and show her the sights of HQ.'

'HQ?' Nina questioned, not objecting to the idea in principle.

'Newmarket is HQ to anyone in flat racing,' Joey said.

He wanted to tell Di to go away and leave Nina with him. But that would have upset the good humour of the lunch party.

'What a good idea,' he said instead. 'There are several things I need to do this afternoon.'

He walked around to the front of the house, where Nina and Di climbed into Di's Peugeot 205 and shot off up the drive.

Joey went inside, switched on the answerphone, and set off for a walk across the broad flat fields of pasture that surrounded his house. Once he issued a sharp, tremolo whistle and listened for the sound of Roger, rustling and snuffling through the undergrowth, until he remembered with a sharp pang of grief that he would never again feel the dog's wet nose barge into the back of his hand.

And as he walked, he nursed his bruised chin and hoped the women's conversation didn't reach the point where intimate details were swapped; although he guessed Di wouldn't be able to resist the temptation.

Di drove at ninety-five with half a finger on the wheel as she extracted a cigarette from a packet of Silk Cut. She poked it into her mouth and managed to light it without taking her eyes off the road.

'How are you getting on with Lord Tewkesbury?' she asked.

'Who's Lord Tewkesbury?'

'He's a well-known breeder – the man who let you park on his stud. I saw him yesterday evening. He'll be very disappointed you've left.'

'Oh. He told me his name was Gerry. He was very nice to me. I went to look at his mares this morning and he gave me some eggs. He said I could stay as long as I liked, but I told him I was moving to Joey's.'

After a long drag on her cigarette, Di shot a glance at her passenger. 'So, I suppose you and Joey had a mad passionate affair when he was riding with you in the circus?'

Nina gave a husky laugh. 'No way! You're not going to believe this, but in those days I thought he was gay.'

'Joey gay?' Di exclaimed, appalled. 'That's the last thing he is.'

'You know from personal experience?'

Di answered with a grin.

Nina felt a sudden surge of envy for the English girl. Then reminded herself she had no justification. It was absurd to expect Joey to have stayed celibate for ten years, and she'd only reappeared in his life three weeks before.

'But what on earth made you think it?' Di was asking.

'Because when he first arrived, he lived in a trailer with a strange little Czech clown who'd always liked other men. And my father told me too, though I guess that was just wishful thinking on his part.'

'My God! Was your *father* like that?'

Nina shrugged. 'Sometimes.'

'What a life you must have had.'

'Maybe, but for me it was normal. Coming here, where everyone has so much land and big houses – that's much more peculiar for me.'

'I hate to disillusion you, but not everyone has big houses here. The trainers – some of them – a few of the top jockeys, like Joey, and some of the big owners and breeders, but for every one of them there are a hundred humble souls like myself, living on a pittance, lurking in grotty cottages and flats. The lowest of the low, the young lads, often live in grim little hostels on no money at all.'

'But not Joey's brother,' Nina said.

'No. Danny's lucky. Luckier than he deserves to be, really. I sometimes wonder why Joey puts up with him.'

'Are you fond of Joey?' Nina asked point blank.

'Yes, I'm not interested in a long-term scene with him, though. He can be a bit too intense, you know.'

'Intense? What do you mean?'

'Well, he can brood a lot, especially lately. I suppose he takes his job very seriously. My boss says he does, anyway. But I've always rather fancied him.'

'Do you have a lover?'

'Sort of,' Di said quickly, turning her attention back to the road. 'Was that madman who turned up before lunch your ex?'

'You mean Ivor?'

'Yes.'

'Of course not. No way! He wanted to be, he kept giving me presents and promising he was buying a great big place where we could live in the winter, but he was full of shit. I loathed him. It was just that I'd got stuck in his circus and didn't seem to know how to get away. It was a sort of inertia. Then last week he . . . well, he tried to rape me.'

Di took her foot off the accelerator and turned to Nina, shocked. 'But surely, if he threatened you with rape, you must do something about it?' Nina was the only person she'd met who'd ever come close to being raped.

Nina tossed her head. 'What? I could never prove anything. It would just be a waste of time and would only cause problems for my friends still at the circus.'

'But you can't just let him get away with it! Listen, if you need help dealing with him, promise me you'll let me know, okay?'

Barry Mannion didn't go to the Brighton races with Joey next day. Joey knew that was probably because he didn't think they'd have a winner. It turned out he was right.

Despite the demands on his attention from the blackmailer, and from Nina, Joey's urge to win was as strong as ever. But that day, not one of his mounts remotely deserved to win a race. It happened like that sometimes, and it often shook Joey's self-confidence.

Driving home, he phoned Barry, in need of reassurance; he wouldn't have admitted it, but his friend knew.

'Joey,' Barry butted in as he was trying to justify his performance, 'you don't need excuses – not like you did with Colombian Prince. It was all their fault today – you'd five rotten horses. I'm sorry. If anyone's to blame, it's me. But frankly, all the winners were tied up. You know how it is sometimes.'

'It wasn't your fault, Barry, and you know it.' Joey recognised he was being humoured. 'Anyway, what's been going on back at the ranch?'

'I've had your Miss Korsakov here in the office, haranguing me for not having her licence yet. She says she's already got three or four rides lined up. I tell you, Joey, that girl's taking this town by storm.'

'Did she leave any message for me?'

'She asked when you'd be back, and I told her. She watched a couple of your races on the box then disappeared.'

Joey said goodbye, put down the phone and drove the

rest of the journey in a state of expectation and frustration. When he got home, he was almost ashamed at how delighted he was to find Nina back in Barry's office.

Barry poured them both a drink. After a few minutes, Joey knew he couldn't evade it any longer and slipped over to the house to see who had rung him during the day.

Among the normal, everyday communications there was just one ominous message, delivered over the phone in that familiar, distorted voice.

'I'll ring again after eight. Make sure you're in.'

It was ten to. Joey went back to Barry's office, where a couple of his friends had turned up and were flirting outrageously with Nina. He managed to take her to one side.

'Do you want to have dinner with me tonight?'

'Oh, yes. Can we go somewhere called Le Picasso? Di told me that's where you took her and it's the best place to go.'

'What else did she tell you?'

Nina grinned. 'Nothing to put me off!'

'In that case, of course we can. The only thing is, I'm expecting a call soon, so we'll have to wait until it's come through. D'you mind?'

Nina shrugged her shoulders. Time had never been much of a factor in her life.

Joey glanced at Barry's friends. They'd be more than happy to entertain her till then. 'I'll get back and wait for this call, then we'll go, okay?'

'Sure,' she nodded. 'Barry says he'll show me some tapes of the ladies' races.'

After twenty minutes of waiting in his house for the

phone to ring and to hear the familiar, eerie voice, Joey didn't know whether to be relieved or alarmed that it hadn't come. As he walked back up the outside stairs to Barry's office to fetch Nina, he put on his best smile and decided to forget things for tonight.

Le Picasso was buzzing. It buzzed even louder when Joey walked in with Nina. In a town where gossip was the staple diet, a new dish was always welcome. During the evening, several people passing their table stopped on some pretext to talk to Joey, but really wanting to take a closer look at Nina.

Between these unsolicited interruptions, they talked, and Joey felt they were recovering some of the ground lost since they'd last been together. At the same time, he could see that she was flattered by all the interest the racing world was showing in her.

'Di says racing is a sexy business,' Nina said.

'I suppose it is,' Joey acknowledged with a wry smile.

'But you don't have a lover?'

'No. I've been waiting for you.' He grinned.

Nina laughed. 'I bet you've had women in and out of your bed the whole time.'

'Only if they reminded me of you.'

'Did you sleep with Di?'

'Did she say I had?'

'No.'

'There you are then.'

'But I don't believe her. She wants to be a friend to me, I think, but I don't trust her.'

'Why not? They don't come much straighter than Di.'

'Is that what you think? She must have a rich boy-friend somewhere.'

'I don't think so. Why do you say that?'

'When I was in her flat yesterday, after we drove around Newmarket, I was in her bedroom and she showed me her jewellery. She's got some fantastic stuff – and yet she doesn't seem like a very rich person.'

'There are lots of girls like that in racing, from posh families with loads of assets they won't sell and no readies. Di's family live in some bloody great house with a thousand acres the other side of Thetford, and her father drives around in a clapped-out old Volvo and wears jackets with elbow patches. You'll probably find the jewellery was left to her by her granny or some great-aunt.'

Nina bowed to Joey's greater knowledge of the arcane code of people like Di Lambert, while he found himself wishing he could buy some jewellery for Nina – if only all his money wasn't being raked in by blackmailers as fast as he made it.

With that thought, the magic of the evening disappeared for him. He tried not to let his disappointment show, but knew he wasn't ready to take her home with him tonight.

She looked surprised when he suggested he would take her straight back to her trailer, but didn't try to change his mind.

'Have you got everything you need in there?' Joey asked.

'Yes, of course. For me a trailer is home, remember?'

'Okay, but is there anything I can do for you?'

'Yes, there is. Fix for me to come and ride with you tomorrow.'

Joey wondered what Dick would think about Nina's turning up to ride out. 'Sure,' he said, with a grin. It would certainly shake up the lads. 'I'll pick you up at seven.'

Nina opened the car door but stayed where she was for a moment. Abruptly, without saying anything, she leaned across and gave Joey a soft kiss on his mouth before she climbed out and disappeared into the blackness of the oak spinney with a backward glance and a wave.

He sat in his car and watched her go, cursing the malign influence of his blackmailer.

Nina's eyes opened wide at the sheer magnificence of Crowle House, the fifty-yard square of fine, brick-built Edwardian stables, the venerable clock-tower, and the time-honoured, organised chaos of morning duties.

Joey parked his Ferrari among the dozen or so cars belonging to Seabourn's lads and work riders and took Nina round to introduce her to the yard.

Dick barely raised an eyebrow when Joey walked into his head lad's office with Nina. He declared that he was more than happy to put her up on a young filly for a little light work.

For once, the lads were dumbfounded. A lot of girls rode work, but none who looked like Nina. Joey noticed that the string was unusually talkative as they walked up to the Heath.

Several versions of who Nina was and her background had already swept through the yard before they had even pulled out.

'What a dream to ride these horses! But more difficult than my Spanish stallions.' She grinned as they pulled up at the end of the all-weather gallop.

'I should think it is,' Joey laughed. 'These little things haven't had ten years' tuition from you, for a start.'

Together they turned to ride over to where Dick

225

Seabourn stood watching with an owner.

'You can come and ride work any time,' he said to Nina, 'just as long as you don't distract my jockey too much.'

'I try not to,' she said with a look at Joey.

They hacked back to the yard and after a quick debrief over coffee in Seabourn's kitchen, climbed back into the Ferrari to drive home.

Joey never locked his car. That morning someone had left a copy of the *Sporting Life* and an envelope with his name on it on the passenger seat.

With a faint feeling of foreboding, he stuffed the envelope into the pocket of his leather jacket and drove Nina back to his house for breakfast.

The angry weather of the last two days had passed. It was a fine, warm morning and they laid breakfast on the cast-iron table under the laburnum tree.

As they ate, Nina talked happily about the horses that had been out that morning – what they had done and what they might be expected to do. She was entranced by them.

She was in mid-flow when the mobile phone beside Joey rang.

He tried to control the trembling which now afflicted him every time he heard it.

'Hello.'

'Joey Leatham, please.'

He sighed with relief. It wasn't the blackmailer. 'Speaking.'

'Oh, great. This is John MacClancy – sports producer for the BBC. We wrote to you about appearing on our quiz show and we haven't heard anything. We were wondering . . .'

'I'm sorry,' Joey said, trying to disguise his impatience. 'There's no way I can do the show right now.'

'But I understood from your agent . . .'

'My agent books rides for me, not TV shows.'

'Fair enough, but would you consider it? I know our audience would be very excited to see you on it.'

'Look, I'm sorry, I have far too many other commitments at the moment. I'll be in touch. Okay?'

'Okay, Mr Leatham.' The TV producer sounded so dejected that Joey almost felt sorry for him as he put down the phone. If the man had rung three weeks earlier, Joey knew he would have said yes.

As soon as he had put it down, the phone rang again.

It was Barry, already in his office, wanting to see him urgently.

Joey pulled a regretful face at Nina, leaving her to top up her coffee and read the racing papers.

While he was up in Barry's office, the phone in the garden rang once more.

Nina picked it up.

'Hello?' she said in her husky Russian accent.

'Oh, hello? I wanted to speak to Joey Leatham.' It was a young female voice, uncertain, obviously thrown by having to talk to a woman. 'Is that his number?'

'Yes, but he's not here.'

'Oh. When will he be back?'

'He won't be gone long.'

'Tell him Laura phoned, and wants to see him. It's urgent.'

'I'll tell him. Goodbye.' Nina switched off the phone with a flourish, poured herself more coffee and settled back in her chair. She had just seen Joey coming back through a trellis arch at the side of the house.

'One of your lovers just phoned. She must see you *urgently,*' Nina said with a broad smile.

Joey shrugged. 'She's going to be disappointed. Did she have a name?'

'Yes. Laura.'

Joey stopped in his tracks. 'Laura?' he repeated.

'Oh? So maybe she won't be disappointed.'

Joey shook his head. 'Laura's not a lover, but she could be a problem. She's Dick daughter. I think she feels that as I work for her dad, I ought to be at her beck and call. And I found her drunk with Danny the other night.'

'The old ugly sister routine,' Nina laughed.

'That's not fair on Danny.'

Nina looked at him closely. 'You don't think you're sometimes just a little too protective of that brother of yours, do you?'

'If I am, it's because blood is thicker than water.'

When Nina had gone back to her trailer, Joey went straight round to Danny's cottage. There was a Mercedes Joey didn't recognise parked in the courtyard, as well as both his own cars. Danny should not have been still at home at this time of day, but it looked as though he was and Joey wanted to find out what had been going on with Laura Seabourn. He was just about to ring the bell by the front door when it opened and Lenny Williams came out. Joey backed away instinctively, as if to avoid contamination.

''Morning, Joey. I hope you can talk some sense into that brother of yours. Things are getting out of hand.'

'They'll get more than out of hand if I see you round here again. Do you realise what you could do to my reputation?'

Lenny grinned coldly. 'Of course I do, and I hate to embarrass you. But maybe you can help me – your brother didn't seem to know. You're riding a horse called Tap Dancer tomorrow, aren't you?'

Joey froze. 'What of it?'

'What's the matter, Joey? I just want to know if you think he'll win.'

He looked at the bookie with utter disdain. 'Just get out of here. If you come here again, I'll call the police.'

Lenny burst out laughing. 'You? Call the police? Yeah, why don't you do that?'

Still laughing, he walked across to his car and climbed in. He gave a couple of farewell toots as he skidded off up the drive.

Joey turned and went into Danny's cottage.

'Dan? Where are you?'

There was a croak from the small living-room. Joey went in. His brother was lying on a sofa bed, unshaven and pale.

'What's wrong with you?' Joey asked.

'I've got a dose of 'flu, that's all.'

'Yet another hangover, more like,' said Joey with a sigh. 'Why did you let Lenny Williams come here?'

'I didn't let him. He just turned up. I owe him a bit, that's all.'

'Oh, Dan! Take my advice and stick to cash betting. At least then you know when you've run out of money. I can't keep on bailing you out, it's bad for both of us. And what have you been doing to Laura Seabourn?'

'Not enough,' Danny said, turning his face to the wall.

'Oh, well, we'll talk about it another time.' Joey stared at his brother's back, wishing Danny didn't find it so difficult to cope with life, knowing that his own success was part of the problem.

As he walked back to the house, he thought about his achievements and the downside it could bring; then, with a sudden sinking in his stomach, he remembered the envelope which had been nestling in his pocket for the last hour.

He wanted the protection of his own four walls, so waited until he was inside before shoving his hand in his pocket and pulling out the unwelcome letter. He extracted a single sheet of paper, printed like earlier ones in Letraset.

'TAP DANCER better not win.'

The name of his best ride the following afternoon at Sandown was highlighted in bright orange.

Chapter Eleven

Joey was booked to ride four races at Leicester in the afternoon. He set off in his Range Rover just after midday with Nina and Di.

As they cruised across country on the A14, he tried to push to the back of his mind the thought of stopping Tap Dancer next day. Meanwhile, his companions were discussing the best way to pay back Ivor Wimsatt.

'You can't just let the bastard off,' Di urged. 'Men like that have got to be shown that they simply can't abuse women as and when they feel like it.'

'But I've told you, I won't go to the police – I don't want him sent to jail; too many other people would suffer as a result.'

'Okay, but there must be some other way of punishing him, mustn't there, Joey?' Di appealed.

He agreed that Wimsatt had to be taught a lesson – one he would not easily forget.

And something Danny had recently done gave him an idea.

In the early-evening, on his own, Joey sat at his kitchen table gazing at a list of all the branches of the Southern Counties Building Society. The money he'd been pouring into it could have been drawn from any one of them, scattered across the south of England, up towards the Midlands. There was even a branch nearby in Cambridge.

For a few irrational moments, Joey considered a plan to stake out the Cambridge branch and watch to see if anyone he knew turned up there to draw money from the 'hole-in-the-wall'. But he knew he was clutching at straws. Nick Allen had made it clear enough that even the police would have had trouble homing in on whoever was taking Joey's money.

He got up and put on the kettle. It was just coming to the boil when the phone rang. He picked it up.

'Hello, Joey. Did you get my note?'

He didn't reply.

'Sounds as though you did. Remember what will happen if you don't do as you're told.' There was a brief pause. 'And we want another fifty thousand, by Tuesday.'

'I can't do it by Tuesday.'

'Yes, you can. And you'd better if you don't want this tape sent to the press and the police. And don't forget, we're watching you.'

As usual, the line went dead as soon as the speaker had finished.

Joey stared at the phone. He was beginning to sense something faintly familiar about the voice. Or was it his mind playing tricks?

He wondered if the threat that he was being permanently watched was just a bluff. Although they'd had no trouble tracking him in France, there'd been no mention of his visits to Lichfield or Chester.

But then, they'd known when he'd been to Yarmouth; Giulio's corpse was testament to that.

Joey stood up and stretched. Determined to take some control over his life, he went and changed. The sponsors of the big weekend meeting at Newmarket were holding a reception at the racecourse, to which everyone was invited. He had asked Nina but to his surprise she'd turned him down; she'd already been asked to a party herself.

In a moment of desperate insecurity, Joey wondered if she had been annoyed by the call from Laura this morning. Perhaps she hadn't believed his woolly explanation about Danny's involvement. But he dismissed the thought as unworthy, and hoped that the reason was Nina's fierce sense of independence.

The reception was in a large, elaborate marquee behind the stands at the racecourse. Few people noticed when Joey walked in; at four foot ten, it was hard to make a grand entrance.

Expensive scent mingled with the smell of cigar smoke and champagne. The indecipherable babble of a few hundred voices talking loudly all at once enveloped him without giving him the buzz it usually did. Occasional camera flashes reminded him of the publicity purpose of the function, and Joey wished he'd never come.

He squeezed his way through the crowd, nodding at most of the people he passed. He hadn't ventured far inside the canvas cavern when he noticed a small group gathered around the man who was currently the town's most fashionable trainer: a philanderer with good connections and an uncanny eye for a horse.

It was natural for Charles Rettingham to be surrounded by rich, laughing men and beautiful women. But on this occasion at the centre of the circle was Nina.

Joey felt a sharp stab of jealousy at her presence. He saw Di, too, bathing vicariously in Nina's popularity. He deliberately skirted round the group, not wanting to be part of it.

'Hello, Joey!' Laura Seabourn greeted him with an extravagant hug and a generous kiss on his lips.

He returned the greeting with as much enthusiasm as he could muster. 'Hello, you wicked little creature.'

'Little? That's rich, coming from you!'

'You won't argue with the "wicked" though?'

'I'm sorry about what happened the other week. You were right, I was being stupid. Poor Danny.'

'I hope you haven't been driving him crazy ever since. Anyway, why did you ring me this morning?'

'I just needed to talk to you,' she said defensively.

'Here I am,' Joey said with a friendly smile; she wasn't much more than a child after all.

'It's just that . . .' Laura was suddenly less sure of herself. 'Well, Mum and Dad . . . Oh, it doesn't really matter.' Her voice trailed off and she reddened.

Joey guessed that the real reason for her call was that she'd heard about Nina from her parents and wanted to find out what she meant to him. Now it looked as if she were too embarrassed to ask. Pretending he hadn't noticed, he managed to get her chatting about horses for a while, until someone caught her eye and she took the cue.

'Joey, I'll see you later.' She leaned down to kiss him on the lips, ignoring a photographer's flash. She may only have been seventeen, but she was a very attractive girl. The next moment, she was gone.

He heard Nina's voice in his ear. 'Hello, I can see you're busy, but aren't you going to talk to me?'

'I didn't think you'd noticed I was here.'

'I hadn't, Di told me.'

'Your new friend.'

'I've got lots of new friends since I came to Newmarket.'

'Who brought you tonight?'

'Gerry and Charles.'

'Well, don't pay too much attention to Rettingham, for a start.'

Nina laughed. 'He already told me that breaking in fillies is his speciality.'

Joey grinned with relief at her evident disdain. 'And has he offered you any rides, yet?'

'You could say that. And he says he has a horse to win a ladies' race called the Newmarket Plate or something.'

Joey nodded. 'The Town Plate. You wouldn't be popular if you won that.'

'Hello, Joey,' a loud, aristocratic voice boomed over his shoulder.

Joey turned round to face a tall man in his early-forties, lean, fit and fine-featured. 'Hello, Rupert.'

The tall man's eyes flickered from Joey to Nina. 'Any chance of an introduction?'

'Nina Korsakov, this is Lord Leamington. He used to be a jockey.'

Leamington looked approvingly at Nina. 'Are you Russian?'

'Of course,' she said in her low voice.

'How interesting. Where are you from?'

'The circus.'

Lord Leamington laughed, already hooked by her unique combination of the bizarre and the beautiful.

'How is Lady Leamington?' Joey asked.

'She's fine.' He nodded over adjacent heads. 'Just over

there, talking to your boss. We've just bought a horse in your yard – Tap Dancer. You're riding him at Sandown tomorrow, I believe?'

Joey couldn't speak at first. What was this? A conspiracy? Fate playing with him, or what? He had been trying desperately to forget the instruction to stop Tap Dancer, and Lenny Williams' subsequent interest.

'You are riding him, aren't you?'

'Yes, I think I am. He should go well.'

'Worth a punt?'

Joey nodded. 'On the form. I haven't ridden him for a while, though. I don't know how well he is. You'd better ask Mr Seabourn.'

'Dick says he's jumping out of his skin.'

Joey's heart sank, but he was saved from making any more inventive excuse by someone else catching Lord Leamington's eye. 'Best of luck then, Joey. I expect we'll see more of you?' He gave Nina a winning smile and walked away.

'My God, what a fantastic-looking man,' she said, and just as abruptly changed the subject. 'But why were you so fidgety when he mentioned Tap Dancer? Don't you think he will win?'

'Was it that obvious?'

'Yes.'

'I don't think he's up to it, but the man's only just bought the horse. I couldn't say, "Well done, you've got yourself a donkey".'

Nina looked at him.

He was irritated to feel himself blush.

She shook her head. 'Joey, you wouldn't ever cheat anyone, would you? You were such an innocent, honest boy when you first came to the circus.'

'I'm still an innocent, honest boy,' he protested.

'Who's this you're talking about?' Barry said, coming up behind them with a grin.

Joey didn't want to repeat the conversation he'd just had with Tap Dancer's new owner. 'Can you convince this woman I wouldn't lie to her?'

'Nina,' Barry said with elaborate earnestness, 'yer man here is probably the straightest jockey in Christendom, but of his qualities as a liar, I know nothing.'

He beamed at them both.

Joey tried to detect some double-entendre from his agent's delivery, but the Irishman's smile was as inscrutable as ever.

'Now, Nina,' Barry went on, 'there's someone over here I'd like you to meet. He may even have a ride for you.'

Joey watched them go, cursing the way this woman had him trembling like a teenager. Why the hell, he asked himself, did this have to happen when he was in the middle of saving his career – his liberty even – from a cunning, opportunistic blackmailer?

He'd already realised he'd need all his wits about him to handle Nina, and had to remind himself of this later when he decided to leave.

He went to find her and she greeted him with a big grin and a warm kiss on his cheek, as she laughed with the group surrounding her.

'Can I tear you away yet?' he asked.

'No, you can't. Di and I have a job to do tonight, remember? And I'm afraid you'd only get in the way.'

'Are you doing it tonight, then? You've worked fast.'

Nina nodded with a grin. 'We strike while we're hot.' Her eyes flashed. 'We got hold of your brother's friend.

Di's been over to Cambridge to get him.'

Joey was impressed. He wished he could do more to help with the plan he'd helped formulate, but Nina had objected. Wimsatt knew him, and that would blow the whole thing.

'Keep out of trouble, if you can,' he told her. 'Come round tomorrow and tell me how it went. I'm going to bed early. I've got a living to make in the morning.'

If you could call this living, he thought to himself as he walked towards the exit from the marquee.

Di was already in the car park, waiting for Nina in her small Peugeot. She had been home briefly to change.

'My God!' Nina gasped. 'You look fantastic! I've never seen anything so tarty in my entire life. He'll love it!'

'Let's hope so. He sounded pretty doubtful when I said I wanted to see him after the show tonight. Said he liked to look at new acts with a clear head in the mornings.'

'Don't worry, as soon as he sees you, he'll forget about that. And when he thinks you're going to sleep with him to get the booking, he'll do whatever you want. He's one of those men who just loses his mind as soon as his prick hardens. Believe me, I know.'

'Right, let's hit the road to Banbury.' Di glanced in her mirror. 'Danny and the chap from Cambridge are right behind us.'

Ivor Wimsatt walked back to his trailer with eager little strides. Over the phone, there had been a husky confidence about the woman's voice which suggested she had more to offer than just a juggling act. He wasn't particularly interested in that, anyway; he already had one of the best female jugglers in the country. But, as his father had always said, it cost nothing to look – especially if there could be a bonus for him in it. And it wouldn't be the first time that such a bonus was on offer.

It had been a good show tonight. Bringing the lion act back had certainly boosted the rural Oxfordshire crowds. Inside his trailer, Wimsatt poured himself a large brandy and tried to stop his hands from quivering at the prospect of his interview with the juggler.

He had left the door open to let in the warm evening air. He caught a waft of her powerful scent before he heard the tap on the door.

'Come in,' he said in a gruff, dry voice.

Long legs in knee-high boots drew his attention first. Then dark tan stockings with black tops showing below a scanty black leather skirt. Above this was a short expanse of exposed midriff, and a slinky, shiny short top barely covering a black lacy bra and big, round breasts.

Only then did the ring-master look at his visitor's face.

Di had enjoyed going to town on her appearance. The make-up methods of the professional seductress were tried, tested and devoid of subtlety. She hadn't attempted to improve on them: a warm foundation, long false lashes, dark kohl around the eyes. Her hair fell in long, loose waves to her shoulders.

'Hello, my dear,' Wimsatt said breathlessly.

Di knew she'd reached first base. 'Mr Wimsatt?'

'Come in, come in. Would you like a drink? Brandy? Champagne?'

'Brandy, please,' Di said in a voice her mother wouldn't have recognised, and sat down on a comfortably sprung, built-in couch.

She saw Wimsatt gulp as she hitched up her skirt and flashed her scarlet knickers at him. She took the large balloon glass he offered her and pretended to drink a mouthful of brandy.

He did the same, and positioned his squat, ungainly body beside hers. He put one podgy arm around her and squeezed. 'Well, my dear, if your juggling is anything as good as the first impression you give, I think we might be able to come to some arrangement.' He cleared his throat. 'Are you married, by the way? I forgot to ask on the phone.'

'No. I was once, but I like a bit of variety, know what I mean?'

'Of course.' Wimsatt tried for a debonair tone. 'I quite agree.'

'Is the circus all yours, then?' asked Di.

'Oh, yes. And my father's before me.'

'Is that big blue Roller outside yours too?'

'Yes, though it's a Bentley.'

'D'you fancy taking me for a spin in it – give us a chance to get acquainted, like?'

Wimsatt hesitated for a moment, balancing up the probability that if he complied he would be rewarded against the certainty that he was over the drink-drive limit.

Lust – enhanced by Di's stretching her legs and offering him another glimpse of her red knickers – took about five seconds to overcome prudence.

'Come on, then. Bring your glass and I'll bring the bottle.'

With obvious glee, he shepherded her down the steps to his gleaming, aquamarine limousine. He opened the passenger door for her and his jaw sagged with excitement as she tucked her long legs under her on the white leather seat.

He scuttled round and climbed into the driver's seat. There was still a faint hint of sun in the western sky, but there was no moon rising and soon it would be pitch dark. Di chose a soul album from the rack in front of her, pushed it into the CD player and lay back in her seat, praying that Nina and the boys were following close behind.

Nina sat beside Sean Delaney, a recently acquired friend of Danny's, who was driving his small Renault van. Danny was crouching in the back, peering between the front seats at the tail lights of Wimsatt's Bentley.

In the Bentley, Di took a deep breath, gritted her teeth and snuggled up beside Wimsatt. Given the reason for the whole exercise, she considered it worthwhile, and it wouldn't last too long. Anyway, she enjoyed giving her performance, and knowing she was playing her part in securing a triumph for Nina.

She had fixed the wing mirror so she could see the lights of Sean Delaney's van.

Three or four miles west of the old market town where the circus was playing, Di slipped one arm around Wimsatt's ample waist and squeezed, while her other hand massaged his upper thigh. He smiled smugly at his powers of seduction – and Di marvelled anew at a male vanity which was so predictable and easy to manipulate.

She gently tugged Wimsatt's arm. 'Let's turn down this lane and find somewhere to stop. I'm beginning to feel very horny.'

Wimsatt nearly overshot the turning in his excitement,

but hauled the big car round at the last moment and nosed into the narrow lane between tall trees.

After another fifty yards, Di pointed. 'Look, there's a little track. No one's going to disturb us there.'

Wimsatt nodded eagerly and recklessly turned the Bentley on to the narrow earth track where it lurched a dozen yards into the woods.

It was nearly ten and night had fallen. Nina, Danny and Sean sat in the van with the window open, listening to the evening calls of the birds and the screech of barn owls waking for the hunt while they waited for Di to work on Wimsatt.

After five minutes, they climbed out, Sean carrying a small case containing the tools of his trade. They trooped in single file down the secondary lane until they reached the point where the track headed off into the woods. They stopped and listened. The Bentley's engine had been turned off and they could clearly hear the CD player now, still belting out soul.

They peered up the rutted track. Out of some strange instinct, Wimsatt had left on the side lights and switched on the interior lighting.

'S'pose he likes to see what he's doing,' Danny whispered.

Nina put a finger to her lips and signalled them to keep still while she set off up the track, comfortable in the knowledge that the khaki waxed jacket she wore over her party dress would make her hard to spot in the dark.

When she was within ten feet of the Bentley, she stopped and waited a moment before creeping forward, right up to the car, crouching with her head well below the windows. She listened to the noises from inside. As far as she could judge, everything was going according to the ad hoc plan she and Di had worked out, giggling over a bottle of Chardonnay at lunch today. There was a rock track playing now and the murmur of two voices – Di's husky and false, and the more intermittent growl of Ivor's, fuddled with drink.

Nina took out the pocket knife she had brought with her and groped around until she had located the nearest of the four big tyres.

She unfolded the well-sharpened blade and began cautiously to press it into the side of the tyre. Quivering with fear and excitement, she started to apply pressure with her finger alongside the blade. As soon as she felt the first hint of escaping air, she pulled back the knife. Within a few minutes, Nina had all four tyres deflating gently. Then she crept back the dozen yards to where the two men were waiting.

Di wasn't particularly enjoying her part of their stratagem, but was at least gaining some satisfaction from seeing it.

Wimsatt eagerly activated a reclining mechanism until both pristine white hide seats were near horizontal – more than flat enough for a comfortable snooze.

Di was quick to take the initiative.

She was getting a buzz from the power that her sexual hold over the man gave her, and submitted to his clumsy pawing of her breasts. The music didn't completely drown the grunting and snuffling sounds he made as his excitement mounted.

'Ivor!' Di said in mock affront. 'You're so keen – like a boy in a sweet shop! Slow down, you're getting over-heated. Let's get you undressed first, then you can undress me – nice and slow.'

'Oh, yes!' he grunted as Di unbuttoned his shirt, unbuckled his belt and unzipped his flies. He fumbled around, helping her to slip down his pants to reveal an unimpressive erection.

Di was careful not to laugh; she knew he was capable of violence if she did anything to injure his pride. She carried on pulling the clothes off his tubby, inebriated body until he was completely nude against the white leather upholstery.

She gritted her teeth and put a hand on his naked thigh, massaging it as much as she could bear, while with her spare hand she picked up the bottle of brandy and put it to her lips. She tilted back her head, carefully ramming her tongue in the neck of the bottle before she lowered it with a contented gasp and passed it to Wimsatt.

He took it in the same spirit of abandon and, less carefully than Di, also tilted it back. The brandy dribbled from the side of his mouth as he gulped down as much as he could.

As he drank, Di scooped up his shoes and all the clothing she'd removed. Wimsatt, busy with the bottle, didn't notice. She quickly let herself out of the driver's door.

'Just going to have a pee,' she said over the noise of the CD, and shut the door. By the dim light of the car's interior, she peered into the gloom of the bushes beside the track.

'Danny!' she hissed.

He came out of the undergrowth, crouched over, a coil of rope over one shoulder. Sean was beside him, with his box of tools. 'Hi,' Danny whispered. 'Having fun?'

'I will be when I see what you can do.' Di dropped the pile of clothes into a plastic bag Danny had brought for the purpose, and opened the car door.

'Hurry up,' Wimsatt bleated. 'I don't think I can hold out much longer.'

Di climbed back into the car and pulled the door shut.

Meanwhile, Danny crept round to the driver's side of the Bentley with Sean, who had been prepared to broaden his usual sphere of activities for the extra hundred pounds he'd been promised. Danny clutched the handle, looked at Sean and opened the door against which Di had managed to press the ring-master's flabby body.

She quickly backed away while the two young men grasped Wimsatt's doughy flesh with gloved hands and heaved him off the reclining seat. It took some strength to manoeuvre his eleven flaccid stones from the car and on to the grass verge between the track and the woods.

For the first few seconds Wimsatt had no idea what was happening. As soon as he started to struggle, half-way out of the car, Danny gleefully punched his fist hard into the flabby, white midriff, and Wimsatt collapsed into a quivering heap.

Di turned off the lights in the Bentley. In the sudden darkness Danny and Sean swiftly dragged Wimsatt a few yards further into the wood to the sturdy trunk of an oak tree. They heaved the naked man against it. Sean propped him up and flicked on a powerful torch while Danny took the coil of rope from his shoulder and lashed Wimsatt with his back to the tree and arms splayed around it behind him.

The ring-master was jabbering with a mixture of terror and fury that he'd been set up. But every time he struggled, Danny punched him and he soon got the message.

'What the hell do you want?' he gasped, blinking into the beam of Sean's torch. 'If it's money, just say so. You don't have to go through all this charade.'

'It isn't money.'

Wimsatt glared into the darkness, not sure if that was Nina's voice he had heard.

'Who's that? Nina? What do you want?'

He shivered as the air grew perceptibly cooler and his penis shrivelled into obscurity.

Nina stepped into the dim torchlight, and laughed. 'You'll find out soon enough.'

Once they were sure that he was securely tied, Sean fetched his tool-box from the other side of the car.

He came back and handed Danny the torch while he placed the box on the ground and opened it to reveal his collection of needles and syringes.

Wimsatt saw them and quivered in terror. 'What the hell are you going to do? You can't kill me . . .' he cried.

Sean looked up at him and smiled. 'We're not going to kill you, Mr Wimsatt,' he said softly. 'It's not drugs in here, it's dye. We're going to tattoo you.'

Wimsatt's face registered complete horror.

'What do you mean? What kind of tattoo?' he asked in a strangled whisper.

'A warning to others,' Nina told him coldly. 'So you don't get a chance to hurt anyone else the way you tried to hurt me.'

Sean stood up with the first needle ready. 'I'm going to do this free-hand, so it won't be the best I've ever done. But then, I don't suppose you'll be showing it off too much,' he added with a humourless grin.

He took a pace nearer and placed the needlepoint on Wimsatt's bare, hairless chest. 'I think here, just above the nipples.'

Wimsatt flinched, and the needle caught his flabby pectoral. He squealed with pain. 'For God's sake!' he pleaded.

'The more you move, the more it will hurt,' Sean said calmly. 'Now, I'm going to do the outline in black, but you can choose the infill colour. What would you like?'

'Fuck you! I'll make you pay for this, you bastard!'

Sean carried on smiling. He was enjoying himself. 'All right. If you won't choose a colour, I will. I think a nice turquoise, to match your car. That'll look good, won't it?'

Twenty minutes later the job was done. Nina, who had been watching silently from the shadows, stepped forward. She raised an automatic camera to her eye. It flashed half a dozen times on the trembling naked figure of Ivor Wimsatt, lashed to the tree, with the word RAPIST emblazoned in two-inch letters across his chest.

He kept up a muttered barrage of abuse and self-pity as he realised they were going to leave him. They had taken his car key, and his spare wouldn't be any use with four flat tyres. Besides, it looked as if they weren't going to untie him from the tree.

'You can't leave me here like this!' he wailed.

Nina reached into the back of his car and pulled out a rug folded on the rear seat. She passed it to Danny. 'Wrap this around him. If he gets much colder, his cock's going to disappear altogether.'

Di and Nina crammed into the little van with Sean and

247

Danny. As they drove away, they crowed with triumph and relief.

'My God,' Nina said. 'I never actually believed you'd get him to drive you into the country.'

'Didn't you? O ye of little faith,' Di laughed. 'It was easy. Once his blood was up, he would have done anything I wanted.'

'I think that'd work with me too,' Danny guffawed.

'Yeah, well, you're not getting the chance to find out. And don't you dare tell *anyone* what we did tonight, or I'll have your bollocks.'

'Yes, please,' he tittered.

'I mean it.'

Danny didn't miss the steely edge to Di's voice.

'But thank you very much, Danny,' Nina said to mollify him. She was glad she'd asked him to help. He'd done his bit well; the whole operation had gone better than she'd dared to hope, and they had inflicted just the right amount of humiliation on Wimsatt in retribution for what he had done to her.

With a great deal of expense and embarrassment, he would eventually be able to get the letters on his chest removed, but there would always be a faint scar to remind him.

They soon reached the circus site, where Di and Nina transferred to Di's Peugeot. She gunned it into life and they headed back to Newmarket.

After a couple of miles, she stopped and pulled into a lay-by. She picked up her mobile phone and dialled the Banbury police.

When the call was answered, she adopted the voice of an upper-crust sexagenarian and told them where they would find a man acting very strangely, almost certainly up to no good, maybe even murder.

Then she put down the phone.

'Do you think they'll go?' Nina asked.

'They're bound to. They couldn't ignore a call like that, just in case it turned out to be genuine. I don't suppose they'll do him for much more than being drunk in charge of a vehicle, but that and the tattoo should keep him away from you for the foreseeable future, shouldn't it?'

'I don't know, but he's the sort of man who hates to look a fool so I guess it'll work.' Nina laughed. 'And it was fun doing it. I should think he's going crazy now. Either I'll never see him again, or he'll come back and try to kill me.' She shrugged her shoulders fatalistically.

Di had started the car again and was driving more slowly now. 'Was it hard to persuade Sean to take the job?'

Nina grinned. 'Not too hard.'

Di glanced at her. 'You're amazing. You've only been here a week, and you've got people running all over the place for you. I'm sure Gerry Tewkesbury fancies you, and he's one of the most eligible men in Newmarket.'

'Well, I don't fancy him.'

'Just Joey?'

Nina nodded. 'Just Joey.'

When they reached Newmarket, Di stopped the car near the centre of the town, outside a large Edwardian red-brick house that had been split into flats. Hers was on the top floor. 'Come on up and have a drink.'

'Thanks, I need one.'

In the small, pretty apartment, Di took a bottle of champagne from her fridge and filled two slender glasses. 'Here's to Operation Ivor.'

They both laughed and drank. Di put on a CD and they settled down on her squashy calico-covered chairs.

'So, tell me all about Joey and the circus?' she invited.

'Have you ever seen Freddie Fielding's Circus?'

'No. Never.'

Nina told her about circus life and Joey's early days there; how he had been taken into her mother's Cossack Riders, then her father's trapeze troupe, and how he was learning to fly when her father and brother had been killed.

'Soon after that, my other brothers left, leaving me and my mother. Ginger moved on, then Joey. I assumed he was going to look for Ginger.' Nina shook her head at her misjudgement. 'Of course, we got a new trapeze troupe – a Mexican family called the Flying Ferraras. I don't think they'll stay with Wimsatt much longer, though, they're a brilliant act.'

Di nodded. 'Yes, I've seen them . . . I think. Or heard of them.'

'Anyway,' Nina went on, 'I never saw Joey again after he left until he turned up in Nottingham two and a half weeks ago.'

'Really?' Di said. 'He just turned up out of the blue, without any warning?'

Nina nodded. 'Yes.'

'What made him suddenly do that?'

'I'm not sure. He said he was looking for Ginger. I gave him the address of Ginger's old partner, Giulio. He went to see him, but a week later the old chap was attacked and died. It was terrible.'

'Do you think Joey's visit had something to do with it?'

Nina didn't want to tell her what she thought. She'd already said too much. She shook her head emphatically. 'No, but Joey was very upset.'

'He must have been. Do you know, he never really talks about the circus. Of course, most people know that's where he came from and where he learned to ride, but I've hardly ever heard him speak about it. It's as if he's trying to forget it.'

'I don't think so – not entirely,' Nina said. 'Though I do know he wasn't always happy there.'

Di got to her feet. 'Refill?'

Nina nodded.

After a couple more glasses of Di's champagne, she turned down the offer of dinner and took a taxi back to her caravan. She climbed into bed, satisfied with her evening's work, and grateful to Di for her help. At the same time, she had an irrational but nagging hunch that there was more to Di's assistance than simple good nature; and she wondered, not for the first time, if the girl still harboured stronger feelings for Joey than she was prepared to admit.

The next day, at Sandown races, Barry found Joey in the weighing room. The agent could barely contain his anger.

'Why the hell aren't you riding Tap Dancer? He'll waltz it – look at the field. There's nothing to touch him. What's going on?'

Joey stood by the rails behind the weighing machine and stared at the large brick fireplace. He couldn't look his friend in the eye. 'Barry, I tell you, I've done something to my ankle. It's bloody agony. I'll have to go and see the quack.'

'But what have you done to it, for God's sake?'

'I don't know. Twisted it jumping down, I think. Does it matter? It hurts like hell, that's all I know.'

'Look, Joey,' Barry pleaded, 'I've backed the horse, and there's no one else much around to ride him.'

'Graham hasn't a ride,' Joey suggested. 'But anyway, it's up to the guv'nor – not you or me.'

'I'll have to go and see Dick and sort it out, then.'

Joey watched Barry rush off and wondered just how much money he had on the horse to make him so anxious for Joey to ride.

Or – he paled as the thought struck him – did Barry just want Joey to have the ride to be sure the animal *didn't* win?

Nothing had happened to eliminate anyone else from his long list of suspects and he had to accept that Barry Mannion's name was still on it.

He walked to the racecourse doctor's office, hobbling conspicuously, trying to be consistent in which leg he was favouring.

The duty medical offer felt Joey's ankle and shook his head. 'Can't feel a thing.'

'Maybe you can't, doc, but it's my leg and I bloody well can!'

'Just try walking on it again,' the doctor asked.

Joey swung his legs over the side of the couch and took a few paces, limping heavily and wincing.

'Oh, well,' the MO said, 'if it's that bad, I'd better sign you off for the rest of the day.'

'Thanks, doc. My agent didn't believe me, I'm afraid.'

'Didn't he? I don't think I do either, but there it is. Please try not to twist your ankle like this again.'

Joey left with a certificate forbidding him to ride

that day and until he'd seen another doctor to pass him fit. He went to look for Dick to tell him the bad tidings. As he'd expected, Barry had got to the trainer first. Seabourn looked livid. 'Do you know where the hell Graham is?'

'I don't know, guv'nor. He was here, and he's got a ride in the last, I think.'

'Well, he's nowhere to be seen now. If you see him in the next few minutes, tell him he's needed. Otherwise there's a young claimer I could put up.'

'Lord Leamington won't mind who rides him, as long as he wins.'

Dick looked at him hard. 'I hope to God there's something seriously wrong with your ankle, Joey.'

'Thanks a lot, guv'nor!'

Joey didn't stay at the races. He couldn't face seeing anyone else and pretending to be injured. The whole incident was making him feel genuinely sick, but at least he'd avoided having to pull the horse.

He found his Range Rover and drove out of the car park. He listened to the race commentary on a premium rate service over the phone, glad for the new owner when Tap Dancer sounded as though he'd won easily.

He didn't want to think about what the consequences would be for him. Instead, he thought of Nina.

He had been hoping to see her that morning, to hear how she and Di had got on with their scheme to deal with Wimsatt. But when he'd rung, she hadn't answered her mobile.

Although usually he didn't believe in revenge, he had never been subjected to the kind of demeaning assault that Wimsatt had inflicted on Nina, and could see how she might well feel purged if the culprit was made to suffer a similar ordeal. Di's eagerness to be involved he attributed to her taste for adventure.

When he got back to Three Elms Farm, Joey ignored his flashing answerphone. Instead of playing his messages he went straight upstairs to lie in a bath with a large tumbler of vodka, and tried not to think about what could happen next.

At last, he forced himself out of the womb-like security of the water to face raw reality. Wrapped in a towelling robe, he went downstairs and played through his messages, dreading the alien tone of the black-mailer.

But the only call was from Laura, asking him if he'd seen the papers and telling him to call her as soon as possible. He decided to deal with her later. Right now, he needed to concentrate on identifying the party or parties who were holding him to ransom.

Like Nick Allen, he was coming round to the view that he must be dealing with someone involved in racing. It could have been anyone who at some point had had access to Ginger's tape, and the opportunity to play and copy it.

He stared at the list of names he had already made a dozen times and willed one to jump out at him.

Graham, Barry, Mike Wade, maybe Lenny Williams through Graham; any of these was still a possibility. So, for that matter, was Ivor Wimsatt. Even though he had no direct connection with racing, it was more than likely he had friends who had.

Joey banged the table in frustration. He had already been up and down this road a dozen times, proposing and rejecting suspects on the flimsiest evidence.

He was still gazing angrily at the names when a soft thud from his study caught his attention.

He stood up slowly and wrapped his robe tighter around him. He padded silently across the hall. The study door was ajar, far enough for him to see into part of the room. He stopped, waited, listened.

There were no sounds from inside the house besides the tock of the grandfather clock behind him. He stood for another ten seconds in complete silence before he pushed the door wider and walked into the room. At first, he saw nothing odd or out of place until he noticed that the door of the long cabinet behind his desk was open a fraction of an inch.

It should have been locked, and he kept the keys to it in his bedroom. This was his gun case, where he stored a twelve-bore for occasional forays across the meadow after teal and pigeons.

Abandoning caution, he walked quickly across the room and pulled the oak-panelled door wide open. The gun wasn't there.

'Looking for this, Shorty?'

Joey spun round.

An anonymous male figure stepped out from behind the curtains. He was wearing a cheap checked shirt, jeans and Timberlands. On his hands were leather gloves and his face was obliterated by a black, three-hole balaclava.

Even in his fear and confusion, Joey recognised the voice at once. It was the man who had beaten him up in France.

'That gun won't be much use to you without any shot,' he said defiantly.

'Maybe, but this way I know you won't be using it either. Now, we want a word. Outside.'

Someone grasped Joey viciously from behind. His arm was rammed up between his shoulder blades. He was spun round and marched to the front door, out across the gravel forecourt towards the spreading shrubbery on the other side of the drive.

'Looks like your ankle's better,' the man with the gun said from behind him.

Summoning up all his strength and speed, Joey jerked round and tried to wriggle free from the grip on his arm. The stock of his own shotgun was smashed into his side as he caught a glimpse of a second hooded man, who twisted him back violently to face the front and frog-marched him towards a wall of lush, full-leaved laurel.

When they reached the bushes, his captors carried on propelling him straight in among the branches, pushing through to a clearing on the inside. They were no more than twenty feet from the public highway, but Joey knew that only two or three people a day walked along it.

Without warning, an iron-hard fist drove brutally into his side, deep between his lower ribs and pelvis.

'We don't want to damage you so much you can't ride. You owe us a lot of money and you need to be able to earn it. But I promise you, this is your last warning.'

The bile that rose in the back of his throat emphasised the bitterness of Joey's defeat. The frustration he felt was almost worse than the pain.

A second blow slammed into his other side, bruising his kidneys, making him retch and gasp again.

'Understand? Next time you're asked to stop a horse, you fuckin' stop it, see? Unless you want to end up like your mate Giulio. I wonder who the Old Bill would look for then? Someone wanting revenge for the death of two men on a trapeze, I should think. The daughter . . . the sister. What d'you reckon?'

For a third time a fist was pummelled into Joey's side, already almost anaesthetised by the previous punches. 'That's who they'd look for: the daughter of the man you killed. They'd be looking for Nina Korsakov – your pretty friend. Wouldn't they?' The man hit him again, laughing.

Joey came close to fainting. Through the mist of pain and fury that dimmed his vision, he could see splashes of a blue-gold evening sky between the blurred edges of dark waxy leaves. The next day seemed a hundred years away, and his house a hundred miles. He wondered if he would ever see either again.

When they hit him once more, he gave up and waited for oblivion.

But it didn't come.

Slowly he realised that they had gone – abandoned him on a carpet of rotting leaves beneath a green canopy of laurels. The sharp pain in his sides had diminished to a dull ache of bruised muscles, and a shameful fear.

Joey heard them go. There was a noisy snapping of branches and rustling of leaves. Then a car revving up out in the road; a faint squeal as it roared off.

He didn't know how long he lay there, but with the return of his strength came a new resolution.

He had to get to these people before they asked him to pull a horse again. And he had to confess to Nina how and why her father and brother had plunged to their deaths ten years before.

If she didn't forgive him or accept the innocence of his involvement, at least he would have had the satisfaction of telling her himself, and not allowing her to hear it from the thugs who had just beaten him.

It was another couple of minutes before he was strong enough to clamber to his feet and push his way out of the laurel thicket. He took the same route as the men who'd beaten him and found a gap in the fence where they had clambered through on to the roadside. On the verge was a trail of skid marks and gravel spewed from the road across the scrubby grass.

He scrambled through the fence and limped back down the road towards his gate. He was opening it when Barry's Porsche appeared at the end of the straight and slowed down to turn in.

Joey hobbled back to the house before his agent could see the state he was in. He'd just banged the front door shut behind him when Barry pulled up outside and walked across to knock on it.

Joey got himself upstairs and opened a window in his bedroom, overlooking the courtyard.

'Hello, Barry. I was just lying down to rest my ankle. I'll come across later if you're staying?'

'Joey, what the hell's going on?'

'I'll tell you later. Nothing to worry about. Tap Dancer won, didn't he?'

'But *you* should have had that winner.'

'Well, you backed him, didn't you?'

'That's not the point. I need to know what's going on.'

'I'll be up in your office in ten minutes, okay?'

'Okay.'

Relieved, Joey watched him go, praying that he hadn't just been sold an elaborate double-bluff. If the agent was genuinely happy at the outcome of the race, he couldn't have wanted Joey to stop the horse – which in turn meant he was nothing to do with the blackmail plot.

Joey wondered if, after all the years he had known him, he could really be sure of Barry.

When he was out of the shower, he picked up the phone by his bed and dialled Nina's number which he already knew by heart.

This time she answered.

'It's Joey. How've you been?'

'I've been having fun. Last night was brilliant! And today I was schooling some horses for Charles Rettingham.'

Joey winced. There could be only one reason why Rettingham should want Nina to school his string – and it had nothing to do with the horses. But he refused to let himself be jealous.

'I'll come over later and you can tell me all about it,' he said.

'Great. I'll make you dinner. Bring some wine.'

'How's the ankle?' Barry asked as Joey walked into his office over the garage a few minutes later.

Joey didn't have to pretend to be lame.

'Bloody sore.'

Barry suddenly looked at him more closely, noticing the cuts and bruises on his face. 'Are you okay, Joey?'

'It's okay. I'm fine.'

'But what have you done to your face?'

'Nothing. I walked into a stable door, that's all.'

'Lucky you didn't do it yesterday.'

'Why's that?'

'Haven't you seen the *Mail* today? There's a lovely picture of you on the gossip page.'

Joey remembered Laura's message and pulled a face. 'No.'

Barry handed him a copy of the paper. There was an eye-catching photograph of Joey and Laura kissing at the reception the evening before; underneath it the caption, 'Joey Leatham: retainership?' and an article speculating about possible marriage plans.

Joey groaned.

Barry laughed. 'They do write the most terrible drivel, don't they? I suppose it stops them getting bored.'

'Never mind that. What will Dick Seabourn think?'

Barry shrugged. 'Who cares? He's not going to get rid of you, whatever you do. Not now. He needs you too much to worry about his daughter rutting below her station.'

'She's not rutting – well, not with me.'

'Not while the lovely Nina's around anyway,' Barry chuckled.

Joey froze. There was no chance that Charles Rettingham would have let the day pass without drawing the article to Nina's attention, and milking it for all it was worth. 'Oh, shit,' he muttered, and sat down at Barry's desk to read the piece in full.

Barry stood up. 'I've left some stuff in my car,' he said. 'Just hang on a minute while I fetch it. There's a couple of things I wanted to talk to you about.'

He hurried off down the stairs. Joey finished reading the fiction about his nuptial plans and glanced at the papers on Barry's desk. His eye was caught by an official police notification of a speeding offence, registered by camera.

It was for Barry's Porsche, on the M56, between the M6 and Chester on Sunday, 7 July.

The day Joey had been up to get Nina.

The wording dissolved into a blur and swam in front of Joey's eyes.

Coincidence?

Joey thought wildly. What could possibly have taken Barry to Chester on a Sunday?

He heard his agent climbing back up the stairs and quickly walked across to the sofa and sat down, as if still reading the paper.

Barry came in. Joey let him carry on with finalising a few arrangements before he said casually, apropos of nothing in particular, 'Did you go to the evening meeting in Chester last Friday?'

'No. Why?'

'When were you last there?'

Barry looked at him, slightly bemused. 'God, I haven't been in two years. Why do you ask?'

'I just wondered.'

Barry looked at him askance and checked two more dates with him before Joey got up, glancing at his watch.

'I'm sorry, Barry, I've got to go.'

'Nina?' He grinned.

'Yes.'

'Best of luck. Dick says you're working Scaramanga early tomorrow. I'll see you on the Heath then.'

Nina had asked him to bring some wine. Joey picked up two bottles of Barolo from the rack in his kitchen and walked down to the paddock in the evening sun, his mind busily turning over the implications of Barry's trip to Chester.

Of course, being caught on the M56 didn't mean he had been to Chester, but near enough for him to have mentioned it when Joey asked – if he'd had anything to hide.

Barry had been one of Joey's closest friends since he had arrived in Newmarket.

Against that, there was no denying that he liked
making money as much as anyone else in this town of
brazen opportunists.

The only thing to do – and Joey should have done it
there and then this evening – was to confront him
directly over the speeding ticket. Resolved that he would
do just that the next morning, Joey clambered stiffly over
the stile, through the belt of trees, and climbed up the
wooden steps to Nina's front door.

When she opened it to him, he saw at once that she
had made an effort to look as good as she could, and
was glad he hadn't let his bruises prevent him from
coming. It made him feel better just to see her.

The inside of Nina's trailer looked as it had on Joey's
first visit to Nottingham – the time she'd invited him in
to eat goulash. He was struck that a mobile home should
have such an air of permanence about it. He guessed it
was the plethora of ornaments and free-standing domes-
tic objects that achieved the effect, as well as the length
of time Nina's family had occupied it.

Joey was impressed to find her already quite at home
in Newmarket after just a few days. It seemed that
everyone was offering her help, advice, jobs – anything to
make her life easier. He was under no illusion that any
spectacular-looking woman of exotic background could
fail to attract a lot of interest, but couldn't help feeling a
little cheated nevertheless.

However, he couldn't blame her.

Nina had carefully made up her eyes, accentuating
their brightness. She was wearing a hand-worked lace
blouse, full at the shoulder and close at the waist, and a
multi-coloured tiered skirt. If it hadn't been for her fair
colouring, she'd have looked like a Hollywood gypsy. As

it was, Joey thought, she looked like a proud and know-ing peasant, about to seduce a young squire.

Her manner was more compassionate. She immedi-ately saw the bruises he'd acquired. 'Joey, what happened to you?'

'If you give me a corkscrew to open this wine, I'll tell you.'

'It wasn't Wimsatt, was it?'

'No, it wasn't your old boyfriend. Why should it be?'

Nina laughed. 'I should think he's mad as hell over what we did to him last night – and ready to take it out on anyone.'

'Do you think it was such a good idea?'

'I don't care whether it was or not. I had to do it, and I'm sure it worked. Anyway, it was your idea, remem-ber?' she added with a grin.

'I'm not so sure how good it was, though – not if you think he's going to come back and make trouble.'

'He was already doing that, wasn't he?'

'I suppose so. Was Danny any help?'

'Sure, he was fine. So was Di, but I still can't see why she's so friendly to me. I think she still wants you.' Nina nodded her head knowingly.

'How's helping you supposed to achieve that?'

'Some women like to be devious,' Nina told him gravely.

Joey jerked the cork out of the bottle and glanced at her. 'So I've heard. But you're okay?'

'Of course I am.'

'But if he does come back, he's not going to be in a good mood, is he?'

She dismissed the problem. 'I'll deal with him if he does. Anyway, it seems to me you're the one who needs protecting. If it wasn't Ivor who came and beat you up, who was it?'

'I wish I knew.' Joey filled two glasses and put them on the polished mahogany table fitted between two upholstered benches. He slid on to one of them, opposite Nina. He smiled then groaned at his own folly. 'There were two of them, both with balaclavas over their heads. I know who sent them – the guy who tried to make me stop Tap Dancer.'

'Lord Leamington's horse? No wonder you thought it wouldn't win. What happened to it?'

'I didn't ride it – I got myself declared unfit. The horse won. These people weren't too happy.'

'Were they going to pay you to stop it?'

'No.' Joey breathed in deeply. 'They said they were going to send a videotape – to you, and to the police, if I didn't.'

Nina stared at him. 'To me?'

He nodded.

'Why to me?'

He refilled their glasses and pushed one across the table towards her. 'I should have told you about this weeks ago, when I first came to see you; and I won't blame you if you never want to see me again after I've told you.'

Nina sat quite still, gazing intently at Joey. It was as if she could see right into his soul. She said nothing.

'It was a tape of us practising on the trapeze the day your father fell.'

Nina's eyes opened even wider. 'You, my father and Mischa?' she said in a whisper.

Joey nodded. 'It's fuzzy and dark, but it clearly shows what took place.'

'But I remember, when it happened, Ginger said there was no . . .' She stopped abruptly. 'You wanted to see him. That's why you came back, isn't it? And why you wanted to find Giulio.'

'Ginger had recorded it – though he'd promised me he wouldn't.'

'Why? Why did he *promise* you? I know he always used to record rehearsals. My father used to bully him into perching up on the poles to get the best angles. And that was going to be a very important rehearsal. That was the day Sol Werner was coming to see the act, don't you remember?'

Sol Werner.

Joey held his head in his hands for a moment until a feeling of nausea had passed. He was telling Nina the truth now, and it might be the only chance he would get. He didn't want to blow it.

'I remember it all right,' he said, not allowing his eyes to waver from hers. 'Ginger promised me he wouldn't make a tape. Said he'd give an excuse to Ivan, say the tape bust – anything – but he wouldn't record the rehearsal because he'd asked me not to catch your father . . . to drop him – as a joke, a cruel joke – to humiliate him in front of Sol Werner.' Joey took a swig from his glass.

He glanced away; couldn't look at Nina for a few moments. 'Ivan had been terrible to us, me in particular; I never knew why. But he'd also upset Ginger – he'd pinched Giulio from him. I didn't know that then, of course, but I didn't care what he'd done. I was quite happy to see him made to look stupid, especially in front of this agent, and maybe put a stop to that crazy idea of his for two flyers to catch him. We didn't want to do the act; it was never going to look great, but he wanted it, so badly, like he was jealous of his own sons for being able to fly.'

Joey lifted his eyes and looked straight across at Nina. 'But I swear to you, I never knew about the nets . . . and I *never* thought he'd take Mikhail with him.'

Nina stared back at him. 'This is all on a videotape?' she asked huskily.

Joey looked closely at her, searching her eyes for any sign of forgiveness. 'Yes. Ginger sent me a copy just before he died. I found the hospice in France where he'd been. The nuns there said he'd seen me on telly, when that mad stallion went for the girl on French Derby day. Up until then he didn't even know I was a jockey.'

'But why did he send it?'

'I don't know. But a few weeks after the tape arrived, I got a blackmail letter, posted from Nottingham, and, of course, I assumed it was from Ginger. It was only when I went to France that I realised he'd died a week or so before the letter was sent. Then I started getting phone calls and notes demanding money, masses of it. A hundred grand!'

'A hundred thousand?' Nina gasped. 'What did you do?'

'I paid it, and a lot more since.'

'Why? How could you pay so much?'

'They threatened to send the tape to the Jockey Club, the press, the police, and then to you.' '

'Joey, I believe what you say – that Ginger asked you to do it. I don't blame you. Of course I was sorry to lose Mischa – heartbroken – but so far as you were concerned it was an accident.'

Her words lifted a weight from Joey's mind.

'But if you saw the tape, you might doubt it, which is why I don't want it sent to anyone. The only people who knew the truth were Ginger and Giulio. And they're both dead.'

'Ginger wasn't murdered?'

'No. He died of AIDS. But whoever is blackmailing me found out that Giulio knew I'd been put up to it by Ginger. And Giulio saw him loosen the pegs on the net guys.'

'And now they ask you to make horses lose?'

'That's almost worse than any money, though I've really run out of that too. The blackmailer who calls knows more or less how much I've made every week, and he always wants a percentage.'

'But don't you have *any* idea who it is?'

'No, not yet. I've got a few ideas, but . . .' He shook his head.

'But you *must* find them, stop them – get rid of them!'

Joey looked at her eyes, fiery with indignation, and knew he had been right to tell her. He wished he'd come clean before; but he hadn't known a few weeks ago just how strong and resourceful this woman was. Now he couldn't help smiling.

'Sure,' he said. 'I'm trying to find them, believe me. But at the moment I'm getting nowhere. All I have discovered is how they're getting the money. I pay it into an account at the Southern Counties Building Society, and somebody draws it out in cash. They can do that at any branch, up to five hundred pounds a time, several times a day.'

'Joey!' Nina said, devastated at the scale of the extortion. 'You must find these people, before they really harm you!'

'Why? Would you mind so much if they did?'

'Don't be such a fool! Of course I'd mind. I'd hate it if anything or anyone took you away from me, like that skinny girl who was crawling all over you at the party last night.'

'You saw the paper? I suppose Charles Rettingham showed you.'

'Yes, he did.'

'Nina, that was Laura Seabourn, Dick's daughter. I told you – I think Danny's after her. But yesterday she said she wanted to talk about her parents – and, well, I suppose they're friends of mine.'

'That was Dick's daughter?' Nina laughed out loud. 'I was so jealous!'

Joey's heart missed a beat. 'You were?'

'Of course. Don't you know that?'

He shook his head slowly, and a broad grin spread across his face.

'Of course,' Nina said, 'since you came to my trailer that first time in Nottingham, and I realised you weren't gay. Why else do you think I've come here?'

'Because you wanted a career in racing?'

'I do, but I want you more.' She stretched her hand across the table, took Joey's and squeezed it.

Joey dried the dishes while Nina washed up in a tiny enamel sink. She had put some Russian folk music on her stereo. Joey felt as if they were a couple of gypsies. They drank the second bottle of wine, and Nina turned down the wick of the oil lamp which had illuminated the caravan since the sun had buried itself among the trees on the other side of the paddock.

At one end of the trailer, taking up its entire width,

was a high brass bed, covered with an elaborate quilt of satin and broderie anglaise.

'I want you to stay, Joey,' Nina said with a shyness he hadn't seen in her before but which didn't surprise him.

'Only if you promise to massage my bruises?'

'Every square inch of your body, if you want,' she promised. She was standing very close, facing him. She linked her arms around his neck. He wrapped his about her waist until their bodies were pressed tightly together. Her open mouth found his and their tongues entwined hungrily in their first real kiss.

The gypsy music on the stereo became quieter, so that they could hear the wind rustling the birch leaves outside in the summer night. Joey leaned back on the bed while Nina, silhouetted against the warm golden light of the lamp, began slowly to undress, swaying in time to the wild cadenzas of the Romany violin.

The faint smell of musk and a haziness induced by heavy Italian wine lent a strange, other worldly quality to the scene. The light gleamed off Nina's earrings and her pale soft flesh as she slid her lace blouse over bare breasts. She wriggled her hips free from the tightly hugging upper tiers of her skirt and slipped it down her bare legs.

When she was completely naked, she sat on the bed and swung her leg over to kneel on either side of Joey's hips. Dexterously, she unbuckled his belt and slid down his jeans.

When he was naked too, they lay side by side for a while, wrapped around each other.

Then she knelt beside him and with her fingers gently caressed the tingling surface of his bruised flesh. The curls of her pudenda gleamed in the lamplight between

firm, flawless thighs and the gently dimpled curve of her
haunches. Her breasts, like a pair of harvest moons,
shone down on him as he flickered his tongue around
her stiffening nipples.

He reached up and drew her down on to him. As their
bodies met, all Joey's pain and worry melted away and
he lost himself in a place he'd dreamed of but never
known before. He never wanted to leave it and deliberately delayed his orgasm, prolonging her pleasure, drawing his own from her sighs and gasps and ultimate
surrender.

Later as they were lying side by side in her big brass
bed, Nina was suddenly struck by a thought and sat up,
shattering the mood of intimacy.

'Joey.' She propped herself on one elbow to speak and
looked steadily into his eyes. 'You can't let this blackmail
go on. How do you know they won't send the tape
because you didn't stop that horse?'

'First, I didn't ride the horse. And second, I was
calling their bluff. After all, the minute they send the
tape, they stop the money coming – and if they damage
me, they damage my earning capacity. Anyway, I've
made up my mind: I'm not shelling out any more. My
biggest fear was what would happen when you found
out. I mean, I have to tell you – on the tape it's
absolutely clear that I deliberately dropped your father. I
still feel terrible about it, even though I'd no idea what
Ginger had planned.'

'Don't feel terrible. No one was sorry my father went –
you know that. And I've already told you, I don't blame
you for what happened to Mischa. I just want to help
you, Joey. What can I do?'

He smiled slowly and reached under the bed clothes to

stroke the soft curves of her thighs. 'I'll tell you what you can do.'

She shivered and gasped. 'Joey!' A big grin spread over her face. 'What are you doing, Joey . . .'

Chapter Twelve

It was strange, he thought; he'd slept less than an hour, yet despite all the pressure being brought to bear on him, he'd never felt so alive and positive as when he jumped down from Nina's trailer to go to Dick Seabourn's early the next morning.

Driving out to the gallops with him, through wisps of early mist, Dick noticed it too. 'You look brighter than you have for a while, Joey.'

'Maybe it's because I stayed with Nina last night,' he said with a grin.

Seabourn looked at him sharply. 'Did you? After that photograph of you and Laura in the *Mail* yesterday, frankly I'm relieved.'

'I presume you don't object to Nina?'

Seabourn gave him what was intended to be a worldly smile. 'Of course not. What you do in your own time is entirely your affair. It's only when it spreads over into my territory that I get worried.'

'Laura's not causing you too much trouble at the moment, then?' Joey asked tentatively.

'No, no. Not as far as I know,' the trainer answered airily. 'Anyway, as I say, it looks as if your new girlfriend's doing you good. I hope it lasts,' he added.

'Ah, excellent. Here comes Scaramanga. There are only nine days to go to the King George. I'd very much like your opinion as to whether we should run him. Personally, I'm not entirely happy.'

They climbed out of his car and waited for the string of twelve horses to reach them.

Joey looked around for Barry, who'd said he would be there to see the gallop. There was no sign of the Irishman. Joey thought with a shiver that maybe his agent was avoiding him, anticipating a confrontation.

Once he was on the back of Scaramanga, he gave the job his total concentration. He had the ability – essential to any top-class sportsman – to clear all other problems from his head and give one hundred percent of himself to the task, whether he was racing or working a horse to assess it for a major race.

Although Scaramanga had run so close in the English Derby, he would have to prove himself in one of the other Group One races if he was to achieve the best possible value at stud the following year.

The King George and Queen Elizabeth Stakes, run over twelve furlongs at Ascot towards the end of July, was a race with almost as much kudos in the breeding world as the Derby itself, pitting the current year's three-year-olds against those of the previous year's classic animals that were still in training.

What was more, Joey had a deal with the colt's owner that if he won the King George on it that season, he would get a nomination to the horse when it went to stud. A nomination would give him the right to send one mare to the stallion each year. And that right could be worth as much as fifty thousand pounds a year – a useful pension if the horse prospered as a stallion and lived a long, fertile life.

But if he ran in the King George and gave a mediocre showing, a lot of the merit achieved by his impressive performance at Epsom would be lost.

Joey was only human; he'd worked like a slave to get where he was, and these personal financial considerations were bound to concentrate his mind. He gathered up the reins and hacked down to the bottom of the gallop.

Seabourn had told him to gallop seven furlongs alongside the stable's most experienced miler, to stretch Scaramanga a little.

'How fast shall we go?' the rider on the lead horse asked as they arrived at the start of the gallop.

'A good strong canter and then quicken up from the three-furlong marker. I'll come and join you for the last two.'

'What do you think?' Seabourn asked as Joey returned.

'He feels fantastic – better than he did at Epsom.'

Joey drove home for breakfast leaving Dick Seabourn in a much happier frame of mind and himself feeling buoyant about his chances in the King George, and ready to launch a fresh strategy in the search for his blackmailers.

First he wanted to see Nina. He parked his car at the farm and walked across the paddock to her caravan.

There was a small Ford in the field beside it. Joey climbed up the steps and knocked on Nina's door.

'Hi.' She beamed at him, making his heart thump faster at the thought of the night they'd spent together. 'This is Harry.' She waved to a slight young man of twenty or so, already installed on one of the benches at the mahogany table. In front of him, scattered so that they covered most of its surface, were several photographs and a copy of the *Banbury Star*. 'Harry's a groom at Gerry's stud, but he says he's really a photographer, so – I gave him the chance to prove it by developing all my shots from the other night. I didn't want to take them to the chemist,' she added with a giggle. 'Take a look!'

A quick glance showed Joey that most of the photos were of Ivor taken from various angles.

'And look at this, Joey!' Nina picked up the paper and leafed a few pages into it until she found a short report which stated that the boss of the circus currently playing in the town had been charged with drink-driving.

No reason was given as to why Wimsatt had been found with three times the limit of alcohol in his blood, naked by a Bentley with four flat tyres.

'You'd have thought they'd have mentioned that he was tied to the tree,' Joey remarked.

'Danny loosened the ropes,' Nina said. 'Just enough so he wouldn't have too much trouble getting out of them. And we left him with a car-rug to wrap round himself. But look at the rest of the story.'

The last paragraph offered the information that Essex police were also investigating a fire at Wimsatt's winter quarters in Canvey Island, in which he claimed hundreds of thousands of pounds worth of equipment had been destroyed, and his eighty-year-old mother had been killed.

'He never kept anything at that place,' Nina said. 'It was just a ruin of a house and a few tumble-down barns where he used to store a bit of hay in the winter. And I never knew his mother was still alive. The funny thing is, none of us in the circus heard a word about this.'

'I don't suppose it made it to the nationals at the time,' Harry said. 'Not a big enough story.'

'I remember him saying how rich his mother was,' Nina speculated. 'Maybe that's how he bought the car and the jewellery he gave me. And he was talking about buying a massive farm near the old one. I'm sure the circus wasn't making enough for all that.'

'I bet he put in a bloody great insurance claim for the fire, too,' Joey said. 'He must be mad at himself – scaring you off by trying to rape you, just when he was thinking he probably had enough bread to land you.'

'The arrogant pig! As if I'd have gone anywhere near him just because he had a lot of money.'

Joey laughed at her indignation. 'Anyway, at least you've got the justice you were after. He seems to be in all sorts of trouble now, as well as having to explain away that tattoo every time he takes his shirt off! I don't think we need worry about him showing up round here again. Serve the bastard right for what he did, especially if the police arrest him for arson, and possibly murder, as well.'

When Harry had gone, leaving the pile of photos with Nina, she and Joey walked back to Three Elms Farm. Joey made some coffee and busied himself cooking a breakfast of eggs, bacon and toast that few jockeys could have got away with. As he ate, out of habit he looked around for Roger to give him the bacon rinds. The old spaniel's absence brought him back down to earth with a vengeance; Nina may have savoured the sweet taste of revenge, but his own problems were far from over.

She sensed the change in his mood. 'Have you heard anything new?'

Joey shook his head, reluctant to involve her any more than he had while at the same time longing to share his troubles.

'I wish I could help you,' she sighed.

'There's not a lot you can do. I'll have to get that private detective back and ask him what he thinks; I'm getting nowhere on my own. If they ask me to stop another horse and I don't, there really will be trouble. And if they ask for any more money, I'm either going to have to hock this place or sell it.'

'But, Joey,' Nina almost whispered, 'you can't! You've worked so hard for all this, you don't deserve to lose it. It's not as though you had any intention of killing Mischa and my father. I could tell that to any court.'

'I wish it would carry some weight if you did, but you weren't even there. And, besides, you haven't seen the tape.'

After breakfast Nina left saying she had some business to attend to, but she refused to tell Joey where she'd been when she arrived back at Three Elms Farm a few hours later. When they set off for Sandown that afternoon, he pressed her to tell him.

'No, I won't. I've been following up some suspicions of my own, that's all. I don't know if I'm on the right track yet. But I'm going to find out.'

As they drove into the jockeys' car park at Sandown, Joey groaned. 'Oh, God. Not again.'

'What is it?'

'See that man leaning on a BMW? That's Lenny Williams. One of the bentest bookies in the business. He's always trying to fix races. I thought he might have been involved in the blackmail at one point, he seemed very interested in Tap Dancer's race, but I think now he must have taken a few large bets on the opposition.'

They passed the car and Joey stiffened. 'Crikey! That's Barry's old BMW and the guy in the driver's seat is Graham Street. There's no way he could afford the ten grand Barry was asking for it – not on what he's been earning recently.'

'But why does that bother you?'

Joey hadn't slowed or done anything to let Graham know he was taking any special notice of him. He carried on, parked and climbed out, leading Nina towards the weighing room. 'Because I've been going round thinking anyone who was in Barry's office the day the tape arrived could be involved. Graham was there, test driving that BMW.'

'Nina! Hi!' Di Lambert had spotted her walking into the Members' Stand and came over to greet her with a hug. 'I didn't know you were coming today. Are you going to have lunch with us?'

'Am I invited?'

'Of course you are! Come on up to the box.'

Once they were inside, there was no scope for private discussion, with people coming and going and Dick being expansive with owners and guests. Nina joined in, alert to any nuances in Di's conversation that related to Joey.

But it wasn't until everyone else had finished lunch and gone off to the paddock to see the runners for the first race that they were alone again.

Nina easily managed to steer the conversation around to the difficulty she was having in getting a particular type of make-up which she liked in Newmarket.

'They said I might be able to find it in Cambridge. Trouble is, not driving, I don't know when I'll be able to get over there. Maybe I can get Joey to give me a lift some time, but he's always so busy.'

'I'm going in on Saturday morning,' Di volunteered. 'Write down what you want and I'll get it for you.'

'Would you? Thanks a lot. You've been so kind to me since I got here.'

'It's no hassle; don't worry about it.' Di waved aside her thanks. 'I'm just pleased it's going so well with you and Joey. It still is, isn't it? I mean, no signs of stress yet?'

'To tell you the truth, Joey does seem to be worrying about something, but I don't think it's anything to do with me. Of course, he says it's nothing. He wouldn't tell me anyway.'

Di looked at her, concerned. 'I wouldn't have thought he had too many problems at the moment,' she remarked. 'He's having a fantastic season.'

'Yes, I suppose he must be.' Nina nodded at her and smiled, looking forward to Saturday when Di would go to Cambridge.

She left the box to place a small bet on Joey's horse in the next race. Nina preferred to deal with the bookies out on the front, rather than the unpredictable, anonymous Tote. On her way back to the stands, from the corner of her eye she caught sight of a profile that was as familiar as it was distinctive, and definitely out of context.

She swivelled her head and found herself looking at a short man wearing a silver mohair suit, a dark red shirt and silver tie. A pair of heavy, black-framed spectacles rested on the bridge of his over-sized nose and his thick, silver hair was brushed straight back from a low forehead. She turned away before he saw her and carried on back to Seabourn's box, contemplating the fact that this particular man was the last person she'd expected to see at the races.

Joey's next horse didn't win, nor had any of his earlier rides. He didn't have a ride in the last race and wanted to get back to Newmarket. After he'd showered, he found Nina in Seabourn's box and they left before most of the crowds. Once they were out of the racecourse and heading for the M25, Nina said casually, 'Guess who I saw today?'

Joey wasn't in the mood for a guessing game but suggested a few obvious racing names.

'No,' she said. 'It wasn't anyone you'd expect.'

'Who then?'

'Sol Werner.'

'Good God!' he gasped, taken by surprise. 'What the hell was he doing there?'

'I don't know. I didn't speak to him. In fact, I only just recognised him; I hadn't seen him for a few years.'

'Are you absolutely sure it was him?'

'Oh, yes. His isn't the sort of face you forget.'

'I wonder why he showed himself now?'

'Why shouldn't he?'

'I didn't tell you the other day because it seemed so crazy, but I thought *he* might be one of the people blackmailing me. And now he's turned up at the races.'

Nina looked at Joey as she considered the possibility. 'Maybe. I certainly never trusted him.'

She was still working on her own ideas, while Joey wondered about a possible connection between Sol Werner and Barry Mannion.

Barry hadn't turned up on the Heath in the morning,

he hadn't been at the races, and Joey hadn't been able to get hold of him on the phone. His secretary said he would be at home in the evening.

'I've got to call round at Barry's place as soon as we get back to Newmarket. That may open a couple of doors for us.'

'Barry? What's he got to do with it?'

Joey told Nina about the speeding ticket issued the day he'd been to see her in Chester. 'I was going to tell you last night, but I thought you'd had enough surprises for one evening.'

'You could say that.' She gave him a wide smile. 'But I'm really surprised if Barry's part of it. He told me he was one of your oldest friends.'

Joey winced. That was what troubled him most. 'I wish I was wrong, but it can't just be a coincidence he was up there the same day I was. He must have been following me, to see what I was doing. That's how they knew about Giulio.'

'Maybe you should go to the police and tell them the truth now, Joey.'

'I can't. I've told you, if they look at that tape, they'll say I killed two men. There's no one left to tell them about Ginger's part in it, and I'm bloody sure the CID won't let it lie.'

'But the blackmailers – Barry, Sol, whoever – would they have gone and killed Giulio themselves?'

'Not a chance. It will be the same people that have already had a go at me twice, and they know what they're doing.'

Joey left Nina at her caravan. She insisted that she would cook dinner if he promised to come back later. He went home first, to check his messages and faxes.

There was nothing unusual waiting for him. He rang Barry and got him at his flat. Without any preamble Joey said he wanted to see him and was on his way round. It wasn't an unusual request, and Barry seemed to take it in his stride.

Joey knocked on the door, and Barry let him into his big, newly built, fourth-floor flat. He showed him into a large, light kitchen/dining-room with wide views over the Heath to the west, dominated inside by an over-sized television and two vast piles of racing journals and sale catalogues. Otherwise, it was unexpectedly clean, tidy and well equipped, with an elaborate espresso machine already spluttering on the work-top.

The Irishman greeted Joey and made him some coffee. 'Did you see what's happened to the price of Scaramanga?' he asked, before Joey had a chance to say anything.

'No. I haven't looked yet.'

'They've cut him from fives to five to two.'

This made the colt favourite over the Derby winner. Several pundits had already expressed the view that it was the shape of the Epsom track that had beaten the colt. But this dramatic drop in price meant that news of how well he had worked was already out.

They talked for a few more minutes about Scaramanga, while Joey tried to detect any suspicious undertone in Barry's voice or manner. Despite his apparent glee at winning on Tap Dancer, Joey didn't underestimate the Irishman's ability to act. He'd seen him in action too many times for that. Listening to him now, Joey realised he was never going to get anywhere by pussy-footing around.

Angry with himself for not coming to the point sooner, he braced himself.

'By the way,' he said, during a lull in Barry's almost incessant talking, 'do you know why I asked you if you'd been up to Chester the other day?'

Barry looked at him blankly and shook his head. 'No. Haven't a clue.'

'You got caught on camera speeding up there, on the M56.'

Barry stared back as if Joey had lost his reason. 'What the hell are you talking about?'

He had to force himself to battle on in the face of Barry's obvious indignation. 'When I was in your office last night, I saw a speeding ticket, for your car on the M56 on the seventh of July. So you must have been there, right?'

'You saw a speeding ticket? Good God! Is that what this is about? And why the hell shouldn't I have been on the M56 on July the whatever?'

'Well, were you?'

Barry shook his head in disbelief. 'I wish I knew where the hell you were coming from, Joey. What's got into you?'

'Barry, it's a simple question. Were you driving along the M56 that day?'

'If you're talking about that speeding ticket, I didn't even notice where it was from. I'm just going to pass it straight on to Graham.'

'Graham?'

'Yes, Graham Street. He was using the car. I sold him my old BMW, and it broke down. He came round here whingeing about it, saying he needed a car desperately, and I told him he could take the Porsche. I wasn't going anywhere.'

'So you're absolutely sure it was him who was speeding on the M56?'

'Yes, yes, for God's sake, I told you – I haven't been up there for years. And anyway, what the hell is so important about it?'

'It doesn't matter. I'll tell you another time.' Joey tried to defuse Barry's annoyance. 'But did you say you'd sold the BMW to Graham?'

'If you can call it "sell". I've only seen ten percent of the money so far – I'm too bloody soft, that's my trouble. I should think it'll be a long time before he comes up with the necessary.'

Joey looked away and took a gulp of his coffee, convinced Barry was telling him the truth.

Whether he was or not, Joey guessed there was no point in further confrontation that evening.

'Okay,' he said, with an attempt at a careless smile. 'That clears up the mystery. Sorry if you thought I was accusing you of anything.'

Barry fixed bright blue eyes on Joey's. 'It hurts, you know, when I feel there's a lack of trust between us, Joey. Next time you've something on your mind, just level with me, okay? You must know by now you can trust me.'

Joey gave a small sigh. 'Yes, of course I do.' He swallowed the rest of the coffee and put the cup down. 'Right, someone's cooking me dinner so I'd better get back.'

'Some spicy hot Russian dish, I shouldn't wonder,' chuckled Barry.

Joey drove a few hundred yards from Barry's flat, round two corners into a road of small Victorian terraced houses which ran along the back of the High Street.

This was a part of Newmarket occupied by the lower rungs of racing's pecking order. Graham had recently moved there with his wife and three children, after his smart bungalow on the edge of the town had been repossessed.

Joey managed to find a tight slot for his Ferrari outside a snooker club opposite Graham's house. He climbed out to a chorus of greetings from local children and walked self-consciously to the front door and rang the bell. There was no sound from inside. After some time he knocked and a moment later the door was opened by a girl of three or four with a grimy dress and a nose that needed blowing. Her eyes were replicas of Graham's.

Joey smiled at her. 'Hello. Is your dad in?'

Before the child made any response, a harassed woman, no more than thirty but already worn out, shuffled through from the back of the house in a T-shirt, a pair of grey leggings and dirty pink slippers.

Even in her unkempt condition and obviously devoid of self-esteem, Joey knew that Angela Street could be – certainly once was – a surprisingly good-looking woman. He hadn't set eyes on her for several years. Graham must have let her down badly to bring her to this, he thought, feeling unexpected compassion for her.

'What do you want, Joey?' she asked ungraciously, registering the Ferrari parked on the other side of the road.

Joey didn't blame her for resenting him. He tried a smile on her. 'Just looking for Graham,' he said lightly.

'He's not here.'

'Any idea when he'll be back?'

'No, and if I had, and told you, he'd go ape-shit.'

Joey pulled a regretful face. 'Could you tell him I called, then?'

'Yeah, s'pose so.'

Joey looked at the small girl who by now had wrapped her chubby arms around her mother's skinny legs. 'Would she like a little present?'

'Like what?' her mother asked suspiciously.

'I was just going to give her something to buy some sweets with.'

'No thanks!' the woman said, pulling the girl closer to her. 'We don't need your charity.'

Joey couldn't think of an appropriate response. He gave the child a small smile, turned and walked back to his car, depressed by the encounter and frustrated that he hadn't had the chance to confront Graham with the speeding ticket from Cheshire.

He drove home, turning the new development over and over in his head. Since he had first come to the conclusion that it must be someone in racing who was extorting money from him, Graham's name had never been far from the top of his list of suspects.

Yet now that it looked to be a distinct possibility, he couldn't understand why, if Graham had been getting his hands on the money, his family weren't looking a lot better provided for.

It seemed to him that no man would willingly let his wife get into that state if he could afford to do something about it. But then, Joey knew from his own experience that human nature was capable of infinite variation.

He would just have to be patient until he got Graham on his own and could study his reactions.

★ ★ ★

The phone was ringing as Joey walked back into his house. Out of habit, he ran to catch it before the answer-machine cut in.

'Hello?'

''Ello, Joey.'

Joey held his breath for a moment. This was a new voice – new in this context, but not unfamiliar.

'Who is it?' he asked calmly.

'You've been talkin' to my colleagues . . .' The voice left the statement hanging, not requiring confirmation, while Joey ran back through his memory bank to identify it.

'You was workin' a horse this mornin' – you know the one I mean?'

'What about it?'

'Worked well, didn't 'e?'

'What about it?'

''E won't win 'is next race, will 'e?'

'He might.'

'If 'e does, you're fuckin' dead. And your girlfriend will take the rap – I'd make sure of that.'

Joey was still absorbing the full horror of what had just been said when the line went dead. Trembling, he slowly put the phone back in its cradle.

And as he did, he knew whose voice he'd just heard. It was the man in the balaclava, who only the day before had beaten him up and stolen his shot gun.

Joey didn't doubt that he'd just heard a genuine threat. His murder, with the crime clearly attributable to Nina, was a far more effective use of the tape from the blackmailers' point of view. However heroic he might have chosen to be in risking his own life, to risk Nina's being charged with murdering him out of revenge for the death of her father and brother wasn't even a remote option.

Scaramanga was due to run in the King George and Queen Elizabeth in eight days' time, which gave him that long and no more to find the blackmailers.

Determined not to be cowed, he pulled a bottle of champagne from his fridge and walked to Nina's trailer.

'To celebrate.'

'What?'

'I just had a call from my friendly neighbourhood extortionist and he didn't ask for money.'

'But, Joey, if they didn't ask for money, what did they want?'

'They want me to stop Scaramanga in the King George.'

'But surely there are other horses that can win it – the Derby winner, Nureyev, he's running too.'

'This isn't about placing bets – it's about laying them. Some big bookie will ease his price, once he's sure Scara won't be winning, and he'll take tens of thousands on it from the punters, and lay it for a few hundred other shops, knowing that he'll keep the lot. He'll be prepared to pay for the certainty that Scara isn't going to win. Trouble is, he *will*.' And Joey grinned at her.

Later, their love-making was even more passionate and profound than the night before.

In the morning Joey woke with Nina still in his arms. At her first slight movement, the excitement returned and they were lost in each other again until it was time to go.

Nina went with him to ride out. He was trying a horse

for Charles Rettingham, for whom he sometimes rode when Dick didn't have a runner. Rettingham was more than happy that Nina had come, and immediately proposed that she should ride too.

It was a perfect morning on the Heath and to Joey it was one of the finest sights in the world. Racehorses had been galloping up the grassy slopes for so many centuries that they were an integral part of the place. A gentle breeze rippled the long grass beside the mown gallops and a haze was lifting gently off the broad horizons of the low-lying landscape. This place gave him a sense of freedom that he would have gone to almost any lengths to defend.

Forgetting all his other troubles for the moment, he smiled at Nina as he leaned forward to give her horse a gentle pat on the neck.

She smiled back and drew in a deep breath. 'I can see why once you came here, you stayed,' she said. 'Do you know, it's amazing the way a shy little boy like you has come to this place and become a king.'

Joey laughed, hoping no one had overheard. 'I'm no king. The trainers are kings here, and the pompous stiffs in the Jockey Club are gods. Rettingham there,' Joey nodded to the trainer, strolling long-legged and languid towards them, 'is at the top of the heap. I just ride what he produces. Even the best jockeys in the world call trainers "sir".'

'At least you get paid for your skill and courage. In the circus we risked our lives, night after night – for peanuts.'

'Well, you've left now,' he said. 'So make the most of it.'

Thanks to her, Joey was feeling in much better spirits

as they later drove over to Seabourn's yard.

Dick Seabourn greeted Nina with his usual, old-fashioned good manners but refused to talk about horses in front of her. 'Have a look round the yard,' he said with an expansive gesture. 'You'll probably find a few animals better suited to the circus than the racecourse,' he added, joking against himself.

He took Joey into the house, to the office, where his manner changed abruptly. 'There's a rumour going round that someone doesn't want Scaramanga to do his best next week.'

Joey froze. He attempted a laugh. 'What! In a Group One race? They'll be lucky.'

'Joey, has anyone contacted you to . . .' Seabourn was evidently having trouble completing the question.

Joey stared back at him, registering horror that Seabourn could even consider such a thing.

'Bloody hell, guv'nor, I'd have told you if they had – you know that. Just don't worry about it. As long as I'm on him, the horse will win.'

'That ankle of yours is all right now?'

'Yes, thanks, more or less.' Joey didn't like having to lie to Seabourn, but he had no choice.

The trainer looked distracted, glancing out of the window every few seconds. Joey followed his gaze to where two surly men in anoraks were walking through the yard with clipboards in their hands.

He and Seabourn talked for another twenty minutes about the horses entered over the next few days. As Joey left, Di walked into the office and gave him a broad smile. 'Are you okay, Joey? You look as though you've been in the wars.'

She was looking at a small cut he'd got on his jaw

during his tussle in the shrubbery. It was healing badly and looked worse than it was.

'It's nothing. Just a scratch. Coming to Newbury today?'

'No, the boss won't let me. Too much to do.'

Joey left the house and went down to the yard. He looked into the office beside the tack room where he found Martin, the head lad and the man who managed the day-to-day running of the yard.

'Morning, Joey,' he said. 'Did Billy go well for you yesterday?'

'Yes, improving all the time.'

'Unlike other things in this yard,' Martin said grimly.

'What are you talking about? We're having a great season.'

'I'm talking about money. This yard is suffering from severe sterling deprivation. Some of the owners who took their horses away last year after the virus struck refused to pay. There's one big one still arguing the toss, says we never did the job properly. Of course, I don't know about these things, that's not my job, but I do know the boss was late with the VAT last month, and the bailiffs turned up this morning.'

'Those two miserable-looking blokes in anoraks?' Joey asked.

'Yes. They're not taking anything away, apparently, but they will if they haven't had the money in a week or so.'

'Good God. Poor old Dick.'

'I don't suppose it's a problem, really. I'm sure his missus will bail him out if it comes to that. They say her dad left her a few million.'

'As long as our jobs aren't on the line,' Joey said lightly.

'No chance,' Martin replied.

'I hope you're right. Anyway, I was looking for Danny.'

'He's already left to go to Thirsk.'

Joey knew Dick had a runner at the Yorkshire track, but didn't know Danny was looking after it.

'Is that one of his, then?'

'No, but he's put in for a lot of travelling recently and the other lad didn't want to go.'

'That's new,' Joey said. 'Where was he yesterday?'

Martin thought for a moment. 'God, we've had so many runners and lads away lately.' He called across to a girl carrying a muck-sack round to the heap. 'Where did Dan go yesterday?'

'Chepstow,' the girl shouted back. 'Came back with a pile of cash, the jammy sod!'

Joey's face paled. In his present suspicious state, the idea of Danny with a pile of cash struck an unpleasant chord.

He rebuked himself for his disloyalty. 'Tell him I was asking,' he said, 'otherwise he feels neglected.'

Martin grinned. 'Yeah, sure. I'll tell him.'

Joey found Nina chatting to two of the girls. As they walked away, he talked normally to her until they were in the car and out of anyone's hearing.

'Danny!' he burst out as they left the yard. 'He went to Chepstow yesterday and came back with a load of cash.'

Nina looked at him, appraising the information. 'So, he took a horse to Chepstow and he won some bets. Is that so unusual?'

'Yes, for Danny. He's a terrible punter.'

'But once in a while he could get it right, couldn't he?'

'I suppose it's possible,' Joey sighed. 'But Martin said

Danny's travelling much more, too. He says he likes it. He's already gone up to Thirsk today.'

'Is there a Southern Counties branch there?'

'No. Not that far north.'

'Then if he comes back with another bundle tonight, that will be from the bookies.'

'Or some punter he's selling information to,' Joey said disdainfully.

'But not your money at least.'

Joey gave a short grunt of frustration. 'Yes,' he conceded. 'You're right. It may not mean anything, but I can't pretend that it's impossible Danny could do something like that.'

'I think you don't realise how loyal he is to you,' Nina said. 'He's just an awkward boy, you know, and lives in your shadow. I think he copes with it pretty well.'

'But he's always been mates with Graham, right from the start, and now he's in with people like Lenny Williams. He hangs around with a lot of dodgy people.'

'But you haven't even seen Graham yet. He might have some perfectly good reason for being up near Chester that day.'

'Do you really think that's likely?'

'No,' Nina admitted. 'But that still doesn't mean Danny's done anything.'

'I hope you're right. Anyway, I'm going to find Graham now. Then we'll know what's going on there. Do you mind waiting in the car for a few minutes?' He had turned the Range Rover into the top of Graham's road and once again found a space near the snooker club. 'I think it'll be easier if I do this on my own.'

'Okay,' Nina agreed. 'I'll stay here.'

He walked across the road and knocked on the door.

This time Graham's wife opened it with a mutinous look in her eyes. 'If you're looking for him, he's over the road.'

Joey turned. 'In the snooker hall?'

'Yes. He's always there, the bastard, or in some slag's bed.'

'Thanks.' He hesitated a moment before taking a fifty-pound note from his top pocket. 'Get something nice for the kids,' he said and offered it to her.

This time she took the money, showing her gratitude with a faint smile, and Joey was glad he had taken the risk. Nodding a brief goodbye, he turned and walked across the road.

He pushed open the swing doors into the dingy stucco-covered building. The snooker hall had been converted from a Methodist chapel in the early-sixties and now helped fill the long leisure hours of the town's less busy men.

There were eight tables, all being used at half-past nine in the morning. Joey spotted Graham about to play a shot on the farthest one and made his way towards him. Everyone in the room recognised Joey and most greeted him cheerfully – apart from Graham who glowered as he glanced up from missing an easy pot.

'I heard you'd been sniffing around. What do you want?' he growled.

'Maybe we should talk somewhere less public.'

Graham stood back while his opponent, ignoring Joey, leaned over the table to take a shot. 'I've no secrets from anyone here.'

'Okay. I want you to tell me what you were doing in Chester three Sundays ago?'

'Why the hell should I tell you what I was doing at any time?'

'Because if I find you were there, I can guess what you
were doing and you'd better believe, I'll have you for it!'

Graham straightened up from slouching against the
table. 'I don't know what the fuck you're talking about!
It looks like success has gone to your head, mate. I'm not
doing anything to you, and Sunday three weeks ago, I
was here all day, playing a tournament which I bloody
well won. You can have a look at the results over there.'
He nodded at a noticeboard on the wall, on which a
knock-out competition chart was displayed. Joey didn't
bother to walk over and check. He already knew from
Graham's eyes that he was telling the truth.

'Then who the hell was driving Barry's Porsche? He
lent it to you, and got sent a ticket for speeding on the
M56.'

Graham looked at him in amazement. 'On the M56?
She said she was going to Windsor, for the polo.'

'Who?' Joey asked hoarsely, sweating at the prospect
of the information he was about to receive.

'Di. She wanted to borrow my car, but that was
buggered, so I got Barry to lend me his.'

'But you didn't tell him Di was going to drive it?'

'No,' said Graham defensively. 'I was borrowing it
because the pile of junk he sold me was knackered. It
wasn't his business who was going to use it.'

'But why did Di want to borrow your car in the first
place?'

'I dunno. Maybe that little thing of hers was off the
road. But she asked me, and I said yes; she never said she
was going to Chester.'

'And you're sure it was that day?'

'Of course I bloody am. Anyway, what's this all
about?'

'Don't worry. If it was Di, it's no problem,' Joey said as lightly as he could. 'I'm glad I cleared things up. Sorry to interrupt your game.'

Graham shrugged his shoulders, apparently mollified. 'Yeah, well. I'll let you know when I need a favour.'

Joey walked out of the snooker hall with a friendly smile on his face and his head spinning.

Outside he had to stop himself from running to the car. But he held in his news until he'd driven down the road and was heading for the country when it burst out of him. 'It was Di! She must have followed me up to Chester.'

'Di?' Nina nodded with an ironic smile.

'Yes,' Joey said. 'You were right about her. I can hardly believe it!'

'Why? Why shouldn't she be a blackmailer, as much as anyone else? Just because she has an upper-class accent and a fresh face doesn't mean she's honest.'

Joey glanced at her ruefully, knowing she was right.

'I've never trusted her from the start,' Nina went on. 'She let slip she'd seen the Flying Ferraras, but also said she'd never been to Freddie Fielding's. That's impossible. Then suddenly she changed her mind and said she'd only heard of them. Anyway, I've already arranged to follow her into Cambridge tomorrow. I'm dropping round to her flat tonight to give her a list of make-up I'd like her to buy. We might get lucky and catch her withdrawing money from a building society.'

'You've planned this?' Joey said with amazement.

'It was just an idea.'

'But, Nina, she'll see you a mile off.'

'That's why I got myself a grey wig and a pair of glasses, and one of Gerry's lads is driving me in his old car. If she even notices, all Di will see is a little old lady and her son going shopping.'

Joey smiled at her. 'Of course, she may not go near the Southern Counties, but you're right, it's worth a try. Do you know, when I saw her at Dick's this morning, she asked me quite innocently if I'd been in the wars – made a good job of it too. I just wouldn't have believed she was part of all this.'

The following morning Joey had arranged to be at the yard early. A fresh strip of grass was being opened, and Seabourn wanted to be first on it.

When he arrived, the yard was full of excitement; the feeling was that they might pull off a treble that afternoon. Joey wanted it, not just for him but for Dick and all the team. Since hearing about his problems, Joey had made a few discreet enquiries. Moves to sue recalcitrant owners had already cost the trainer nearly a hundred thousand pounds for debts of just under a quarter of a million, and neither sum was likely to be recovered.

And Seabourn was a mere tenant of his wife's family trust. Factor in the general downturn in the racing business since the nineties recession started, and the informed view was that poor old Dick was suffering, and too proud to ask his wife to bail him out.

Joey could believe it. Dick Seabourn had always seemed to him the epitome of honour – the kind of man who would die rather than ask for help.

He wondered what the trainer would think if he knew he was harbouring a blackmailer in his yard; someone whom he trusted completely, and who was cold-bloodedly arranging for his best horse to fail in one of the biggest races of the year.

★　★　★

Nina had left Di's flat after one the night before and had taken a taxi back to her caravan. Joey had called in on his way to work the next morning. He wanted to hear what she'd found out, but she'd learned nothing new beyond the fact that Di's first sexual experience had been with a boy who had come up from London to pick vegetables on her father's farm.

Nina had a feeling this might be one of the men they were looking for.

'But why do you think he might be helping her now?' Joey asked sceptically.

'She talked about him as if he had been on her mind recently,' Nina told him. 'You know, remembering in a way that was connected with the present.'

'It certainly isn't Sol Werner who's been ringing. His German accent's so strong you'd hear it through the fuzz-box or whatever it is he's using. Not just the accent but his grammar, too. I'm sure the guy who calls me is English; and the bloke who came and thumped me is definitely an East Londoner.'

'How do you know they're not the same person?'

'I don't, but when the heavy phoned, he didn't even bother to disguise his voice – maybe because he knew I'd heard it already.'

Joey left Nina in her caravan to change into her simple disguise and wait for Gerry Tewkesbury's lad who was going to pick her up and drive her round to wait near Di's flat.

The King George was now seven days away. He still hadn't told Nina the full story of the last threat that had been made. It was more than he could do to admit to her that if Scaramanga won, and they still hadn't found the blackmailers, there was the threat he'd be killed – and in such a way that the evidence of the videotape and whatever else they could plant would make her a very strong suspect.

He had prepared a document to lodge with his solicitor, giving every detail he knew of what had happened since he had first received the tape. For whatever pressure was put on him, he intended to ride the horse, and ride to win.

That afternoon, to prove to himself and anyone else who might have been interested that he wasn't allowing the threat creeping up on him to affect him, he produced the trio of winners the yard had been hoping for.

For a few hours, being the most popular man in Newmarket helped him forget his troubles. He only wished he could have put a bigger smile on Seabourn's face as the trainer collected his trophies.

Still, Joey reasoned, it could only be a matter of time before everything came right for his boss. For a start, they were going to win the King George next week.

Nina arrived at the course halfway through the afternoon, transformed from a morning spent as a frumpy fifty-year-old. She called Joey from the changing room.

Outside, she said quietly: 'Di went to the building society.'

'Did she take anything out?'

'Yes.'

'How much?'

'I'm not sure. I was too far away from her when the money came out, but it looked like quite a lot to me.'

Joey found he was trembling but beamed at the news.

At last!

At last he knew with whom he was dealing. The connection with the man who had been relaying the demands they could deal with later. At this stage it was enough to know it was Di who'd been behind extracting the money – though part of him still found it hard to believe.

'She must have got her hands on the tape somehow,' he said. 'Probably made a copy of the one Ginger sent and put the original in the office for me to find that evening when I came back from York. If she did, the chances are she's keeping the copy hidden at home.' He thought for a moment. 'I wonder if we can get into her flat somehow,' he said, keeping his voice to a whisper. 'We'll have to do it when we know she's away for a few hours.'

'That's no problem,' Nina said. 'I'll find out what her plans are. She said she was coming here to give me the make-up she bought for me.'

Joey grinned at her. 'What would I do without you?'

'I'm doing it for me, really,' she said. 'I want you all to myself, with no distractions.'

Joey had one more ride, in which he passed the post halfway down the field.

Nina was waiting for him outside the weighing room.

'Did you see Di?' he asked as they walked towards the car park.

'Yes. And guess who I saw her talking to?'

'Not another guessing game, please – not now,' Joey protested.

'It's the same answer as last time.'

He stopped. 'Sol Werner? I knew it! I knew he had to be in on it too.'

301

'Di told me he'd been pestering her to see Dick about sending him some apprentices from the circus. He got the idea from you, he told her, and I suppose he thinks there's more money in handling jockeys than trick riders.'

'Why did Di tell you about him? Did she know you'd seen him?'

'No, I don't think she did, but I guess she was just covering herself because she knew I'd recognise him.'

'They must be working together to rip me off.'

Nina agreed. 'Anyway, we can have a look in Di's flat tomorrow; she's going off to Norfolk to stay with her parents.'

'Are you sure?'

'Yes. She asked if I wanted to come too.'

'And did she remember your make-up?'

'Yes, she did,' Nina said thoughtfully.

Joey rang Di's number several times on Sunday morning, but got no reply. This didn't prove she had gone to Norfolk, so Nina rang her parents' number and asked if she was there.

She wasn't but had phoned her mother to say she was coming to lunch.

'I wonder where she was last night?' Nina said. 'We'd better wait till nearer lunchtime before we go to her flat.'

The uncertainty that they wouldn't be disturbed made them nervous but didn't put them off. Joey had a plan for getting into her flat without breaking in. He knew there was an old caretaker who lived in two small rooms in the basement. He went round to the back of the building and knocked on the old man's door.

'Mornin'. What can I do for you?' If the janitor recognised Joey, he didn't show it.

'I've a birthday present for Diana Lambert on the third floor. It's a great big plant and I want to leave it in her flat as a surprise. I wondered if you could let me in?'

The old man looked him up and down, assessing him for criminal tendencies. Joey was hoping he would simply hand him the key and tell him to help himself, but the old man took it off a rack behind him and shuffled out.

'All right then. I'll let you in.'

Joey's plan two would have to be implemented. 'Perhaps you could give me a hand with the plant?' He jingled some coins in his pocket to underline the request.

The caretaker nodded and followed him to the Range Rover where an oversized yucca in a heavy terracotta pot was crammed into the back.

Nina was nowhere to be seen.

The two men heaved out the plant and carried it into the building and up the three flights of stairs. When they reached the door to Di's flat, the porter unlocked it and pushed it wide to let them in.

'Can you give me a hand carrying it through to the kitchen, do you think?' Joey asked.

The old man grunted, apparently in the affirmative, as he bent down to take up his side of the pot once more.

As soon as the two men were halfway down the hall, Nina, who had flitted up the stairs behind them unseen, darted in through the front door and into Di's sitting-room, just in time to hear Joey and the old man walking back, the porter making a performance of pulling the door firmly behind him to ensure it was locked.

She heard two sets of steps clattering down the stairs, and a few minutes later a single set ascending much more quietly. She went to the door and opened it. Joey slipped in.

'Okay,' he said. 'We'd better be quiet, just in case she's got nosy neighbours.'

'What sort of people live in flats like this?' Nina asked.

'I can tell you exactly who lives here. There's a young bloodstock agent, a journalist from one of the racing mags, and a junior vet, but I don't know how public-spirited they are.'

'Okay. Where shall we start?'

'I'll do the living-room, you do the bedroom. I wouldn't feel right rummaging around among her knickers.'

'I wouldn't mind if you did, as long as she's not wearing them,' Nina said in a whisper and let herself into the bedroom.

Fifteen minutes later she came into the living-room where Joey was prodding desperately under the corner of the fitted carpet. He looked up. 'Any luck?'

She shook her head. 'Nothing, not even a dirty love letter.'

'Okay, try the bathroom. I'm just going to run the first few seconds of these videotapes to check they're what they say on the sleeve.'

There were twenty or so tapes. When Joey had checked them and found nothing, he went through to the kitchen and searched all Di's cupboards, making sure he left everything as he'd found it.

Nina came in, shaking her head in disappointment. 'I've searched her spare bedroom. There's nothing in there, either.'

'I've got a few more things to check here. But you could have a look through all the books on that shelf in the living-room. I forgot to do it.'

Ten minutes later, he admitted defeat in the kitchen and went to see how Nina was doing.

In a corner of Di's sitting-room there was a small, tidy desk with a fax machine and a word-processor on it. Joey had already searched the contents of its single drawer, but Nina was sitting at it, studying a piece of paper.

'What's that?' he asked.

'It's the last bill for Di's phone card.' She passed him the itemised call breakdown. 'Do you recognise any of the numbers?'

Joey ran his eye down the long list. The only one that registered with him was Dick's. 'Let's take a copy of it and we can check them out later.' He fed the document into the fax machine and set it to copy.

Nina was rummaging in the drawer. Something caught Joey's attention which hadn't the previous time he'd looked – a small packet of Letraset type, partially used.

He leaned over Nina's shoulder and picked it out. 'Two of the notes I've had were written with this stuff. I wonder if there's any way of proving they came from these sheets?'

Nina nodded. 'There could be. Let's take it and check.'

'No,' Joey said. 'We've got to leave everything exactly as we found it. Now we know it's her, we have the advantage. Did you find anything in the books?'

Nina shook her head regretfully. 'No.'

'Too bad. We'd better get out of here, then. You go down to see the caretaker and keep him chatting for a few minutes while I get that plant back into the car. If I look out of Di's kitchen window, I'll be able to see you at his door.'

'Okay, see you back in the car.'

Joey went back into the kitchen and craned his neck to watch her coming round to the back of the house and knocking on the caretaker's door. Once he could see her talking with her usual animation, which would keep the old man happy for as long as she chose, he heaved the big plant on to the landing outside Di's front door. He went back in to make sure they hadn't left any sign of their search before firmly clicking the door shut and carrying the yucca down to his car.

Back at Three Elms Farm, Joey and Nina looked at the list of phone numbers Di had called.

Most of the Newmarket calls were to her boss. Some were to Barry, others to Graham and several racing people whose numbers Joey verified from his own address book.

That left a few dozen calls to other parts of England which struck no immediate chords.

'I bet one of those numbers is Sol Werner's. When I rang you from Paris the other week, you gave me his number. I think I wrote it in my diary.' Joey reached across his desk for his Filofax and leafed through it. When he found Sol's number, he ran his eye down the list on Di's bill.

'That confirms it!' The London number cropped up twice, towards the bottom, dated ten days previously. 'Di Lambert and Sol Werner!' He thumped the desk with glee. 'Now we'll get them.'

'What about the man who beat you up and rang you to stop Scaramanga?'

Joey gave a pained smile. 'And the guy who was ringing before that.'

'How can we check these other numbers?' Nina said.

'I tell you what. With that sexy voice of yours, no man's going to hang up in a hurry. You dial them and when they answer, keep them talking. I'll turn up the speaker on the phone, and see if I recognise any of them.'

They were rewarded with several unanswered calls and two female voices, similar to Di's, who dealt brusquely with Nina's enquiry: 'Is John there?' These were interspersed with several business answering services and followed by a man who denied there was anyone called John on the premises, but wondered if he would do.

Joey, listening, shook his head, and Nina put the phone down.

The next one was also answered by a man, to a background of heavy metal.

'Is John there?'

'John who?'

'He never told me his other name.'

'And what's yours, darling?'

'Maria,' she lied. 'Can I speak to John?'

'What d'you want to talk to him about?'

Nina glanced at Joey, who was straining his ears to hear the voice over the music. He grimaced and shook his hand from side to side to indicate his uncertainty.

'Maybe I'd rather talk to you,' said Nina.

'If you came round here, I'd make sure of that.'

Joey stiffened. Exactly that phrase had been used by the man who had phoned telling him to stop Scaramanga; the accent and intonation were identical. He glanced at Nina and gave her a thumbs up.

'I bet you would,' she laughed into the phone. 'I'll be round later.' She put the phone down then let out a gasp and looked at Joey. 'Was that him?'

'I thought it was from the start, and then he used words identical to ones he used to me on the phone the other day. I'm sure it's him. Di must have been communicating with this guy so it's more than likely his number would be on her bill, right?'

'Okay,' Nina said. 'If you're right, we've got a number for one of the men working with Di and possibly Sol. What do we do next?'

Joey flipped open his Filofax. 'We call in the pros.' He picked up the phone and dialled his solicitor's home number.

'Bruce Trevor.'

'Hello, Bruce, Joey Leatham here. Sorry to call you on a Sunday afternoon. I need to get in touch with Nick Allen.'

'Nick? Sure. No problem. I'll get him to call you. Are you at home?'

The private investigator rang within fifteen minutes. He cut Joey short from telling him any details over the phone, saying he would report for duty at eight sharp the following morning.

Joey and Nina knew there was nothing useful they could do about pursuing Di and her accomplices until then. Instead, they cooked dinner on a fire beside the stream and pretended they didn't have a care in the world. As the last glimmer of daylight left the sky to the stars, they went to bed in the caravan and happily lost themselves in each other until the first thrushes whistled their alarm call.

Chapter Thirteen

Next morning, after riding first lot, Joey found it hard to concentrate on what Seabourn was saying to him. He was too impatient to get out of the yard and into his car so that he could phone Nina at the farm.

'Is Nick there yet?'

'Yes. And I've just spoken to Di. She told me she'd been home to see her parents and got back late last night.'

'Okay. What are the chances of keeping her busy for a couple of hours this morning, well away from the flat?'

'I can try. She did say we should get together soon.'

'Tell Nick, and say I'm on my way home. I'll get out of doing another lot.'

Joey rang off, confident that Nina would manage to find some way of distracting Di. In the short time since he'd got to know her again, he'd learned that if Nina said she was going to do something, it was done.

He arrived to find her sitting with Nick at the kitchen table, with a large pot of coffee before them.

Nick jumped to his feet and shook Joey's hand.

'Nina's told me most of what's been going on. I've already got someone tracing the name and address of the guy whose voice you recognised.'

'And, Joey,' Nina added, excited, 'Di wasn't at home so I phoned the yard and Dick told me she's already gone to Lambourn with some horses for him. She has to do some paperwork or something, he said.'

'Do you know where in Lambourn?' Nick Allen asked.

'Yes.'

'Get the number and leave a message for her. Ask her to call you on your mobile when she gets there.'

'What are you going to do then?'

'Search her flat, of course.'

'We already have,' Joey said, 'every square inch of it.'

'I know.' Nick smiled. 'I hope to hell you didn't give yourselves away.'

'Nina says we didn't.'

'Maybe not, but as soon as we know she's well away, I'll go in there and do the job properly. Did you happen to see if she had a second VCR in the flat?'

'No. Just one.'

'So if she made a copy of the original, she probably did it in your agent's office – where there are two?'

Joey nodded. 'Yes, that seems the most likely possibility.'

'Okay. I'll need to take a second VCR with me and a blank tape.'

'No problem. I'll sort them out for you now.'

While they were waiting for Di to return Nina's call, Joey went over to Barry's office and tried to pretend this was just another Monday with a big race to look forward to at the end of the week. That afternoon, he had two rides in Bath. If they hadn't been good ones, he might have passed them up. As they were he arranged to fly down so he wouldn't be away from Newmarket for too long.

He was still talking to Barry when, through the window, he saw Nick Allen walk from the front door with a video recorder under his arm and get into a small BMW. A moment later the car was heading up the drive and out of sight.

Joey excused himself and hurried back to his own house.

Nina was waiting for him.

Di had just rung her back.

'She's in Lambourn now. I asked her if I could have lunch with her, but she said she wouldn't be back until around four. I told Nick and he went straight off. He said he'll call if he needs anything.'

'Great. I hope he does better than we did.'

'What do we do now?' Nina asked.

Joey grinned, wrapped his arms around her and drew her to him.

'Something to make the time pass quicker while we're waiting.'

Nick Allen had entered hundreds of private residences illegally, and had never been caught yet.

When he saw the mellow red-brick Edwardian building, he didn't think this would prove to be the exception. With Joey's VCR and a blank videotape stowed in a suitably anonymous khaki rucksack slung over one shoulder, he let himself into the main door of the block with a rudimentary skeleton key.

Three flights up, he took one look at the simple lock and flipped open his wallet. From half a dozen credit cards he plucked out the least worn and slipped it between the door jamb and the curved face of the bolt until it had been pushed back into the lock far enough to disengage and let the door swing open.

He closed this quietly behind him and, in almost complete silence, started his search.

Twenty minutes later, he was considering ringing Joey to ask why he was so certain Di Lambert was the blackmailer. Apart from the Letraset sheets, which were inconclusive, Nick had found no sufficient evidence to support their claim.

He sat down at the desk and hunted through it for a third time.

He flipped open the spring-backed telephone directory and checked all the numbers in it against those on the itemised phone bill. He couldn't find the one which Joey and Nina had identified as belonging to the man who had beaten up Joey.

Flipping through it for a final time, his eye was caught by a nine-figure number, written in isolation on the reverse of the "A" card.

He stared at it, knowing it was out of place. It wasn't a phone number – there was no "01" at the beginning – and he knew he'd seen it before somewhere.

'Yes!' he hissed to himself as he pulled his notebook from his jacket. He leafed through a few pages, until he found it – the number of the Southern Counties Building Society account where Joey had been instructed to make his payments.

He stood up. This was all the confirmation he needed that Di was involved.

And if she was, all his professional experience told him there must be something else in the flat to link her with the blackmail plot.

He resumed his meticulous search again, overlooking nothing.

After half an hour, without anything to show for it, he started on the kitchen for the second time. He had already checked all the cupboards and the fridge-freezer, but this time he took all the packets out of the deep freeze and placed them on the draining board by the sink.

He picked up and checked each of them until he found a couple that had already been opened. An apple-pie carton that seemed a little more tightly packed than it should have been caught his attention, and an under-weight slab of folded puff pastry.

He took the cling-film wrapping off the pastry, but it was too frozen to pull apart. He ran it under the hot tap for a while to make it more pliable. Then, carefully, he unfolded it until he was rewarded with the discovery of a bundle of fifty-pound notes.

He extracted them, counted them and found around five thousand pounds in five-hundred pound batches of consecutively numbered notes. He jotted down the serial numbers in his notebook and carefully folded up the money again and rewrapped the outer casing of puff pastry.

He turned his attention to the apple-pie carton, from which he pulled a videotape, tightly packed in bubble wrap and cling film. And with the tape was a single folded sheet of cheap squared paper on which a letter had been written in a spiky hand.

Nick carried the tape and the note through to Di's sitting room. He quickly connected up the VCR he had brought with him and used it with Di's player and the blank cassette to make a copy of the tape he had found. After a few minutes' more activity, he ejected Di's tape from her player. He made a copy of the letter on the fax machine, and put it back with the tape into the apple-pie carton exactly as he had found them.

He repacked the freezer and wiped down the draining board to remove any trace of his presence there.

In the sitting-room, he disconnected the second VCR and replaced everything in the room as he'd found it. Satisfied, he tucked the VCR and the copy-tape under his arm and headed for Di's front door.

He had his hand on the small metal catch of the lock when he heard footsteps coming up the stairs.

Knowing the lay-out of the flat, he slipped into a tiny spare bedroom, scantily furnished in pine and Laura Ashley chintz. He let himself into an empty built-in wardrobe and shut the flimsy door behind him just as a key was turned in the lock.

'How did you manage to get back so quickly?'

Nick heard the voice clearly through the thin partition walls. It was a man's voice, but it had neither Sol Werner's thick German-Jewish accent nor the heavy's East London, both of which Joey had described to him.

'I left the lorry driver with the paperwork. He knew what to do.' Di Lambert's confident tones rang out clearly as she and the man walked past the spare room and into the sitting-room. 'I drove back like a hare with a pair of lurchers on its tail.'

'Lucky lurchers,' the man chuckled.

'You're the lucky lurcher,' she said.

No one spoke for a few moments.

Nick guessed they were kissing and fondling. To his practised ear, they sounded like two people in the middle of a lustful affair.

'Do you want a drink, you horny beast?' Di asked.

'No, let's get to bed while we've got the chance.'

Their footsteps moved from the sitting-room to the main bedroom next door.

The two bedrooms had evidently been constructed from one larger room, and the dividing wall was simple studding and plaster board. The sounds of full-blooded love-making seeped through the flimsy partition. Nick listened dispassionately as Di Lambert and her lover reached a vigorous, noisy climax.

There was a lull in the noise, then a quiet murmuring which rose to a normal conversational level.

'That was fantastic!' the male voice said. 'What a succulent, wicked little creature you are!' The voice became more downbeat as it went on. 'But if we want to keep this up, we're going to have to find another really big injection of cash from somewhere soon. What we've been getting out of Joey doesn't go halfway to what we need.'

Nick carefully opened the door of the cupboard just enough to let some light in.

'Don't you worry,' Di was saying. 'I've got a couple of other irons in the fire that'll bring in plenty. Then we can start our own yard and really show those cynical bastards.'

'What else have you got going?' The man sounded concerned. 'You never told me about that.'

'Don't worry. Billy's handling it.'

'Billy? Do you have to use him?'

'There's no point in being snotty about him. He's been bloody useful and you know it.'

'I hope you've got him under control?'

'Of course I have. As long as he can get his bets on, he's happy to do what's necessary.'

'Why did you have to get him involved any further?'

The man seemed alarmed at the prospect. 'I suppose you have to use him for threatening and so on, but I wish you hadn't got him so mixed up in it. I really don't trust him.'

'Don't be so bloody pathetic!' Di said with an icy scorn which didn't fit Joey's description of an affable, easy-going Sloane Ranger. 'He'll be okay. As long as the money keeps coming – he'll do anything for money.'

'Yes, well,' the man sighed. 'Won't we all?'

'I'm not doing *this* for money.'

Nick guessed what she was doing from the man's contented sigh. A few moments later, the sounds of energetic sex reached him once more through the wall until suddenly the man seemed to panic.

'Christ! Look at the time. I've got to get back.' There were sounds of someone jumping out of bed and stumbling about, getting dressed in a hurry. 'People will smell a rat if I don't turn up for lunch.'

'Some rat!' Di laughed. 'Maybe you're right. I'll see you later.'

In his cupboard Nick prepared to leave. The man made a hurried exit and ran down the stairs. The faint bang of a car door being slammed echoed up from the street outside.

Di seemed to be taking her time, though. Nick heard her go through into the kitchen and evidently prepare something to eat. He listened intently for any sign that she'd noticed things had been moved, but after ten minutes of normal activity she walked back down the corridor to the bathroom where she spent some time in the shower.

An hour and a half after she and her lover had come in, she left the flat – Nick presumed to go back to her duties at Dick Seabourn's stables. Cramped and stiff, he slowly stepped out of the cupboard, keeping an ear cocked for sounds of Di returning. But from one of the bedroom windows he could see her, getting into her car and driving off.

He let himself out of the flat carrying Joey's VCR and the copy-tape in his rucksack. Making sure that no one saw him leave, he walked to his car and drove back to Three Elms Farm.

Half a mile from the house, he stopped and punched in Joey's number on his mobile phone.

Nina answered.

'Is Joey there?'

She recognised his voice. 'No. He had to go racing. We thought you'd have been in touch much earlier?'

'I'll tell you about it later. Is anyone else there?'

'Only Barry.'

'Ring me as soon as he's gone. And tell Joey to ring me if he can.'

Joey pushed the Ferrari hard on the way to his house from Newmarket racecourse where his plane had landed. He was edgy with frustration. Nick Allen had already been at the farm more than two hours, and Joey had made him promise not to let Nina see anything – the videotape or the note – until he got home.

At the same time, his heart was pounding with excitement now they had definite, unequivocal proof that Di was one of the prime movers in the conspiracy to blackmail him.

At first, when Nick had told him over the phone that he'd found the tape, Joey had been more shocked than angry. He realised that until that moment, he'd refused to believe that anyone from Di's background could possibly be a criminal.

When he drove into the farm's courtyard, he was relieved to see that there was no sign of Barry or anyone else in the office. He parked right outside his front door and ran in, to be greeted with a kiss from an excited Nina.

'My God, Joey! It feels as if we've been waiting days for you to get back, and Nick won't show me anything.'

They walked into his study where the private detective was waiting. 'Hi, Joey. Shall we get on with it?'

He nodded, and sat down on the sofa. He was dreading what their reactions were going to be when they saw the tape, dreading Nina's response most, despite all the understanding she had expressed to him.

But this moment had to be faced.

They laughed at the first sequence of the Cossack Riders: a nervous, waif-like Joey, aged sixteen going on twelve, riding round the arena in an oversized *feska*; a chubbier eighteen-year-old Nina, with blonde hair even longer than it was now, flowing behind her.

Joey looked down at her, sitting on the floor with her back against the sofa. It seemed astonishing that so much had changed in the ten years since the film had been shot. She glanced up at him, and smiled, thinking the same thoughts.

The riding sequence came to an end.

All Joey's muscles tightened, as if to withstand the shock of what he knew was to follow.

After a few seconds of flickering static, the interior of the circus big top came into view. Joey had watched this scene on tape only once before, but every second of it was etched on his memory so clearly that he was pitched right back into the whole terrible nightmare.

★ ★ ★

Joey's knees quivered as he gazed down at the safety net, ten feet by forty, stretching the distance of the arcs of the trapezes to either side of the big top. It was suspended under tension between eight angled poles at the sides and each corner. The poles were secured with wire hawsers which disappeared beneath the banks of raked timber seating where they were anchored to the ground. The net was there to save lives, but it still had to be treated with respect. If you landed wrongly, you could do serious damage. No trapeze artist ever ate for several hours before a session, to avoid choking if he hit the net.

Joey and Mikhail, side by side on the specially made wide trapeze, swung themselves up together, keeping perfect time between them, maintaining the balance and precise momentum needed to be at the exact spot when Ivan would let go of his own swing and hurtle down towards them.

At the top of the arc, they turned themselves over and swooped back, hanging from the rail by their knees.

Ivan stood perched like an eagle on a cliff top, watching them, counting the timing of each swing. As Mischa and Joey were halfway down their return swing, he stood on tip-toes, lifted his own trapeze and launched himself, diving with none of an eagle's grace towards the centre of the tent.

Joey and Mischa were already swinging back towards him as he started to drop. They had performed the cycle once more when Ivan gave a low grunt at the top of his swing; Joey braced himself for the violent tug when both his hands would grasp one of Ivan's large fists.

The young men had done the routine so many times they knew instinctively what each other was doing; there was no need for them to see or hear.

Ivan, swinging by his hands, let go of his bar halfway up its forward curve and dropped like a lead weight towards his pair of pint-sized catchers.

Together they took the sudden massive strain of Ivan's weight as his hands slapped their wrists and instinctively clutched them.

They swung back with Ivan dangling below them. His weight sent them hurtling down and back up, almost to the crow's nest on their side.

The strain on their shoulder muscles intensified at the top of the swing as Ivan's sixteen stones were whipped out by centrifugal forces. The three of them careered through another half-circle. When they reached the top at the apex of the tent, they released Ivan, who twisted through a hundred and eighty degrees and caught his original trapeze as it came up to meet him. Two seconds later, he placed his feet with a thud on his home base.

Mikhail and Joey had spun themselves over to sit on their bar and carried on swinging. Ivan turned and growled across the upper void of the canvas cathedral. 'That was okay,' he admitted grudgingly. 'Did you get it, Ginger? I want to see it afterwards.'

'Sure I did, Ivan,' the clown piped from his perch in the darkness. But Joey knew he hadn't; he had promised he wouldn't.

'Good,' Ivan bellowed. 'Now Mr Werner has arrived, so we do it again.'

Joey's pulse quickened as they began the routine again. He and Mischa tipped themselves over to hang by their knees and launched themselves towards the summit of the big top.

The air rushed through their hair and pressed against

the flesh of their cheeks. They swung twice. Ivan launched himself again.

The catchers swooped back. At the bottom of their arc, Ivan reached the top of his. He let go, and dropped like a boulder towards them.

Joey gritted his teeth and uttered a short prayer. When the precise moment came to extend his hands for the catch, he held back, withdrawing them a few inches until the critical fraction of a second had passed.

He heard Ivan's big right hand slap into Mikhail's wrist while the other groped wildly in the air in front of Joey's face, seeking the absent hand. He even saw Ivan's eyes, angry, black, terrified, and knew that the punishment for his betrayal would be vicious.

Joey shouted at his partner: 'He missed me, Mischa! Let him go!'

Too late. The slender young Russian had taken all his father's weight, which tore at his shoulder for a moment of excruciating pain. He had tried to release the large hand, but Ivan wouldn't let go. His left arm flailed furiously just short of Joey's grasping hands.

Mikhail's only option was to drop from the swing. He straightened his legs at the top of the arc, detaching himself from the swing, and tumbled down to the net, pulled by the wrist still in his father's grasp.

Joey saw the double fall as he swung back. Passing over them, in the split second before he was hurtling up to the top of the tent, he saw them hit the net . . . and carry on, as if it didn't exist.

It felt like minutes before he swung back and turned himself over to land on the platform where they'd started. He dropped the trapeze and left it dangling above the terrible spectacle below where the net had collapsed into a heap of knotted nylon cord over two broken bodies.

His heart stopped for several seconds. He didn't breathe until the full implication of what had happened hit him and he exhaled in a long, loud gasp. 'Jesus Christ!'

Just then, Ivor Wimsatt walked briskly through the curtained door into the arena and stopped as if he'd walked into a stone wall. He immediately started yelling for help in a voice that was surprisingly loud and clear in the still aftermath of the fall.

Within moments, people were running in and scurrying around the tangled net, opening it out to reveal the bodies of the two fallen men.

Joey watched from above, trying not to believe what he saw, until he heard Tatyana wail: 'My God! Mischa, my little Mischa . . . Dead . . . Dear God, he's dead!'

More calmly, Wimsatt's voice echoed through the shocking stillness of the great tent. 'So is Ivan.'

It was Nick Allen who picked up the remote control and turned off the VCR.

Joey carried on staring at the blank screen. He didn't dare look at Nina, until he felt her hand on his knee giving it a gentle squeeze. Her eyes were brimming with tears of compassion, not accusation.

'I understand,' she whispered. 'You didn't know about the net.'

He gazed back at her silently.

'Is that true?' Nick asked.

'Yes,' Joey replied. 'I told you, it was all Ginger's idea – just to make Ivan look a fool in front of Sol Werner.'

'I've got to tell you, anyone looking at that sequence

would say you'd deliberately dropped the guy, and it would be hard to convince people you didn't know the net was sabotaged.'

'I know,' Joey said grimly. 'And the only people who knew that Ginger rigged it, were him and Giulio. Di and her mates worked that out pretty quickly. Anyway, thank God you've got their copy of the tape now.'

'I haven't. This is a copy of their copy.' Nick explained what he'd done at the flat, and the importance of Di's not learning they had found her tape.

'But I don't care if she knows we've found it! I just want her to stop the blackmail and give me my money back.'

'What?' Nina said indignantly. 'You don't want her punished?'

'Listen,' Nick said to Joey, standing up to make his point. 'You're the client, and you give the orders, but I can tell you, there's enough evidence here for the police to get a conviction – at least against her. And I guess it wouldn't be too hard for them to get a case against whoever murdered Giulio too.'

'But Giulio wasn't murdered, he died from a heart attack.'

'Any court would say that was a direct result of the attack, though. She could get ten to fifteen for conspiracy to blackmail and murder.'

'And what would I get if I'm found guilty?'

'You'd be charged with manslaughter, not murder, and if they convicted, you could be looking at five years.'

'Five years!' Joey exploded. 'I've struggled too hard to risk all that. I'm not doing five days, never mind five years.'

'But, Joey,' Nina was looking at him, 'you *can't* let Di

get away with it. She was a friend of yours, and tried to be a friend of mine. You trusted her.'

'I don't care. I'm not risking my freedom and my career for the sake of revenge.'

'Okay,' Nick said, in a mollifying tone. 'We'll deal with that later. There's also this note I found with the tape.'

He passed Joey the Xerox he'd made of the sheet of cheap, squared paper. It took Joey a few moments to recognise the sloping, foreign hand.

It had been sent from the hospice in France, dated 3 June, the day after the French Derby.

Dear Joey,

It's been a terrible long time since I saw you. I thought about you often, and wondered what you were doing. Then I saw you on the television, saving the girl at the racecourse, and I see you are a hero and a great jockey.

I am very proud for that.

But I am dying now, very close. I want you to have this tape. There is something on it you won't ever want to see again, but it is the only one, and you can destroy it yourself. It was my fault what happened. I have terrible guilt about it always. I unhooked the guys for the net. I knew what would happen. Ivan had been very cruel to me but I did not want his son to die.

Forgive me, Joey.

With much love from your old friend,

Ginger

(Heinrich Calaval)

Joey read the letter twice. He could do nothing to stop

the tears welling up. He passed the piece of paper to
Nina without a word. She read it, and looked at him.
Her eyes showed that she understood without any further explanation what it all meant. His story had been
corroborated from beyond the grave.

'How did Di get the tape and this letter?' she asked.

'It came in the post – in a padded bag. I was out, so
it went up to the office. It had a French post-mark on
it; I guess everyone assumed it was the Prix du Jockey
Club video. Barry said he didn't have time to watch it.
There were other people in and out all day. Di must
have picked it up, opened it and realised from the note
that it wasn't the race and might be worth watching.
She could easily have been in there on her own long
enough to have a look and make the copy which she
took home. And she obviously realised it was worth
something.'

'And she was right,' Nick said. 'But I haven't made the
connection with Sol Werner yet.'

'What about the other guy?' Joey asked. 'Did you get
anywhere with the phone number?'

'Yes. He lives in Epping and his name's Billy Duckett.
I think you were right; he's your thug, but Di Lambert's
much more involved with someone else. They talked
about setting up a yard. She spent an hour showering
and messing about after he'd gone,' he said. 'That's why I
didn't get back before you left for Bath.'

'But who the hell was she with?' Joey said. 'Has she
told you about a new boyfriend?' he asked Nina.

'No. Nothing. But it's not so surprising, and it must be
someone who knows you.'

'That could mean anyone in Newmarket,' Joey said
without vanity.

'It has to be someone in racing,' Nick nodded. 'Someone who would consider taking up training.'

'A jockey, maybe.' Joey shrugged. 'A bloodstock agent; another trainer's assistant. You say he had an upper-class accent?'

'Yes, same as Di's.'

'There are plenty of those round here,' Joey said thoughtfully. 'But I can't think of any involved with Di, or who's bent enough.'

'You never can tell,' the private detective said.

'Yes,' Joey agreed ruefully. 'I realise that now, thanks to Di.'

'She sounds a right scheming bitch to me,' Nick commented.

Joey clenched his fists and looked at Nina. 'The bastards! How can people like that, with so much going for them, sink so low? I wouldn't blame them so much if they'd had nothing – if they'd had to fight their way up from nowhere.'

'They're weak, and they're cowards,' she said, voice husky with anger, 'and they're greedy. We *must* take back everything they took from you and more. And they must pay for killing Giulio.'

'All the evidence is there, Joey,' Nick said. 'The tape, the money – you'll find they can prove that's come from branches of Southern Counties. The account number is in Di's writing on her phone directory. Then there's Ginger's note and the Letraset sheets, in conjunction with the notes you've had. Also it's an odds-on chance this bloke Billy dealt with Giulio, and he seems dozy enough to have left something behind in Yarmouth.'

'Maybe we could get them done for that, without

bringing the blackmail into it?'

'I doubt they could pin anything on Di Lambert without it.'

Joey stared at a large oil painting of a group of horses behind the start on Goodwood racecourse. But he didn't see it.

Why had these people tried to tear his life apart like this?

What had he ever done to them?

In the silence, the phone on his desk rang. The answerphone was on so Joey let it ring.

There was a click as the tape finished and the caller came in with a message, amplified over the speaker.

'Oh, hello, Joey. Dick Seabourn here. I tried to get you earlier but I couldn't get through on your mobile. Well done on the filly; she went much better than I'd hoped.' The trainer's cultivated voice conveyed his customary charm. 'I'd like to chat about her, and a couple of things for tomorrow. Could you give me a ring, please, as soon as you've a moment? Thanks. 'Bye.'

'I never asked,' Nina said. 'Did you win?'

'I did, as a matter of fact.'

'Never mind that.' Nick was staring at them in agitation. 'Who was that?'

'That was my trainer. Why?'

'That's the guy who was in bed with Di Lambert!'

There was complete silence in the room for a few moments.

Joey felt his jaw drop. 'Don't be crazy. That was Dick Seabourn. He's a respectable, middle-aged man, old enough to be her father and happily married.'

'All that may be true, but it's never stopped anyone before. I heard him in bed with Di Lambert and they weren't playing tiddlywinks. Plus he's involved in what's going on.'

'My God!' Joey strode back and forth across the room. 'I can't believe it! Dick, for Christ's sake! The whole world's going crazy!'

'If he's your trainer, why would they be talking about getting their own yard?' Nick asked.

'Crowle House belongs to Veronica, Dick's wife. He rents it from her trustees. He's never had a lot of money of his own.'

'And now he's having a steaming affair with his secretary.'

'I just can't believe it,' Joey said again.

'It's probably happened a million times before,' Nick said. 'It's the weak, middle-aged men, flattered by some young girl's attention, who do the craziest things – quite out of character. But what do you want to do about it?'

Joey picked up a salt pot from the sideboard and fiddled with it for a moment as he thought. 'Now we know Seabourn's part of it, that makes it even harder.' Joey turned the problem over in his mind. 'I don't want Veronica to go through the embarrassment and disgrace of seeing him sent to prison.'

'He wanted to speak to you, didn't he? If you rang him back and asked him to come round here, would he?'

'Maybe.' Joey glanced at his watch. 'They'll be starting evening stables soon, but he sometimes leaves that to Martin.'

'See if you can get him over,' Nick urged.

Joey looked at the phone for a moment before picking it up and dialling Seabourn's number.

Veronica answered.

'Evening,' Joey said as calmly as he could. 'Is the guv'nor there?'

'He's just out at the yard.'

Joey detected an unusual breathlessness in her voice. 'Are you all right?' he asked.

'I'm fine.'

There was a pause. Something in her voice told Joey she was far from fine, but he didn't press her.

'Dick wanted to see me,' he said, 'and I was wondering if he'd mind coming round here? There're a couple of things I need to show him.'

'I don't see why not. He'll be in any moment, I'll get him to go straight round.' She said it in a way that left him in no doubt her husband would come.

Joey put the phone down, not looking forward to the imminent confrontation. He knew, though, that they had to talk to Seabourn before Di. Of the two, the trainer was most likely to capitulate under pressure.

He turned to Nick. 'What are we going to say when he comes?'

'You leave that to me.'

'My God!' Joey said, striding up and down the room again. 'When I think of all the people I suspected were in on this – and I never once considered Dick! Bloody hell! I thought it was everyone but him. I even thought it might be my own brother!' He stopped and looked at Nick. 'But Sol Werner could still be a part of it.'

'The circus man you told me about, the one Nina saw at the races?'

'Yeah. It was him who told me to go to that place in France where I got beaten up.'

Nick shook his head. 'That doesn't mean he had you thumped. Di obviously had Billy following you around, when she couldn't do it herself. I would say it's more than likely she found out about Giulio and realised he had to be bullied into keeping his mouth shut, but her mate Billy overdid it. As for Sol Werner –' Nick shrugged '– from what you've told me, and what I've seen and heard myself, he's not involved at all. Di was – probably in some kind of partnership with your Dick Seabourn, and with a bit of hired muscle from this Billy Duckett.'

Dick Seabourn arrived twenty minutes later. Joey saw as soon as he opened the front door that the trainer was apprehensive.

'Ah, hello, Joey. Veronica gave me your message.'

'Thanks for coming.' Joey ushered his boss across the hall. 'I thought it might be better to talk here.'

Seabourn stiffened and half turned as he walked into the study. 'Something confidential, eh? I hope you're not thinking of going freelance again?' He attempted a chuckle which died when he saw Nina and Nick Allen standing in the room.

'I might have to,' Joey kept the conversation going, 'if what I've just heard is true.'

Seabourn stopped dead just inside the door to the study. Taking in Nick's no-nonsense expression and Nina's obvious scorn, he turned and looked at Joey like a nervous stag which knows it has just been cornered.

'What . . . What have you heard?'

'I heard it, Mr Seabourn,' Nick said matter-of-factly. 'I heard a conversation you had while I was searching Miss Lambert's flat this afternoon.'

Seabourn, who had taken a few steps further into the room, visibly sagged at the knees.

'Why not sit down?' Joey waved him to a chair. 'Do you want a drink?'

'Yes . . . yes, please. A whisky,' the trainer said faintly as he lowered himself into one of Joey's deep, wing-backed chairs.

'I've been working for Mr Leatham,' Nick went on dispassionately, 'trying to find out who's been blackmailing him.'

Seabourn's head, already hanging, dropped lower while his eyes lifted. He looked at Nick, then, wincing with shame, at Joey. He said nothing.

The detective walked across the room and sat behind Joey's desk. Without any further announcement, he retold Seabourn and Di's conversation to Joey and Nina.

Seabourn's specific reference to Joey caused the trainer to close his eyes and shake his head remorsefully.

He straightened his back, sitting bolt upright in the chair. He turned to Joey. 'I will never be able to express my shame and regret for what I've done.' He walked across to the window and gazed out silently towards the meadows behind the house, where the sun had started to lengthen the shadows of the alders by the brook.

When he spoke, he didn't turn to face his listeners. 'I never wanted to get involved, but Di's a lot sharper than you might think. And, you see, I was obsessed with her. Of course I love my wife, and respect her deeply. It's just in recent years she seems to have lost any interest in the physical side of our marriage. I understand it happens sometimes and I shouldn't take it as any reflection on myself. But it's very hard not to. I have the usual male urges, and Di is a very attractive, very physical woman.'

Nick, seated at the desk, nodded. 'What my client

wants to know is, where's the money?'

'The money?' Seabourn said vaguely, as if that were the least of the problem. 'Di was transferring it to another building society account, drawing it out from the one where I'd told Joey to put it.'

'*You* told him?'

Joey was nodding. 'Now I know, I can tell Dick made the first phone calls. Not from his accent, nor through that voice-distortion box, whatever it was, but from the words he used and the way he phrased things.'

'Yes, it was me,' Seabourn said quietly.

'Asking me to stop those horses?'

'What horses? What are you talking about?'

'Colombian Prince. Tap Dancer. Scaramanga.'

'No! No, I never asked you to stop them. I'd heard a whisper that someone had, or at least I had a suspicion from something Di once said. But of course I wouldn't have asked you to lose a race.'

'Who was it then?'

Seabourn said nothing.

'Come on. We know, but give us a name: confirm it for us.'

'He's a chap Di knows. Nothing to do with me. I never got involved with him or wanted him to do anything.'

'Like beat the shit out of me in France, and then again right here in my own garden?'

'That was Di's idea. I didn't know what she was up to but she said it was to encourage you. She said it was just like you were paying an extra tax – half your earnings was no worse than paying for an ex-wife after a divorce. She made it sound quite reasonable.' Seabourn's voice was breaking by now. 'I don't know how I let myself be carried away by it all.'

'You still haven't told us the bloke's name,' Nick reminded him.

'Billy,' Seabourn sighed. 'Don't ask me his surname.'

'Billy Duckett,' Nick said. 'The muscle from Epping; one of Di's previous bits of rough. Give her her due – she has a catholic taste in men. What about Giulio?' he snapped suddenly.

Seabourn blinked. 'Giulio? Who's he? What's he done? She never said she had anyone else helping her.'

'All right,' Nick said. 'We'll forget Giulio for the time being. Let's get back to the money.'

'I haven't got it,' Seabourn said. 'We decided it would be too risky if I had anything to do with the account. There are already enough people snooping around trainers' finances. But anything I can do to get it back, I will.'

Nick shook his head with a cynical smile. 'It's a bit late to start offering to give it all back and trying to do deals.'

Seabourn turned around to face them across the room – Nick at the desk, Joey leaning against the fireplace and Nina sitting on the edge of the sofa.

Drawing together the tattered remnants of his dignity, he looked Joey straight in the eye. 'I have behaved abominably. You've been utterly loyal to me . . .'

'No, I haven't,' Joey said. 'I stopped Colombian Prince.'

'You didn't have much choice, by the sound of it. Anyway, I suppose I was to blame – indirectly.' Seabourn sighed and gazed down at the carpet. 'What's going to happen now?'

Joey stared at him. 'We'll see,' he said quietly. 'Go home now. We'll let you know.'

From his study window, Joey watched Dick Seabourn climb back into his Mercedes. It gave him no pleasure to see the older man suffer and he hoped that Seabourn's fears for his future would not come true.

Exhaustive discussions with Nick had convinced Joey that he and his blackmailers were at a stand-off.

If he wanted to see Di convicted for blackmail and conspiracy to murder, he would have to let the police see the tape with which she was blackmailing him.

However he then argued his own innocence, there was a strong chance he himself would be charged with killing Ivan and Mikhail, and suffer all the ignominy which Dick Seabourn now dreaded. And besides, although he wouldn't have fallen from such a height within the racing establishment as the trainer, his high public profile would make him a much more newsworthy subject.

And bringing down Di meant bringing down Dick Seabourn. Which would inevitably involve Veronica.

Billy Duckett was a different matter.

As soon as Seabourn had driven away from Three Elms Farm, Nick Allen dialled a number Joey had given him.

'Detective Inspector Jacobs? . . . Hello, Inspector. I'm told you're dealing with the death of Mr Giulio Santini . . . The man who did it was Billy Duckett of 15 Pychard Way, Epping. I expect your colleagues there know him.'

Nick put the phone down with a grin. 'That's him dealt with, we hope. Now, what about Miss Lambert?'

'Nina's on the phone, arranging to meet her.'

'Does she trust Nina?'

'As soon as Nina turned up here in Newmarket, Di latched on to her – presumably to keep a close check on me and divert suspicion. As it happened, she got that all wrong. Nina thought there was something wrong about her from the start.'

Nick grinned. 'I learned a long time ago not to underestimate what they call "female intuition". Of course, it's not intuition, just a natural cynicism more highly developed than ours!'

As they spoke, Nina came into the room. 'Okay. She said she'd meet me at the stable where she keeps her horse. I told her I wanted to see him.'

'What horse is this?' Nick asked.

'An old racehorse she keeps,' Joey said. 'She likes to hack around the Heath on him.'

'Where's the stable?'

'On the edge of town. It's just a couple of boxes and a small paddock she rents.'

'Sounds ideal. How are you going to get there, Nina?'

'Danny just came in. He says he'll take me.'

'Okay. We'll follow.'

'Good-looking woman,' Nick observed appreciatively.

He and Joey were in Nick's car, under the cover of a great, spreading oak. They watched Di park her car twenty yards away and walk down a short track to a small block of two timber stables and a tack room.

Nina was waiting for her, leaning over the post and rail of an over-grazed paddock beside the stables, in which a big, handsome chestnut horse was nudging at an empty feed-bowl.

'What do you think of Hector, then?' Di asked proudly.

'He's lovely. Was he a good racehorse?' Nina asked, glancing over the animal with an expert eye.

'Yes, he was a useful stayer – won over two miles. He'd have made a good jump stallion if they hadn't cut him.'

'He's still got the look of a stallion about him.'

They admired the horse and talked about him until Di suggested they go into the tack room while she mixed his feed.

'Right,' Nick said from the cover of the car. 'That looks an ideal place for the little chat you're about to have. Let's get down there and get on with it.'

Joey pushed open the door of the ten-by-ten wooden tack room.

Di was leaning over a feed-bin with a scoop in her hand. She glanced up at him, startled.

Nina feigned surprise. 'Joey! What are you doing here?'

'I came to see her.' He nodded at Di.

Her eyes narrowed in a hint of alarm. She glanced at Nina to see how she was taking what could be construed as an act of infidelity on Joey's part.

Like Joey, Nina smiled. Di grew visibly nervous.

Nick appeared in the doorway behind Joey.

'This is Nick,' Joey told Di. 'He's what you'd call a private investigator.'

'Oh?' Di said. 'What are you investigating up here? An equine paternity suit?'

'No. Someone's been extorting money from Joey with a threat to send a potentially incriminating videotape to the police. He asked me to look into it, so I searched your flat today.'

Di looked away sharply to conceal her reaction. Apart from a sudden tightening of her jaw and fists, little showed. She picked up a bridle and fiddled with it for a

336

few seconds until she'd recovered. Then she turned back and addressed Joey.

'What on earth's he talking about?' she asked in a self-righteous tone. 'Why should he be searching my flat?'

'What would he have found, Di?'

'Nothing. He didn't find anything.' She turned to Nick. 'Did you?' she challenged.

He didn't answer. The very fact that she showed no indignation at having her flat broken into was a de facto admission of guilt.

Joey calmly sat down on a corn bin and folded his arms. 'He found the number of the account I've been putting all my money into. Over a hundred and fifty grand I've paid in! How much is left?'

Di stared at him, defiant and scornful. 'I don't know what you're talking about.'

Joey shrugged.

'He found the sheets of Letraset, matching up with the notes you sent me.'

'What does that prove?' she asked contemptuously.

'What could it prove, Di?'

'Nothing. I don't know what the hell you're talking about.'

'Let me explain something to you. Just for the moment, you can take it we've got so much evidence we could drive you round to the nick in the High Street and have you banged up tonight – for blackmail, conspiracy to defraud, and murder.' Joey grinned at her encouragingly. 'The only problem is that I'd have to let the police see a video of an accident which happened ten years ago, which makes it look as if I deliberately allowed two men to fall to their deaths. Even though I didn't have any

intention of doing that and thought they'd land safely in
the net below, it would be hard for me to prove, and the
publicity would finish me as a jockey.' He paused. 'I
don't know why I'm telling you,' he added. 'You obviously realised it all as soon as you found the tape and the
letter in Barry's office.'

Di sat down on a saddle rack and stared back at him.
She clearly wasn't planning to admit anything yet.

'Unfortunately the only two people who knew who
had sabotaged that net were Ginger, who did it, and
Giulio – his lover. Luckily for you, Ginger died just after
he sent me the tape, and you had Giulio killed. So, it
looks like a stand-off. Nick, you tell her the score.'

'It *is* a stand-off, but not an even one.' Nick spoke
authoritatively. 'I can tell you, even without any wit-
nesses for the defence, if Joey gets convicted at all, it'd be
of manslaughter and he'd get about five years. But you
would definitely go down for what you've done, for
something nearer fifteen.'

Joey looked closely at Di as Nick spoke. Her hands
were shaking.

'So I suggest,' Nick went on, 'you listen very carefully
to what Joey has to offer.'

'It's simple enough,' he took over. 'You give me back
my money and your copy of the tape, and we'll do
nothing. You'll get off scot-free.'

Di tilted back her head and laughed.

'That's absolutely pathetic! Just the sort of thing I'd
have expected from a tight-fisted little shit like you.' She
stood up and walked across to the door, opened it and
looked outside. Evidently satisfied, she closed it and
turned back to them.

'I see your dozy brother's standing sentry for you.' She

shook her head. 'Anyway, listen to me. You can't pin a thing on me. The account's not in my name. All I've got is a card and the PIN number to get the cash out. Your private detective here may have found the Letraset, but he didn't take it, and I burnt it when the caretaker told me this afternoon he'd seen someone snooping around. And you don't think I did it all on my own, do you?'

Joey grinned. 'No, of course not. Dick was round at my place earlier. He left half an hour ago. By the way, he asked me to tell you he's posting your P45 and a cheque in lieu of notice – no need to go in to pick them up.'

Di's face contorted into an ugly mask of fear and spite. 'The despicable, cringing bastard!' she hissed. 'Of course, Veronica'll always have him back and forgive him, because she feels guilty she never lets him screw her.'

'Probably,' Joey agreed.

'Listen, even though he was going to end up with a yard of his own, the cowardly shit didn't have much to do with it – apart from making a few phone calls. You won't find much on him.'

'Maybe, but I haven't told you everything. Nick also found a telephone bill in your flat, listing a string of calls to someone called Billy Duckett.' Di squeezed her eyes tight shut for an instant. 'He's an old boyfriend of yours, isn't he? The police from Yarmouth will be picking him up – just about now – for killing poor old Giulio.'

Di's healthy colour faded from her face.

'B-but even if they pull Billy, he'd never tell them about me.' Her confidence returned. 'And they can't do anything without the tape, and I've still got my copy. I can take a punt too, Joey. From where I'm standing, it looks like you've a lot more to lose than me.'

'That depends,' he said with a shake of his head, 'on how many copies you made.'

Her eyes shifted uneasily.

'If the only one you had was the one in your deep freeze,' Joey went on, 'I'm afraid you'll find it's been wiped. Isn't that right, Nick?'

Di was quivering with rage now. 'What? What the hell are you talking about? You didn't find it . . . It's still there. Why didn't you take it? You didn't wipe it – I checked this afternoon. I played it!'

'All of it?'

Suddenly limp, Di stared at him and didn't answer.

'He didn't erase the nice footage of Nina and me as Cossack Riders – there was nothing very embarrassing about that. But if you'd bothered to play it all, you'd have found the bit I don't want anyone to see isn't there any more. And we've got the serial numbers of the five grand in notes in the pastry packet. They'll be traced straight back to Southern Counties – or do you want to take a punt on that too?'

She took two hesitant paces towards the door. Joey stood aside. 'If you want to go and have a look at that tape and get the money, Danny'll take you. He'll make sure you don't come to any harm.'

Di opened the door stiffly and stepped out like a sleep-walker. Joey followed and signalled to Danny. The Range Rover roared into life and rolled down the track towards the woman walking slowly towards it.

Barry was waiting in his office when Joey arrived back at Three Elms Farm with Nick and Nina.

'Will someone tell me what's happening?' he asked plaintively. 'Dick Seabourn sounds so miserable, you'd think every damn' horse in his yard had just died. And then you ring me demanding my presence, as if you were going to read a will.'

He waved his three visitors to the sofas in the middle of the room and got them drinks.

'So, what's the big occasion?'

Joey took a grateful slug of the vodka Barry had poured him and launched into an account of the complicated chain of events which had led to his suspecting almost everyone in Newmarket of blackmail – and the extraordinary developments that had taken place since he'd found the speeding ticket on Barry's desk.

His friend was dismayed, though eventually realistic, when he heard that even he had fallen under suspicion. 'I tell you, though, I'm almost relieved to know you stopped Colombian Prince. I was seriously worried about your competence for a few days after that. Of course, I always knew Dick would be feeble under pressure.'

'But can you believe it?' Nina asked. 'Joey couldn't accept that people like Seabourn or Di would stoop to blackmail.'

'I do find it hard to believe,' Barry admitted. 'And when we Irish decide to be cynical, we're good at it.'

They were interrupted by the sound of a car pulling up outside. Nick went to the window and looked down into the yard. Danny was opening the door for Di – not, it appeared, out of an excess of politeness.

A few moments later, he was ushering her into Barry's office.

When she walked in, Di seemed to Joey like an entirely different person from the one he'd always known. There was a resentful hardness about her he'd never seen.

A few steps inside the door, she stopped and gazed at him with undiluted hatred.

He stood up to face her, acutely conscious of the eight-inch difference in their heights.

A second later, a pale object flew through the air, caught him hard on the side of his head and thudded to the ground behind him.

'There's five grand, gift wrapped in puff pastry!' Di advanced a few more steps and flung a videotape at him. 'You miserable little bastard!' She was screaming manically now as she pulled an envelope from a pocket of the cotton jacket she was wearing. She scrumpled the paper into a ball and hurled it at the floor.

'You sort it out. I opened the account in the name of Jennifer Hartwell. I've signed a blank draft. All the money's still there, except the five grand in the pastry and ten more that's gone, and you can bloody well piss in the wind for that.'

She stopped and glowered at Joey, shaking her head. 'My life's ruined now, thanks to you, you selfish *dwarf*! What do you need all that money for anyway? You've got no one to spend it on.' She shot a spiteful glance at Nina. 'No woman's going to hang around long for a lousy little prick like you! Think you're a star in bed, don't you? Well, let me tell you, a boy-scout on beginner's knots could do a better job than you.' She tossed her head, spat at the documents on the floor and walked from the room.

There was a stunned silence in the office, broken only by the sound of her footsteps clattering down the wooden stairs outside.

'Jesus!' Barry hissed. 'I wouldn't have believed she could change like that.'

'She never changed,' Nina said in a low voice. 'She was always a bitch, kidding she was a good old jolly-hockey-sticks type. Joey, you can't let her get away with it! Ten thousand pounds – stolen from under your nose.'

'Leave it,' he said, struggling to keep his voice even. Di's scathing reference to him as a dwarf had hurt him as much as her theft of his money.

'She's bloody mental,' Danny said. 'But like Nina says, you can't let her get away with it.'

'It's my money. And provided I get the rest of it back without any trouble, I'm not going to stir anything up. That's the way I want it left.'

'You must be crazy.' Barry was looking at him in amazement. 'If anyone ripped me off for ten grand like that, then abused me the way she just did, I'd not only want her guts for garters, I'd want every sinew in her damn' body. You *can't* let her get away with it.'

Joey looked at him. 'Barry, I don't give a damn what she said to me. She's barking mad and I'm happy to lose ten thousand quid if that's an end to the whole business. So let's leave it.' He turned to Nick Allen who, with professional impartiality, had not expressed a view. 'Nick, thanks. I'll let you know if I need any more help.'

The private detective thought of saying what was on his mind, but Joey had made his intentions clear, and that, Nick guessed, was that.

Barry drove Joey back to Newmarket the evening after the King George and Queen Elizabeth Stakes. Joey had just ridden the race of his life, Scaramanga looked set to become one of the great horses of his generation, and Dick Seabourn had been acclaimed for a supreme display of training.

Joey tilted the passenger seat of the Porsche as far back as he could. 'God, what a wonderful feeling!' he sighed.

'Winning the King George at last?'

'No. It's great but I wasn't thinking of that.'

'Is it knowing you'll be going home to a lovely Russian tonight?'

Joey laughed. 'I'm just getting used to the idea of not having to worry about phone calls and threats and who's going to see that video.'

Barry chuckled. 'You looked very pleased with yourself, burning that last copy of it the other night.'

'I was. That was all I wanted – that and getting the money back.'

'All bar ten grand,' Barry growled.

'I've told you, I can live without that.'

'I don't know how you can stay in the same town as that woman, after what she did.'

'There's not a lot I can do about it, not without stirring up more hassle than it's worth for ten grand.'

'Well, I won't tolerate you being treated like that.'

'What's it to do with you?'

'What's it to do with me? You're my best friend, for God's sake! I have a vested interest in your well-being, and that includes your pride. So you'll understand when I tell you that Nina and I, and Danny, all felt Di deserved a little something for what she did to you.' He glanced at his watch. 'As a matter of fact, Danny should have delivered it by now.'

Joey sat up in his seat. 'What? What the hell are you talking about? What have you done?'

'None of us have to do anything now – that's the beauty of it.'

★ ★ ★

Di Lambert parked her car near the stables where she kept her horse. It would be dark soon and a sharp night was forecast. An unseasonal northerly wind was blowing.

She hurried down the track to the tack room and opened the wooden door. Inside, she rummaged around, moving a stack of blankets and sweat rugs to uncover a well-used jute rug. As she gathered it up, she took little notice of the strong, vinegary smell which lingered on it.

Out in the cold night, she made her way round the side of the stable block to the paddock. The horse had his front end in a lean-to, eating hay. She climbed over the fence and walked towards his strong chestnut quarters. The evening breeze gusted behind her and rippled the jute rug on her arm.

'Hector,' she called. 'Come on, old man.'

The horse lifted his head and turned towards her.

She knew at once that there was something wrong. This was not Hector. The animal's nostrils were flaring; he was showing the whites of his eyes and he was wearing a leather head-collar.

A second later, he had pirouetted his half-ton weight and was charging towards her with his head down.

The horse lunged forward in a frenzy of fear, triggered by memories associated with the acrid odour of the disinfectant spray in which the rug had been soaked.

As his head rose up, the dying light caught the brass name-plate on his head-collar and, etched on it, two words: Sudden Spin.